The Hol

Hannah Treave is the pseudonym for Fiona Ford, an experienced freelance journalist and prolific novelist. She has written for weekly women's magazines for the past fifteen years and is the author of six novels – two under the penname Fiona Harrison, *A Pug Like Percy* and *A Puppy Called Hugo* (HQ, 2017), two WWII sagas for Orion (*The Spark Girl* and *A Wartime Promise*) and a series set during the Second World War, the first of which, *Christmas at Liberty's* (Penguin Random House), was a bestseller in 2018.

Also by Hannah Treave

The Notekeeper
The Holder of Hope

the
holder
of hope

HANNAH TREAVE

CANELO

DK Penguin
Random
House

First published in the United Kingdom in 2025 by

Canelo, an imprint of
Canelo Digital Publishing Limited,
20 Vauxhall Bridge Road,
London SW1V 2SA
United Kingdom

A Penguin Random House Company
The authorised representative in the EEA is Dorling Kindersley Verlag GmbH.
Arnulfstr. 124, 80636 Munich, Germany

Copyright © Hannah Treave 2025

The moral right of Hannah Treave to be identified as the creator of this work has been
asserted in accordance with the Copyright, Designs and Patents Act, 1988.
All rights reserved. No part of this publication may be reproduced or transmitted in
any form or by any means, electronic or mechanical, including photocopy, recording,
or any information storage and retrieval system, without permission in writing from
the publisher.
No part of this book may be used or reproduced in any manner for the purpose of
training artificial intelligence technologies or systems. In accordance with Article 4(3)
of the DSM Directive 2019/790, Canelo expressly reserves this work from the text and
data mining exception.

A CIP catalogue record for this book is available from the British Library.

Print ISBN 978 1 80436 131 3
Ebook ISBN 978 1 80436 130 6

This book is a work of fiction. Names, characters, businesses, organizations, places and
events are either the product of the author's imagination or are used fictitiously. Any
resemblance to actual persons, living or dead, events or locales is entirely coincidental.

Printed and bound in Great Britain by Clays Ltd, Elcograf S.p.A.

Look for more great books at
www.canelo.co | www.dk.com

1

Prologue

The medal was warm as she turned the keepsake over in her lily-white hands, the blue-and-cream ribbon around the clasp still damp.

She had found it hours earlier in a flooded street, of all places, and at first, thought it was a sweet wrapper. But bending down to take a closer look, she realised it wasn't litter, it was a medal, a precious keepsake. Something that once lost, could never be replaced. With a sense of urgency, the woman had scooped the medal up and dried it off as best she could.

After hours of knocking on doors with no success, frustration gnawed at her. She had returned home, the medal still in her pocket, determined to uncover the rightful owner.

Upstairs, she had tapped lightly on the door of her spare room that also occasionally doubled as home to her best friend. Finding it empty, she had gone inside and stared up at the shelf where she kept a handful of her own treasured mementoes.

A photograph of her parents, another of her and her husband on their wedding day a year earlier, and in the centre, a snap of her and her best friend taken the day they had started secondary school. Already friends for several years, the two girls held hands and grinned into the camera, both wearing new, shiny blazers that were far too big for them.

As she held the medal, her eyes drifted to the small gold necklace resting on the shelf – a simple chain with a star-shaped pendant. Though it didn't look much at first glance, it was her most treasured possession. Sometimes, when the memories weighed too heavy, she would wear it, a fragile reminder of how easily things could be lost, how the past could slip away if she didn't hold on tight. Of all her treasures, this necklace deserved pride of place on her shelf, amongst the people she carried in her heart.

Now, as she held the medal aloft, she caught sight of a name along the rim: TPR Hakeson. How had she missed this before? Her mind tumbled with ideas. She thought for a moment – realising TPR must stand for Trooper. But who was Trooper Hakeson? And how did he lose his medal on a flooded street?

The sound of footsteps at the doorway pulled her back to the present. Turning around, she came face to face with the woman from the school photograph and gave her an affectionate smile.

'What are you going to do with it?' her best friend asked, gesturing to the medal.

The woman sighed. 'Find its owner. Something as precious as this deserves to be where it belongs.'

Her friend took a step forward and leaned against the doorjamb, her golden locks framing her face.

'What if it's already where it belongs?' she asked.

Her words made the woman pause.

'What do you mean?'

'What if this medal is exactly where it's supposed to be? What if it's supposed to be with you?'

The woman shook her head.

'It's not mine. I can't keep it.'

'But what if you found it for a reason? What if you're meant to take charge of this medal until the time is right to reunite it with its owner?'

The woman thought for a moment. She hadn't considered the possibility that the medal was supposed to be something she found. She stared at the talisman once more. Could there really be a reason she had found it? The medal wasn't hers to keep hold of, the memories it contained not hers to own, but what if the keepsake was hers to safeguard? At least for a time?

She looked up at her own shelf of precious memories, each one filled with hope in its own way. In that moment, the woman knew just what to do with the medal and instinctively placed it next to her necklace.

She glanced at her best friend standing steadfast beside her, her presence never failing to offer comfort.

'Good,' her friend said approvingly. 'Some things are meant to be found in their own time.'

Chapter One

Twenty-four years later

The smell of spaghetti bolognese wafted through the stair-well as Ava Ryan made her way towards the kitchen.

She let out an inward groan of despair when she saw her station manager, Miguel Fernandez, at the top of the stairs.

Clipboard at the ready, he jerked his head towards the kitchen.

'Hope you've got an iron stomach,' he said in his rich and burring Bath accent. 'Big Stu's cooking for the family tonight.'

Ava rolled her eyes. 'I thought he was banned after last time.'

Miguel laughed. Big Stu's cooking skills were legendary amongst the Blue Watch, not to mention the Green, Red and White Watches that made up Bath Fire Station. An old timer, on the verge of retirement after thirty years of dedicated service, Big Stu had unfortunately always been a terrible cook. The old joke that he could burn water had followed him around for years, and he'd only ever mastered one dish: baked beans on toast. Blue Watch had tried to encourage him to expand his reper-toire, even bought him a cooking course for his birthday one year, but Big Stu had been so bad, the course teacher threw him out of his kitchen.

Last month, things had taken a sinister turn when Big Stu had attempted to cook chicken hotpot but hadn't realised the chicken he'd used was more than a week past its use-by date. When his colleagues questioned the pong, he simply shrugged and said he thought that's how chicken was supposed to smell.

The mere memory of that narrow escape made Ava's stomach turn, and she looked pleadingly at her boss.

'Have I got time to nip out for a sandwich?'

'You know the rules, Ava love,' Miguel said. 'We eat as a family, or we don't eat at all.'

'I'll take the last option,' she quipped.

Pushing a lock of raven hair behind her ear, she saw Miguel was about to unleash one of his familiar lectures about the importance of teamwork and pulling together in times of crisis, when someone, somewhere, must have taken pity on her. The glare of the station lights flashed on and off, followed by an ear-piercing alarm and a loud, disembodied voice that screeched, 'Mobilise. Mobilise.'

Blue Watch now had sixty seconds to get into the engine and onto the road. Ava wasted no time making her way down the pole chute to the muster bay, which contained her boots and protective gear. In seconds, she was sitting in the back of the fire engine, her colleagues following swiftly.

As watch manager, driving the fire engine wasn't her job or Emerson's, who was crew manager. Instead that task was down to firefighters like Big Stu, Phil, or trainee Jodie who made up the rest of the watch. As Big Stu set himself up in the driver's seat, Jodie jumped in beside him and handed him the tip sheet – a printout of the incident details.

The experienced fireman ran his pale grey eyes across the sheet. Ava caught the look of grim resignation flicker across his face.

'Blaze at a block of flats up west,' he said. 'Us and another unit from Bath North are going out.'

Emerson sighed. 'Bloody kids.'

'It might not be,' Jodie said, brightly, her demeanour overflowing with enthusiasm. 'It might be a chip pan fire got out of hand.'

'And I might be married to Justin Timberlake!' Miguel teased as he clambered in alongside them. Ava didn't mind. Although it was unusual for station managers to join a shout, she and Miguel had known one another for years and liked working together. 'Come on, Jodie love, it's November – you know that's our busiest month of the year.'

Ava's hazel eyes met Big Stu's in the rear-view mirror and they shared an eye roll. Miguel's quick wit was legendary, usually funny, but occasionally mean. Turning her gaze to the trainee, she saw Jodie had coloured a deep red that clashed with her auburn tresses, neatly piled into a bun. Leaning forward, she squeezed the young recruit's shoulder. Jodie had only been with the watch a month and was still finding her confidence.

Ava knew the men in her watch weren't always as patient with Jodie as she thought they ought to be. But Ava herself remembered only too well how nervous she had been when she started as a fire officer over two decades ago. Back then, she had been one of only two female firefighters. Now there were at least twenty-five on the payroll in Bath alone.

They had to stick together, and Ava wanted to encourage the young woman.

'To be fair, that's a good instinct, Jodie,' Ava said gently. 'It could be a chip pan fire, but most likely, it's a firework through the letterbox that's got out of hand because it's Bonfire Night tomorrow. Remember your training and you won't go far wrong.'

Jodie smiled gratefully at Ava. 'Sorry, I'm just nervous. This is only my fourth real shout, not counting that cat stuck up a tree.'

'You'll get there,' Emerson encouraged.

Ava nodded, her eyes crinkled with kindness. 'I'll only put you in if I really need to.'

Big Stu swung the engine around the corner and the flames from the block of flats at the top of the hill came into view.

The blaze was huge. Experience told Ava that half an hour of breathing equipment wasn't going to be enough. She looked back at Jodie, her blue eyes as wide as saucers. There was nothing she could say. Jodie would have to learn through experience, like they all had.

As Big Stu parked the fire engine and turned off the siren, Ava clambered out of the cab and saw the police up ahead, busy closing the roads.

Throngs of people were gathered on the pavement, dressed in an assortment of dressing gowns, pyjamas, coats and hoodies. They surveyed the scene in horror, as they used their hands and sleeves to cover their mouths from the billowing plumes of smoke.

She followed the onlookers' gaze and allowed herself to briefly feel their terror, their stricken faces taking her back to the day when her own world had been upended and her life took a turn in a way she had never fully come to terms with.

Quickly, Ava pushed the unwelcome memories from her mind. No good would come from remembering the past.

She strapped on her helmet and found Miguel, who had already set up a command centre with the police. The sound of a rhythmic thumping overhead caught Ava's attention.

'Helicopter's out,' she observed.

'It's windy,' Miguel shouted over the noise. 'We need to monitor the conditions, this could get out of hand quickly.' Turning to Ava, he smiled. 'You ready?'

'As I'll ever be.' She smiled back, tapping her breathing tank.

'See you in thirty minutes,' Miguel said firmly. 'And don't try and be a hero.'

Miguel's words of advice could sound corny to the untrained ear but as station manager it was his job to ensure that every firefighter returned alive. Five years ago, Miguel hadn't been so lucky and had lost one of his brigade during a house fire when the firefighter had decided to keep fighting the flames even after his breathing apparatus had run out. It had hit Green Watch badly, but Miguel had taken it personally, blaming himself for not being firmer with his team. Now, he insisted every single member of each watch followed his instructions, especially when he was in the field.

'I'm never that,' she replied.

'No, but you get caught up in situations, Ava.' Miguel's tone was sharp. He caught himself. 'I'm just saying, this fire's too big for you to start trying to salvage precious memories, for you or anyone else.'

Ava said nothing as she scanned the scene. Instead, she focused on issuing quick orders to Phil, Emerson and Jodie to check the upper floors and secure the stairwell. With the team in motion, she grabbed the thermal-imaging camera from Big Stu to sweep the room herself. This was her strength, and she needed to ensure nothing was missed. Fires like this were notoriously tricky – unpredictable and dangerous.

She knew well how a single spark from a firework could set off a chain reaction, turning a small blaze into something uncontrollable.

She walked towards the blaze. Stepping inside the building, the roar of the flames pounding in her ears, the hundred-degree heat already making her sweat. Immediately, the screen of the camera lit up with black-and-white shapes that revealed the heat levels in the room. As she swept it through the smoke, the shapes started to glow – furniture, walls, but no signs of trapped heat signatures.

'Clear,' she called to her watch, as she breathed through her apparatus. At least in the fire she felt in control. Unlike the battles waiting for her outside.

But fighting her way through the thick black smoke, she remembered her promise to Miguel and pushed it from her mind.

But Ava knew that if she found precious treasure, she'd do all she could to make sure the memento was returned to its rightful owner. Ava knew better than anyone how much those keepsakes meant when faced with tragedy.

Chapter Two

As the sun began to rise, peeping over the traditional Bath stone chimneys like an artist making the first strokes on fresh canvas, Ava sat on the floor of her spare room, legs curled beneath her.

Clutching a cup of coffee, she gazed at the shelf above the small desk in the corner that was full of what looked, at first glance, to be nothing more than junk. At the front of the shelf stood a small toy tractor, next to it a dog-eared photograph of what Ava suspected was mother and daughter at a graduation ceremony, followed by a gold fob watch, a battered Madonna concert ticket, a first edition of Oscar Wilde's only novel and her first treasure that she'd found soon after beginning her career as a firefighter: a 1993 Gulf War medal.

This eclectic mix of treasures – or memories, as Ava preferred to think of them – weren't just random clutter, they were precious mementoes that once upon a time had meant the world to their owners. These keepsakes were items Ava had rescued from the debris of blazes she had attended over her career – all in the hope of one day reuniting them with their owners and preserving that precious memory attached to every memento. Most of the keepsakes she collected from the disaster scenes she attended were reunited with their owners within weeks or days. But the items in Ava's Nostalgia Nook – as Cassie teasingly referred to it – had remained for years, their owners never traced, despite Ava's best efforts. Some, she imagined, had lost their value now, such as the tractor, but the medal still puzzled Ava. She refused to believe someone would have parted with something so meaningful so easily. As she ran her eyes over it, taking in the familiar clasp, Ava felt a sense of peace. After a long shift or tough day, Ava often found comfort staring at this wall of treasures. Each item reminding her of the power of lost connections, and above all else, giving her hope that one day those connections would be rekindled.

As her gaze landed on her own keepsake – a gold star-shaped locket she'd had since she was a child – she reached for it and slid it around her neck. Instantly she felt comforted.

Taking a sip of her coffee, she felt the caffeine begin to work its magic. Her shift had just finished and she'd only just returned to her traditional mid-terrace in the south of the city. It was not the most glamorous of houses, certainly not compared to some of the grand houses that routinely featured in period dramas, but to Ava it was home.

Leaning back against the wall, the door to the room opened a crack and she smiled as Monkey, her old rescue tabby cat, snaked through her legs.

She tickled his chin. 'How are you, eh?' she whispered, his loud purr rivalling a motorbike. 'You sleep well?'

The cat purred even louder as Ava crooned into his ear.

'You talking to me or the cat?' A loud voice boomed from outside the door.

At the sound of the voice, Monkey looked up and Ava followed suit.

Dressed in grey pyjama bottoms and an old biker's T-shirt, Steve's grey hair was sticking out in different directions and even from here Ava could see his round, nut-brown eyes that looked like pinpricks against his olive skin. She frowned; he clearly hadn't had enough sleep.

'Morning,' Ava said softly as she stopped tickling her cat.

Upset the attention had stopped so abruptly, Monkey glared at Ava before stalking out of the room.

'That cat's too spoilt,' Steve grumbled, planting a kiss on Ava's cheek. Suddenly he recoiled. 'Jeez, you stink.'

'Thanks!'

The night had been long. The watch had finally put their pumps down shortly after two in the morning but their job wasn't over. Escorting people to temporary accommodation, ensuring each resident was in contact with victim support, then there had been the clean-up, which always took a while. The Red and White Watches would be down at the scene today. They'd continue the clean-up and help the investigation team determine the cause of the fire, which Ava was sure was down to kids messing about with fireworks.

Steve's expression softened as he sat on the floor beside her and rested his head on her shoulder. He smelt of sleep and curry. Ava was sure he'd taken advantage of a night alone and treated himself to a biryani from the takeaway at the bottom of the road.

'You had a big shout last night then?'

Ava nodded. 'The big block of flats up by the park.'

Steve groaned. 'Fireworks?'

'I think so,' Ava replied. 'This time of year it usually is.'

'Any casualties?' Steve asked, his tone gentle as he cut to the heart of the matter.

Sliding her hand through his, Ava tried not to mind. They had been together for twenty-six years, she was used to his ways by now. But even so, there were times she wished he would empathise rather than ask for straight-out facts as if he was a statistician.

She shook her head. 'No, but the whole place is decimated. Nobody will be moving back in there for a while.'

'Ouch,' Steve replied. 'Poor buggers, at this time of year, too. Where will they all go?'

'They'll be housed temporarily,' Ava said, stifling a yawn. 'Or stay with friends and neighbours. Social Services will sort it.'

She closed her eyes, the warmth of her husband's body relaxing her aching muscles. She was tired but knew sleep wouldn't find her for a long time yet, that her mind would be too busy thinking about the people who suddenly had no home. She thought of the one little boy who had been sobbing in his mother's arms as he wept for his lost blanket, his mother doing her best to comfort him as she stood on the pavement, herself in threadbare pyjamas.

'Don't forget we're going to the adoption agency information event,' Steve said, interrupting her thoughts.

Ava's eyes flew open and a familiar sense of dread unfurled within her stomach at the word 'adoption'.

'This afternoon?' she asked, doing her best to keep her tone neutral. 'I thought that was next week.'

Steve got to his feet and Ava sensed his irritation.

'Glad to see this is so important to you,' he said drily.

'Don't be like that,' Ava sighed. 'I'd just forgotten after everything that happened last night.'

Steve ran a hand through his hair, his brown eyes softening. 'I know, sorry, it's just that this is important, to me at least.'

'It's important to me too, Steve.' She set her mug on the desk and stood up, sliding an arm around his waist.

Leaning her head against his chest, she wondered when this action started to feel so alien. When had touching her husband gone from being one of the most natural things in the world to suddenly being so difficult?

'Sometimes it doesn't feel important to you,' Steve said now, his voice small above her head. 'Don't you want to have a family any more?'

At the question, Ava felt a renewed sense of tiredness. She pulled away from Steve and looked into his eyes.

'You know I want a family. What sort of question is that? I'm just not sure adoption is the best way forward, I have said that, and I think it's something we both need to agree one hundred per cent on.'

Steve shook his head and pulled away from his wife. 'This again.' He raised his eyes heavenwards. 'Ava, we can't go through IVF again. We can't afford it for a start, never mind what it's done to your body. All those hormones, those chemicals, it's awful.'

Impatience gripped Ava. 'We've had three goes at IVF, Steve, but I want us to try again. We deserve a family. We need a family.'

Steve paused, then said patiently. 'We've been at IVF for years, Ava. You're forty-four now, I'm forty-five, I don't want to sound rude but we're not getting any younger. Our chances of success are getting slimmer. How much more can we take? We could give a child a home now, instead of waiting around for a miracle that might never come...'

His voice softened as his sentence tailed off, but Ava heard the plea underneath. He wasn't just offering an alternative – he was losing hope.

For a moment they looked at each other feeling help-less. Then Steve pulled Ava back into his arms and kissed the top of her head.

'I don't know why you won't think about adoption. The event is just a chance to get more information.'

Ava bristled. She was tired of having to explain herself to her husband. He was the one person in the world that was supposed to know her best, and yet her feelings about adoption weren't something he seemed able to wrap his head around at all.

'I don't want a child we choose,' Ava said patiently as she felt she had said a million times before. 'I want a child that's ours. Yours and mine, that we created together.'

Steve paused again and Ava could tell he was doing his best not to say something that would start a row.

'I think we need to find other ways to be happy,' he said eventually.

He let her go and, rather than look at her husband, Ava found her precious cat who had come back into the room and was now curled up in the window. She picked him up and held him to her chest. He was old now at sixteen, but to Ava he was still that same fluffy kitten she had fallen in love with at first meow.

'You were quite happy to rescue a cat,' Steve said sharply. 'Why not a child?'

Ignoring her feelings of irritation, Ava took a deep breath.

'Adopting a child is different.'

Steve let out a hollow laugh. 'It's always different.'

She turned to look at him and saw him glance at their small, ordered hallway that led downstairs to a small but equally ordered kitchen and sitting room. Emptiness echoed throughout the house. Their home needed chaos.

'I want my life to mean something,' Steve said. 'A family will give us that. Does it really matter whether that child is biologically a part of us? Surely the important thing is we get to be parents.'

As Steve took a step towards Ava, his eyes now brimming with love, she felt wrong-footed and angry. Just because Ava had been adopted, it didn't mean she automatically understood the need to adopt other children. If only Steve would realise it wasn't as easy as he made it sound. Adoption wasn't just a matter of choosing a child. It meant months of interviews, social workers digging into their lives, home visits where every corner would be scrutinised. And what if they weren't considered good enough? It wasn't the adoption process itself that scared her – it was the uncertainty that came with it. Her own past had left her feeling incomplete, and she wasn't sure if she was ready to inflict that on herself again or another child.

Setting the cat down, Ava backed away from Steve. He was always like this in an argument, reasonable but forthright, determined to get what he wanted. But Ava knew she was too tired after the night she had endured, and didn't want to say something she might regret.

Instead, she pushed past her husband and walked calmly down the stairs and into the entranceway. She reached for the smoky jacket she had only recently taken off and slipped it back on.

'Where are you going?' Steve asked, incredulous.

'Out.'

'But you've just got home,' Steve pointed out. He followed her, confusion written across his face. 'You need to sleep.'

'I'm fine.'

Ava picked up her bag, reached for her car keys and opened the door. She needed to breathe.

'What about our appointment later?'

But Ava couldn't speak. She was too consumed with frustration as she stepped into the cool morning air and slammed the door shut behind her. There was only one place she wanted to be.

Chapter Three

The rich smell of coffee jolted Ava awake. Sitting upright on the narrow sofa in her best friend Cassie's lounge, she saw her pal standing over her, two steaming mugs of coffee in hand.

Ava smiled gratefully, blinked the sleep from her eyes and took the proffered cup. 'What time is it?' she croaked.

Cassie sat next to her, a lock of long, blonde hair falling into her mug of coffee.

'Just after one. I left you as long as I could but Steve rang, said you needed to be at the adoption agency by three.'

Ava felt a stab of irritation that she had been so predictable. If she wasn't at home or the fire station, there was only one other place she'd be, Cassie's house. Ava looked at Cassie, wondering what she was thinking. As usual she gave nothing away. Typical Cassie. Always steady and even-tempered. The kind of soul you wanted around in a crisis.

The sight of that warm expression worked its usual magic and Ava began to feel calmer. She and Cassie had been best friends since the first day of primary school when they were shy five-year-olds. Aside from a fortnight in Year Seven when they'd fallen out over a chicken sandwich of all things, the two of them had been inseparable ever since.

'I'm not going. I'm tired after last night,' Ava said mutinously.

'The fire up at the flats?' Cassie quizzed, sensing it was best to leave the subject of adoption alone. 'I heard about that on the news. Sounded awful.'

'One of the worst I've been to in a while,' Ava replied. She checked her watch and groaned. Her head was fuzzy from sleep. Standing up, she ran a hand through her knotty dark curls. Even after all these years, some fires stuck with her. The heat and smoke faded, but the forlorn faces of those who had endured the worst day of their lives lingered. No amount of debriefing or downtime could ever erase that.

'What time are you starting work?' Cassie asked.

'Five.' Ava yawned and stretched. 'I've got to go back up to the scene before then. You?'

Cassie was a community charity leader on the estate she lived in and worked all sorts of odd hours.

'Day off.' Cassie beamed.

'All right for some.' Ava yawned. If there was one thing she could do with, it was a bit of time to herself. She reached for her jeans and pulled them over her hips.

'So, are you going to meet Steve?' Cassie asked.

'No time.'

Cassie straightened the cushions on the sofa, clearly playing for time.

'Does Steve know that?'

Ava didn't miss a beat. 'I've told him, I'm not sure he heard me. You know Steve.'

It was true. Ava had begun dating Steve when she was eighteen and she had got an after-school job working for an insurance company. The two had bonded over a shared hatred of filing and Steve had learned quickly that dating

Ava meant forming a relationship with Cassie as well – the two were a package deal.

Cassie prodded Ava gently in the ribs. 'I know Steve has his faults, but he does listen.'

Anger flashed through her. 'Whose side are you on?'

'Give over,' Cassie laughed, Ava's anger seeming absurd. 'But you can be such a stubborn cow-bag you don't half make it difficult sometimes.'

Just like that, the tension diffused and Ava giggled. 'Nob!'

'Whatever,' Cassie teased with a shrug of her shoulders.

Sticking her tongue out at her friend, Ava reached for her trainers, the insults water off a duck's back to the pair of them. The two women knew each other better than they knew themselves. Calling each other out was as much a part of their lives as boozy lunches, direct messages filled with memes and a shared love of yoga and over-indulging in chocolate cake.

'Look, I'm not getting involved. I told Steve the same thing,' Cassie tried again. 'But don't you think adoption is worth a shot?'

'How can you of all people ask me that?' Ava said exasperated. 'You've carried your own child, you know how precious a gift pregnancy is.'

As if on cue, the back door opened and in walked Cassie's eight-year-old son, Dylan.

Wearing a slightly too small football kit and covered in mud, Cassie's pride and joy walked towards his mother, not thinking about the dirt he was trailing inside.

'Less of a gift and more of a sodding nightmare at times,' Cassie quipped, backing away from her son. 'Stop right there, mister. Not another step.'

Aghast, Dylan did as his mother said, the wet, muddy coat he was holding dripping onto the floor. Ava watched the scene unfold. Cassie might have been a single mother, but she handled everything Dylan brought into the house with the combined strength and grace of two parents.

'Ah, for crying out loud,' Cassie groaned as she examined the prints all over the vinyl flooring. 'Back in the kitchen with you and get all those filthy clothes off and in the machine.'

She turned back to Ava. 'Grass isn't always greener. You sure you want this? Your home's like something out of an interiors mag.'

'And that's the problem,' Ava grumbled. She picked up her mug and followed mother and son into the kitchen. 'I want mess and chaos.'

'I don't!' Cassie quipped.

Ava looked at Dylan and rolled her eyes, sending the little boy into fits of giggles.

Cassie bustled behind them, filling her ancient washing machine with muddy clothes.

'You two better not be ganging up on me like usual.'

'Never, Mum!' Dylan promised.

Ava winked at him. She had always adored Dylan and the feeling was mutual. Ava had been Cassie's birthing partner when she gave birth and had been the second person to hold Dylan just minutes after he was born. 'You'll be in his life as much as I will,' an exhausted Cassie had said, beaming at the two.

The machine sprang into action and Cassie stood up.

'You, in the shower,' she said to her son in a tone that brooked no argument. Dylan disappeared and Ava blew him a kiss. 'And you, talk to your husband,' Cassie said firmly.

'I don't want to,' Ava said obstinately.

'You sound like Dylan,' Cassie pointed out. Then more gently, she said, 'I know it's hard, Ava, but I'm just asking you to be open.'

Ava shook her head, resolute. 'I want to carry my own child.'

'But what if you can't?' Cassie asked, not unkindly. 'You'd make a great mum, you're so good with Dylan, never mind all the kids you come across through work. I just think this fixation you have of only having a child one way isn't healthy.'

Ava sighed. She knew if it was Steve talking to her like this, she'd have screamed at him, but with Cassie it was different.

'I wish I didn't feel like this, Cass, it would make life a lot easier, but I've got to try this. I'm not ready to give up yet and sometimes IVF takes loads of tries.'

Cassie wrapped an arm around her. She smelt of baked beans and CK One, a scent she had adopted in the late Nineties and never given up. Ava found it strangely comforting.

'I know that. But all those hormones, wreaking havoc through your beautiful body. Not to mention all that disappointment. Surely you've had enough now? It broke my heart every time it failed for you, I can only imagine how you must have felt.'

'I'm strong,' Ava insisted, lifting her chin a little.

Cassie raised an eyebrow. 'Nobody's doubting your strength, Ava. But sometimes, the strongest thing to do is the hardest.'

Ava said nothing. Reaching for her smoke-scented jacket, she threw it over her shoulders, hating the fact she knew her friend was right.

'Where are you going?' Cassie asked.

'To do what I need to do.'

A look of relief passed across Cassie's features. 'I get why you're hesitant, but you're focusing on the wrong thing. Adoption isn't just about having a biological connection. It's about giving a child a chance at life, at family. Isn't that what matters most?'

Ava said nothing and simply kissed her friend on the cheek before she opened the door. Stepping into her trusty Vauxhall Astra she started the engine and thought for a moment. Just where was it she really needed to be?

–

As Ava drove the short distance to her destination, doubt plagued her. By the time she pulled into the first available parking space, she still wasn't sure she was doing the right thing.

Slamming the car door shut, she caught the still acrid smell of smoke hanging in the air. Looking across at the block of flats she and her colleagues had done battle with until the early hours of the morning, she felt despair wash over her.

Ava had turned up to these flats numerous times in her career. Chip pan fires in the early 2000s, then car fires, and now, more recently, for talks to residents on fire safety, including the importance of storing fireworks away from little people.

Sadly, no matter how many talks Ava gave, there was only so much that seemed to sink in. Making her way down the road, the November drizzle damp against her skin, she flashed her fire brigade pass at the police officer standing guard.

'You've just missed the investigating officers,' he said. 'Head in.'

Ava nodded and smiled at the policeman and entered the site. She had unfinished business to attend to and hoped it wouldn't take long.

For a moment, all she did was stand in what had recently been the communal hall. This hall was where she and the rest of her team believed the fire had begun. The source point had been a box of fireworks set off in the corner by the lifts.

Gingerly, she picked her way through the scene. There was very little left. Hopes and dreams gone, precious treasures wiped out in an instant. All because of one thoughtless action.

She pulled on her gloves, the charred remnants of the building still a hazard even hours after the fire had been put out, and with just her personal torch to guide her, carefully began a detailed search of the wreckage. Ava moved through each flat as if she were a forensic investigator. Everywhere she looked there were burned-out signs of lives disrupted mid-flow. Discarded handbags, IDs on the floor. All belonging to people whose lives had changed immeasurably in an instant.

Despite all the years Ava had been working as a firefighter, every burned-out shell of a building reminded her of her parents, Janet and Sam.

When she was eighteen they'd celebrated their twenty-fifth wedding anniversary with a week in Madeira. But on their final night a kitchen fire had swept through the hotel, killing them and other guests in an instant.

Over twenty-five years later and the pain of grief could still upend Ava. She had never forgotten the call from a Portuguese police officer that caused her to throw up.

Neither had she forgotten the harrowed call to Cassie, who came round immediately, helped her throw clothes into suitcases and accompanied her to the Portuguese island.

Ever practical, Ava's parents had always insisted that not only did they never want a funeral, but that if they were to die abroad then they didn't want their bodies repatriated.

'Just leave us where we fall,' her father had always insisted.

With Cassie's support, Ava had followed their wishes. She would never have survived such tragedy without her best friend, and a fire officer named Raoul.

With a shiver, she brought her attention back to the present.

As her feet crunched over the rubble she told herself it was lucky nobody had died in the blaze. There had been some injuries, one lad, high on something, had jumped out of a first-floor window instead of using the stairs. Luckily, he only broke his leg.

Reaching the last flat, the inky black of the late afternoon sky gathered pace. She increased the brightness on her torch only for her eyes to latch onto a photograph. She bent down to pick it up and blew the debris from the glass; three faces beamed out at her. Two girls and an older man who, she guessed judging by the likeness, was their father.

This wasn't just a picture, it was a fragment of their lives, preserved in this moment before everything changed. How many times had she held onto photographs like this after her own parents had died.

Carefully, she slipped the photograph into her pocket ready to place her latest find in her Nostalgia Nook when she got home. Just until she could reunite the print with its rightful owner.

She knew more than anyone how much keepsakes could mean. Raoul had given her a similar treasure before she left Madeira.

'I found this in the wreckage, in what was your parents' room.'

She had looked at him in surprise as he held out a small tissue-wrapped parcel.

Unwrapping it, she was astonished to see a simple gold necklace with a star-shaped pendant. The necklace was as familiar to her as her mother's face.

'Where did you find it?' Ava had gasped. 'I thought everything was gone.'

Raoul had given her a kindly smile. 'Sometimes all is not lost, it just looks like it is.'

Ava had immediately taken the necklace and put it around her own neck, the treasure providing unexpected but much needed comfort over the years.

Returning home from Madeira, Ava had felt lost, unsure of her place in the world, apart from one thing: she knew she wanted to be a firefighter.

Back outside, she took her phone off silent and checked the time. It was almost five. Her shift started in twenty minutes. Miguel would be fuming if she was late; he didn't tolerate tardiness from anyone in his watches. But worse, there were ten missed calls from Steve and three voicemails. She hurried to her car and threw the phone in the glovebox. The last thing she needed was to do battle with another blaze.

Chapter Four

Two days later and Ava still hadn't seen her husband. She had successfully managed to avoid him, ensuring their paths didn't cross when her night shift finished and his day began. She also took care not to walk into town past Steve's office, just in case he happened to emerge when she was nearby. She hadn't even spoken to him. Instead, she'd been playing phone tag when she knew he was in a meeting, leaving messages and apologising for the fact they were ships in the night, but that they would talk soon.

It was cowardly.

Childish.

Stupid.

She knew all of that. But still, Ava wasn't brave enough to face her husband. She couldn't bear to think of him in that adoption office by himself and the longer she left it, the worse it got.

Come Friday, Ava knew she couldn't avoid Steve any longer. The design agency he ran with his business partner had teamed up with the fire station several years ago to support a local children's charity. That evening, the station was hosting an event in the charity's honour.

Usually, Ava hated this sort of thing and would go to all sorts of elaborate lengths to get out of socialising. This time, Miguel refused to take no for an answer when she had tried to wheedle her way out of it.

'If I'm going, you're going to at least show your face!' he'd told her. 'Every other watch manager will be there.'

They were in the locker room, Miguel dressed in a dinner suit and bow tie, Ava sat on a bench behind him offering sartorial advice.

'Aren't you on shift tonight?' she asked.

Miguel shook his head and fiddled with his cufflinks. He looked at his reflection in the cracked mirror that hung in the locker room and straightened his bow tie, making micro adjustments until he settled on perfection.

'I'm not needed tonight as station manager. Instead, my role is belle of the ball.'

Ava rolled her eyes at Miguel's obvious excitement at getting out of his navy uniform and playing dress-up for once.

'And who am I supposed to be? The beast to your beauty?'

He chuckled. 'You might have a few more crow's feet than when I first met you, love, but even I draw the line at beast.'

'Sod!' Ava laughed, throwing her trainer at him and narrowly missing his head.

'Harassment in the workplace!' Miguel called loudly. 'Harassment in the workplace!'

'Oh yeah?' Ava raised an eyebrow and bent down to undo her other shoe. 'Keep it up and I'll throw the other one.'

'Okay, okay.' Miguel laughed, sat on the bench and leaned back against the lockers. 'You're going to have to see Steve some time, this has gone on long enough.'

Ava said nothing. She knew Miguel was right. She also knew that Steve was looking forward to the event. He had mentioned the benefit the previous Sunday when they had been flicking through the papers companionably around the fire, Monkey sat in between the two of them.

'The firm's provided all the booze,' he'd smiled. 'Be nice if you were there.'

She'd tucked her feet into his lap and given him a rueful smile.

'If you don't, people'll think we're getting a divorce!'

They had giggled at that, as if the idea was unthinkable. It had all been boring but lovely. Cosy. The epitome of married life. How had so much happened in a week that the idea of doing the same this Sunday seemed alien? Ava had stared at the lost treasures on her shelf after every shift that week hoping one of them might give an answer to her own life.

The Gulf War medal had always bothered her. Highly polished, complete with a cream, red and blue ribbon and clasp, Ava knew this wasn't an honour given out lightly. She reached for it and saw the service number she knew by heart along with the name on the rim: Hakeson. She had been trying to reunite this medal with its owner since 2000, after finding it in a flooded village high street. Despite her best efforts, she had never managed it, but Ava hadn't given up.

'Might be better to face Steve tonight,' Miguel suggested, pulling her back into the present. 'Big crowd and all that, he can't make a scene.'

'Steve's not the type for a scene,' Ava countered.

Miguel brushed an imaginary piece of lint from the arm of his jacket.

'Maybe not normally, but he might be a bit cheesed off at the moment, don't you think?'

Ava said nothing, too embarrassed to admit Miguel was right.

'Where were you anyway?' Miguel asked.

'When?' Ava replied, stalling for time.

Miguel looked impatient. 'When you stood up your husband?'

Ava paused. Miguel didn't always understand her passion for finding lost treasures. She wasn't sure now was the time to enlighten him.

'Nowhere.' She shrugged. 'Just needed some air.'

She stretched her arms overhead and checked her watch. The party started in less than half an hour. Surely Miguel would let her keep out of the way?

'Let me guess, you went back to the fire alone, after the investigators had finished,' Miguel snapped.

Ava groaned. Was she that easy to read?

The station manager rolled his eyes heavenwards. 'Who's the lucky recipient this time?'

'A single dad. I found a picture of his family amongst the wreckage of what was the top floor flat,' Ava said in a small voice.

'And where is he now?' Miguel asked.

'Staying with his sister nearby.' Ava had already managed to do some successful detective work. 'I thought I'd take it round to him tomorrow before shift. Was hoping you might come with me.'

'And if I do?'

'What do you mean?' Ava asked, though she had a sinking feeling she knew where this was going.

'I mean, if I do this for you, what will you do for me?' Miguel's brown eyes twinkled.

'I shouldn't have to do anything for you,' Ava pointed out. 'You should want to come with me out of the goodness of your heart. Surely it makes an old firefighter like you happy to see people reunited with their prized posses-sions.'

Miguel snorted with laughter. 'I tend to think that saving their lives is enough, but whatever.'

Ava shook her head, lips twitching. 'All right, what do you want? And don't say you want me to come to the party.'

'I want you to come to the party,' Miguel immediately answered. 'Cassie's coming as well so you've no excuse not to put in an appearance.'

'Argh, Miguel!' Ava got to her feet and threw her hands in the air. She had forgotten her friend was attending, all in a bid to try and secure publicity and donations for the estate. Cassie was keen to develop the community centre and get the kids involved in more projects.

'Stop being such a baby,' Miguel said pompously. 'You're a bloody grown woman, though there are times you'd never believe it. Now come with me for an hour, meet some people, keep the charity happy and make nice with your husband.'

'Fine,' Ava sulked, 'but if there's no jelly and ice cream for pud, I'm off!'

Politely declining a glass of Prosecco, Ava instead helped herself to an orange juice from one of the waiters doing the rounds. She had to admit the fire station's func-tion room looked smart. Tatty trestle tables were now covered in pristine white tablecloths, neatly decorated with hydrangeas in their centres, crystal glassware and highly polished cutlery. A sound system was playing elegant chamber music in the corner of the room and the chandelier which hung from the ceiling, that normally looked so out of place in the station, tonight seemed well-suited for once.

The room was filling up nicely with Bath's well-heeled and Ava felt conspicuous in her uniform, which was earning glances of admiration from around the room.

'I feel like an idiot,' she hissed in Cassie's ear. They were standing by the fire exit, and Ava longed to make use of it.

'Don't be such a grump,' Cassie whispered. She was wearing a simple green shift dress that showed off her tanned skin and lithe figure. Dressed in her bulky uniform, Ava felt like an elephant in comparison.

'I'm not,' Ava hissed. 'I just think that as this is Steve's thing, I shouldn't be here.'

She was about to say more when the man himself entered the room. Dressed in black tie, which she knew he had hired, she felt herself melt a little. Even after all these years he was still gorgeous, still had the power to take her breath away. She raised her hand, determined now they were in the same room to remain friendly, but he didn't see. He was engrossed in conversation with the tall woman beside him, who unlike the rest of the guests was dressed in a pair of dark jeans, heeled boots and a blazer.

Ava recognised her immediately as his business partner, Christina. A stand-offish, introverted woman, who'd moved here from China in her youth, with a wicked sense of humour in the right moment. Ava liked her enormously.

Steve must have sensed her looking at him and lifted his head. For a moment he stared and Ava froze. Would he ignore her? But before she could wonder any more, he whispered something in Christina's ear, then walked towards Ava.

'Hide me,' Ava hissed in Cassie's ear.

'What?' Cassie asked, bewildered, before catching sight of Steve and giving her friend a nudge. She opened her arms in welcome. 'Steve,' she cried warmly, pulling him in for a hug.

Ava watched Steve fall happily into her friend's arms then his eyes landed on Ava.

'And here's my loving wife! Who said she'd moved out?'

Miguel, who had now joined them, let out a raucous but fake peal of laughter.

'Just been busy, you know how it is when I work nights,' Ava mumbled.

Clamping an arm around her shoulders, Miguel pulled Ava towards him protectively.

'She's been fighting the good fight, haven't you, Ava love?' Miguel said, supportively.

In that moment Ava could have kissed him.

'Honestly, we'd be lost without this woman,' he continued theatrically. 'She practically dealt with that fire single-handedly at that block of flats the other day. Bravery,' Miguel clutched his remaining free hand to his heart at this point, 'you don't know the half of it. If only all my watch managers were as brave and disciplined as my Ava.'

'That's as maybe, but it would still be nice to see my wife when she's not saving the world,' Steve said coldly.

'But that's our Ava, and we wouldn't have her any other way,' Cassie put in loyally. She winked at Ava, then stepped forward to kiss Miguel on the cheek.

'How are you doing?' she asked. 'And when are you coming over again? Dylan is dying to see you. He wants you to show him how to tie a tie in a hundred different ways.'

Miguel beamed at her. 'Of course he does. The boy has style.'

'Well, your husband does,' Steve teased.

'Ouch,' Miguel winced at the mention of his much younger Brazilian husband, Xavier. 'Someone's got their claws out.'

'And usually you say it's me,' Ava put in.

The little group laughed, lifting some of the tension.

'So, who's got Dylan tonight?' Miguel asked, changing the subject.

Cassie saw a passing waiter and helped herself to a glass of bubbles. Everyone apart from Ava followed suit.

'My neighbour Dolores. I've told him to behave himself. I swear at the moment he's like a boy possessed!'

'He's not that bad,' Ava countered.

'Yes, he is.' Cassie laughed. 'One minute he's like a baby, the next like a little man! I can't keep up. The other day he had a full-on breakdown because I wouldn't let him watch *Iron Man* before bed. Cries of, "I hate you," could be heard from the top of our street.'

'Grim.' Miguel winced then took a large gulp of Prosecco.

'Grim is right,' Cassie agreed, helping herself to another glass of wine from a waiter.

'Can't Dylan's dad ever help out?' Miguel asked.

Ava gave her friend a hard stare; he knew Dylan's dad had never been in the picture.

Sensing he'd put his foot in it, Miguel clamped a hand over his mouth. 'Sorry, I forgot.'

'It's all right.' Cassie shrugged. 'I like to try and forget he buggered off before Dylan was born myself. But we don't need him, we've got each other.'

'Doesn't Dylan want to know who his dad is?' Miguel persisted.

'Miguel!' Ava hissed.

But Cassie waved her friend's concerns away. 'I suppose he will one day. Dylan's never asked and I never put his dad's name on the certificate – largely because I only ever knew his first name was Pete and honestly that might not have been his real name.'

'Come off it, Cass,' Steve laughed. 'Course you knew his name.'

'We were only together for a couple of dates or so. It was casual,' Cassie said lightly. 'Anyway, when did you get so judgy?'

'Not judgy, just surprised. You're so organised with your work and everything, it just seems unlike you not to know who Dylan's dad was,' Steve explained.

'What can I tell you?' Cassie said bluntly. 'I wasn't myself.'

Ava gave her friend a sympathetic smile.

Cassie had been going through a bad time nine years earlier. She'd divorced her then husband, lost her home and her job in public relations within a month. Ava had been there for every drunken night out and after every one-night stand while Cassie regained her confidence and sense of self. A baby had not been part of Cassie's plan, unlike Ava who had been trying for a baby unsuccessfully for two years by that point. Yet Dylan had been the catalyst for Cassie to turn her life around. With someone else depending on her, she'd found the courage to retrain as a community support worker and in turn find a home on the temporary housing estate made from prefab huts. She was only supposed to have been there for a few weeks but Cassie loved the place so much, along with overseeing all the comings and goings of new residents, that she and Dylan had never left.

Cassie gave her friend a weak smile and looked around the room. 'This place is beautiful. Did you transform this, Ava?'

Miguel let out another whoop of laughter. 'You've got to be joking. Too busy saving souls this one. No, Steve did it.'

'Well, actually Ronnie my PA did it,' Steve said, looking uncomfortable as Ava and Cassie let out unbridled jeers. 'They're very creative,' he tried again.

As Steve coloured, Miguel, Ava and Cassie rocked with laughter.

'Leave it out, the last thing I need is you lot ganging up on me.'

'Awww, diddums,' Cassie teased. 'I should probably mingle anyway. Lovely Emma Higginson is here from the Sean Ben Foundation and I must go and say hi.'

'I'll join you,' said Miguel, sensing the lingering tension.

When her friends walked away, Ava felt Steve take a step towards her.

She took a deep breath, aware she needed to grow up.

'I'm sorry about the other day,' Ava said above the noise of the party.

'Oh?' Steve's tone had an edge to it.

'I should have called you,' she admitted, 'at the very least.'

There was silence as Steve let out a snort of furious laughter and then turned around and walked back to Christina on the other side of the room.

Chapter Five

Ava had returned the following morning to find Steve asleep on the sofa, Monkey curled up beside him.

The sight of him asleep, vulnerable, should have comforted her. Instead, it made her stomach churn – how had they got to this point?

Feeling unsettled, Ava had left him to it, making herself a coffee in the kitchen. When she heard him stir, she seized her opportunity.

'Please can we talk about the adoption thing?' she asked, as he got up from the sofa.

But Steve ignored her and walked upstairs to the bathroom, locking the door behind him.

Ava heard the shower start to run.

'I'm trying to talk to you,' she persisted, waiting for him to emerge.

Eventually, Steve opened the bathroom door. Finding Ava sitting on their bed, he stalked past her, pulled a football shirt from the wardrobe and slid it on. He helped coach a kids' football team on Saturday mornings, though Ava suspected it was the midweek beers with the other lads who helped out that was the real incentive.

'I can see that but I'm trying to get ready for this morning's session,' Steve replied.

Ava tried to swallow the irritation she felt. She knew she had behaved badly but surely Steve recognised that they had to talk sometime?

'This is important,' she said gently. 'We need to talk about what happened.'

'But there's nothing to talk about.' He reached for his shorts and pulled them on. 'I went to the adoption event, I got the info, I met the social workers and other prospective parents, you didn't.' Despite his calm tone, there was an edge to his voice.

'I couldn't face it.'

A hollow laugh escaped from Steve's lips. 'I gathered that from the fact you didn't turn up.'

'I handled it badly,' she croaked. Ava was tired from worry and a lack of sleep. Staying even tempered was hard but she was doing her best.

Steve whirled around to face her, his eyes flashing with anger.

'Yes, you did,' he hissed. 'You've handled all this badly. I appreciate this is hard for you, that you're desperate for a child of your own, that you don't want to adopt, but I thought we were a team, if nothing else. You could have picked up the phone. I might not have liked what you said but at least I wouldn't have been at an adoption event by myself, like a loser, loads of people asking me if I was going it alone and telling me how brave I was!'

'I'm sorry,' Ava replied, meaning it.

Steve's jaw tightened. 'I feel like we're going around in circles, Ava. Every time I think we're making progress, you pull away again. I'm not sure how much more of this I can take.'

He turned away and ran down the stairs.

A stab of fear darted through Ava's chest and she chased down after him. 'What do you mean?'

'I mean we can't keep doing this dance, Ava. I've got a low sperm count, you've got a hostile womb. Together, our chances of having kids naturally are unlikely. We need to change our vision of what our family looks like. I've caught on, but you haven't.'

The even temper Ava had been holding onto was out of her grasp. 'You know I want kids. I think we should have another go at IVF. Just one.'

'No. We only got one go for free on the NHS. Now, we've spent nearly ten grand on another two rounds.' Steve's voice was low, controlled.

'Which I paid for out of the money Mum and Dad left me,' Ava hissed.

'But what's the point in pouring more time, money and pain into something that may not come off?' Steve cut in.

Ava felt the familiar knot of guilt tightening.

'It's worth it,' she muttered, but Steve's silence said otherwise.

'Steve, come on,' she tried again. 'I adored my parents and they gave me a loving home. I know adoption works – of all people I get that – but for me, I need a child of my own.'

Steve sighed. 'We could give some lovely child a happy home, without all this torment of IVF. We could be us again.'

A sense of helplessness and frustration began to seep through Ava's veins. How could she explain this to him? It wasn't about dismissing the idea of adoption; it was about the deep, aching need to see her own eyes, her own smile and her own history in a way she'd never been able to see in her adoptive family. She loved them, deeply. But having a family of their own was about something more that she couldn't put into words without it sounding selfish or unfair.

She had never really considered the idea that Steve would refuse to give IVF another try. Her parents had left her their house when they had passed away. After the mortgage had been repaid there had been enough left to give her and Steve a deposit for their own home and a few pounds in the bank which had helped fund the IVF they had tried so far. Ava thought there was enough left for at least another round.

In the past, Steve had always seemed to understand Ava's desire to have a child of her own. He realised that as a child of adoption, Ava needed to feel a blood connection to her own family. Even though he understood, that hadn't stopped Steve trying to get Ava to think about adoption differently. He frequently reminded her that she had no idea where, or who, her roots belonged to, and it didn't matter. Her eyes fell on a framed photo of her parents. She'd always believed Sam and Janet were her parents, regardless of biology. But now, with Steve pushing for a child of their own, the questions she'd buried were starting to rise. Who was she? Where had she come from? And why had she been rejected? By and large these questions were ones she'd ignored. After all, her life had been filled with love, but lately, more than ever, she'd been thinking about where she had come from. All she really knew was that her biological mother was from Dublin and Ava had been desperately wanted by her adopted parents. They had taken her from Ireland and brought her back to England when she was just a few days old.

But there was something about having a baby of her own... Ava wasn't even sure she understood herself, but there was a primal need inside of her to have her own baby. She wasn't ready to let it go.

Reaching for Ava's hands, Steve pulled her towards him and rested his forehead against hers.

'I want to be with you, Ava. I want us to have a family and I don't care what that looks like,' he said softly.

Tears pooled in Ava's eyes; she hadn't heard Steve talk so intimately, so tenderly, for a long time.

A tear slid down Ava's nose and Steve wiped it away with his thumb.

'Please think about adoption.'

She looked up at him. His eyes were so full of hope and desperation. She thought back over the years they had shared together. They had grown up together, been part of one another's lives for so long, and now here he was, begging her to help make their dreams of family a reality. All the love she felt for him rushed through her core. Like Cassie, Steve was her family. Didn't she need to try and bury this primal instinct or whatever it was? For her husband? For her marriage? For her life?

And so, reluctantly, Ava found herself nodding in agreement.

'All right,' she whispered.

As Steve threw his arms around her neck and sobbed his thanks, Ava couldn't help wondering how one person's joy could make someone else feel so lost and broken.

The drive to the west of the city barely took ten minutes from the station, but that still didn't stop Miguel asking Ava why her face was pinched, angry and red.

'It's not,' Ava said hotly.

Miguel knew better than to pry and Ava was glad. Her friend meant well, but that morning's conversation with Steve had left her feeling unsettled.

Furious, tortured questions gnawed away in her mind as they drove past Poet's Corner and then out onto the dual carriageway ahead. Why had she agreed to something she knew in her heart she couldn't do? She was only making life worse for herself later down the line.

The satnav interrupted her train of thought as the disembodied voice advised her the Livesay family lived five minutes away. Turning left when instructed, she drove smoothly past Cassie's estate.

'Perhaps we could pop in on Cassie on the way back,' Miguel said. 'I think we're due to give a fire safety talk there soon.'

Ava smiled, she'd been thinking the same thing herself. 'Maybe you could talk to Dylan while we're there about a hundred ways to tie a tie?'

Miguel laughed. 'And teach him how to dribble. He'll never play for Bristol City if he can't get better ball control.'

'You're going to teach him, are you?' Ava asked drily.

Miguel was an avid football supporter and adored West Ham, but he could barely spell keepy-uppy, never mind perform one.

'I know a thing or two,' Miguel said through pursed lips. 'In Spain it's practically a crime if you can't dribble.'

Ava said nothing as she pulled into a space outside the Livesays' home.

'Thanks for coming with me,' she said, getting out of the car.

Miguel shrugged. 'It's good to do something positive every now and again.'

As they strolled down the street, the unusually bright winter sunshine upon them, she hoped that the family wouldn't mind they were calling on a Saturday. Ava had got so used to working shifts she'd forgotten Saturdays and Sundays were days off for normal people, as she thought of them.

Knocking sharply on a brightly painted red door, Ava and Miguel stood in the warmth of the winter sunshine. It didn't take long for the door to be answered by the man in the photo, Mr Livesay himself.

He looked at the two firefighters warily.

'We're not fundraising,' Miguel said quickly. 'We have something for you.'

At that Ava reached quickly into her bag for the photo. She was quite proud of it, having taken it to a framer she knew to get it repaired. It was as good as new now, she thought, as she handed it over to Mr Livesay.

'We found this in the wreckage of your flat,' she explained.

At the sight of the photo, the man let out a gasp of delight. 'My children.' He looked at Ava and Miguel with incredulity in his eyes. 'But I thought there was nothing left, the police, the family liaison officer, all told me very few possessions had been found. I'm staying with my brother and even living in his old clothes.' He gestured apologetically to the shirt that was clearly two sizes too big for him.

Ava smiled. 'I came across this, thought it might be worth salvaging.'

Wordlessly he gazed down at the frame and ran a finger across the photo.

'You've replaced the frame,' he whispered. 'It's beautiful. Better than the original. I never thought I'd see this again,' he said through tears. 'It sounds silly, I left everything behind when the fire started but what I really wanted to grab was this photo. The children gave it to me before they left.' The man took a pause for breath and looked up at Ava and Miguel. 'The kids live in South Africa now,' he continued. 'Their mum took them back with her two years ago when we split. I haven't seen them since.'

This was too much for Ava, who decided that whilst a hug might be too much, a gentle pat on the forearm was more than appropriate. 'I'm sorry.'

Nodding, Mr Livesay turned to her. 'We split up, you know, all the rows, not good for the kids. So when she went back home I couldn't object. It wasn't good for them to see us fight and I knew they'd have a good life there. But this photo...' He jabbed at the frame now. 'They gave this to me before they left and I thought it was gone forever.'

In that moment he looked as if he was going to break down again but instead smiled, glancing back at Ava and Miguel.

'I can't thank you enough. Can I offer you a drink at least, to say thank you?'

'We're fine, thank you,' Ava said, with a shake of her head. 'Knowing you're happy, that's more than reward enough.'

And before Mr Livesay could say anything else she smiled and gave him a small wave before walking away.

Hearing the front door shut behind them, Ava let out a huge sigh of relief.

'That went well,' Miguel said brightly.

'You sound surprised,' Ava remarked as they walked along the road back to the car.

'Not surprised,' Miguel said carefully. He opened the passenger door of Ava's Astra and got inside. 'Just always astonished at how much these treasures mean to people. You've got a gift, Ava, the way you push and fight to reunite the things that matter with their rightful owners. You never give up.'

At the praise, Ava felt a rush of pleasure. If she was honest, finding lost treasures and then reuniting them was the favourite part of her job and not one that was ever found in any firefighter job description.

The sound of Miguel's phone pinging pierced the silence. He pulled out his phone and his eyes widened in horror.

'What's wrong?'

But Miguel didn't answer and instead handed her the phone.

Ava looked at the phone and let out a gasp of her own.

According to the email Miguel had received, the powers that be were considering cutting jobs.

Chapter Six

It was a long weekend for Ava. She and Steve had spent most of it going around in circles about IVF and adoption. It was the same conversation, over and over again – Steve, optimistic but frustrated, pushing to move forward, and Ava, caught in a spiral of doubt, retreating every time the decision felt too close. The pressure was mounting, and Ava could feel it pressing in from every side, at home, at work. Everywhere she turned, there was something to lose.

Then there was the possible loss of her job and those of her colleagues hanging over her head like a black cloud. Naturally, the news had hit all four watches at the station badly, but Miguel was devastated.

Ava spent much of her day shift that Monday hosing down the rigs with the rest of Blue Watch in the muster bay. As watch manager, she wasn't expected to get her hands dirty any more, but she liked to lead by example and would never ask one of her crew to do something she wasn't prepared to do herself. But as she sloshed water over the rigs, she found that her mind was no longer on job losses but the evening ahead. She and Steve were going out on a date later that night, and if she was honest with herself, she was dreading it. Things between them were dismal, and truthfully she felt they'd be better off

47

pretending to spend quality time together by watching the telly but actually scrolling idly through their phones.

Her mood wasn't helped by the fact that every time she looked up through the windows she could see Miguel pacing up and down in his office, brow furrowed and jaw clenched.

Dropping her sponge into the bucket, she wiped her hands on the back of her trousers and made her way upstairs. Rapping lightly, she poked her head around Miguel's office door.

'I was worried about the carpet,' she teased.

Miguel looked up at her quizzically.

'The pacing,' she explained. 'I thought you might have worn a hole in it, you're doing that much walking up and down.'

'I'm fine,' Miguel said in a tone that said the opposite.

Ava walked inside and shut the door behind her. As she sat in the chair opposite her boss's desk, she waited for him to open up.

'I can't stop thinking about this review committee that are looking into job losses. The union's already been informed,' Miguel added, his voice low. 'There are rumblings of a fight to protect jobs, but...' He trailed off, his eyes reflecting the doubt neither of them wanted to voice.

'You don't know that,' Ava reasoned.

Miguel said nothing, his silence saying more than words ever could.

'Why don't we think about how we can move forward. Be positive?' Ava suggested brightly.

Miguel raised an eyebrow. 'That's unlike you.'

She rubbed her hands up and down her arms trying to encourage some warmth into her body. The time cleaning the rigs had left her frozen to her bones.

'Maybe it's time for a change of heart,' Ava said with a smile. 'Either that or fake it until you make it.'

The well-worn phrase was something she had been saying to herself repeatedly since deciding to give Steve what he wanted and look at adoption.

Her heart wasn't in her decision. Deep down she was hoping that she might get pregnant by accident. She'd read about it all the time in women's magazines. Women like her thought they were hurtling towards the menopause and then found themselves pregnant. Or had gone through rounds and rounds of unsuccessful IVF only to wind up pregnant naturally after they'd stopped trying.

Miguel offered her a wan smile. 'Like every firefighter here, I'm lost without this job, Ava, it's everything. It's not just a job, it's a home, it's family.'

'I know,' Ava said softly.

She felt the same. Even though she wanted a family of her own, her station crew were already family to her, and she knew she'd be lost without the fire station and the firefighters that made up the watch.

Suddenly she had an idea.

'What if we ask Cassie to help?'

Miguel gave Ava a sceptical look. 'I know she's your best mate but how's she going to help?'

'The community.' Ava's eyes glinted with determination. 'If we want to save the fire station we need to get the community behind us, and Cassie's estate is all about community. Get them on side and we can prove how needed we are.'

Miguel still looked doubtful. 'We'll never do it. I don't know exactly how long we've got, but no doubt the powers that be will want to make decisions as soon as they can.'

'There'll be plenty of time,' Ava countered. As the idea grew, she felt a swell of optimism. 'We can design a programme for the kids, and also encourage other schools to get involved. What about holding events here or up at the community centre on Friday nights? You said you wanted to do more for the community, now's your chance.'

Her eyes fell on a 'Back to the Eighties' poster on the noticeboard inside Miguel's office. When she was a child, her mum and dad had not only routinely taken her to Saturday morning cinema but they'd also got her involved in community events. She'd helped out at old people's homes, played netball for a local team even though she was terrible and, of course, helped out when the fire station held charity car washes.

Janet, Ava's mum, had been insistent they all gave back. Although her mum had worked full-time for the city council, she had volunteered every other Saturday at the local women's refuge, and was always sending her dad, Sam, to the shelter with old shoes and clothes Ava had grown out of for the children. Sam, like his wife, believed in the power of community. He had once been in the army and was the first to help as a volunteer with any community endeavour. Caring for those around her was a vocation for Ava.

'We'll start this Friday night, assuming Cassie agrees. Bring Xavier with you,' she instructed. 'And I'll bring Steve, if he'll come,' she muttered.

'Why?' Miguel looked puzzled again. 'What do they know about firefighting? Xavier runs comedy nights and he's planning on catching up with *Bake Off* while I'm out.'

Ava rolled her eyes. 'We'll do a boot camp exercise session with them all. Cassie will join in with Dylan. It will show those kids and everyone else on the estate how important community is to all walks of life, how valuable firefighters are.'

'I don't really see how Xavier and Steve will do that.' Miguel still looked doubtful.

Ava battled her impatience. 'Because it shows that no matter who we are or how busy we are, we can still make time to come together for community.'

'And you really think it will work?'

'I don't know.' Ava sighed. 'But I know we have to try, and that's probably more important than *Bake Off*. We're not going out without a fight.'

-

Despite the chill of the November evening, the rooftop bar at the top of the city gave off a distinctly Mediterranean vibe. As she sat on a bar stool next to a window that offered views of the floodlit city, Ava smiled. There were times she really did feel lucky to have grown up and now live in such a beautiful city that brought tourists in from all over the world.

From her vantage point, she could see the lights of the shopping district and the orange glow of the Pump Room. She had no idea how the evening with Steve would turn out. Of course, he'd accepted her apology on the surface, but he was distant and Ava could only feel the gap between them widening. She looked over at him now, at the bar ordering them each a drink. He'd been an hour late to meet her, claiming that work had got on top of him. For the sake of good relations, Ava had chosen to believe him, but a part of her believed his thoughtlessness was a punishment, or worse, a sign of indifference towards her and their relationship.

She leaned back in her chair and tried to stop her head from spinning. She'd had two glasses of wine while she waited, a decision she was now beginning to regret. She continued to watch her husband. Still as handsome as the boy she had met all those years ago.

Would they have got married if her parents hadn't died? At just eighteen, her need for security had hung heavy and Steve had offered her a chance to feel anchored. Had she really loved him? She thought so, but was it enough?

When she and Cassie had flown back from Madeira, her heart gripped by loss, she'd found Steve waiting for her at Bristol airport, armed with a hug and a huge bunch of flowers. The sight of him waiting for her had grounded her. It wasn't until later that she had found it strange he never suggested accompanying her. Years later, when she'd asked him why he'd never offered to fly with her, he'd shrugged and said that he thought it was obvious Cassie would be her first choice.

'She's been a constant in your life, far longer than I have,' he explained. 'She was your family before I was.'

He was right, there was no getting away from the fact Cassie and Ava were more than friends and always had been. Steve had been a lovely addition and since they met had always proved a reliable constant, with the love she and Steve shared blossoming over time.

They moved in together when Ava was nineteen and at twenty, Steve proposed to her in a pizza restaurant as they celebrated the dawn of a new millennium. A delighted Ava had screamed yes over and over and they'd married a year later buying the mid-terrace they still lived in.

It was only now Ava wondered if she'd chosen to marry Steve because she'd been desperate for connection, or because she had truly wanted him. Had she really made a choice or had she allowed herself to get carried away by circumstance?

Looking back, the only choice Ava felt she had ever really made was becoming a firefighter. It had been before she and Steve had got engaged and she remembered how at the time Steve had railed against it, claiming it was dangerous, but Ava had held firm. She had written to Raoul before she joined and with his support she had completed her training. Slowly, Steve had come around, and in the end become her biggest cheerleader.

Now, as Steve carried their drinks towards her, she wondered if her fear of having to strike out on her own was the real reason they couldn't have kids. Was that why her womb was hostile?

'What's all this?' Ava asked.

'An apology for being late and an opportunity to celebrate a rare night off together,' Steve said, setting down a tray with a bottle of champagne and two glasses.

Ava was doubtful. Much as she loved a drink, up until tonight she'd been avoiding indulging too much for the past few months, doing everything she could to get her body baby ready.

Steve caught her concern. 'Come on,' he encouraged. 'No need to worry about booze intake now. You can treat yourself, another advantage of adoption.'

Ava swallowed the rush of anger that swelled inside her. She didn't want to ruin the night and say something before their evening had truly begun. She had to give Steve a chance. Something Cassie had reminded her of earlier that day in a WhatsApp message.

> Just enjoy yourself and for one night let the baby stuff go. You can row about it in the morning. Cx

Like so much of Cassie's advice, it was blunt but fair. So, Ava plastered on a smile and took a large sip.

'Any news on the fire station?' Steve asked.

Ava shook her head. 'Miguel's worried though. Big Stu says the authorities will see us as the dream team we are, but I don't know.'

'If they don't, surely you'll be able to go somewhere else?' Steve asked.

'I don't want to go somewhere else.' Ava took another sip of her wine. 'I like it at Bath City, which is why we're going to hold a boot camp fitness day for the kids at the estate and we need your help.'

Steve widened his eyes in surprise. 'What do you want me to do, climb ladders and shimmy down poles?'

'Not quite,' Ava laughed. 'Xavier will be there, too.'

'Xavier's half my age!' Steve protested.

'You're exaggerating, and Cassie will also be doing it.'

Steve moaned. 'Cassie runs half marathons for fun.'

Ava laughed. Cassie had always been a fitness freak. She lifted weights watching telly as a way to relax.

'We just need bodies to show it's easy,' Ava said. She put her drink down, reached forward and held her husband's hand. 'It's a way of helping some of the kids on the estate and showing them that there are other things to do than play with matches and start fires.'

'I don't know what's wrong with kids these days,' Steve said, his expression growing weary. 'When I was their age, we used to hang about the streets asking for a penny for the guy at this time of the year.'

'All right, Granddad,' Ava teased. 'Times change. The kids want more excitement than your mum's old tights balled up into a sack with a face drawn on it.'

'You do paint a lovely picture of life in the Eighties.' Steve laughed. He gave his wife's hand a squeeze then leaned back in his seat.

'I just say it as I see it.' Ava smiled, pleased with herself for following Cassie's advice, and despite her worries, was beginning to enjoy herself. 'So, are you in?' she asked. 'I'm seeing Cassie tomorrow to finalise details, it'd be great to tell her you'll be there.'

'Doesn't seem as if I have much choice.'

Ava smiled. 'Well done. Think about the exercise.'

'I exercise,' Steve protested.

'Not enough,' Ava warned. 'Especially if we're planning on kids.'

She bit her lip. She hadn't meant to mention kids. But at the suggestion of fatherhood Ava could see Steve's face relax.

She touched her glass to his. 'The future.'

'The future,' he echoed.

Whatever it may hold, she thought.

Chapter Seven

On Friday evening, Ava pulled into Cassie's estate, feeling almost happy. Her night out with Steve had been the tonic she hadn't known she'd needed and she was still glowing.

For the first time in weeks, the tension between them seemed to have eased. It wasn't that their problems had disappeared, but the weight of IVF and adoption felt a little lighter, at least for now. But as good as it had felt, Ava knew they weren't out of the woods yet, even if their night out had obviously done Steve good, too.

He'd been cheerful all week, whistling in the shower, kissing her without invitation or prompt. The only thing marring her mood now was the anniversary. She'd been feeling so light, she'd almost forgotten what day it was. Then she'd sat up and remembered, the pain of realisation almost as cutting as the moment she'd received that heady phone call all those years ago.

Pushing her grief to one side, she got out of the car and walked towards the community centre looking forward to seeing her friend.

Just as she'd expected, Cassie had been eager to help the station's cause and jumped at the chance to hold an information evening that Friday. It was typical Cassie, always leaping into action to help, but she was full of good qualities, like the way she could always help Ava see things more clearly. It was one of the things Ava loved most about their friendship. It was a balance to the emotional chaos of her own life.

She passed Miguel's car as she went and spotted her boss and Cassie through the window of the centre, heads bent over charts and posters. Ava's heart sank; these kids would want to hear about danger and escapades not graphs.

'What have you got there?' she asked walking inside, in an overly bright voice that was trying to mask her negativity.

Cassie turned and gave her a megawatt smile. 'We were just talking about you! As well as the boot camp, Miguel's got some graphics he thinks could be good for the kids. We thought we'd start with an introduction to it all tonight.'

Ava peered over Miguel's shoulder. 'Wouldn't pictures of the ladders they can climb down at the station drill area be better?' Ava suggested.

'We have to reach the parents. Can't make it all fun for the kids,' he pointed out.

Miguel was right but Ava wasn't sure he was going about it in the best way. She also knew now wasn't the time to try and change his mind; Miguel had that determined look about him. Better for her to focus on something else. Cassie had asked her a month or so ago if she'd have a chat with a hoarder that had been with them since the estate was developed. He was well known to the fire service, as all hoarders were, but Cassie was worried about him. He had become more of a recluse and more parcels continued to arrive at his door.

'How about I go and talk to Mr Hopkins,' she said instead.

'Good idea,' Miguel said without looking up. 'I'll join you in a minute.'

'I'll come with you,' Cassie said. 'He's a bit prickly these days.'

Shooting Miguel a sunny smile, she hastily followed Cassie out of the centre and into the street.

Soon, they were standing outside a rundown house, with books piled up at the windows and newspapers stuffed in between. It was impossible to see inside and Ava dreaded to think what else they might find.

'Mr Hopkins,' Cassie called, rapping on the wooden door. 'The fire service is here. They'd just like a quick word.'

Ava waited for the sound of footsteps to come to the door but there was nothing beyond the noise of traffic from the A-road behind them.

'Mr Hopkins,' Cassie tried again.

Still nothing. And with so much pressed up against the windows it was impossible to tell if there were any lights on and someone home.

'Hmmm, that's unusual,' Cassie said with a frown. 'He's always around at this time.'

'Could he be with a relative? Be a bit late perhaps?' Ava asked. She hated hoarder interviews. Being a natural neat freak, she always wanted to start decluttering the moment she was inside.

'Unlikely,' Cassie said. She checked the time on her phone. 'I suppose he could be with his sister but that's not something he usually does in the week.' She looked around, thoughtful for a moment, as if expecting Mr Hopkins to suddenly pop up at any moment.

'Let's wait, see if he comes back.' Cassie gestured to the bench opposite Mr Hopkins's house and Ava nodded.

Sitting beside her friend, she rubbed her hands together to keep warm.

'Thought you'd have all the gear to keep the cold out,' Cassie said good-naturedly.

'Only for fires,' Ava explained. 'All that heat protective stuff costs money, we have to suffer like everyone else.'

Cassie smiled and rubbed her arms to try and keep out the cold. 'You really ought to get onto them about that, Aves. Time you enjoyed a few perks the rest of us don't.'

Ava chuckled. 'The Salvation Army has started upping the biscuits they're doling out at a rescue lately.'

'Ooh nice.' Cassie looked animated. 'You know I love a Jammy Dodger.'

'You're so old fashioned!' Ava chuckled. 'You're more likely to be offered a triple chocolate cookie or gin and tonic-flavoured, sugar-free layer cake now than a custard cream.'

Cassie laughed and stamped her trainer-clad feet on the floor in a bid to warm them up.

'You ever think about doing something different?'

'What do you mean?' Ava looked at Cassie blankly.

'The service,' Cassie said. 'You've been doing it so long now. You ever think the world's trying to tell you something with all this threat of closure business?'

'Cass!' Ava exclaimed. 'How can you say that? You know how I feel about the service.'

At that, Cassie laughed. 'I know. I s'pose I'm jealous. I love the community aspect of this place but I'm so fed up at the lack of dough to actually help people. Look at Mr Hopkins, the poor bugger needs real support. All I can do is offer to whip round with a duster when I've got a minute.'

Ava linked her arm through her friend's. 'You're doing your best. That's all you can do.'

'Never enough though, is it.' Cassie sighed and turned to her friend. 'You all right today?'

Ava felt her throat constrict and the tears she'd been holding back since that morning were now trickling down her face.

'I almost forgot,' she whispered. 'For the first time, I forgot.'

Cassie wrapped an arm around her friend's shoulders.

'It's okay, it's just part of the process. Doesn't mean you loved your mum and dad any less, you know.'

'I know.' Ava sniffed. 'But it feels like they're slipping away from me. As though not remembering means they're lost to me again.'

Cassie said nothing. She simply held her friend, and Ava let the tears fall onto her shoulder as she had so many times before. This time, she allowed the memory to run through her mind like a film.

The call from the Portuguese paramedic just as she'd come back from college for lunch. The dismay, the disbelief, as she took in the news. The way Cassie had never left her side, only when Ava went to the morgue to formally identify her parents' bodies. The way they'd looked so still, so similar but so different. The way Ava had just wanted to pull the covers around her mum's chin to keep her warm, and the way her dad's hands were by his side rather than folded on his lap – the way he always held his hands, even when he was asleep. Then there had been after, the endless paperwork Cassie had helped her deal with. And of course, the only bright star – a wonderful Portuguese firefighter named Raoul who had taken care of her. Driven them both to the site of the hotel, the soothing tones he used to explain her mum and dad would have felt no pain.

Even now they stayed in touch.

She lifted her head from Cassie's shoulder, her eyes bright with tears. Cassie squeezed her hand and the warmth of her friend's skin was as reassuring today as it had been all those years ago. It was comforting – the simple joy of friendship, finding someone who knew you as well as you knew yourself.

She ran a hand over the necklace she always wore when she wasn't fighting fires and felt its strength ground her. Only a few close to her knew the real reason she wanted to be a firefighter and why it was more than a job. Most people assumed when they heard the story of how her parents died that it was because she had been moved by the firefighters who had tried to save them. That was certainly part of the reason, but not all of it.

Yes, of course Raoul's kindness had moved her, but something else convinced her she wanted to be a firefighter. She ran her fingers across the necklace as she always did when she felt nervous.

'You know how Raoul managed to find this for me amongst the wreckage?'

'I do,' Cassie said. She leaned back and touched the necklace around Ava's neck.

The locket caught the morning light, flashing a beacon of gold as she did so.

'Raoul thought I might like something that had been important to Mum. He said he'd been firefighting for over ten years and liked to try and reunite those that had lost loved ones with something important, give them a happy memory to treasure.'

'I remember,' Cassie said softly.

Ava nodded. Her hands were trembling now as she reached around her neck and undid the chain. But she knew what she was about to do was worth it. This talisman that meant so much deserved another chance at love.

'This necklace means the world and my mother knew it; it was why she carried it with her.'

Cassie nodded. 'It's something I never understood. I always thought this necklace was yours.'

Dread shot through Ava's stomach. Cassie only knew part of the story. Today it felt right to share the rest.

'I think I told you that we had a row... Mum and me, the day before they went on holiday,' Ava said shakily, holding the necklace in her hand now. 'I threw it on the bed. Told her I didn't want it any more, that it meant nothing.' She paused and Cassie reached out and held her hand, encouraging her to go on. 'I treasured the necklace, wore it all the time.'

Cassie nodded. 'You said your birth mother gave it to you, along with a white robe.'

Ava nodded. Over the years, she'd tried to find out more about the people that had made her. Cassie had even tried to help, when they were teenagers. But the Irish adoption system prevented her, and since her mum and dad had died she'd shied away from wanting to find out more about her biological parents. It had seemed disloyal somehow, as though she was saying Janet and Sam weren't enough.

But there were times, especially lately with her own quest for a baby, that Ava had wondered where she had come from. Every time she did, she shook the thought free from her mind. She had tried to find out the truth when she was eighteen and look what had happened.

'What I've never told you is that just before Mum and Dad went to Madeira I kept on asking them questions about my adoption and couldn't understand why they didn't have the answers,' Ava began. Her voice was shaking but she knew it was time to unburden herself. 'All they kept telling me was that I was chosen, that I was loved very much. It wasn't enough, I felt as if I didn't know who I was. I wanted to know about me. Mum kept telling me I should write my own story, that it didn't matter where I came from but what mattered was where I was going.'

'Your mum was always wise,' Cassie said quietly.

'She was,' Ava agreed, her voice now tinged with regret. 'I didn't know how much. I pushed her and pushed her for answers. Then we had this terrible argument about it all.'

At the memory, Ava closed her eyes, the horror of the words she had flung at her mother as cruel as weapons. They still haunted her to this day.

'I told her she couldn't understand what it was like for me,' Ava explained, her voice faltering as she bared the very worst of herself. 'That she might have thought I was chosen but I felt differently. I always had, since that day at primary school when I'd had to give my birth certificate into the school office and instead could only give them the Certificate of Entry into the Adopted Children Register. The teacher looked surprised and then pitiful, it made me feel terrible, like I'd done something wrong.' Ava didn't want to reveal the true horror of the words she had said, the pain she had no doubt caused the woman that loved her unconditionally. It still hurt.

'Oh Ava,' Cassie gasped. 'That's awful.'

'And then I threw this necklace at her.' She swallowed past the lump in her throat. 'Told her it was worthless if she couldn't tell me what I needed to know. That it would mean more to Mum than me. She picked it up and I assumed she thought I would want it myself one day.'

'Maybe a way of keeping you close,' Cassie whispered. 'You know all those treasures you keep hold of? Maybe your mum was doing something similar. Waiting for the right time to reunite the keepsake with you one day.'

There was a pause as Ava realised how right her friend was. Maybe that was why she had this compulsion to reunite people with lost items. Memories, treasures and keepsakes. They weren't about the objects, they were about the connections people made through life. A way of keeping a loved one beside you, no matter what.

'The thing is, Cass, I didn't realise Mum didn't know, herself,' Ava continued. 'I thought she was keeping things from me.'

'But she'd always been honest that you were adopted?' Cassie quizzed.

'Yep, stupid, wasn't I?' Ava sighed, frustrated with herself. She spread her long, pale fingers out before her and examined the skin. So many callouses and lines now compared to the young hand that her mother would have seen curled into a fist as she threw the necklace. A whole life lived.

'I was too young and naive to piece things together,' Ava said. 'And now this necklace has so many memories attached to it.'

She held it up to the light, then pressed it into her friend's hand.

'Time to make new memories now.'

Cassie looked at her blankly. 'What?'

'I want you to have it. It's yours. It's a connection between us now, that's what I want this necklace to mean.'

Cassie looked at the piece of jewellery that lay in her hand. She opened her mouth, about to speak, but Ava cut her off.

'You're my family, Cass. You've been with me through every step of my life. This necklace, it seems right I give it to you today.'

'I—I—I don't know what to say.' Cassie was crying now, tears streaming down her golden-brown face. 'I wasn't expecting this, Aves.'

'Neither was I,' Ava said, laughing as she wept. 'But this just seems right. I love you, Cass, I want you to know that.'

Cassie looked at the necklace in her hand and pressed it to her heart, clutching it until her fingers were white.

'And I love you,' she whispered. 'You and Dyl are my favourite humans in the world.'

There was another pause as each woman looked into the eyes of the other. The silence between them saying so much more than words ever could.

Silently, Cassie slipped the necklace around her neck, the star catching the soft light as it lay against her olive skin.

'I'll never take it off.'

Just then the sound of footsteps coming towards them broke them apart.

They looked up in unison to see Miguel walking towards them.

'Are you two coming back? It's chaos in there. The kids are running riot. Poor Steve's close to tears and Xavier's fuming – one little horror is diabolical. He keeps trying to trip me up as I walk past him.'

'Little sod,' Cassie snapped, getting to her feet and wiping away her tears with the back of her hand. 'I bet that's Jolie Nelson's eldest. I'm always trying to reason with him.'

A scowl passed across Miguel's face. 'Trust me, Cassie, if he comes near my freshly pressed trousers again, I'll be doing a lot more than reasoning.'

Cassie shuddered while Ava stifled a laugh.

Together they got up and walked across the courtyard back to the centre. Ava didn't have the heart to tell Miguel his freshly pressed trousers had a rip in the back. There were some things in life that didn't need mentioning.

Chapter Eight

Over the next few days, Ava found home and work kept her busy. She had reluctantly agreed to go to another adoption event later that week with Steve and this time, for the sake of her marriage if nothing else, resolved to at least try and plaster on a smile. But no matter how hard she tried, the idea of adoption still sat heavy in her chest, a reminder of the life she wasn't sure she was ready for. In truth, she couldn't help but wonder how long she could keep pretending.

Since her heart-to-heart with Cassie the other day, Ava had been thinking. Giving Cassie her necklace had felt like the most natural thing in the world. A chance for old memories to merge with new ones as Cassie now took on the talisman. Giving away such an important piece of her past had also made Ava feel lighter. For so long Ava had felt rooted in her history, the necklace perhaps helping keep her there. Now, she felt readier to embrace the future – whatever that looked like.

Then of course there was her job. The threat of job losses hung over the Blue, Red, Green and White Watches like an angry cloud, but Ava refused to worry. She believed there was still hope. Her Nostalgia Nook was proof of that. After all, today she was hoping to reunite one of her lost treasures.

A month earlier she had attended a fire at a DIY store. Thankfully, the blaze had started at night so there were no casualties. But amongst the wreckage Ava had found a gold and emerald eternity ring with a small inscription. The task of finding its owner had been painstaking, the ring jutting out of her shelf almost teasing her, but two days ago she had worked out who the rightful owner was. And today, before she began her shift, she wanted to return the ring, hopefully with someone she knew needed cheering up.

Tapping lightly on Miguel's office door, she saw his head millimetres from the computer screen in front of him. He was staring intently at rows of numbers.

Ava had no idea what Miguel was looking at, but knew columns of figures that looked like that weren't something that would easily bring joy.

'Come on, we're off out,' she called to his back.

'I can't,' Miguel moaned. 'I've got a meeting with the group manager in two hours.'

But Ava wasn't ready to be dissuaded.

'This won't take long, we're just going into town for a bit.'

Sensing when he was beaten, Miguel stood up and followed Ava outside, heading to his car. But Ava shook her head and pointed towards the path.

Together the two set off down the busy main road into the centre of town.

Silent for a few moments, both were happy to enjoy the warm winter sunshine that made the city glow. It was easy to forget how beautiful this city was, Ava mused as they rounded the corner of the main shopping street and began their descent past the bookshop and ice cream parlour. Bath was such an old city that had been built with the purpose of entertainment in mind. It was easy to take for granted the sheer beauty of every Georgian building, the creamy stone often dirty from pollution, but nonetheless glorious with every inch of architecture offering something new to look at.

They passed the old Mineral Water Hospital and wound their way through the narrow streets bursting with coffee shops and bakeries, before crossing the road and stopping outside a pub.

'Come on.'

'A drink?' Miguel looked puzzled. 'I'm on duty.'

'We're not drinking.' Ava rolled her eyes and simultaneously tugged at his sleeve as she pushed the door open.

This pub, The Cow and Cello, had been a favourite in her teens. With its sticky floor, dark interior and cloud of cigarette smoke, it had been the perfect place to drink beer – or rather alcopops – back then.

Now, the place had changed into a gorgeous gastropub with rich blue walls, stripped wooden floorboards and a gleaming brass bar. Striding towards it, Ava caught sight of a burly barman. Dark and wearing a checked shirt, she hoped she'd found the right person.

'Josh?' she asked brightly.

The barman looked up, his thick head of dark curls bouncing on his shoulders as he did so.

'Who wants to know?'

'I do,' Ava said. 'I'm a firefighter with Bath Fire Station and I think this might be yours.'

Fishing into her pocket she reached for the ring she had found and held it aloft.

'Ava, what are you doing?' Miguel hissed.

Josh looked at her, curiosity dancing across his features, and Ava laughed and winked at Miguel.

'Relax, I'm not asking him to marry me.' She turned to Josh. 'I promise. I found this in the fire over at the DIY store last month.'

'Did you?' Miguel looked even more puzzled. 'But the place burnt to a crisp.'

Josh sucked in a sharp breath as he gingerly took the ring from Ava's outstretched hand.

'However did you find this?'

Ava shifted from foot to foot. She didn't want to admit she'd spent hours combing the wreckage until she'd found something that she could take to someone.

Josh broke the silence. 'I do security a couple of nights a week there, or at least I did.'

A look of knowing passed between Miguel and Ava. The cold hard truth of firefighting was that very often people were injured or died. In a way it was lucky, much as they would hate to say it, that Josh hadn't been at work when the fire started. He would have been looking at a very different ending if he had.

Finding the ring was a happy accident, something good to have come from something so awful. Ava was thrilled to hand it over now.

Josh turned the band over and held it up to the light. 'It's even got the inscription,' he marvelled.

'"Indira my rock",' Ava murmured.

'My mother,' Josh said quietly.

Then pressing the ring to his heart, Ava saw tears pool in his eyes.

'I thought this was gone forever. This was the only thing I had left of her.'

'I'm so sorry,' Miguel murmured. 'What happened?'

'She died,' Josh said flatly.

'Not in the fire?' Miguel exclaimed. He turned to Ava looking concerned. 'I didn't think there were any casualties.'

'There weren't,' Ava said. 'It was an empty building. The fire was caused by faulty wiring in a routing box.'

'Mum died when I was a teenager. Long story.' He looked down at the ring, clearly not wanting to explain more. 'I'd planned to take it down to the jeweller to get it resized so I could propose to my girlfriend, Siobhan, after my shift. But it must have fallen out of my pocket during my last shift. I didn't realise until I got ready for bed and got undressed. Then I heard about the fire and thought that, as well as losing my job, I'd lost the ring.' Eyes glistening with emotion, Josh kissed the ring and put it securely in his shirt pocket, buttoning it closed.

Ava looked concerned. 'Haven't you got anything a bit more secure?' she asked. 'I'd hate to think of you losing it again.'

Miguel shook his head in despair. 'For crying out loud Ava, stop mothering the lad.' He nodded at Josh. 'It'll be fine in your pocket. I'm just glad we could get you your ring back in one piece.'

'I'm never letting it out of my sight again.' He patted his pocket, almost checking the security after Ava's words. 'How can I ever thank you? You've done the unthinkable. You've brought me back my mother.'

Ava looked away, suddenly feeling embarrassed. 'We did nothing. Just reunited this ring with its rightful owner. And as for your mum, well, she was always here.' Ava gestured to her heart. 'She was never lost.'

At that Josh looked as if he might start crying. Sensing a full-scale weeping fest between Ava and Josh, Miguel smiled at the bartender and took hold of Ava's elbow.

'We'll let you get on with your day,' Miguel said kindly now. 'You take care.'

'I will,' Josh said, wiping away the tears with the back of his hand. 'And thank you. If there's anything I can do for you, free drinks!' he called with sudden excitement to his voice. 'They're on me.'

'Not necessary,' Miguel called from the doorway.

On the pavement, Ava turned to Miguel and looked at him triumphantly.

'See?'

'See what?'

'Don't you feel joy?' Ava pressed. 'This is why what we do is so important.'

Hanging his head, Miguel scratched his chin then suddenly pulled Ava in for a hug.

'You daft old sod. Where would I be without you?'

Releasing her, he squeezed her shoulder. 'Thanks. I think I did need reminding that what we do is about much more than paperwork and that all this –' he gestured to the pub around him '– is worth fighting for.'

'Exactly,' Ava agreed.

She linked her arm through his and together they set off back up the hill towards the fire station. Inspiration could be found anywhere; Ava was pleased she had managed to help Miguel find his to keep fighting for what they both knew was important. If only she could find the courage to do the same.

Chapter Nine

Despite the success of their outing, there wasn't long to bask in the glory of Josh's find for Ava and Miguel. No sooner had they returned to the station than there was a shout.

'Anything serious?' Ava called.

'It's something up on Cassie's estate,' Jodie called as she raced to the pole chute. 'Mr Hopkins's house is on fire.'

Ava's heart sank. This was the very real worry when it came to hoarders. They, of course, had every right to live as they pleased, but the simple truth was that too many belongings blocked exits and caused fires to spread more quickly; there was simply more material to burn. Ava, like the rest of her colleagues, had the utmost sympathy for those that struggled with hoarding tendencies, but the truth was hoarding could be a serious fire hazard.

In one practised fashion she slid down the pole and into the muster bay.

'Has it spread?' she asked, glancing at the rest of the watch.

'At least to the houses either side,' Emerson replied.

Reaching for her neatly laid out kit, Ava dressed quickly. This wasn't good news for her or anyone else.

Scrambling into the back of the cab, she waited for Big Stu to take the wheel while Jodie and Emerson climbed in the front and Phil and Miguel, who felt the incident was likely to be larger than initial reports suggested, got into the back. The whole cab was silent as they made their way towards the container, even Jodie was quiet, mentally processing what they could expect.

They arrived just behind the unit from Bath North to thick plumes of smoke and Ava jumped out of the engine to take in the scene. Not only was there thick smoke but the stench of so much burning was an assault on her nostrils.

Casting her gaze wider down the street, her heart sank when she saw bright orange flames licking what had once been the windows of Mr Hopkins's home. Not only were the houses next door on fire, but the blaze had travelled the length of the street and was currently destroying the community centre too.

It seemed Miguel had been right.

The sound of nervous chatter behind Ava was getting louder. She turned and saw the usual throngs of people, astonishment and shock on their faces as they tried to absorb the devastation.

But amidst the shocked faces, Ava saw Cassie clutching Dylan. Her home was a few doors down from Mr Hopkins's, and the desperation on Cassie's face shocked Ava to the core. Ava had always been her protector, even when they were kids. And now, as the fire raged dangerously close, she felt that old instinct rising again. For a moment, all Ava wanted was to run to Cassie and put her arms around her and tell her everything was going to be okay. Just as she had when two bullies in Year Nine had flushed her head down the loo. Ava had been so incensed at what had happened to her friend, she had helped wash and dry Cassie's hair then found the bullies responsible and given each a hard shove into the lockers and a slap around the face in the process. She had earned herself a week's suspension for violence but Ava hadn't cared, her friend had been hurting. That was all that mattered.

Today, the bully in question was a fire, destroying everything her friend held dear – the best thing she could really do for Cassie was her job.

Miguel, along with the station manager from Bath North, quickly established the command centre. Ava knew that they were in for a long night. Although there were a lot of people on the street, search and rescue would be a vital part of their operation. Residents and animals may not have managed to find safety and paramedics could be needed, even though all firefighters were trained to deliver urgent, life-saving care.

Though it wasn't her usual task as watch manager, Ava stepped in to help Jodie, ensuring the hose was ready to tackle the blaze. They worked silently and swiftly, each movement efficient as they connected the hose that would allow the jets of water to unfurl across the flames.

The operation took seconds as Big Stu, Phil and Emerson hooked up their breathing apparatus and went inside. Miguel looked on and nodded at Ava, urging her to keep an eye on the breathing gauge.

For hours, Ava and the watch worked to bring the fire under control, all under the scrutiny of residents who watched eagerly in the background, awaiting to see how this, their very own real-life drama, would unfold. Cassie seemed to instinctively keep out of Ava's way – holding onto Dylan for dear life as she soothed residents' fears and helped distribute the cups of tea and biscuits that the Salvation Army had provided. The only communication the women had between one another was the odd comforting smile. For Ava it was enough to keep going, when her back ached and her lungs hurt, that smile reminded her that she had survived tough times and she would survive this too.

That smile also helped when Big Stu emerged with what looked like a non-responsive Mr Hopkins in his arms. Ava's heart sank. People always thought they had more time in a fire, that they could grab those precious items, not realising that the thick plumes of smoke they were inhaling would cause them to pass out, making escape impossible.

Blue Watch, together with the White Watch from Bath North, carried on like this for hours. Between them they found another two people who hadn't escaped their homes and brought them to safety, all the while battling the blaze. At a little after three in the morning, the fire was officially brought under control. Ava was spent.

'Take a break,' Miguel instructed. 'I'll take over here. You go up to the bridge and check in with command.'

Ava didn't need telling twice. Although she was used to manning the water pumps for hours, Jodie wasn't and Ava had had to take over from her to give the new recruit a break more than once. Her eyes were dry and sore and her whole body was exhausted, but that didn't mean she could stop. The fire might be under control, but the estate was decimated.

'Control, this is Watch Manager Ava Ryan,' she called into her radio. 'Road closures need to remain in place until at least first thing.'

'Copy that,' the disembodied voice replied.

Ava turned her gaze to the thermal-imaging camera for the properties, relief flooding through her as the colours dulled. Her finger hovered over the radio, ready to report that all the houses were clear. Then she froze. A bright orange figure suddenly flared on the screen, glowing hot against the cooling backdrop. Ava's breath caught in her throat. Something wasn't right. The figure burned brightly, a heat signature that stood out starkly against the rest.

She peered closely at the screen and gasped. The figure was in Cassie's house! Ava scanned the crowd for her friend. Seeing Cassie standing with her neighbour Dolores, she let out a sigh of relief until she realised something was missing. Dylan. He was no longer by Cassie's side.

Ava took a deep breath to steady herself, reminding herself not to jump to conclusions before knowing all the facts. She glanced again at the camera, wondering if her tired eyes had deceived her. But no matter how exhausted she was, there was no mistaking the orange glow now moving around. Years of training had taught her to trust her gut, but this felt different somehow, more personal, more dangerous.

Could it really be Dylan? She had drummed into him how dangerous fires could be ever since he was old enough to walk – hadn't the message hit home?

But there was no time for recriminations. Whoever was up there wouldn't have much chance of survival. Plumes of orange flames, intertwined with thick black smoke were spilling from what was left of the window. Any chance of rescue was becoming slimmer by the second.

Her heart pounded as she radioed Miguel, her voice calm despite the adrenaline flooding her system.

'We've got movement on the top floor. A heat signature, likely a person. Possible snatch rescue on the top floor,' Ava said steadily. 'I'll move fast and get out before it spreads.'

'Roger that,' Miguel replied calmly. 'Backup's on standby.'

Ava knew the importance of clear communication. As a firefighter, nobody was ever alone.

Blue Watch was so well seasoned when it came to working together that Emerson had arrived at the fire appliance before she'd even finished speaking to Miguel.

'You going with the nine-metre for the second storey?' Emerson asked, reaching for the ladder.

Emerson had been on the job almost as long as Ava, but even he looked concerned at the idea of a rare snatch rescue.

Ava nodded. 'Can you help me get it straight? Then I'll go up there once I've got my breathing apparatus on.'

Ava had thirty minutes with her breathing apparatus. She wasn't wasting a second. Once the ladder was positioned under what was left of the window, Ava carefully made her way up the rungs. She had almost reached the top when she heard screams from the ground below.

'Ava,' Cassie roared. 'What the fuck do you think you're doing?'

The panic in her friend's voice was audible, but Ava wasn't about to waste time answering her. In this moment, her only concern was who was inside.

Reaching the top of the ladder, she opened the sash window of Cassie's bedroom just enough to squeeze her body through. Inside, the smoke was thick, the visibility poor. She kept the thermal-imaging camera in one hand, scanning the room as she moved. The heat from the fire grew stronger, licking at the walls as she pressed forward. The flat was a maze of overturned furniture and smoke, but the camera showed the path clearly, the bright orange figure just ahead, lying still.

Ava's pulse began to quicken. She knew she was looking for Dylan and she wasn't leaving the house without him. Every breath through her mask felt heavier than the last, the heat searing against her gear. Her movements were slow, deliberate.

Determined to remain in control, Ava padded her way through the room before moving out onto the tiny landing and into Dylan's bedroom next door. The smoke wasn't as thick in here and Ava could immediately see the single bed and stack of toys in the corner. It was then her eyes fell to a lump on the floor.

Ava sprang into action and rushed across the floor to reach the figure. She dropped to her knees as she grabbed his arm. Dylan. His small body lay limp, as he clutched a small teddy bear in his hands.

Her throat constricted, as her eyes roamed across his body. Seeing the slight rise and fall of his chest she felt a surge of relief.

'Dyl, it's me, Auntie Ava,' she said loudly. 'We're going to get you out of here. Stay low, keep still.'

At the sound of her voice Dylan lifted his head and peered at her through her mask. She could see the fear in his eyes.

'I wanted to get Bry, my teddy, from my bedroom. I've had him since I was a baby,' Dylan said.

A mix of sorrow and anger swept through the firefighter. Had Dylan really risked his life for a teddy bear? She wanted to scream, until an image of her Nostalgia Nook came to mind. Weren't these everyday treasures the very bedrock of connection? Of course, Dylan wanted to keep hold of something that had meant so much.

'No more talking and do as I say.'

Ava wasn't sure how long Dylan had been exposed to smoke inhalation, but she had taught him well over the years and Ava was pleased to see he'd had the sense to stay low to the ground in clearer air.

She grabbed a small blanket at the base of his bed and wrapped it around his face, covering his mouth and nose.

'To protect you from breathing in the smoke while we get out of here,' she said over the roaring flames.

Dylan remained silent and, with bellies low to the ground, they crawled back through Cassie's room and out towards the ladder.

Ava hefted Dylan over her shoulder, his weight feeling like nothing compared to the pressure of the flames closing in.

The safety of outside was almost in reach as Ava pushed the window fully open. Her grip on Dylan tightened; she wasn't losing him now.

Carefully, Ava fed one leg out onto the rung below. She peered down and was pleased to see Emerson still firmly holding the bottom, Cassie beside him. Her friend's eyes widened in horror as she took in the sight of Dylan in Ava's arms. She opened her mouth about to call out again, but Ava gave a brief shake of her head. Of all the times she needed silence in order to concentrate, it was now.

Cassie understood and promptly closed her mouth. Ava turned around, her front facing the ladder, Dylan firmly in her grasp. Then she began her descent.

'You're doing great, Dylan,' she said.

By now a huge crowd of onlookers had gathered. Ava could hear their shocked gasps as she got closer to the ground. 'Not long now, just keep Bry pressed to your face and your eyes closed.'

Reaching the ground, the cold night air hit her like a wave. She collapsed to her knees, Dylan still in her arms, gasping for breath but alive.

Cassie flew to her and Dylan immediately, her strength enveloping them in a tight embrace. Ava could sense her fear and relief as she wept, holding them both close.

'Oh my god, oh my god, oh my god,' she screamed into their ears.

As Ava felt her friend's arms around her she began to fully understand the risk she had taken.

'I can't believe you did that, Aves,' she wept. 'I can't believe you risked your life for my boy.'

Ava wrestled free from her grasp and looked down at Dylan, who was clutching his mother's leg as if he were a koala.

'Ah well, didn't have much to do tonight,' Ava said with a small smile. 'Fancied a bit of excitement.'

'You stupid bloody cow,' Cassie whispered, her voice cracking with emotion.

'There's bloody gratitude for you,' Ava laughed through tears. The adrenaline was leaving her body now and she was beginning to shake.

'Come on you,' Gayle, a paramedic Ava knew, called from behind them. 'I hate to break this little party up, but you and the lad want looking at.'

'We'll talk later,' Ava whispered as another paramedic led Dylan and Cassie away.

Gayle reached for a sheet of thermal foil, the kind that was used to wrap around marathon runners. She pressed it against Ava's body and led her to a waiting ambulance.

Sitting on the edge of the bed, Ava went over the events of the last few minutes. Had she really just rescued Dylan from a burning building alone? She'd never done a snatch rescue before. Turning to look over her shoulder, Ava could see Dylan now in the ambulance parked next to hers, rescue workers still thrumming about. The paramedic was pressing an oxygen mask over his little face and talking to him in low, gentle tones.

She caught Cassie's eye. Her friend had her arms wrapped tightly around her son.

'I can't believe you did that.'

'I'm fine, Mummy,' Ava heard Dylan say. 'Auntie Ava threw me over her shoulder.'

Cassie pressed another kiss on Dylan's forehead.

'Is he going to be okay?' she demanded, looking at the paramedic.

'Should be,' the paramedic replied. 'We've given him oxygen. With rest and some recovery time, he'll be back to himself soon.'

Ava could see the relief on her friend's face as she took in the news and hugged her boy tight.

'I'm just going to find Auntie Ava, I'll be back in two minutes,' she promised.

Then turning around, Cassie immediately locked eyes with Ava. The two friends said nothing as Cassie pushed through the throng of people and made her way to Ava's side.

'What you did...' Cassie was speechless.

'It's my job,' Ava whispered.

'Ava, that is not your job. I don't know what that was, there are no words to describe what you have just done.'

At Cassie's words, silence fell across the pair. There was so much to say that it was all better left unsaid. Each woman knew just how much they meant to the other and what they had nearly lost if the rescue had gone differently.

'Spare bed's made up if you both want to kip over at ours,' Ava said, eventually. 'Come and go as you please.'

A deep frown etched across Cassie's face. 'I hadn't even thought. Aves, I've lost my home.'

At that, they both turned to look at the blackened ruins of buildings that had once been homes.

'It's not as bad as it looks,' Ava consoled.

Cassie raised an eyebrow. 'Really? Because honestly it looks pretty shit.'

'Fair,' Ava chuckled. 'I tried.'

Once again the friends lapsed into silence as Miguel rushed towards them.

'Ava! A snatch rescue. Well done!' He pulled her into his arms and Ava could feel her station manager tremble.

'I saw a figure on the camera,' she explained.

'I know,' Miguel whispered as he released her. 'I'd have done the same. But you had me worried.' He cast his eye across the people with smartphones still filming the scene. 'This'll have them going for hours.'

'You'll be all over TikTok tomorrow!' Cassie put in.

Ava groaned. She had a horrible feeling her friends were right.

Events like this one had a tendency to go viral and Ava could well do without being the centre of attention. Not when there were more important things to think about.

'I need to be with Dylan,' Cassie said, catching the paramedic's eye in Dylan's ambulance. She kissed the top of Ava's head. 'I'll never forget what you did tonight, Ava. Never.'

Chapter Ten

Two days after the estate fire, on a sunny but cold Saturday afternoon in early December, Ava found herself in a cafe at the top of the city, surrounded by the excited chatter of prospective parents.

The cheerful atmosphere felt at odds with the chaos she'd left behind just days earlier. It was hard to shake the feeling that she didn't quite belong here, not yet. She felt like an outsider, watching a world she wasn't sure she was ready to step into. Adoption was still a distant, uncertain possibility.

For the past hour she had been doing her best to look as interested as everyone else as they chattered away, answering and batting questions back about the adoption process. Ava watched on, unsure what to say, certain it was obvious her heart wasn't in adoption.

A couple next to her were talking animatedly about their home visits, how the social worker had pointed out every detail.

'They're thorough, but that's a good thing,' the woman said, smiling.

Ava forced a nod, but the thought of someone picking through her life felt invasive.

And so, as her neighbour excused herself to go to the loo, Ava turned her face to the window and allowed the winter sunshine to warm her face. Closing her eyes, she felt Steve's hand on her leg.

'You okay?'

She blinked open her eyes, resentful that her chance to gather herself had been disrupted.

'Fine,' she said.

'It's all going to be okay this time.' He patted her leg reassuringly, mistaking her irritation for nervousness.

'I'm sure,' Ava said lightly. Giving Steve a tight smile, she turned her face back to the window, even keener now to find a few moments of calm.

Steve was swept up in excitement. He'd already started planning what their life might look like, turning the guest room into a nursery, talking about potential names. It was hard for Ava to match his energy when her own doubts weighed her down.

'Your cuts and bruises seem to be healing well. Are you tired?' he asked gently.

Irritated, Ava's eyes flew open again. He meant well, she reminded herself.

'A bit.' She turned to face him.

'I suppose that's to be expected. Not often you have a rescue like that.'

Steve's face was earnest; he was trying as hard as she was, Ava realised.

'No,' she said softly.

'I'm just grateful you're in one piece. When Cassie called me, I was terrified something awful had happened.'

He leaned forward and kissed her hand. His touch anchored her as always, and for the first time that day she was glad Steve was with her. When he had heard about the fire from Cassie, he had rushed to the estate and fought his way through the crowds just as the paramedics had finished checking Ava over. His face was red and pinched. Ava could see he had obviously been crying and she felt a pang of guilt for causing Steve so much pain.

'Thank god,' he said, rushing forward and wrapping her in his arms.

'She's fine,' Gayle said. 'Looks a lot worse than she is. You can take her home.'

Steve had immediately taken her back to their house, just as Dylan and Cassie were being taken to the hospital. At home, Steve had run her a bath and kept a watchful eye on her all night – something he had been doing ever since. She was grateful. Since the fire, life had become chaotic. Her face had been splashed across the local news websites as well as social media. She had been branded a local hero, pictures of her carrying Dylan over her shoulder with the blaze behind her were available for all to see.

It had made for uncomfortable reading, if she was honest. Being thrust into the media spotlight, becoming the poster girl for the firefighting service, wasn't who she was. Not that it had done her any good. There was hope for a couple of days that her heroics might have proven the worth of firefighters, but it had only made the powers that be wonder if so many firefighters were necessary when one had just been holding a ladder while she performed a rescue.

Blue Watch had been furious when the news from headquarters filtered down.

The idea that she might lose her job filled Ava with a greater dread than any other she could think of. Just the thought filled her eyes with tears, and she was almost grateful when a tall, pink-cheeked woman clutching a clipboard approached them both.

'Steve,' she said, 'lovely to see you again.'

'You too,' Steve said warmly. 'Nikki, this is Ava, Ava, this is Nikki, she's a social worker.'

Nikki smiled broadly again at Ava. 'Nice of you to join us today.'

'Yes, sorry.' Ava felt another stab of guilt. 'I wanted to be here last time, but there was an emergency at work.'

'I'll bet – you're a firefighter aren't you?' Nikki's eyes crinkled in recognition. 'Weren't you in the paper the other day? You rescued that child from a burning building.'

Now it was Ava's turn for her cheeks to redden.

'Erm, yes.'

Nikki slapped her clipboard against her thighs and let out a gasp of wonder. 'No need to ask whether you're committed to children if you're rescuing them from burning buildings then!'

As Nikki laughed at her own joke, Steve and Ava nervously joined in.

Taking it as an invitation to sit down, Nikki sat opposite them both and pulled her chair in closer, her face serious.

'So, how are you finding things this afternoon? Chatted to lots of people like yourselves?'

'Good,' Ava said hurriedly. She felt Steve squeeze her leg again. 'We're having fun meeting people and finding out more about the process.'

'Excellent!' Nikki leaned back in her chair and Ava was pleased she'd given the right answer.

But then Ava saw Nikki's face change as she looked through her notes.

'So, Steve gave us some information about your circumstances at the last event, but I thought I'd run through everything with you now, check we have everything we need and ask if you want to make your

87

Registration of Interest now so we can set you up with a caseworker?'

Ava felt blindsided, panic forming on her face.

'Our what?'

'Formal application,' Nikki said kindly.

'We do,' Steve said quickly before giving Ava a chance to reply.

Nikki smiled, but this time it didn't reach her eyes.

'I know you do, Steve, but I need to hear it from Ava.'

Ava felt Nikki and Steve's eyes bore into her. She suddenly felt immense pressure.

'Of course,' she gulped.

Nikki nodded, her curls moving as vigorously. 'Okay then, so to let you know where we're at, I'd be lying to you if I didn't let you know that we had some concerns.'

Steve removed his hand from Ava's leg and leaned forward in his chair.

'Concerns?' he echoed. 'Is it because Ava wasn't here the other day?'

'No,' Nikki confirmed. Then looking at Ava, she said, 'But if you decide adoption is the right path for you, we would appreciate it if you could prioritise us where possible.'

'Of course,' Steve said solemnly. 'But just so you know, it's not likely to be a problem again. Ava might be getting made redundant.'

Ava stared at her husband in surprise. Had he really just blurted that out?

'Oh, I'm so sorry.' Nikki looked concerned.

'It probably won't happen,' Ava said, reminding herself to haul her husband over the coals when they got back. 'Everything is very up in the air at the moment.'

'But even if it doesn't happen, Ava wants to prioritise a family. She won't let her job get in the way of that,' Steve put in quickly.

Ava was aghast. What on earth was Steve playing at?

'Okay,' Nikki said evenly, 'but it's not your job that's bothering me, Ava.'

Ava appreciated Nikki's blunt approach. She always preferred straight talking and something told her Nikki felt the same way.

'What is it?' Ava asked.

'It's your IVF situation. Your last round was what, four months ago?' Nikki asked, checking her clipboard again, though Ava strongly suspected she didn't need to check.

'That's right,' Ava said. 'We've had three attempts and each one has been unsuccessful.'

'I understand.' Nikki smiled sympathetically. 'We see a lot of couples where IVF has failed and they decide to try adoption instead.'

'So it's not a problem we've had IVF?' Steve said hurriedly.

'Not at all,' Nikki replied. 'But we prefer that your last attempt is at least six months from the start of the process. We also like to think that you're not coming into adoption and seeing it as a consolation prize.'

'We would never see adoption that way,' Ava said and meant it.

'Course not,' Steve added. 'I mean, Ava's adopted herself, I think I told you. If anyone understands that, it's us.'

Nikki said nothing, glancing between the pair.

'I can see that you really do want to be parents, but I'm concerned you might be rushing into this in order to fill a gap in your lives. Do you think that's the case?'

'Yes,' said Ava.

'No,' said Steve.

Nikki sighed.

'I can see you're good people, and, Ava, your commitment to children is obvious, as is your desire to be a father, Steve,' she said. 'But I'm wondering if you might benefit from a bit more time to think things over. I can't help wondering if IVF was offered again, would you take it?'

'Yes,' Ava said in a small voice.

She knew the truth was hurting Steve but she also knew there was no point lying.

'And you know as well as I do that an adopted child isn't a consolation prize,' Nikki said gently.

'No,' Ava said. 'My own parents never made me feel any less loved because I was adopted, every child deserves that level of love, adopted or not.'

'Then as a child of adoption you know how important it is that we're careful about placing children with the right family,' Nikki said gently.

Ava nodded.

She had often wondered what would have happened if she'd been placed with a different couple.

Nikki smiled and stood up, indicating the meeting was over.

'You are both very welcome to take your application to the next stage. You're just who we're looking for and I think you'd make wonderful parents, but perhaps a bit more time to make sure this is what you both really want is the best thing.' Nikki's tone was kind. Then, looking at Steve, she added, 'Come back to us when you feel more settled.'

With that she turned and walked away.

Once she was gone, Steve jumped to his feet, his cheeks flushed with anger.

'Steve,' Ava called.

But he merely reached for his jacket and slipped it over his shoulders.

'I can't believe you told her that, Ava,' he said, jaw clenched.

'I was just honest,' she replied. 'Every kid that's up for adoption deserves the adults around them to give them that.'

'Yeah?' Steve zipped up his coat. 'Well, let's be honest, this isn't working. There's my truth.'

With that he turned and walked out of the cafe, his steps quickening as he reached the door. All Ava could do was stare – she didn't have the strength to go after him.

Chapter Eleven

After Steve left, Ava remained rooted to her seat, gazing out of the window, her fingers tracing the rim of her cup. She wasn't sure how long she'd been sitting there, but the movement around her felt distant, like background noise she wasn't a part of.

In what seemed to be a too regular occurrence, Ava found herself on the verge of tears. Annoyed, she wiped them away with the back of her hand. It felt like all she did these days was cry. Blinking her eyes open, she saw something that made her spirits lift – Cassie. How was her friend always able to show up just when she needed her?

'What are you doing here?' she asked.

Cassie gave a half-smile and sat beside her friend.

'Thought I'd see how the adoption event had gone.' Cassie looked around the cafe. 'Steve in the loo?'

'He's gone,' Ava replied flatly. 'We had a row.'

'Ah.' Cassie looked sympathetic. 'What happened?'

With a sigh Ava briefly outlined the cause of their latest argument. As she brought the explanation to a close, Cassie winced.

'Ouch.'

'Ouch is about right,' Ava agreed. She leaned back in her chair. The last thing she wanted was to talk any more about it. Her own life was even boring her. 'Tell me what's going on with Dyl,' Ava insisted.

Cassie smiled but the usual joy she expressed to the world didn't reach her eyes. He'd been in the hospital the last three nights, Cassie sleeping beside him on a camp bed at his bedside. 'He's absolutely fine. Just about to pick him up now and take him back to yours.'

Ava watched as Cassie picked at a loose hem on her sleeve and tapped her feet up and down. She seemed agitated.

'What's wrong?'

'That obvious?'

'To me,' Ava said softly. She leaned forward in her chair and waited for Cassie to speak. Her friend was terrible at talking about her feelings. For all the care she gave to others, Cassie always preferred to keep things bottled up, never speaking up until she felt ready.

'I had a letter this morning,' Cassie began.

'Oh?'

'From my dad.'

Ava's mouth dropped open in shock. Cassie hadn't spoken to either of her parents in over twenty years. Her mind was spinning with questions. Why had he got in touch now?

'He read about the fire and saw the picture of you carrying Dylan,' Cassie explained. 'He knows your address from back in the day and guessed I would be staying with you and thought it would be a good time to get in touch.'

There was a pause as Ava tried to take in everything her friend was telling her.

'Where's the letter?'

Cassie's face grew red with anger. 'I threw it away. Didn't want that filth in my possession,' she said fiercely.

Ava nodded. She wasn't surprised. Cassie's parents had treated her appallingly. Paul, her father, had been caught cheating with Sheryl, a girl they had gone to school with. When Cassie told her mother, she refused to believe it and threw Cassie out of the house. But far from being homeless, Cassie had stayed with Ava and Steve, going to work at the local council until she had enough money to go to Bristol University the following year, but she always returned to them in the holidays.

As for her parents, Cassie never spoke to either of them again. Not when she married, not when she divorced and not when she gave birth to Dylan. Cassie had always said that even if you were related to someone that didn't necessarily make them family, insisting she and Dylan were better off without her parents. Ava understood, but over the years wondered if it would be better if Cassie had someone linked by blood and genetics she could rely on. Blood family was a precious link, something to cherish.

'And what else did the letter say?' Ava asked gently. 'Did he apologise?'

A look of incredulity spread across Cassie's face. 'My father *apologise*? You must be joking. He just said some shit about how when tragedy strikes it's a reminder of how precious life is and we ought to make the time count with the people that matter. I thought, well, you don't matter to me, mate, and you haven't done for over twenty years, so sod off.'

Ava winced. Cassie was always upset when she spoke about her family, which was rare. There had been times over the years when Ava had privately wondered if life would be a bit easier for Cassie if she made up with her father, especially when her mother died two years earlier.

On the surface it looked as if Cassie was fine with being estranged from her family, but deep down, Ava felt there were a lot of emotions her friend hadn't processed and it would be better in the long run for her and Dylan if she did. Wasn't this the perfect opportunity to do that if Paul was offering an olive branch?

But now wasn't the time to make this observation, not least because Cassie looked as if she wanted to throw Ava's coffee cup at the wall.

'Probably the best thing to do,' Ava said slowly. 'I'm so sorry that's happened, Cass. What a stupidly selfish thing to do.'

'Typical Paul. Never thinking, "Ah, perhaps my daughter and her son need time to adjust to the fact they've lost their home." No, he saw it as an opportunity to get something for himself. He doesn't care about me – never has.'

'It's really shit,' was all Ava could say, wishing she could express something more helpful. 'I take it you're not going to contact him?'

Cassie let out a loud belly laugh.

'What do you think? Dylan thinks his grandparents are dead. I'm hardly about to tell him his grandfather's risen from the grave like some sort of horror film. Actually, if Dylan had to meet his grandfather, that *would* be like a plot of a horror film.'

'Oh, Cass.' Ava got out of her chair and pulled her friend in for a hug.

'I'm fine,' Cassie whimpered. 'I'm not letting that tosser get in my head. Not today, not when I'm about to get Dylan. Today is about him, not that arsehole father of mine.'

'What time are you getting him?' Ava asked, recognising Cassie wanted to change the subject.

'About an hour,' Cassie said, checking her watch. 'Thought I'd stop in for a coffee first but I know Dyl's excited to see what you've added to the nook! He can't stop talking about all the treasures you might have added to it since he last saw it.'

Ava laughed. 'You can tell him nothing has been added, but something's been removed since he last saw it – although that Gulf War medal is still there in pride of place.'

'Bloody hell,' Cassie marvelled. 'That has to be your oldest find, doesn't it?'

Ava nodded. It still bothered her that something so precious hadn't been reunited with the right person.

'Are you really still looking for the owner?' Cassie asked.

'I guess,' Ava replied, 'though I have to confess it's fallen to the bottom of the priority list.'

'Well, maybe me and Dyl can help,' Cassie mused. 'As a thank you for letting us stay.'

'Not necessary, you doughnut,' Ava said affectionately.

'Well, that's kind, but I hope we won't be cluttering up your place for too long. We're hoping to get the estate rebuilt pretty soon.'

'Really?' Ava blinked in surprise. She'd expected her friend to start looking for private accommodation for her and Dylan.

'Yes, really.' Cassie laughed. 'I've spoken to a few of the residents and they all love living on the estate. It has such an old-fashioned community feel, you know. We had a meeting last night at the pub, and we're going to try and organise more units, get things started up again, talk to

96

the housing association.' Cassie grimaced. 'Course, these things take time, but that's why I've set up a committee to get everything moving.'

Ava shook her head in astonishment. 'How do you pick yourself up off the floor and find the enthusiasm, the drive, to start again like that? The fire was less than a week ago!'

Cassie shrugged. 'You know me. Don't like sitting on my hands. Had to do something while I was sitting at Dylan's bedside, and everyone has been so kind. Though I think all those social media posts of you and your heroic rescue might have helped. Do you know we've even had builders offering to pitch up and help for free! It's incredible.'

Ava rolled her eyes. She always felt awkward when people tried to call her a hero.

'So, what are you and Steve going to do now?' Cassie asked, changing the subject.

'No idea.' Ava shrugged and looked heavenwards. 'We need to talk, but I can't face it.'

'You're going to have to face him sometime,' Cassie warned. 'You've only just got over the last row you had.'

'Tell me about it. It feels like we're on this never-ending hamster wheel, we go round and round in circles.' She reached for her long cold coffee and took a sip. 'I should let you go and get Dylan. He'll be wondering where you are.'

'Come with me?' Cassie invited as she picked up her handbag.

'Looking like this?' Ava gestured to her face, knowing that she was red and blotchy. She had never been an elegant crier. 'I'll put the poor boy off his dinner.'

'True.' Cassie laughed. 'But it's never stopped you in the past. Now come on.'

And with that Ava allowed herself to be pulled to her feet by her friend and dragged out of the coffee shop. Ava hated to admit it, but Cassie had been taking care of her since they'd met. Secretly, there was a part of her that never wanted her to stop.

—

Dylan was right at home the moment he was discharged from hospital, and Ava loved watching her favourite boy take up space.

A handful of days later and he was comfortably lolling on the sofa, remote in hand as he channel-surfed. Ava would have happily waited on Dylan night and day but Cassie had other ideas. Returning from the supermarket, Cassie's eyes landed on her son accusingly.

'We don't want to take over your house, Ava,' she said, dropping the bags. In one fluid movement she removed the remote from Dylan's hand and swiped his legs from the sofa, onto the floor. 'It's enough we're here at all.'

'Honestly, it's a pleasure,' Steve said gently. 'We've got all this room and nothing to do with it.'

His words hung in the air. Things between them had been more than strained since the adoption event but for the sake of Cassie and Dylan they were going out of their way to be polite to each other whilst both avoiding the source of their never-ending rows.

Now, Ava looked at him and felt the pain as keenly as he did. They had bought this house, renovated it, turned it from a two-bed into a three, all with the hope of creating a gorgeous family home. The fact they hadn't managed it was a stark reminder of their failed dreams. Far better for Dylan and Cassie to make use of the room they did have.

'Can I help?' Ava asked as Cassie finished unpacking the groceries.

Cassie reached for a saucepan and poured in a tablespoon of olive oil. 'Absolutely not, you've done more than enough.'

'It's no trouble.' Ava got to her feet and opened the fridge door. She could see that Cassie had bought a stack of vegetables and minced meat – looked like spaghetti bolognese was on the menu. She knew it would be a lot better than Big Stu's.

'Seriously, Ava, sit down and relax.' Cassie's tone brooked no argument. She walked out of the kitchen and into the living room. 'Dylan, can you come and help me with dinner?'

Guilt washed over Ava. The little boy was still recuperating after his misadventures. Cassie caught her expression and rolled her eyes.

'Ava, it's important that boy knows how to look after himself if he wants to contribute to society. One of the best ways he can do that is by learning to cook and clean. He's well enough to do that and it's how it's always been.'

'I'm saying nothing.' Ava pulled out a bottle of white from the fridge and waved it at Cassie, who nodded eagerly, and Ava poured two glasses.

'In hindsight, my mum let me get away with absolute murder. I never lifted a finger, she did everything and worked full time.' Ava took a sip of her wine and thought about how her mum was always run ragged by the weekends, her father happy to sit in his chair even though her mother had worked just as he had.

'It was the Seventies and Eighties,' Cassie said with an explanatory shrug. 'We've come a long way since then.'

'Cheers to that.' Ava lifted her glass to toast her friend. Cassie laughed and took a sip just as Dylan walked into the kitchen with a scowl on his face.

'I'm tired.'

'Me too,' was Cassie's immediate reply, 'and so is Ava. Everyone's tired and everyone has to eat, so help me by washing up that chopping board please.'

Clearly knowing better than to argue with his mother, Dylan did as instructed and Ava watched mother and son work together in harmony, Dylan soon getting over his initial irritation and laughing at his mother's jokes while he told her all about school that day.

'And then everyone wanted to see my burn scar,' Dylan said triumphantly. He pushed back the sleeve of his jumper to reveal the bandage he still wore.

'They should be more impressed with yours and Ava's bravery,' Cassie said firmly.

Dylan and Ava smiled. As the firefighter took another sip of her wine, her eyes fell on the paperwork spilling out of Cassie's bag. Architecture plans for the new estate, along with committee meeting minutes were splayed out across the table.

'Looks interesting,' Ava said, gesturing to the notes.

'It will be.' Cassie smiled as she supervised Dylan pouring in the tomatoes. 'That's it, love, give them a stir,' she encouraged. Then, turning back to Ava, she continued, 'We're all really committed to getting the estate back on its feet as soon as possible. Some aren't living in such luxuries as I am.' She waved her hand to the kitchen around her and then the wine. 'We're all going to do as much work as we can, the community centre is the one place we really want to focus our attention. If we get that up together sooner, then some of our residents can still come back from wherever they're living and see their friends in their clubs, the kids will have after-school care, we'll even be able to go back to running sports training and give the older folk a hot meal. It's helpful for people to have something to focus on.'

'You've got it all worked out,' Ava marvelled.

'Dunno about that.' Cassie looked momentarily sheepish. 'I'm just trying to make the most of everyone's enthusiasm. It's the clean-up job that's the hardest. There's still so much mess.'

'Always is,' Ava said knowingly. 'Even once the fire investigation is complete there's debris to clear and dispose of. But as this is a community matter then perhaps more people could help.'

An idea whirred in Ava's mind. Slamming down her wine glass, her eyes were alight with excitement.

'What if the fire station helped? We could get this project off the ground, rebuild the estate faster. I'll talk to Miguel, he'll love it.'

Cassie blinked in surprise. 'Are you sure? It's your first day back. Take it easy.'

Suddenly Ava felt butterflies in her stomach at the thought.

'You'll be fine,' Cassie said watching her. 'Firefighting is in your blood, Ava. The moment you set foot in the fire station all those nerves will disappear.'

Chapter Twelve

As Ava pulled into the fire station the following morning, Cassie's words rang in her ears. She wouldn't say it aloud, but the snatch rescue had hit her hard. If she had a child, would she still have put her life at risk like that? Fire-fighting was in her blood, but would it stay that way if she had more to lose?

Ava wasn't sure she knew the answer, and that troubled her. There was always a price to pay for every fire-fighter the moment they stepped into any fire. Despite the precautions they took, there was always risk.

Entering the station, the whole watch was there to greet her with cries of well done and slaps on the back. Big Stu pulled her in for a hug then hoisted her on his shoulder and ran around the station.

'You're brilliant, Ava,' he shouted. 'Bloody brilliant.'

'Will you put me down, you wally,' she laughed.

Only Miguel was quiet as he sat in his office, glasses perched on the end of his nose.

'More stuff about job losses,' Phil whispered when Big Stu set her down and she glanced in the window. 'He's been like that all week.'

Ava frowned and turned away. Perhaps today wasn't the right time to talk to her boss. If she was honest, she had her fill of preoccupied, miserable men at home. Despite the joy Dylan and Cassie had brought to the house, she and Steve were hardly speaking to each other and doing all they could to avoid one another. Neither of them was seemingly able to talk about more than what they wanted for dinner or whether they needed more almond milk.

Ava pushed her marital difficulties to the back of her mind and concentrated on her shift which thankfully passed uneventfully. She had decided to focus on helping Jodie cook her first meal for the watch, which had been incredibly tasty.

'Vegan tofu burgers?' Big Stu had said, eyeing the plate in front of him with suspicion.

Ava stifled a laugh. Big Stu had always been a meat and two veg man, add in a pint of gravy and he was happy.

'And what are these?' he asked, picking up what looked like orange chips. 'Fried Wotsits?' he asked hopefully.

'Sweet potatoes,' Jodie said triumphantly, setting the last plate down for Miguel, whose place was still empty as he remained buried in paperwork.

'Sweet what?' Big Stu prodded the chips with his large forefinger and looked terrified.

'They're good for you,' Phil insisted, putting a handful in his mouth.

Ava tucked in. Jodie had cooked such a lovely team meal, that even Big Stu eventually devoured the lot. Afterwards she was sure she'd overhead him take Jodie aside and ask if he would be able to get hold of sweet potatoes too or if he'd have to go to a special shop.

After her shift, she stood in the car park and stared at the keys in her hand. She couldn't face going home, not when she knew Steve would be there and they'd have to endure another night of forced politeness in front of Cassie and Dylan. Although the three of them had known one another since they were little more than kids, Ava didn't want to inflict such torture on Cassie. Not when she was already coping with so much.

Reversing out of the station car park, Ava found herself driving towards the north of the city. She tried to tell herself that she wasn't sure what she was doing or where she was going but she knew in her heart where she needed to be.

Sure enough, ten minutes later, Ava arrived at Cassie's estate, or what had once been. Something in her needed to see the damage that had happened that night. Parking in a space near what was left of the community centre, she winced as she got out. Even in the pitch black the devastation was evident – only shells of buildings remained, littered with charred metal and the outlines of ghostly black shapes, having once contained memories and lives, only to be upended so brutally quickly.

Making her way along the road, Ava tried to move silently but there was still so much debris, her feet seemed to seek out every crunch.

Instinctively, she went straight to what was left of Cassie's house. Despite the fact she felt glad to be back at work, the rescue had been playing on her mind all day. It was as though she needed to return to the scene of the crime, to remind herself of the danger she had put herself in and the life she had saved.

The moment she took in the building that had once been so familiar, a shiver ran down her spine, but she had to go inside. The blaze was out and the place considered safe enough for emergency services to access, but it was no longer a home. Her foot crunched on the broken glass as she pushed open what was left of the front door, the acrid stench of burnt materials stinging her nostrils.

Her eyes roamed over what had once been the kitchen. Using the light of her torch she could just about make out what had once been kitchen cabinets, and above, a pinboard that still had some notes from Dylan's school and a shopping list with BREAD written in block letters.

Ava felt a sudden surge of despair. There was so much mess. Cassie might think she could rebuild the estate, but she'd need all the help she could get. All her life, Cassie had been her rock, now it was Ava's turn to be the one to pull Cassie up.

–

The next day, at work, she made a beeline for Miguel who was busy making tea for the crew. Seizing her chance, she outlined Cassie's plan to rebuild the estate and suggested the watch get involved, too.

'A mate of mine's a builder,' Miguel said his eyes gleaming with excitement. 'We could get him to help, perhaps some of his guys as well.'

Ava immediately had an image of burly builders running around in steel-toe-capped boots and hard hats. She let out a snort of laughter, well able to imagine why Miguel wanted to get involved.

'What?' Miguel growled.

'Nothing,' Ava laughed, holding her hands up in protest. 'Nothing at all.'

Miguel didn't look convinced and went back to making the tea. 'I know you're picturing the Village People, Ava, but grow up. Just because I'm gay doesn't mean I dress up in a Navy uniform at the weekend and perform choreographed dance routines.'

'Er, didn't you say that's exactly what you were doing in the BottleHop the other night?' Ava quizzed, referring to Bath's legendary LGBTQ venue in the heart of the city.

Miguel scowled. 'I was just saying I think we can get some free help. Get this project sorted properly. And you're right, it would be good for the station, show how important we are to the community, that they can't afford to lose any of us.'

She took a moment to look at Miguel properly. There were bags under his eyes and his usually immaculately coiffured hair looked matted.

'Everything all right?' she asked quietly.

'Why? Doesn't it look all right?' Miguel snapped, snatching up his tea and taking a large gulp. 'What's up with you? You seeing things on top of everything else?'

Ava shrank back. 'No, no you're fine.'

She didn't know what was up with Miguel lately, he seemed ready to pounce at the slightest misdemeanour. Yesterday, he'd had a go at poor Emerson for being two minutes late after he'd been stuck in traffic following a road accident. He'd offered to help White Watch, who had been called out, and earned himself an earful from Miguel.

Reaching for a handful of mugs, she placed them on one of the tea trays, ready to dish them out to her colleagues scattered about the station. Only as she did so, Miguel called her back.

'Ava,' he said abruptly. 'I'm sorry, I didn't mean to snap.'

She turned around. 'Are you sure everything is all right?' she asked.

To her astonishment Miguel's jaw was clenched as he fought back emotion.

'Miguel, what is it?' Ava set the tray down and guided him to one of the chairs at the back of the room, sitting down next to him.

'It's Xav,' he mumbled, his voice catching.

'Xav,' Ava echoed. 'What's happened?'

'We've split up.'

Ava's jaw dropped open in astonishment. This had to be a joke, Xavier and Miguel were the strongest couple she knew. They had been together for twelve years and finally tied the knot two years earlier in a glittering ceremony with the celebrant dressed up as Elvis.

'But you can't. Surely whatever it is can't be that bad?'

But as Miguel brought his face up to meet Ava's and she saw his deep brown eyes shining with hurt, fear curled around her heart.

'Miguel, talk to me,' she coaxed.

'We've been living separate lives. Different interests, different goals. All we do is argue now,' Miguel admitted, his voice low.

Ava frowned. Was that why Miguel had been out dancing the night away so often? Ava had just assumed it was work that had been getting under his skin, but it seemed there was more to it than she first thought.

'Surely it's not that bad.'

Miguel's face fell. 'It is. We've had moments when it feels like the old days, but we want different things.'

'Like what?'

Miguel let out a deep sigh. 'Xav wants to travel. Thinks I should take redundancy if they offer it and we should explore South America – he wants me to understand his home country. Get to know his family. We talked about doing it when we first met but like most things it had been shelved.'

'Oh.'

Ava's mind began to whir. Just how well did Xav know his husband if he thought redundancy would be something he'd want?

'We had a row about it. Awful, it was.' Miguel's cheeks coloured at the memory. 'I told him he couldn't possibly be serious, that firefighting was my life. He said that was my problem, I never put him first. After that it was downhill all the way.'

Shock rippled through Ava like a wave. If Xav and Miguel couldn't make their relationship work, what chance did she and Steve have?

Miguel looked bereft. In all the years she'd known him, she'd never known him to be anything but calm and together.

'Where is he now?'

'No idea,' Miguel said angrily.

'Oh, Miguel.'

Ava leaned forward and wrapped an arm around her boss's shoulders. To her surprise he started weeping, the sleeve of her shirt fast becoming wet through with his tears.

'I feel like I don't know what's happening in my life any more. First the fire station and now Xav.'

'I'm sorry, Migs,' she whispered. 'When did all this happen?'

'Last week,' Miguel admitted through tears.

She had no idea of the pain her friend had been in all this time. Guilt ate away at her. She had been so wrapped up in her own life she had completely neglected the fact Miguel hadn't been his usual self. She had done a great disservice to her friend and wanted to make it up to him.

'Come over tonight. You can talk, vent, whatever you need,' Ava said, her voice gentle.

Miguel shook his head. 'I don't know. I'm not up to company.'

'You shouldn't be alone,' Ava said gently. 'Besides, Cassie's cooking.'

Miguel lifted his head and raised an eyebrow. 'You mean the poor woman's doing your household chores as well as being forced to live with you?'

'It's not like that,' Ava laughed. 'You know Cass, loves taking care of people. Plus, she likes to teach Dylan the value of hard work.'

At the last part Miguel looked doubtful.

'Come on. It'll do you good, a real heart-to-heart and we can even talk about the fire station, get a plan together with Cassie.'

'All right.' Miguel sighed again and got to his feet. 'Anything has to be better than a night at home staring at Xav's photo on my phone wondering what he's doing now.'

'Exactly,' Ava agreed. 'You can always do that at my house.'

Chapter Thirteen

The chill of winter was definitely in the air, Ava thought, as she took her turn to slosh water over the fire appliances. It was a cold Saturday morning two weeks before Christmas and the engines had been out all night in country lanes, covered in soot and dirt. Cleaning them was a rotten job, but she was always happy to take her turn, even if it did mean her hands were left chapped and cold. And, looking at the team of kids Cassie had rounded up from the estate to help, she knew how important it was to lead by example.

It had been ten days now since Miguel had come over for dinner, and together with Cassie they had talked about how the fire station could work in tandem with the estate rebuild committee. Although they hadn't been working together long, so far they had all made good progress. On their days off, firefighters from every watch at the Bath Fire Station, as well as Bath North, had joined forces to help clear the debris on site. That in itself had given Ava ample opportunity to sift through the wreckage and find treasures for her Nostalgia Nook. So far, she had amassed two photos of grandchildren in frames, a Liverpool football shirt and a signed novel with the inscription, 'Treasure this forever – Jan'. Items she had so far arranged to successfully reunite.

As she threw another bucket of water over the engine's windscreen, Ava tried to ignore the swell of sadness deep within her core. Miguel's broken relationship was only serving to remind her how broken things were between her and Steve.

The idea of a child was getting further and further away. Something she wanted to say to her husband, but couldn't find the words. The day before yesterday they'd had the house to themselves and Steve had wordlessly pulled her into his arms for a hug.

She'd thought that was his way of letting her know things were all right between then, or at least they would be. Unable to help herself, she'd seized her moment and fished out her phone as he released her.

'What's this?' he asked, looking at the open webpage on her browser.

'It's a blog from a woman I follow. New post today,' she said breezily. 'Thought it made interesting reading.'

Steve frowned as he read.

'She got pregnant after her seventh round of IVF, Christ, how much money does she have? And apparently she had –' he peered closer at the screen '– almost given up.' He turned and stared at her, disappointment radiating from his eyes. 'This isn't our story, Ava. Why can't you see that?'

Anger reared inside her.

'Why can't you just give other ideas a chance?' she snapped.

She felt like a broken record, and she and Steve were only capable of playing one very broken song.

'We've given IVF a chance,' Steve said, his voice weary. 'We can't afford another round, and I can't keep hoping for something that may never happen. It's time to move on.'

With that he turned on his heel and walked out the door. The only thing Ava could do was get ready for work, her heart as heavy as one of the battering rams she sometimes used to break into a house and put out a fire.

But the fire destroying her own marriage wasn't something she seemed able to extinguish. Consequently, it was no surprise her troubled marriage had been on Ava's mind all morning. It was time for a break so, drying her hands, she walked up the stairs to the office and instead thought about the medal she had found. The one item she was still no closer to reuniting with its owner despite renewed efforts. Over the past week she'd tried all the usual outlets. The local police had filed her new request but she needed a revised plan.

As Ava neared Miguel's office, she saw the door was wide open and Cassie was sitting opposite her friend, the two in deep conversation.

'Hi, stranger,' Ava said in surprise.

Cassie's head whirled around and she smiled. 'Just the person. I was hoping to take you for lunch.'

'Oh.' Ava felt blindsided. She assumed she had the afternoon to herself.

'I want to say thanks for letting me and Dylan stay,' Cassie said. 'I've been trying to convince Miguel to join us but he says he's too busy.'

'Meetings,' Miguel said with a sigh.

'I'd love to,' Ava said. 'I finish in half an hour. Want to wait for me in the cafe across the road?'

'Perfect.' Cassie got to her feet and left the office.

Once she'd gone, Ava turned to Miguel.

'Are you sure you can't come out, just for a bit?'

'I wish.' He ran a hand across his face. 'The powers that be want us to cut at least one person from every watch. Me and the station manager from Bath North are all determined to talk them out of it but I can't see how.'

A stream of messages pinged on Miguel's phone and she quirked a brow. 'Something important?'

'Xav,' Miguel said, glancing at the phone before pushing it away. 'He keeps texting. Like I'm interested.'

'Except you are,' Ava said softly.

Miguel hesitated for just a second, then gave a shake of his head.

'No, Ava, I'm not. It's over and that's the end of it.'

With that Ava found herself wondering for the second time that day why the men in her life seemed particularly cruel.

-

Cassie was already waiting for her as she walked into the cafe.

'Got you a latte,' she said, pushing a mug towards Ava. 'You looked like you needed it.'

Ava smiled and took a grateful sip. 'So, what is it that really brings you here?' she asked.

Cassie shrugged. 'Thought I'd see how you are.'

Ava ran her tongue over her teeth and surveyed her friend. She knew Cassie better than she knew herself – her friend wasn't being honest.

'Out with it,' Ava said.

Her friend paused, her grey eyes now filled with uncertainty.

'I heard you and Steve arguing this morning. Seems like it's happening a lot. I'm worried.'

At the admission Ava felt herself grow hot. She thought she'd been doing well at hiding how bad things were between her and Steve.

'Sorry,' she said embarrassed. 'I thought we'd been good at keeping it down.'

'No need to be sorry,' Cassie said lightly. 'But you need to sort this out, Aves.'

Ava felt weary. 'We can't give each other what the other wants. Steve wants to adopt, I want IVF. Stalemate.'

'Is there really no moving on the point for either of you? You love each other, surely you can work this out?'

Ava took another sip of her latte and studied the sandwich menu. Cassie's words were hard to hear but she knew she was right. She and Steve had been through a lot together. They'd been each other's rock, with Cassie their convenient but lovely third wheel. But did they really still love each other? If they did, surely they wouldn't be in this mess?

'So I have a favour to ask...' Ava said changing the subject.

'Oh?' Cassie's tone was hesitant.

'I'm determined to find the owner of this medal and I want your help. I wondered if one of your old souls on the estate might have some ideas of how I can find who it belongs to.'

'Why not post the medal online? Try those local veteran groups,' Cassie suggested.

Ava had been stuck for so long, Cassie's suggestion felt like a breath of fresh air. Finally she was moving forward in one area of her life.

'So, if I help you with this, will you help me with something?' Cassie asked, interrupting Ava's train of thought.

'Aren't I already helping you by letting you stay in my spare room?' Ava mumbled as the waitress set down their avocado on toast.

'Don't split hairs,' Cassie said, her face a picture of determination. 'I want you to think about something.'

Locking eyes with Cassie, Ava could see she looked nervous and suddenly dread began to swirl in Ava's belly. Why did she have a feeling she wasn't going to like whatever it was Cassie had to say.

'Go on,' Ava said reluctantly.

'I think it's time you found your birth family,' Cassie said, her voice soft but sure.

Ava's mouth fell open in surprise. Of all the things she was expecting her friend to say, that wasn't it.

'Where has this come from?' she managed.

Cassie's voice softened. 'You deserve answers, Ava. You deserve to know where you came from, even if it doesn't change anything. I keep looking at your Nostalgia Nook and honestly, I think you're struggling to move forward in life. Sometimes when you can't move forward you have to go back. I think finding your birth family and finally getting some answers to those questions that have always dogged you about your roots will help you work out what you want to do next about a family of your own.'

Chapter Fourteen

Ava stared at Cassie, her mind fizzing. She had tried to find her parents once before and the authorities in Dublin told her she was entitled to a basic information sheet. However, as the agency that arranged the adoption had shut down, she had to go to the adoption board, who assigned her a social worker. That had been as far as Ava had got. The social worker told her the priest had been terrible at keeping records and couldn't tell her anything else.

Cassie leaned forward and clamped her hands around Ava's. 'I've been doing some research. Things have changed since you last tried. The Birth Information and Tracing Act has really shaken things up for people adopted in Ireland.' Fishing her phone out of her bag, Cassie brought up Google and punched in a few key words. Within a few seconds she had brought up a news report and showed it to Ava. 'See.'

Ava read with interest. Cassie was right, the adoption laws in Ireland had changed. People were now entitled to openly access their adoption records, information could no longer be held back. Ava read on, astonished to hear tales of men and women who had been reunited with their relatives, welcomed into the family after years of searching. Then there were parents who had been interested in trying to find the children that had been taken from them, had searched for years, desperately trying to find what had happened to their offspring who they believed had been lost for good.

By the time Ava reached the end of the piece her eyes had dimmed with sadness. How could she not have known about this? Here was a very real chance for her to find out the truth about what her life story was.

Back at home later that day, Ava walked into the living room full of resolve and found Steve watching *Taskmaster*. Shucking off her coat, and nearly tripping over Monkey, who was attacking the baubles at the base of the Christmas tree, she sat next to him.

'I'm thinking about finding my birth parents,' she said quietly, barely recognising her own voice. She handed him the iPad with a slow exhale.

Steve scanned the article, his brow furrowing deeper with every line. When he finished, he set the iPad down and turned to her. For a moment, they sat in silence, the weight of unspoken words between them. Finally, he pulled her into a gentle embrace.

'I thought you'd let all this go,' he murmured.

Ava stiffened, feeling the familiar knot in her chest tighten.

'I'll never let it go,' she whispered, her voice almost lost. Her gaze dropped to the online article. 'I've wanted this my whole life, to know where I came from. And now, for the first time…' She gestured weakly. 'I have a real chance.'

Steve sighed. 'I just don't want you getting hurt. There's been so much already… the IVF, the adoption…'

'I can see that.'

He got up and walked into the kitchen, Ava followed and found him leaning against the sink, peering out of the window, arms folded. He looked worried.

'Steve?' she asked hesitantly.

'I just don't want you to get hurt, Ava. There's a lot going on at the moment and I worry you're taking on too much. Finding out about the IVF, rescuing children from burning buildings, job cuts at the station, now this. I think it's great you want to find your family, but I wonder if now's the right time. I don't think you need any more stress in your life.'

Unable to help herself, Ava let out a sigh of frustration.

'I need this, Steve. I need a win.'

She put her arms around his middle as she had a hundred times before. To her horror she felt his shoulders shake.

'What's wrong?' she whispered.

'I'm sorry,' he croaked. 'I think everything that's going on between us is getting to me. I don't feel like I know you any more.'

Ava said nothing and instead wrapped herself more tightly around him. She ought to have been hurt, but her husband was right.

'All we do is row,' Steve said. 'I can't take it any more.'

This time he pulled away and turned around to look at her.

'I know,' she admitted. 'I don't know what to do.'

'I don't either,' Steve said, his voice faltering. 'I love you, and yet with all this mess I feel like we've forgotten we're in a relationship.'

Steve lent his forehead against hers. She felt his warm breath against her lips as he spoke.

'I've been thinking it's getting a bit cramped in here with Cassie and Dylan,' he began.

'You're kicking them out?' Ava gasped.

'No, course not.' Steve replied. Ava noticed an edge to his voice. 'But I wonder if maybe I should move out for a bit, give us some space.'

Ava felt winded.

'You're leaving me?' Her voice was thin.

Immediately Steve's face crumpled. 'No!' He peppered her face with fierce kisses. 'I love you, Ava, that will never change. You're my world.' He glanced at her and held her hands. 'But we need a break – the way we are isn't good for either of us. I thought I'd go and stay with my brother for a few days. Give us a chance to reset.'

Ava had her doubts – about a million of them – but looking into her husband's eyes, she could see his mind was made up.

'When will you go?' she asked, aware her knees were trembling.

'Today,' Steve said firmly. 'I think it's best. We can still see each other, I think in fact we should see each other. Go back to dating for a bit. It could be exciting.'

He gave her a hopeful smile but all Ava felt was sadness. She was married, she didn't want to date.

'Fine,' she said, turning away from him. 'I'll get out of your way, let you get on.'

She passed him, fighting back tears. Wasn't a break really just the first step towards a divorce?

–

It took an hour for Steve to pack his bag and leave. Ava sat numbly on the sofa, holding Monkey in her lap. As the door closed behind him, she was struck by the silence. Would this be her life now? No more shared breakfasts, no more weekend walks.

The silence was deafening.

Her eyes drifted to the Christmas tree, its twinkling lights mocking the dark reality of her life. Monkey nudged her hand, but Ava barely felt it. The ache in her chest was overwhelming, a dull, constant throb she couldn't escape.

She replayed the last few months, the endless arguments, the failed treatments, the growing distance.

Was this really the end?

This wasn't supposed to happen to her: childless, single and an orphan at forty-four. She was scared. As her tears fell into Monkey's fur, the animal seemed to sense his human friend needed comfort and he allowed Ava as many strokes and cuddles as she needed.

She felt the weight of her decisions pressing against her chest. Each choice had led her to this moment. Had she been too stubborn, too focused on her own desires? Or had Steve given up on them too quickly?

Ava wasn't sure how long she sat on the sofa after Steve said a quiet goodbye. She was still reeling. He'd used the word exciting. How was it *exciting* for them to date? Or was that just a ruse, something he was saying for a quick exit? It felt like an easy out, a soft blow to end the misery of their marriage. Was Steve out there now looking for someone else? Had he already met someone? Her heart started to race. Was this all part of a plan? Had he dreamed this up all along and this was something he was just waiting to do?

'Aaagh,' Ava let out such a sudden, sharp cry that Monkey jumped off her lap, startled.

Uttering apologies to the cat, Ava got to her feet and paced the living room. She was driving herself mad and was grateful she had the place to herself. Dylan and Cassie were out shopping and she was relieved they couldn't see her spiralling.

Perhaps this was for the best after all? It could give them both a chance to calm down, get some distance and have a think about what they both really wanted. She went to bed unsettled, her heart having taken up a constant, dull ache.

–

The following morning was Sunday, and after a sleepless night Ava remembered she had promised Cassie she would join her at the estate to help with the rebuild. Checking the time, she let out a loud grumble as she saw it had gone ten. Cassie and Dylan would have been there for hours. Why hadn't they woken her?

Quickly, she ran a brush through her hair and pulled on her jeans and a sweatshirt. Grabbing her car keys, she ran from the house. Thankfully, it didn't take long to reach the estate. And she was surprised when she arrived to find Miguel already picking up rubbish and sweeping away debris.

'Didn't expect to find you here,' Ava said as she got out of her car.

Miguel shrugged and she could see the weight of the world on his shoulders.

'I had no place to be so thought I might as well be here.'

'Any word from Xav?' Ava asked.

'He messaged,' Miguel said, continuing to sweep. 'I wish he wouldn't. It's over, what else is there to say?'

Hearing the word over, a fresh round of pain rose from deep inside and she let out an unexpected cry of anguish.

Miguel looked at her in concern.

'Ava? What is it?'

'Steve's left me,' she said.

Suddenly saying the words made what had happened seem more real.

Wordlessly, Miguel guided her to a bench and put an arm around her. Then he listened without judgement as Ava told her friend about the decision she had made to find her birth family, how Steve thought it was a bad idea, and how after yet more cross words he had left, claiming space would be good for them. By the time she'd finished she was exhausted and spent from revealing so much of herself.

Miguel wrapped his arms around her.

'Sweetheart, I'm so sorry. You don't deserve any of this.'

Ava shrugged just as Miguel had done earlier.

'You don't always get what you deserve in this life.'

'No, but you should,' Miguel said softly, his usual bravado softened. 'Steve's not thinking straight. You know that. He's just overwhelmed, like you are.'

He paused, and Ava allowed his words to sink in before he spoke again.

'You need a holiday.'

'Oh yeah? Singles? Think I'm a bit old for eighteen to thirty,' Ava joked.

Miguel smiled. 'You were always too old for eighteen to thirty holidays, even when you were eighteen! But seriously, a break could do you good. Long weekend or something? I'll give you the time off anytime you like.'

Ava raised an eyebrow. If Miguel was being so generous with leave, something must be seriously wrong.

'All right,' she said at last. 'Maybe in a couple of weeks' time – after Christmas in the New Year? When everything is miserable and dreary in January.'

Miguel nodded in approval. 'Good idea. Let me know when you decide where you want to go and the exact dates.'

'I already know where I want to go,' Ava said, her voice quieter than usual.

'Go on.' Miguel rubbed his hands together in anticipation.

'Ireland,' she finally said, the word hanging in the air between them like a challenge to herself.

She knew the decision to find her birth family wasn't one she'd made lightly, but the thought of returning to Ireland, to the unknown, made her heart race. She hadn't shared this with anyone but Cassie or Steve. Could she really go through with it?

Miguel looked at her in astonishment. 'What the hell do you want to go there for? There's no sun in Ireland! You're heartbroken girl! You need sun, sea, sand and—'

'Serenity,' Ava said cutting him off. 'It's time for me to go back and do what I was meant to do. Maybe then I can make sense of my life.'

Chapter Fifteen

The following evening, Ava found herself knee-deep in research, books on Ireland spread across the kitchen table and dozens of tabs open on her laptop. After Steve left, all she wanted to do was run away from her emotions, distract herself from what felt like the inevitable breakdown of her marriage. What better way to do that than to find out more about her roots?

The only fact Ava had ever really known about her start in life was that she had been born in St Joseph's Hospital, on the outskirts of Dublin at 10:42 on a Thursday morning. As it was the only detail she had, it was one she had treasured growing up, holding onto it and trotting it out to childhood friends as if it were some sort of revered secret.

Ava wondered if the fact she had been born in a hospital meant she might have been planned. Her mind started to spiral. If she'd been born to a young unwed mum, was it possible she might have been born in one of the famed Magdalene Laundries or another home for unmarried mothers? Or was there a chance that whoever knew about her existence had felt a hospital birth was best? Either way, there had been an element of care, and Ava wasn't sure if that was a good thing or a bad one. Had her biological mother been forced to give her up? Had she decided after looking at her that she didn't want Ava in her life?

The more she thought about it, the more her chest tightened. Every scenario, every possible reason her mother had given her up gnawed at her. Was this search going to fill the void, or just open it wider?

Ava reached for her glass of wine, and followed her father's mantra: if you couldn't make your mind up about something then you needed more information. Armed with Dutch courage, she'd spent much of the evening filling out the Birth Information and Tracing Form. This would then be passed onto the Adoption Authority that held her information and the process would begin.

The form was long. There was so much information she needed to fill out. She was asked if she wanted a copy of her birth certificate and early years information. But the more information she wanted, the more information there was to fill out. By the time she was finished she was physically spent, but her mind was on fire.

As well as looking at flights to Dublin in early January, she started writing emails to the hospital where she had been born. Suddenly, this challenge felt very daunting. She poured herself another glass of red wine just as Cassie and Dylan walked through the door, armed with several bags of what appeared to be Japanese food.

'What have you got there?' Ava asked, her tummy rumbling at the smell of miso soup wafting through the house.

Cassie held the bag aloft. 'Dinner for all. Where's Steve?' She looked around the house as if expecting him to pop out from behind the television at any moment.

Ava's appetite disappeared. She hadn't been able to have a private moment since Steve left and so hadn't managed to tell Cassie about her marriage. If she was honest, there was also a part of her that didn't want to tell her friend.

It was as if by telling the person she was closest to, what had happened with Steve would be real. But now Cassie was standing in front of her, she knew it was time to face reality.

Slowly and with as little detail as possible, aware that there were young ears listening, Ava explained what had happened. Cassie hung on to every word, and they were both grateful Dylan was more interested in playing with Monkey.

'Oh, Aves,' Cassie exclaimed by the time Ava had finished. She pulled her into her arms and Ava inhaled the familiar scent of CK One as if it was medicine.

'I'm sorry,' Cassie whispered, though her voice caught for just a second. 'I'm so, so sorry.'

They stayed like that, enjoying the safety of one another's arms for the best part of an hour. The takeaway food slowly growing cold.

'He really said he was excited to start dating again?' Cassie eventually whispered.

Ava nodded as she pulled away.

'Never had Steve down as a wanker.'

Ava blinked, feeling a sting. Was Cassie right? She should be angrier, she thought. But instead, she just felt numb.

'What a fucking mess,' Cassie exclaimed.

The unusual outburst caused both Ava and Dylan to gasp.

'You said a bad word, Mum,' Dylan sputtered.

'Yeah well, sometimes it's necessary. Sorry,' Cassie said with a shrug. 'Trust me, sweetheart, you're going to hear these words as you go through life, it's best you hear them from your mother first.'

Cassie's blunt honesty caused unexpected laughter to bubble up in Ava's throat. 'That's one way of looking at it.'

'Can I start swearing then?' Dylan asked eagerly, as he joined them on the sofa.

'No,' Ava and Cassie declared in unison.

Cassie reached for the open bottle of wine, topped up Ava's glass and went into the kitchen to fetch a second. She switched on the oven to reheat the takeaway and returned to her friend's side.

Together they watched Dylan scoop Monkey up into his arms, the cat purring loudly as he did so.

'He's a natural,' Ava remarked.

'Always been good with animals that one,' Cassie added. 'I have a feeling he might be a vet when he's older.'

'There's more money in that than firefighting,' Ava joked. 'Similar danger levels too, if you're regularly putting your hands up cows' bums.'

At the image both grimaced and took another glug of wine. Cassie nodded at the books.

'So, it looks like your search for your birth family is gaining momentum then.'

'It is.'

Ava played with the stem of her wineglass.

'I've thrown myself into it. You're right. I need to move forward to find out what I really want from life.'

'Excellent.' Cassie's beam radiated across the table.

Ava hesitated for a moment. She wasn't sure if this was something she should tackle by herself, but the thought of facing it without Cassie by her side felt unbearable.

'I was hoping you might come with me,' Ava said in a small voice, suddenly afraid her best friend might think it was something she had to do alone.

'Of course I will!' Cassie beamed again and ran a hand through her long blonde locks. She glanced across at Dylan who had fallen asleep on the sofa, Monkey curled up on his lap purring softly.

'It'll be good for him to have a break after all he's been through. I might take him to the zoo while we're there. Get his mind off things a bit.'

'That's a nice idea,' Ava mused. 'We could turn it into a bit of a holiday.'

'Agreed. And no matter what happens when we're there, I think it's going to do you good to draw a line under your past.'

A sudden thought struck Ava. What if she found out something horrible? What if her mother was an axe murderer? What if she was a prisoner who had only been allowed to give birth in the hospital because there were complications? Ava took a deep breath. She was spiralling.

'Knowing is always better than not knowing,' Cassie offered, sensing Ava's doubts. 'Whatever the outcome, you'll deal with it and you'll be stronger for it.'

The oven timer beeped, indicating the takeaway was ready. The women walked into the kitchen and began to help themselves.

Lost in thought, Ava sighed. Life seemed such a mess all of a sudden. She'd believed that losing her parents at such a young age would protect her from later hurts as an adult. She had been naive at best, stupid at worst, she could see that now. Her eyes darted back across the kitchen table, the pile of books on Ireland threatening to topple over. Was she chasing answers or opening doors that should stay closed? The truth lay just out of reach, but with it came a terrifying possibility – what if knowing her past only made the future harder to face?

Chapter Sixteen

After another sleepless night, Ava arrived at work for her day shift to a surprise. Outside, a small cluster of protestors had arrived armed with banners and placards that declared 'Save Our Firefighters!'

The sight made her pause, a mix of bemusement and a faint sense of pride washing over her. Were they really here for them?

'You seen this?' Ava jerked her head towards the protestors as she spotted Miguel trudging over, coffee in one hand, paracetamol in the other. The dark circles under his eyes mirrored her own exhaustion, and she raised an eyebrow in question.

Miguel smirked and popped a couple of tablets, washing them down with a swig of coffee.

'Probably still pissed from last night,' he muttered, nodding towards the protestors.

Ava looked again and saw one or two of them looked familiar. She was fairly sure she had seen them in some of the gay bars she had visited with Miguel and Xav on occasion.

Slowly, realisation dawned.

'You went out last night, didn't you?' she accused, her voice low, but more amused than angry.

Miguel shrugged, trying to appear nonchalant.

'So what if I did?' he said, though the guilt was written all over his face.

'You and Xav should be sorting things out.' Ava sighed. 'How are things going to get resolved if you're out on the pull?'

'I didn't pull anyone,' Miguel said, then catching Ava's face, relented. 'All right, just the one.'

'Just the one!'

'I mean, it was just a snog,' Miguel said quietly. 'For fuck's sake, Ava, I needed a bit of fun, back off.'

Ava said nothing, recognising now wasn't the time. Instead, she changed the subject.

'That still doesn't explain why the people you met from last night are protesting about our station.'

'Got 'em whipped up into a political frenzy, didn't I?' Miguel chuckled. 'And this lot'll do anything for a bit of drama.'

'Not sure it's going to do us much good though,' Ava grumbled.

Miguel shrugged. 'Who knows. It's better than a poke in the eye.'

Ava wasn't so sure as the chants grew louder.

Miguel looked terrible, but she imagined she didn't look a whole lot better. It had taken far more concealer than usual to cover the dark circles under her eyes and her second coffee of the day hadn't done anything to jolt her into action. She walked into the kitchen, looking for another.

But there was no time to think as the sound of bells rang throughout the station alerting her to a shout.

'Another fire at the estate,' Emerson said, moving into the kitchen, clutching the tip sheet.

Ava's mind whirred. There was barely anything left of the estate as it was. Reaching the muster bay, she was relieved to see they were just mobilising one appliance. That usually signalled a small fire, though with the wind picking up, things could always escalate quickly.

With the blues and twos blaring, Blue Watch arrived at the scene within minutes. The fire appeared small, contained to the kitchen, though Ava knew better than to let her guard down. Small fires could turn volatile in seconds.

As Big Stu pulled up right outside, Ava saw the homeowner, a lady she knew called Mrs Connor, sitting on a bench outside her home. Her hands were trembling in shock as she stared at the smouldering remains.

Ava offered what she hoped was a comforting smile, and after issuing instructions, the watch got to work manning the hoses, checking that the water pressure was steady as they aimed the jets at the base of the flames.

Ava directed Jodie to carefully monitor the smoke and surrounding walls, ensuring the fire wasn't spreading to other areas through the building's structure.

After an hour, Ava could see Emerson and Phil had the situation under control, and the blaze was almost out. As the team systematically checked the house for hotspots, Ava knew this would be a good training exercise for Jodie. The new recruit would get valuable experience, especially in keeping an eye out for residual heat pockets and ensuring full extinguishment.

As the fire continued to cool down, Ava saw her chance to check on Mrs Connor. After ensuring that a paramedic had been called to assess her for shock, Ava took a seat next to the old woman.

'How are you feeling?' she asked softly, mindful of the homeowner's trembling hands.

The resident barely noticed Ava's presence, her gaze was fixed so firmly on the fire.

'I can't believe I've been so stupid,' Mrs Connor muttered.

Ava frowned, Mrs Connor was rocking backwards and forwards, her fingers curled around her lips. The woman was clearly in shock, Ava could see that. She loosely slipped her arm around the woman's shoulders, and smiled as Mrs Connor turned, recognising someone was sitting beside her for the first time.

'Mrs Connor, whatever happened was an accident,' Ava said kindly.

There was a pause for a moment as if Mrs Connor was taking in everything Ava was saying.

'I didn't mean to do it,' she whispered, her voice trembling.

'I know that, but it doesn't matter now.' Ava smiled kindly. 'The fire's almost out, look.'

She pointed over at the house.

Emerson and the team were nearly done suppressing the fire, and the damage appeared minimal, mostly confined to the kitchen. A thermal scan confirmed there were no hidden hot spots lingering in the walls.

'It'll need a bit of a clean-up, and the smell of smoke might linger for a while, but luckily the fire didn't spread beyond the kitchen,' Ava assured her. 'The team will do a final check to make sure everything's safe.'

'I was trying to make chips,' Mrs Connor said now, as if she hadn't heard Ava. 'It's Tuesday, we used to have chip butty club at the centre on a Tuesday. I wanted to give the girls the same treat.'

Mrs Connor's gaze returned to her home again.

Ava understood immediately. Mrs Connor had been trying to connect with her old pals, keep the heart of the estate going by maintaining the traditions that held the place together so succinctly.

'I'm sorry,' Ava said gently.

Old-fashioned communities like this one were hard to come by. Now, thanks to an accident, it was on its last legs and the residents who remained were doing all they could to cling onto what was left. It was no wonder a fire like this had broken out, it was a miracle it hadn't been bigger.

'We'll get this sorted,' Ava promised. 'This place will be back to its old self in no time.'

Now it was Mrs Connor who looked at Ava with sympathy in her eyes.

'If you believe that, flower, you're dafter than I am.' She turned back to the fire. 'I know you're all doing your best to get this place back together, but it'll take a miracle, and we've fast run out of those. That Cassie, she's the salt of the earth. Nothing's too much trouble for her, I don't know how she does it with a child to look after and a full-time job to boot. Yet she's always here, looking out for us, looking out for everyone. She puts the heart into this community and without her we'd be lost. But even with everything she's – you're – doing, this community is gone and I was stupid to think I could bring a little dash of sunshine by making chips. Look what's happened.'

Ava slid her arm around Mrs Connor's shoulders and squeezed tightly.

'I promise you that we will get this place back on its feet,' she vowed.

Turning back to watch Miguel finish putting out the fire, she knew that she wouldn't rest until this estate was restored exactly how it had been. It was clear it was more important than perhaps any of them realised and she would move heaven and earth to make it happen.

—

Later that evening, when Ava and Miguel sat in the pub across the road from the fire station, she felt as if any remaining sense of triumph was being drained out of her.

'You can't be serious, Ava, we're doing enough as it is.' Miguel set his bottle of beer on the table and ran a hand through his hair.

Folding her arms, Ava stared at her friend, hoping she was giving him the required level of seriousness with her stare.

'I'm perfectly serious. We need to sort this out now, and to do that we need funds. That estate is at the heart of half the city. We've got to do more. How about we team up with Bath North – they'd be happy to pitch in.'

'Maybe,' Miguel mused. 'They're under a lot of pressure. Two firefighters have just quit.'

Ava raised an eyebrow. 'They've done what?'

'They heard about the redundancies and thought they'd make things easier. One of them had applied for the police a few months earlier and been accepted. She's decided to go down that route. The other one can't cope with the stress anymore.'

As Miguel drained his pint, Ava's thoughts turned to Jodie. The rookie had been under a lot of strain.

'Have you noticed Jodie's been struggling a bit lately?' Ava asked, shifting the conversation.

'Yes,' Miguel sighed. 'I had, and I've no idea what to do about it. She seems frightened of everything.'

'Don't be like that,' Ava said. 'She just needs more hand holding. She's really good at helping the victims.'

'Which we've really got time for,' Miguel said, irritated. 'Don't think I didn't notice you telling her all about your Nostalgia Nook. I don't need another bleeding heart like you looking for treasure, Ava. It's enough that you do it, never mind encouraging Blue Watch's trainee to join you in the madness.'

Ava felt anger rise but said nothing. Miguel was under a lot of pressure and always lashed out when he was under stress. But mention of her Nostalgia Nook had her suddenly remembering the medal. Cassie had suggested she post something on social media, but she'd been so preoccupied lately she'd completely forgotten. Pulling her phone out, she caught Miguel's glare of disapproval.

'I thought we were being social.'

'We are,' Ava said, jabbing at her phone and opening up Facebook. 'But if I don't do this now, I'll forget again and it's important.'

'What is?' Miguel asked, his interest piqued.

Ava typed out a post for Instagram, using relevant hashtags, then tapped out something similar for Facebook taking care to upload it to local groups that might share it, then she showed the post to Miguel.

He took her phone and peered at it.

'Is that the medal you and I found when you'd just finished your training?' Miguel asked, aghast. 'You've hung onto this all that time?'

Ava shifted uncomfortably in her seat. 'What's it to you?'

'Nothing at all,' Miguel said affectionately. He clinked his pint against hers with a smile. 'You're full of surprises,

Ava Ryan. Here, give Kenny, my mate from the British Legion, a ring.'

Miguel reached for his phone and pinged a number from his device to Ava's. 'He's retired now, but he served in Iraq. Might know something.'

Ava's heart leapt with a renewed sense of hope at all these new leads. Surely she'd get the medal back to where it belonged soon.

Spotting Ava's delight, Miguel smiled and took another sip of his drink.

'Heard from Steve?'

'Not a word,' she said bluntly.

'What a silly boy,' Miguel sighed.

Ava gave a wry smile. 'That what you think about Xav?'

To her surprise, Miguel looked stricken.

'What's happened?' she asked.

'Nothing, I'm being daft,' Miguel whispered. 'I just miss Xav. Splitting up is hard.'

Ava said nothing. She knew how Miguel felt.

'Maybe this trip to Ireland will help get your head straight,' Miguel offered.

'Maybe,' Ava replied.

She had now booked flights for the end of January and was feeling mixed emotions at the thought of her upcoming trip.

-

The following day, all thoughts of Ava's Irish connections were put on hold when she sat down to breakfast. Working a late shift, she had the luxury of the kitchen to herself with Dylan at school and Cassie at work. Intending to check her emails, she was astonished to find the tell-tale red dot on her social media apps, alerting her to her notifications. Not only had her post about Trooper Hakeson's medal been shared multiple times, but someone had responded with a comment: *Try contacting the regiment leader of the squadron or you could try contacting the Household Cavalry Museum. It could be that this medal had been sold through a dealer and they may be able to help. Or you could try a medal locator service.*

Ava felt a burst of hope. This was the strongest lead she'd had so far and although it wasn't much, it was something. Quickly, she typed out a reply of thanks. The poster had given her a lot to think about. She'd never thought that the medal might have been stolen or sold – maybe that was why nobody had stepped forward to claim it.

Her mind whirred with possibility. The medal deserved to be reunited with its rightful owner, and the memories preserved just as they should be.

Chapter Seventeen

Christmas passed in a blur for Ava. She did her best to ignore the day. Cassie had taken Dylan to see her great aunt in the Lake District, and Steve was with his brother's family. Cassie had invited her along, but Ava didn't feel like celebrating – she preferred to work.

At the fire station, Emerson, Phil and Big Stu cooked a huge turkey dinner. Afterwards, Ava played Uno with Jodie and helped tidy up. Only one call-out came, a cat stuck in a tree. They arrived just after the King's speech and found a Maine Coon halfway up an oak tree, wrapped in tinsel.

'He wanted to look festive,' the cat's owner, a middle-aged woman wearing a party hat, insisted as Ava got the ladder.

Ava said nothing, determined to maintain the spirit of Christmas. But as she hoisted the poor animal from the tree, she was grateful she wasn't scratched or clawed to death as she cut the cat free of the tinsel.

'Oh, he doesn't look festive now,' the woman said mournfully as Ava handed her back her prize animal without Christmas decorations.

'No, but he does look alive,' Ava snapped. She gave the animal one last stroke before she left and hoped his owner gathered a bit of common sense and left the tinsel for the tree next year.

New Year thankfully also passed uneventfully. There had been one drunken party where revellers had got carried away with some indoor sparklers, but other than that, one of the worst days in a firefighter's calendar had been easy.

Not a word Ava used lightly.

And not one that applied to her personal life either. Though, in a way, it had been easy. Steve had largely kept his distance. They'd exchanged a couple of Happy Christmas and New Year texts but other than that they hadn't spoken.

She had missed him. Of course she had.

But the truth was, she wasn't sure if it was him she missed or his family. Steve's bright, noisy relatives strewn halfway across the UK and Greece all gathered together during this season. When they had first met, she and Steve, along with his mum, dad, sisters and brother had all made the pilgrimage back to Athens, but these days they stayed in the UK, their lives and jobs making it more difficult for them to get away.

But no matter where they were, the festive season was always brighter and louder. It was as though someone had turned the volume up on their lives for a month and Ava loved it. When she was little it had only ever been her and her parents, who she adored but she always wished there were more people, more love. Without Steve and his family, the festive period had felt a lot quieter.

It had helped she'd had the medal project to throw herself into. Not only had she written to the suggested regiment asking for help but she had also contacted the museum in London and left her details. She also checked with the police again, but her inquiries yielded nothing.

'It's probably been sold through a dealer,' one of her police friends said. 'It's more common than you think.'

'There's really a market for other people's medals?' she asked in surprise.

The PC had laughed. 'They're hugely collectible, especially ones from the Gulf War campaign.'

It had been food for thought, but now it was the first week of January and she was keen to get on with the next stage of her life: Ireland.

This morning she had received a letter from the adoption services in Dublin. Sitting down at the kitchen island, she felt a shiver run down her spine as she read.

Dear Ms Ryan,

Many thanks for your application through the Birth Information Tracing Service, which we received on 5 December.

We can confirm that we are able to identify both of your birth parents, but it is important to note that both have registered a No Contact Preference on the Contact Preference Register. This means that we are unable to provide any information beyond their names and last known addresses at the time of your adoption.

The records we hold indicate the following:

1. Mother: Bernice Collins, born 3 November 1947
2. Father: Fintan Collins, born 28 October 1944
3. Last known address at time of adoption: 424 Bourne End Drive, Rathmines, Dublin

Your birth was registered by Maeve McNally, who was listed as being present at your birth. Her address at the time of your birth was 57 Green End Lane, Rathmines, Dublin.

We hope this information assists in your search. Should you require further assistance, please do not hesitate to contact us, and we will be happy to help.

Yours sincerely,
Eimear Flanagan
Head of Adoption Records

Ava stared at the letter. Finally, she had names. Bernice. Fintan. Her parents. Her hands trembled as she re-read the words. For so long, she had wondered. And now, here it was, staring back at her from a screen.

Gazing out of the window at the creamy Georgian architecture, she thought back over her life. Did Ava Collins belong in Bath? Was she supposed to be here or was she supposed to be back in Ireland? Was that where she belonged?

'What's up with you?' Cassie asked, walking into the kitchen.

'I've found my mother,' she whispered, turning the laptop screen towards her friend.

Cassie read greedily, her jaw wide open with shock as she scanned the text.

'Bernice Collins,' she mused, reaching the end.

'I know.' Ava let out a shaky breath. 'I know who I am.'

'Your father, too,' Cassie murmured.

Ava blinked. She hadn't even noticed his name.

She looked back at the screen, reading the email again.

How could she have missed it? Her father – Fintan.

'My dad,' she muttered. Suddenly her joy turned to confusion as she peered back at the screen.

'But why is he on here?' Ava's brow furrowed. 'I thought fathers weren't usually listed in cases like mine.'

Cassie paused, thinking. 'Maybe... they weren't unmarried.'

Ava's eyes flicked back to the email. 'They have the same surname. Were they married then?'

She hadn't put that together when she read the email, too overwhelmed by seeing their names. All her life she'd assumed her mother had been a hard done by single mum, what if she was wrong?

'But why would they be married and give me up for adoption? And why did someone called Maeve register my birth?' She peered at the email again and took in the other woman's name. 'I mean, Bernice would have been, what, thirty-ish when she had me? Not exactly young, especially not in those days.'

Cassie frowned. 'Perhaps they'd fallen on hard times. Couldn't afford you. Perhaps Bernice was so traumatised by her circumstances she wasn't capable of registering your birth. Perhaps Maeve had to do it.'

Ava leaned back, her head resting on the cool wall. 'I've always assumed my mother was a young, single mother. Not a married woman in her thirties.'

'Maybe she and her husband divorced?' Cassie suggested.

Ava shot her a withering look. 'In Ireland? In the 1980s? Come on.'

'Fair point,' she conceded. 'But she could have been a domestic abuse victim. Perhaps Fintan made her give up her child.'

142

She looked back at the email and shook her head in disbelief. How incredible one letter could upend her world. She already wasn't who she thought she was.

'You know you have to keep going, right?' Cassie said gently, as if almost reading her thoughts. 'Even though they've said they don't want to be contacted. You can still find out more about them, more about their lives. Maybe even see where they lived, where you could have grown up. It might help you settle things in your mind and besides,' Cassie's words hung in the air for a moment, 'you've come this far.'

'I know,' Ava whispered. Her head hurt. The stress of all she had uncovered beginning to take its toll.

But she also knew she had to take a chance and uncover the real reason behind her adoption. Ava's thoughts swirled. Could she really handle finding out the truth? What if it wasn't what she expected, or worse, what if it was? With a deep breath, she reached for a pad of writing paper. Her hand hovered over the page for a moment, the weight of the pen suddenly heavy. She stared at the one name that hadn't indicated no contact: Maeve McNally. Taking a deep breath, she began to write.

> *Dear Mrs McNally,*
> *I hope you don't mind me writing to you but I*
> *hope you might be able to help me...*

Chapter Eighteen

Before Ava could deal with her past, she had to deal with her present. Her separation from Steve had lasted longer than she had anticipated. They had now been apart almost seven weeks and Ava felt the distance between them growing. The dates Steve had seemed excited about had amounted to nothing, and Ava had found herself keeping things from him that she would normally have told him in everyday conversation.

Ava had told him her adoption news in an email. She'd reduced the most significant news of her life to a few sentences in a digital message. Likewise, Steve had informed her with a single sentence in a text that he'd taken on a new contract at work.

These two events were things that in the past, they'd have spent whole evenings discussing rather than just a few words. What did that say about where they were now?

All Ava found herself doing was magically hoping that things would right themselves between them. Whilst her feelings for her husband had shifted, they had been together too long for her to imagine a world without him. Something she thought about now as she surveyed the contents of her wardrobe and wondered what she should wear. She and Steve had agreed to meet for a drink that night – whether her husband saw it as a date, Ava wasn't sure. She saw it as something to feel nervous about and wasn't sure why. It didn't help that for the past two weeks she had been anxiously checking the post. Since writing to Maeve she had hoped every day there would be a reply, but so far nothing, and the lack of response made Ava anxious.

Reaching for her favourite pair of jeans, the sound of the doorbell made her jump.

'I'll go,' Cassie called from the kitchen below.

Expecting it to be a delivery, Ava went back to picking outfits. She wasn't sure she wanted to see Steve or that she was ready. But she knew they had to start making some progress towards their future, whatever that looked like. The silence from Maeve felt like a rejection from her past all over again. Ava sighed and slipped on her jeans. Only then did she hear raised voices drifting up the stairs.

Cassie never shouted, but now, as Ava rushed downstairs and towards the hallway, she could hear her voice becoming progressively louder.

'I don't know why you're here, but I'll repeat what I told you all those years ago: I never want to see you again.'

Rounding the corner, Ava stood rooted to the floor in shock as she saw Cassie, pink-cheeked with fury, her hand on Dylan's shoulder, almost as if she was holding him back.

The man standing on her front step was elderly and dishevelled. With grey hair, flushed cheeks and holding a bicycle, Ava's heart sank at the sight of him. Cassie's father.

Yet Cassie's outburst did nothing to deter Paul, who now crouched down so he was at Dylan's eye level.

'You must be Dylan,' he croaked. 'What age are you now? Six?'

'I'm eight,' he said proudly, then, looking up at Cassie, he grinned and said, 'but I'm nine next week, we're going out for pizza. You can come if you like.'

'Now, I'd love that.' Ava couldn't miss the look of affection in his eyes as he reached out a hand to touch Dylan, but the little boy hid behind Cassie.

'He won't be coming to your party,' Cassie said to her son, her eyes never leaving her father's. 'Go into the kitchen please, Dylan. Now.'

Cassie's no-nonsense tone told Dylan that his mother wasn't joking and he slunk off towards the kitchen, head hung low, feet scuffing along the carpet.

As Dylan passed Ava in the corridor, he rolled his eyes.

'I don't know why she's so upset,' he said sulkily. 'If I want my granddad at my party I should be allowed.'

Ava said nothing but felt a white hot, burning rage at this man on her doorstep. He had lost his right to interfere in Cassie's life years ago and had no right at all to ambush her. She walked quickly to the front door and locked eyes with Paul. He hadn't changed much since the last time she had seen him. A lot older now, but his eyes still full of boyish charm.

'You heard what Cassie said,' Ava said in a low voice as she stood shoulder to shoulder with her friend. 'She doesn't want you here. Go.'

At the sight of Ava, Cassie's father smiled.

'Ava love, it's been a long time.' He looked between the two of them and Ava felt the warmth of Cassie's arm as she linked it through hers. 'Still as thick as thieves then.'

'And you're clearly just thick if you haven't got the message, Paul,' Ava said darkly. 'You've been repeatedly told to go away, I don't want to tell you again. Go.'

'Girls, please don't be like that,' Paul said. 'I want to talk. I heard about the fire, how you'd lost everything, Cassie. I wrote you a letter. Didn't you get it?'

He looked at Ava almost accusingly and she felt the rage in her chest grow. She was about to say something, only for Cassie to speak.

'I got your letter,' she said calmly. 'I threw it in the bin where it belongs. You don't care about me, you only care about yourself. Mum's been dead a few years and you're getting older, feeling sorry for yourself. Sheryl not looking after you in your old age is she?'

At the mention of their former school friend, Paul blushed.

'I was wrong. I did some stupid things.'

'Too little, too late,' Cassie snapped.

Ava could feel Cassie's hackles rising. At that Ava slung an arm around Cassie's shoulder.

'Your lies and manipulation aren't welcome here.'

'But Cassie, please.' The man looked distraught and if Ava didn't know the truth about Paul she would have felt almost sorry for him.

'There's no *Cassie, please*,' she said firmly. 'You, Mum, all of you, you made your choice years ago. I didn't want or need you in my life then, and I certainly don't need you now.'

With that Cassie stepped forward and slammed the door shut in the man's face.

Only when Ava could see the man slink away did Cassie crumple to the floor, her shoulders heaving with sobs that racked through her body. Ava's chest tightened. She knew how much Cassie had been hurt by this man, but seeing her friend stand her ground stirred a fierce pride in her. Paul didn't know how much he'd lost throwing away his daughter like she was yesterday's trash when in fact she was precious treasure.

–

'And she had no idea he was coming?' Steve asked incredulously.

The two were in their favourite pub at the top of the city near the Assembly Rooms. Heads buried in two cold pints of lager.

'None at all,' Ava replied. She had been in two minds as to whether to come out tonight but Cassie insisted she needed some time to herself. Ava wasn't sure but wanted to respect her wishes.

Steve interrupted her thoughts by sliding his hand across the table and squeezing her fingers.

Ava felt a flash of warmth as she looked into her husband's eyes. She had forgotten the look of love he'd worn in the early days of their relationship. The way he'd made her heart skip a beat with a simple crinkle of his brow.

'So,' Steve said after a pause. 'When are you off to Ireland?'

'Saturday,' she said, her stomach full of butterflies at the thought. 'Just for five days. You don't mind looking after Monkey?'

Steve shook his head. 'It'll be nice to get out of my brother's spare room for a bit.'

'You can come home,' Ava said in a small voice. 'I know we've a house full at the moment but it's our home, Steve.'

For a moment, sitting across from Steve, she almost allowed herself to imagine they could be who they once were.

She spoke those words around a lump in her throat. She hadn't realised until that moment just how much she wanted Steve to come home and for their lives to return to normal.

For a second, Steve said nothing.

'I know. I want to,' he said eventually, 'but we need to sort our lives out first, Ava. My views on IVF haven't changed.'

The imploring look on Steve's face dashed any hope she had for their future. For a brief moment Ava had felt like she used to, when it was just her and Steve against the world. But as his words reminded her of their stalemate over IVF, the hope fizzled, leaving behind the familiar ache of distance. Steve caught Ava's expression and rubbed his forefinger along her thumb.

'I know it doesn't seem like it, Ava, but I'm not deliberately trying to hurt you. I do understand how you feel about wanting a child of your own, but I can't find anything to convince me to give it another try.'

Ava gave him a weak smile but didn't trust herself to start speaking.

'How's the medal hunt coming along? Think you'll reunite your oldest piece soon?' he asked brightly, recognising the subject of adoption had left them both at an impasse.

As he reached for his pint, Ava groaned. 'It isn't.'

'Why?' Steve looked concerned.

'I've drawn a blank. The regiment can't tell me anything and neither can the Household Cavalry Museum.' Ava reached for her drink and took a welcome sip. 'I've started contacting dealers hoping one of them might have sold it and can give me more information but it's like looking for a needle in a proverbial haystack.'

'You'll do it,' Steve said confidently. 'You always reunite people with their memories, never seen you fail yet.'

Ava wasn't sure, her eyes strayed to the corner of the pub. There was a man there she recognised but couldn't place. Sitting next to a blonde woman, his arm slung around her shoulder, she watched the woman tuck a lock of hair behind her ear, a large diamond ring nestled on her left finger.

Of course! It was the bartender, Josh, who had lost the ring and planned to propose. But there it was, safely on the woman's hand, and the pair of them looked happy, with eyes only for each other.

Despite her misery, Ava felt a flash of joy. There it was, a little reminder that she still had the power to help people reclaim happiness. If she could do that for others, surely she could untangle her own mess. Knowing she had in a small way been instrumental in bringing these two together was proof that her work, her value to the community, was important.

The couple exchanged a kiss and Ava felt a renewed vigour. She realised how much she loved Steve; she wanted him back in her life for good. And with his support and love, she would find her birth family, she would help Cassie, she would reunite the medal with its rightful owner and get the estate back on its feet. Most of all, she would ensure everyone around her would thrive. After all, look at the happiness she was capable of bringing.

Chapter Nineteen

That happiness was something Ava felt utterly incapable of bringing as she gathered with the other watch managers and Miguel for a meeting with Group Manager Colleen Peterson, the following week.

Colleen's face was grave as she gestured for them all to sit down.

'I want to talk to you about the job losses,' she said, going straight to the point.

Ava and Miguel exchanged concerned looks.

'Final decisions have been made.'

'Oh,' Miguel said flatly, his jaw clenched, a muscle ticking in his temple, his emotions barely held in check.

'How many losses are we looking at?' Pete, Green Watch Manager, asked.

Colleen looked at the assembled group sympathetically. 'We're cutting one position from each watch – five in total – at this station and Bath North.'

'That's impossible,' Miguel snapped. 'We'll never manage!'

'Believe me, it could have been worse,' Colleen said, her expression softening. 'We were originally looking at double the number of cuts. This is the best outcome we could negotiate.'

But the fact they were going to lose someone from the watch didn't feel like a win to Ava.

'Is there really nothing more we can do?' Ava begged.

Colleen folded her hands on the table in front of her. 'We've fought hard to reduce the impact. Now, there's a consultation period coming up, and there'll be opportunities for voluntary redundancies or even early retirement packages where applicable.'

'Voluntary?' Miguel muttered, still unconvinced. 'We don't have many who could afford to volunteer for this.'

Colleen nodded, acknowledging his frustration. 'I understand, but we need to see if anyone steps forward first. In the end, if no one volunteers, we'll have to decide based on operational needs.'

Miguel and Ava exchanged another concerned look. How were they supposed to decide something so awful? Every single one of the watch was invaluable, and they all had responsibilities. Emerson had an elderly mum he supported, Phil and Big Stu a wife and two kids. Then there was Jodie, though only a trainee, she had just moved in with her girlfriend, who had cerebral palsy. A job loss now would hit Jodie's training, confidence and personal life hard.

'Is there any more specific guidance?' Ava asked desperately. 'Any criteria to help us?'

'We're looking at several factors,' Colleen said with a sigh. 'We'd prefer not to lose a trainee, and if anyone qualifies for early retirement, we'll look at that too. But beyond that, it's going to come down to who the station can operate without.'

'How long do we have to decide?' Miguel asked.

'Until the middle of May, so we have time to properly consult with employee representatives and trade unions,' Colleen said, getting up from her desk. 'Once the consultation is over, I'll expect suggestions from all watches by then.'

Ava couldn't help but notice the irony of the deadline. Spring was usually a time of hope and new beginnings, but for some, it would mean the end of their career.

–

The following morning, all that was left for Ava to do was worry she had forgotten to pack something. She rifled through her bag one last time, her anxiety mounting.

'Stop worrying,' Cassie's voice called from the doorway, breaking her spiral.

'I'm not worrying,' Ava said, checking her bag for the seventh time.

'You are. I've heard you pacing up and down since four this morning,' Cassie put in.

Ava scowled at her friend just as Dylan appeared. At the sight of Ava's case, he smiled and pointed to his own bright pink case.

'We're going on holiday!'

'We certainly are,' Cassie said, smiling at her son. 'And we're also going to find out about Auntie Ava's family, remember?'

Dylan looked serious for a moment. Both Ava and Cassie had taken the young boy out for a pizza as promised to celebrate his birthday. Over a Pepperoni Passion they had explained that although they were going on holiday, they had an important quest.

'We're looking for the people that made me,' Ava had said simply.

Dylan took a bite of pizza and looked confused.

'But I don't know all the people that made me. I know Mum, but she says my dad just gave a bit of himself, and that was it.'

Ava stifled a giggle and she looked at Cassie for clarification, who shrugged.

'You're right, Dyl,' Ava had said. 'But you know your mum and I don't know anyone that made me and I'd like to find out.'

'Okay,' Dylan said as if she had just announced she was going to the shops. 'But we're still going to the zoo right?'

Now, Ava returned to her bag, just to check once again her passport hadn't somehow disappeared in the two minutes since she'd last checked. As she did so she heard the sound of a familiar tread on the stairs.

'Relax, you know she worries about everything before getting on a plane,' Steve called.

She turned to see him lolling against the doorjamb of their bedroom next to Cassie.

'Checked everything five hundred times?' he asked, smiling.

Ava nodded.

'Then I'd say you're set,' he said cheerfully. 'Go on, I want to hear all about it when you get back.'

Filled with a fresh sense of resolve, Ava set her shoulders determinedly. She had come this far, she wasn't about to stop now. Flashing Steve a grateful smile, she walked out of her bedroom, head held high.

The journey to the airport was a dream, as was security and passport control. By the time they were sat on the plane, Ava was feeling relaxed and hopeful. But stealing a glance at her friend who was sitting beside her, Cassie looked anything but.

Cassie's forced cheerfulness had been grating on Ava since Paul's visit, her overly bright smiles concealed something much darker.

'You heard from Paul again?' Ava ventured now. She was too full of jangling nerves to bother being polite.

Cassie raised an eyebrow. 'Talk about direct.'

'Sorry,' Ava replied. 'But you haven't answered the question.'

Cassie shifted uncomfortably in her seat. Ava knew her friend too well. The reappearance of Paul had shaken her, opening old wounds that Cassie had spent years burying, just like Ava had with her own family.

'I'm sorry, Cass,' she whispered.

'I'm not,' Cassie replied. 'I've all the family I need right here.'

Ava smiled and reached for her friend's hand. Together they sat like that in companionable silence for the rest of the flight. Each comforted by the other's presence.

–

An hour later and the plane touched down on a strip of concrete surrounded by rich and lush green fields with a ripeness not found anywhere else. She had never been back, but she felt immediately a connection to the place. This was the land of her birth, a place where history lingered in every stone and shadow. As Ava stepped off the plane and breathed in the Irish air, she felt those familiar nerves return. Ireland wasn't just a destination, it was the key to unlocking who she really was. This was where her story began.

Chapter Twenty

Having driven out to the little cottage on the outskirts of the city, Ava was feeling chuffed with her choice of accommodation. Large enough for them to have their own space, there was even a huge garden with a swing for Dylan to play on if he got bored, that was if it ever stopped raining.

But despite the cosiness of the cottage, Ava was keen to get started on the point of her visit. There was still no reply from Maeve, but now she had arrived, Ava thought she would pay the woman a visit.

'You're not going to this Maeve's house now?' Cassie gasped.

Ava frowned and picked at a loose thread on her jumper. 'Why not? It's the whole reason we're here. Well, it's why I'm here – Dylan wants to go to the zoo.'

'We're here to support you,' Cassie said gently. She took hold of Ava's hand. 'You can't go to Rathmines without us.'

'I'll be fine,' Ava insisted.

Cassie looked annoyed. 'For god's sake, Aves. God knows who this woman is! She might be violent! You said she hadn't replied to your letter either, you can't just show up.'

'What choice do I have?' Ava countered. 'If I don't at least try then there was no point coming here.'

Cassie's reaction was verging on the comical. Her friend had been the one that had encouraged her to do this, now she seemed to be changing her mind.

'You're right, this is your business not mine.' She reached into her pocket for her mobile and waved it. 'Call me if there's even a hint of trouble, okay? Evil lurks bloody everywhere!'

Ava smirked.

'Okay.'

An hour later and Ava pulled up to a smart semi-detached house, with a small but well-kept front lawn and large sweeping gravel drive. She took a deep breath. Switching off the engine she took a moment to gather herself before, as she knew the Irish liked to say, she lost the run of herself.

She smiled at the expression, hoped she would earn the right to use it after finding out more about her Irish roots.

Opening the car door, Ava stepped outside. The air was crisp and fresh and she inhaled it greedily; the place already seemed so pure. But as she neared the house, her feet crunching noisily on the gravel as she did so, her knees began to knock together and nerves jangled. Was this what she really wanted?

'Get a grip of yourself,' she muttered under her breath.

Steeling herself, she made the short walk to the front door and pressed the bell.

The door was opened moments later by a short woman with a pleasant, open face, friendly grey eyes and a thick mound of grey hair.

She smiled curiously at Ava.

'Can I help you?'

For a moment Ava just stared at the woman who had opened the door. She seemed so normal, so nice. Would she remain that way once she revealed the reason she was here? She opened her mouth to speak, but for some reason no words would come out. The woman stared at her, silently encouraging her on.

'Are you Maeve McNally?' Ava eventually managed to sputter.

A look of wariness passed across the woman's face as she nodded.

'Do I know you?' she asked coolly. 'I don't buy or sell at the door.'

Her confidence faltered, but she wasn't giving up. Lifting her chin slightly, she looked Maeve in the eye.

'I'm looking for Bernice Collins,' Ava continued, her confidence growing as she warmed to her theme. 'I believe you and her were good friends back in the Seventies. Possibly even now.'

At the mention of Bernice's name Maeve's look of concern grew.

'Who are you?' she demanded.

Maeve's pleasant demeanour had vanished and Ava felt her newfound resolve weaken.

'My name's Ava Ryan, I wrote to you a few weeks ago,' she said hesitantly.

The woman gasped and her grey eyes widened as if she had seen a ghost.

'I didn't think you'd just show up here,' she said at last.

'You did get the letter then?' Ava said as gently as she could.

Maeve's eyes hardened for a moment. 'It's all in the past, best forgotten.'

She moved as if to close the door, but then her gaze softened slightly as she glanced at Ava's face, filled with determination and her eyes brimming with sadness.

'Five minutes,' she relented, stepping outside, closing the door behind her.

'You were just a few days old when I last saw you. A quiet little thing, you hardly cried.' Maeve's eyes shone at the memory, but there was a tightness in her voice. 'And then you were gone. Just like that, without a word.'

Ava bristled at the cold finality of it. Maeve made it sound as though she'd been kidnapped.

A thought struck her. Was that how it was? Had someone persuaded her mother and father they knew what was best?

Suddenly Maeve looped an arm through hers and pulled her away from the house.

'Maeve,' a man's voice called from the garden. 'Who is it?'

'Bobby Miller's girl,' Maeve called cheerfully. 'We're just having a gas about the fundraiser for the church next week.'

'Oh, right so,' the man's voice called again.

'My husband, Gerry,' Maeve said quickly. 'He knew nothing of Bernice's pregnancy and he doesn't know about you. He'd be ashamed of me, for the part I played in all this.'

Ava winced but questions tumbled through her mind as quickly as somersaults. Why would Maeve's husband be ashamed?

'I'm sorry. I'm not here to cause trouble,' Ava said. 'I just wanted to talk to you about my birth parents. Your name was in the adoption folder. You registered my birth.'

Maeve nodded and closed her eyes. Ava could almost see the memories of the past forty years playing out across her mind.

'Come with me.'

Together they walked briskly along the street and only when they were halfway down did Maeve slow her pace.

She turned to look at Ava, and there was kindness in her eyes.

'I can't believe you came even though I ignored you,' Maeve said, her grey eyes roaming over Ava as if wanting to drink in every inch of her. 'Even though I knew it wasn't sensible, especially not with Gerry knowing a thing about you, I always hoped I'd see you in some form, find out what you were up to but I never thought it would happen. And now here you are – the absolute spit of Bernice.' Maeve broke off and shook her head regretfully. 'Ava,' she murmured. 'They kept the name I gave you then.'

'You gave me?' Ava asked, shocked.

Suddenly Maeve looked embarrassed. 'Well, it was my idea. I told Bernice she'd regret giving you up, I can remember sitting down to write her a letter letting her know.'

'Why did you call me Ava?' she asked.

This was new information. She had always assumed, perhaps naturally, that her mother had been the one to name her.

Maeve's gaze softened. 'It comes from the Germanic word for desired. I wanted you to know that you were wanted, even if, well, even if you were being adopted out.'

Silence fell across the pair as both women considered Maeve's words. Ava played the word on repeat in her mind. Desired, desired, desired. Had she been? Was she now?

'I take it you had good family?' Maeve said. 'The couple seemed nice that took you. I watched from my car window when they came to get you.'

Ava felt dumbfounded. Who was this woman that had taken such an interest in her?

She shook her head free of the questions that were threatening to take over her mind. She had to stay focused.

'I've been trying to find Bernice,' Ava said. 'The adoption agency gave me my birth certificate and folder. She and Fintan had both ticked the no contact preference on the register but I have to see them, or at least try.'

Ava's heart began to beat faster. Hearing the words out loud made all this seem more real.

Maeve said nothing and continued to walk. Ava took it as an invitation to join her, the cool Irish wind blowing the hair away from her face.

'I tried to find her of course, and Fintan, but I couldn't find anything online. It's as if they've disappeared,' she finished, trying to keep the desperation out of her voice.

'They haven't disappeared,' Maeve said briskly. 'They're divorced. About fifteen years ago now. Bernice uses her maiden name.'

'Oh.' Ava felt a stab of surprise. Of all the possibilities she had considered, this hadn't been one of them.

'It was a terrible shock to the families,' Maeve continued. 'Fintan was dreadfully upset, he moved to New York—'

'New York?' Ava's mind whirled. She hadn't expected this, hadn't anticipated Ireland wouldn't be far enough.

Maeve's next words were like a punch to the chest. 'I'm sorry, love, he died six months ago.'

Gone. Disappointment flooded through her. The man who had helped create her was dead, and she'd never know what he was like, never be able to ask him why.

'And Bernice?' she asked now, hope giving way to manners. 'Did she move away, too?'

Maeve wrinkled her nose. 'Sort of. She's in Cork now on her own, possibly with another fella. I'm not sure, we lost touch a while back.'

'Cork?' Ava felt a flicker of hope rise within her, a light breaking through the disappointment. Cork was close – at least closer than New York. Maybe, she'd find the answers she needed there. Cork was doable, it was easy to drive down there in a day.

'Do you have an address?' Ava asked shyly.

Nodding, Maeve stopped again, her brow furrowed.

'I do… but, Ava, love, I can't give it to you. Bernice won't want to see you. I know this is hard to hear, but I'm doing this for your sake, not just hers.' She shook her head, eyes full of regret. 'I wish I could give you more.'

But after all these years, it wasn't about what Bernice wanted, it was about what Ava needed to know.

Ava studied Maeve's face, there was something more than just reluctance there, almost a glimmer of guilt. What did this woman know that made her so hesitant? She wasn't just protecting Bernice, was she?

Sensing Ava's despair, Maeve sighed. 'It'll do you no good, Ava love. You don't want this.'

But Ava had spent far too long as a firefighter not to know how to use her persuasive skills. She took a step towards her mother's friend, her voice firm.

'You don't understand, I've waited my entire life for this. I deserve to know where she is. Whatever the consequences, they're mine to face. Please, Maeve, I need to know.'

Chapter Twenty-One

Despite the fact it was a Saturday afternoon, Dublin Zoo was surprisingly calm. The January sun had briefly reared its head and was peeping out from behind the clouds, giving the day an unexpected, but much needed, burst of warmth. Ava felt her shoulders loosen and the knot in her stomach start to unfurl.

Meeting Maeve had been a shock and back at the cottage, Ava was surprised to find she was shaking. Had she really been so forceful? When Maeve had refused to give her Bernice's address, she had lost all sense of reason, it was as if a red mist had descended on her. Something on her face must have shown how upset she was, because Maeve's face crumpled.

'Ava, I'm sorry. I don't know what to say. I'm genuinely pleased to see you after all these years, but going to look for Bernice won't help you. Leave it, love. I'll answer any questions I can.'

Ava glanced at Maeve's lined face and saw the worry in her eyes. She felt a wave of guilt. In her quest for information, she hadn't once considered how this search might affect Maeve.

'I'm sorry,' Ava said.

Maeve gave her a tight smile. 'You're all right, love. But I won't give you any details. Trust me, it's for the best.'

'I think it's me that should be judge of that,' Ava said firmly. 'I want to know who my mother is. I want to know why she gave me up for adoption.'

Maeve looked uncomfortable. 'It wasn't the right path for Bernice, is all I'll say. She had her problems.'

'Problems?' Ava echoed, her mind racing. What sort of problems? Was Bernice sick? Had her birth caused some sort of trauma for her mother?

Maeve paused for a moment as if weighing up how much she should say. She moved out of the way to a bench at the end of the street. Ava followed her.

'Your mother and I were the best of friends,' Maeve began, sitting down. 'We knew each other since school, even shared a saint's day. She and Fintan met at the same time I met my husband, Gerry. The four of us would go out dancing together. But then she fell pregnant and for reasons best known to Bernice, she gave you up. To be honest with you, Ava, I'm not entirely sure I understand them. I've thought about it a lot over the years and I still haven't got to the bottom of it, not really. I think it was the wedge that finally drove us apart. I could never understand why she did it, and Bernice couldn't understand why I was so against her decision.'

Ava frowned. 'But she and Fintan were married by then?'

'They were.' Maeve nodded, her lacquered grey hair hardly moving. 'Had been for about ten years, we'd both been married roughly the same length of time. They were happy times and then Bernice fell pregnant and had you adopted.'

'But I don't understand why Bernice adopted me out?' Ava said. 'She was married.'

Maeve sighed. 'She was. But her and Fintan, they were always different, you know. Wanted different things, never happy.'

Ava felt as if she was going round in circles. Nothing made sense.

'I have to talk to her,' Ava said again. 'Please, Maeve, you helped me before, please help me again.'

She sensed a shift in the older woman as Maeve silently reached into her pocket and pulled out a phone. With a few taps, Ava felt something on her own mobile.

She fished it out of her jeans pocket.

'I've airdropped you something,' Maeve said with surprising efficiency.

Surprised, Ava clicked accept and saw a message flash on her phone – a business card bearing the name *Bernice Collins, Life Coach, 15 Dunmore Park Lane, Cork.*

She stared at the screen in surprise and then glanced back up at Maeve.

'A life coach?'

Maeve looked nonplussed.

'Don't warn her you're coming.'

With that, Maeve had got up and walked away, leaving Ava in the street alone.

Now, a couple of hours later Ava was standing what felt like a million miles from Rathmines, in a zoo, with animals and screaming children. The place was bursting with life and precisely what she needed after her strange conversation with Maeve.

'So, are you going to find Bernice?' Cassie asked.

She linked her arm through her friend's and together they sauntered along the path, Dylan running on ahead.

Ava nodded. 'Tomorrow.'

Cassie looked surprised. 'So soon? Don't you want to let the news settle?'

'It's why I'm here.' Ava's voice was firm.

'What if you find something you don't like?' Cassie asked. 'It sounds as though Maeve was trying to warn you off.'

Ava had thought of nothing else on the drive back to the house. But she also knew she couldn't leave things now. She had to get to the bottom of her story no matter what it was.

She was about to say as much when she saw Dylan run straight towards them.

'You've got to come and look at the penguins,' he said breathlessly. 'The keeper's about to feed them.'

She and Cassie exchanged knowing looks. Neither of them fancied watching penguins eat fish, but Dylan's excitement was infectious, and she couldn't say no. 'Thing is, Dyl,' Ava said, bending down to meet the little boy's eye. 'I'd really rather have a beer and an ice cream.'

Dylan giggled at Ava's honesty.

'I don't like beer,' Dylan said defiantly. 'But I do like ice cream.'

'What's that got to do with me?' Ava asked, still crouched down.

The little boy thought for a moment.

'Well, it means that if you come with me to look at the penguins you can buy me an ice cream afterwards.'

Ava threw her head back and roared with laughter. She had to admire Dylan's cheek.

She brought her laughter under control and surveyed Dylan. 'Tell you what, we go see the penguins, I buy you an ice cream, but you buy the beers all right?'

'All right,' Dylan said, clearly not having thought the deal through. 'Let's tell Mum.'

Ava stood up and glanced around for her friend, but Cassie was nowhere to be seen.

'Where is she?'

'Up by the penguins,' Dylan said, skipping ahead. 'She said she was feeling a bit woozy and wanted to sit down.'

Ava frowned and reached out her hand for Dylan to hold. He took it quickly, giving Ava a smile that made her melt.

Within a couple of minutes, they had all reached the penguin enclosure and found Cassie sitting down, frantically puffing on her inhaler.

Ava sat beside her. 'Are you okay? You just disappeared.'

Pulling the inhaler from her lips Cassie gave her a weak smile. 'Change in air, I'll be fine in a minute.'

Ava wasn't so sure.

'You haven't had an asthma attack for ages.'

Ava remembered all too well the attacks Cassie used to suffer at school. She was constantly being sent to the nurse's office to recover. Some kids thought Cassie was doing it deliberately to get out of double maths. If only! Cassie hated being the centre of attention and would rather have faced endless algebra than be sent out of the room while everyone stared and gossiped. Ava would always find her straight after the lesson and tell her exactly what she had missed – which according to Ava, wasn't usually much.

She rested her hand on Cassie's back, just as she had when they were children. Immediately Cassie's shoulders softened and her breathing became less laboured.

'You always did have the magic touch,' Cassie said quietly.

Then, reaching for Dylan, Cassie pulled him towards her and peppered his scalp with kisses.

'Are you all right, Mum?' Dylan asked, his voice full of doubt.

'I'm fine,' Cassie promised.

She got to her feet, Ava reaching out to help her, which Cassie batted away.

Instead, Dylan reached for her hand and Cassie's. Together the trio walked slowly along the path.

–

It was the heady scent of fried eggs and bacon that woke Ava the following morning. Clambering out of bed, she was surprised to see Dylan sitting around the pine breakfast table in the kitchen, Cassie ladling eggs onto hot plates.

'Blimey, am I in an episode of *The Waltons*?' Ava remarked as she walked into the kitchen.

Cassie looked up and smiled. 'We've got a big day today. Want to make sure we're all fired up on full bellies.' She gestured to the teapot standing in the middle of the table, the box of Barry's Tea, standing beside it. 'Help yourself and sit down.'

Ava cast her a suspicious glance but did as she was told. Cassie famously believed breakfast should consist of nothing more than a coffee. The fact she was making eggs before eight in the morning filled her with concern. Deciding it was too early to worry about it, Ava poured herself a mug of builder's brew and looked at Cassie expectantly.

'What's the big day?'

'You, silly,' Cassie said, setting down a plate of eggs in front of her. 'You're going to Cork, we're coming with you. We're not taking no for an answer this time.'

'That's right,' Dylan said, tucking into his eggs. 'You're not leaving our sight.' As Ava chuckled, Dylan's grin widened. 'It's what you said this morning, Mum.'

'Oh, she did, did she?' Ava looked sharply at her friend.

'We were just chatting,' Cassie said airily, before sticking her tongue out at her son. 'You're such a tattletale!'

Dylan giggled, dolloping tomato ketchup all over his eggs and Ava joined in. Cassie and Dylan were so easy to be around, she found herself wishing she could start every morning like this.

'Guys, I appreciate the sentiment, but I can go to Cork alone. I think it's best.'

'Not on your life,' Cassie said sharply. 'You might need support if you meet Bernice. We won't come in with you. Me and Dyl will wait in a cafe nearby.'

Ava raised an eyebrow. 'You've thought of everything.'

'The cafe was my idea,' Dylan pointed out, egg now all up the sleeve of his pyjamas.

Ava reached for his toast and took a bite, earning herself a gasp of horror from Dylan.

She giggled and took another bite, enjoying the shock on the little boy's face. With a hint of mischief in his eye, Dylan reached for Ava's cup of tea and took a long gulp, giggling at the silliness of it all.

'Besides, it's not an easy drive to Cork, it's long,' Cassie said, turning off the hob. 'We can share the driving. And you might not feel like it if things don't go well with Bernice.'

Cassie set down a plate of eggs in front of Ava and watched in surprise as Dylan reached for a slice of Ava's toast.

'I don't know what's got into you two this morning.'

'Must be something in the air,' Ava said, winking at Dylan.

—

Later that morning, Ava was driving down the motorway, Cassie beside her and Dylan in the back.

'Steady,' Cassie admonished as she saw Ava was going twenty miles over the speed limit.

'Sorry,' Ava said, taking her foot off the gas.

'You all right?' Cassie asked gently.

'Fine. Nervous.'

'Understandable,' Cassie replied, then paused before asking, 'Want me to drive?'

'No,' Ava said forcefully. 'Thanks, but I need something to focus on.'

'Well then try and stop being so jerky with the driving, Auntie Ava,' Dylan groaned. 'I'm getting whiplash!'

'Oi!' Cassie chuckled. 'Don't be so rude.'

'He's all right,' Ava said. 'Besides, he's got a point.'

'Even so, I won't have it,' Cassie said firmly. 'Nobody wants a rude kid.'

Ava caught Dylan's eye in the rear-view mirror and stuck her tongue out at him. Dylan retaliated by making a face.

'Kids!' Cassie rolled her eyes catching sight of their antics.

'What can I tell you, some of us have never grown up.'

Ava laughed as she indicated right and took the exit off the motorway, following signs to Cork.

After another ten minutes of driving, they came to a country road with a row of neat, detached houses with large, lush green lawns laid to the front.

It felt like butterflies had taken up residence in her stomach as she pulled up outside number fifteen, Bernice's house.

Silencing the engine, she looked at Cassie and Dylan.

'It takes more than a few pushes and a couple of tugs on some gas and air to be a mother. Don't forget that,' Cassie said softly. 'You don't owe this woman anything.'

Ava felt a wave of love for her friend. Reaching out to hug her, the affection she had seen in Paul's eyes as he stood on their doorstep a few weeks earlier came to mind.

'Have you really never thought about making up with Paul?' Ava blurted as Cassie released her.

The moment the words had left her lips she regretted them. Cassie looked so horrified Ava wished she could take the question back.

'Never,' Cassie breathed.

She glanced at the back seat. Dylan was jabbing at his iPad.

'I will never forgive that man. You know that.'

'I do know that,' Ava said, staring at the house straight ahead. 'But you've got family, Cassie, you've no idea how much I envy you that.'

Cassie let out a deep sigh and folded her arms.

'Ava, some family isn't worth having. Just because you're related doesn't mean you have to get on. I'm going to put this madness down to the fact you're off to find out more about your birth mother and you're not thinking straight. But trust me when I say this, I want nothing to do with any of my family. I hope you have a better outcome than I did, I really do, but honestly, I don't want to talk about this again, so let it go.'

Cassie set her mouth in a firm line and Ava took it as her cue. She opened the car door and began walking towards Bernice's home. It was time to find out who she really was once and for all.

Chapter Twenty-Two

As a firefighter, Ava thought she knew everything there was to know about danger. She had ventured into situations where most would run. She had faced discomfort and routinely made agonising decisions to save the lives of others. But in this moment, as she prepared to face the woman who had given birth to her over forty years ago, Ava didn't think she had ever been so terrified.

She glanced back at the car. Cassie and Dylan watched, silently willing her on. Ava offered a weak smile, then turned back to face the wooden, Scandinavian-style door.

Lifting her hand, she knocked lightly at the door, half hoping that Bernice wouldn't answer.

Yet almost as if she had been expecting her, the door opened straightaway and Ava came face to face with a woman who appeared to be the spitting image of her. With her large hazel eyes, sloping Roman nose and high cheekbones, Ava let out a gasp of astonishment. This had to be Bernice.

Only the woman didn't seem to see what Ava did as she squinted at the woman on her doorstep.

'Are you here about the bake sale?' she asked brusquely. 'Because I already told Marie O'Riordan I couldn't help today. I've to take Barney to the vets, silly sod's got another rose thorn stuck in his paw. If I've told him once, I've told him a million times not to chase the cat next door, but will he listen to me? Will he hell.'

As if on cue, a loud but mournful bark rose from inside the house and Ava felt her nerves dissipate ever so slightly. A woman with a dog had to have a kind soul, surely?

'I'm not here about the bake sale...' Ava began.

The woman blinked at her curiously. 'Then what do you want? I've no time for cold callers.'

'I'm not a cold caller,' Ava said firmly. 'Are you Bernice Collins?'

'Yes,' Bernice replied, this time with more impatience than Ava had offered. 'Who are you?'

Nerves fluttered to the top of Ava's stomach again as she pressed a hand to her heart.

'I'm Ava Ryan. You might have known me as Ava Collins. I think you gave me up for adoption forty-four years ago.'

Bernice dropped her cup, tea splashing Ava's legs as the mug shattered on the doorstep.

'You're what?' Bernice gasped, her face paling.

'I'm your biological daughter,' Ava said.

Bernice just stared at her open-mouthed, completely unaware that tea was seeping from the broken mug out onto her immaculate step.

'You can't be,' she said eventually. 'I specifically signed the no contact preference.'

Doubt gnawed at Ava's heart. Perhaps she shouldn't have ambushed Bernice like this. She had only been thinking of herself, but the reality was that Bernice would be feeling – well, Ava had no idea at all what Bernice was feeling, Ava realised, as she stared at the woman who seemed catatonic with shock.

'I'm sorry,' Ava said eventually. 'I shouldn't have dropped in unannounced like this.'

As Ava spoke, Bernice seemed to come to. Standing up straight, she saw the broken cup on the floor and bent down to pick up the pieces.

'I'll sue,' she hissed, looking left to right from her doorway as if the entire adoption board of Ireland were there ready to take note. Bernice paused for a moment as if to gather herself, then looked Ava up and down. 'I take it Maeve gave you my address.'

Ava nodded. 'I found her yesterday. I begged her.'

'You wouldn't have needed to do much begging,' Bernice said in a clipped tone. 'Maeve always did like sticking her nose into other people's business. Now you're here, you'd better come in – I don't want a showdown on my doorstep.'

She held the door open, tea dripping down her leg and Ava walked inside, choking down feelings of nervousness and excitement. This was the day she had been dreaming about since she was a little girl and had first learned she was adopted – or chosen, as her mother and father always insisted. This was the day to finally get the answers to all those questions she had been thinking about over all these years.

As Ava followed Bernice down the immaculate hallway, she was struck by just how clean and neat the whole place looked. Mirrors shone, as did the parquet flooring underfoot. The hallway was freshly painted in a shade of taupe Ava knew was straight from the Farrow & Ball catalogue.

'Would you like tea or coffee?' Bernice asked as she walked into a kitchen the size of Ava's entire downstairs. With a shiny marble island taking centre stage, Bernice gestured to Ava to take a seat at one of the high barstools that offered views over the lush, green garden.

'Whatever you're making will be fine,' Ava said, not really caring about her beverage choice as she tried to drink in Bernice's home instead.

'I'll make coffee,' Bernice replied stiffly, then fired up an expensive-looking machine that looked more like a spaceship than a coffee pot.

There was silence as the machine whirred into life and Ava tried desperately to think of something to say.

'You've a lovely home,' she offered.

'Thank you,' Bernice said tightly. 'I bought it after the divorce.'

'And you live alone?' Ava tried again.

But her question was drowned out by the sound of the coffee grinder. Turning her gaze away from Bernice's stiff shoulders and back to the garden, Ava thought she could see a glimpse of the Atlantic.

'The view of the sea is better from the bedroom upstairs,' Bernice said, following her gaze, as she placed a black coffee in front of Ava. 'It's why I bought the house, I'd always dreamed of a place with a sea view. After the divorce I was able to have it.'

Bernice pushed a sugar bowl towards her, and Ava shook her head.

'In my line of work, we drink that much coffee to stay awake, if I added sugar I think my teeth would fall out as well.'

'What is it you do?' Bernice asked. She took a seat at the end of the island away from Ava.

'I'm a firefighter.'

Bernice looked at her wide-eyed in astonishment. 'Well, that's a surprise.' She thought for a moment as if weighing up this new information. 'But then my father was a great one for danger. He did a parachute jump on his eightieth birthday! Would you imagine that? We all told him he was a fool, but he loved it.'

Bernice lifted the coffee cup to red lipsticked lips and Ava ruminated over the idea of a grandfather who had been prone to risk. Was that where she had got her desire to face peril head on?

'Are you like your father?' Ava asked; she had so many questions, and no idea where to start.

Bernice thought for a moment.

'No, not really. I've always made considered decisions.' She turned to Ava and shot her a brief smile. 'Even when it came to having you adopted.'

And there it was.

The elephant in the room had been addressed and Ava felt suddenly nauseous. She glanced around the immaculate kitchen, as if looking for an escape. But then she knew that this was her one opportunity. If she didn't ask now, she had a feeling she'd never get the chance again.

'Why did you have me adopted?' Ava asked in a small voice. She tried to keep her nerves steady, when what she really wanted to know was what made her so unlovable, so unworthy, that this woman didn't want to raise her?

To her horror, tears began to pool at Ava's eyes. She took a sip of coffee and hoped Bernice hadn't noticed. She didn't strike Ava as the sort of woman that did sentimentality.

But as Ava set her coffee cup down, she could see Bernice had noticed the tears and her mouth was set in a disappointed line. She regarded the woman she had birthed and sighed.

'I don't wish to be cruel – you seem like a nice enough woman.' Bernice slid a box of tissues along the worktop towards Ava and gave her a tight smile. 'And even though you've surprised me like a bolt from the blue, I don't blame you for wanting answers. There's no easy way to say this.' Bernice's gaze was steady. 'But the simple truth is I never had any interest in being a mother.'

Chapter Twenty-Three

As Bernice made the admission, Ava let out a hollow laugh. After all her years of wondering, surely there had to be more to it than the fact Bernice didn't want kids.

'But you were married? Catholic?' Ava said.

Bernice nodded and clasped her hands in front of her as if she were addressing a bank manager.

'True, but I never saw myself as a mother, never had the patience for kids, never wanted to raise one.'

Ava tried to process Bernice's words. She had never wanted children?

'Was it me?' Ava blurted, all her insecurities coming to the surface. 'Was I not good enough?'

'Not at all,' Bernice said, her barely lined face crinkling with amusement. 'It wasn't you – I didn't know you, Ava. I didn't even name you Ava. I thought your parents could have the honour, but Maeve wanted to call you Ava. Had a notion. Who was I to stop her? She was so hell-bent on it, thought it would be a nice parting gift, I think she called it, so I didn't stop her.'

'Did you hold me?' Ava asked, her head beginning to spin with all this new information.

Bernice nodded again, then closed her eyes as if remembering that day. 'Briefly. Maeve told me it would either cement my decision or make me realise that being a mother was natural. She and Jerry were hoping for a family and kept telling me about the power of mother-hood and how wonderful it could be. How I needed to be sure before I gave up a child because once I had there was no going back.'

At that, Bernice rolled her eyes and took another sip of her coffee.

'Did it help?' Ava asked, unsure which answer would make her feel better.

'No,' Bernice said honestly. 'I appreciate this is probably hard for you to hear, Ava, but I didn't feel anything other than you weren't supposed to be mine.'

Ava bit her lip, trying to suppress the inappropriate belly laughs that were threatening to rise up inside her. Here she was, longing for a child of her own, desperate to be the biological mother she had never had. And yet, the woman standing before her, the one who had brought her into the world, couldn't care less about being a mother at all.

A lump in her throat began to form instead. Ava stared at the woman who had created her. Had her birth really had such little impact on Bernice that she hadn't even thought about her? Or, was it possible Bernice had suffered from post-natal depression that had gone undiagnosed? But, looking at Bernice now, gazing out of the window towards the sea, Ava knew she was reaching for an excuse. Bernice didn't look as if there was any hint of regret about the decision she'd made and was merely presenting the facts as she saw them.

'What about my father? Did he ever want me?' Ava asked.

There was a pause as Bernice turned from the window and looked at Ava.

'You remind me of him,' she said not answering the question. 'Fintan was always like a dog with a bone. Never gave up until he got his answer.'

'And?' Ava persisted. 'You said you never wanted kids, but did he?'

Bernice shook her head and turned back to look out of the window.

'Neither of us did. Ireland back then was not the multicultural melting pot it is now. It felt constrained, so many people were leaving for the UK or America. Back then, your father and I wanted to see something of the world. Children weren't part of the plan. He was a good man, would have supported whatever decision I made, but he was relieved when I said being pregnant changed nothing. That I still wanted us to travel the world, have new experiences without kids.'

'But you're still in Ireland,' Ava pointed out. 'And worse, you're not even together.'

'Touché.' Bernice smiled. 'I had a career to think about and all I wanted to do was provide for myself and have a wonderful future. Both Fintan and I came from very poor families. We started a business together, importing and exporting. We did all right, and the business grew. After a childhood of nothing, now I was the one who could pay for the meals, the nights out, even the girls' trips away. Fintan and I were happy, we didn't want or need anything or anyone else but the business and each other, but over time we grew apart and we got divorced, like many couples. I moved out here and Fintan set up in New York, of all places, before he died.'

As Bernice spoke, Ava couldn't ignore the irony. She had been fighting tooth and nail to start her own family, to love a child unconditionally. But here stood the woman who had given her life and felt nothing at all.

Ava shook her head. To her, family was the cornerstone of everything, she simply couldn't make sense of Bernice's life.

'So when I came along, I was, what, an unhappy accident?' Ava said, unable to keep the bitterness creeping into her voice.

Bernice missed Ava's tone and nodded. 'In short, yes. I was mortified. I didn't want an abortion, never mind the fact it was illegal. Of course, I could have gone to London like a lot of women, but I couldn't organise it all in time. I had no choice but to go through with it and have you adopted.'

'But what about your family? Didn't they know?' Ava asked.

'Fintan's mother was dead,' Bernice explained. 'And I just claimed I was too busy with work to visit my family during the latter half of my pregnancy, so they never knew. The only one who did was Maeve, who was with me when I gave birth. Back then, fathers didn't enter the delivery room and Maeve and I were close.' Bernice sighed and pushed her empty coffee cup away. She glanced at Ava, an expression of pity across her features. 'I'm sure this isn't the story you were looking for.'

'No, it's fine,' Ava said, feeling anything but as her heart thudded painfully in her chest. She didn't want to let this woman into how she was really feeling.

'I don't want to lie to you, Ava,' Bernice said gently. 'The simple truth is I felt nothing for you at the time and I feel nothing now. I never wanted to be a mother, Ava, I just wasn't built for it. I wish you no harm and never have, I've just never thought about you.'

Ava stared at the woman who had birthed her, and it felt like staring at a hollow shell. How could someone feel nothing for the life they created? It was so far from anything Ava could imagine. Her longing to be a biological mother, to give her child what she never had, seemed like the cruellest of situations to find herself in now.

'Not once?' Ava pressed.

Bernice considered the question. 'The odd thought might have slipped through my mind. Realising you'd be sixteen, an adult, that sort of thing, but that was about it.' She closed her eyes, took a deep breath and shook her head. 'I did hope you had a happy childhood, with good people. Did you have that?'

Ava nodded. 'They were the best parents I could have wished for. Loving, kind and generous. They always wanted children but couldn't have them. Then I came along. Mum always said I was meant to be her daughter, that the world had it worked out just right.'

A flicker of satisfaction crossed Bernice's face. 'That's all I could have hoped for. You weren't meant to be mine. Your family were the ones that were meant to be yours, I was just your carrier, nothing more than that.'

Watching Bernice get up and walk to the sink to rinse her coffee mug, Ava felt as if she was sliding into a vortex, her mind whirring with thoughts. This woman might as well be a stranger on the street than her own flesh and blood. Ava hadn't quite known what to expect, but this woman who was entirely indifferent towards her was not it.

Bernice offered her a wry smile as if reading Ava's mind.

'I've disappointed you, haven't I?'

'No, it's not that,' Ava began. A million thoughts raced through her mind.

'The necklace,' she blurted. 'You gave me a necklace when I was adopted. You wanted me to have something of yours, Mum told me. She said it had been a family heirloom, that it was to give me safe passage.'

She reached into her bag and fished out her phone. Scrolling through her photos she soon found a snap of her wearing the necklace she had recently given to Cassie.

Ava's eyes blazed with triumph as she held the phone in front of Bernice's face, almost daring her to object.

But there was no reaction from Bernice beyond a grimace.

'That necklace isn't mine,' Bernice said quietly. 'That belonged to Maeve. As well as giving you your name, she wanted you to have something and tucked it into your cot at the last minute. Told the social worker it was mine, I think. She said she hated thinking of you going into the world with nothing. I told her she'd lost the run of herself, that she was a sentimental fool.'

As Ava digested Bernice's words, a roaring filled her ears. It was the sound of her heart breaking. It was Maeve who had cared after all.

'Ava, there was a reason I never wanted to be contacted by you or think about you all these years,' Bernice said gently. 'It wasn't because I wanted to be cruel, it was because there was no point for either of us. I have nothing to tell you, no wisdom to share, no love to give. There are no strange diseases, no troublesome genetic defects in our families. Me and Fintan had an accident and our accident went on to make you, your mum and your dad very, very happy.'

Ava could take no more, the disappointment and pain of discovering that the flame she had been carrying for her biological mother meant nothing.

'My parents died in a hotel fire when I was eighteen,' Ava snapped. 'I've been an orphan since then. I didn't come here today looking for a tearful reunion, some chance at getting a second mother. I had a mother and she was a bloody good one, but to not feel anything? If you'd have sworn at me and told me I'd ruined your life, or even that I was some horrible secret, that would at least be something, but you genuinely feel nothing!' Ava let out a short laugh and Bernice's expression hardened.

'I never asked you to come here. I never signed the Adoption Contact Register, not because I want to hurt you, I don't know you—'

'And that's it isn't it?' Ava had heard enough. 'You don't know me. I'm a stranger, even though you gave birth to me. Love, connection, family. They're just words to you, aren't they? You've got all this –' Ava jerked her head towards Bernice's prized sea view '– and you haven't worked out that it means nothing. Not compared to connection.'

As her voice trailed off, Ava put her phone back in her bag then got up awkwardly from the bar stool and walked across Bernice's kitchen.

Reaching the door, she turned to look at Bernice who was still standing by the sink.

'Thanks for your time,' was all Ava could manage.

Bernice nodded. 'Good luck in the world, Ava.'

But what could Ava honestly say to that? There was nothing. Empty, she opened the door and stepped outside, determined not to look back as she joined her friend, who unlike the woman that had given birth to her, had never once left her side.

Chapter Twenty-Four

'I still can't get over it,' Cassie said, slamming her pint of Guinness onto the table.

Ava remained silent. The dark pub was busy, customers standing shoulder to shoulder with one another as they laughed over shared jokes. The scent of beef stew wafted from the kitchen and despite her heartache, Ava had to admit it smelled good.

She turned to Cassie and wondered if they could change the subject and get something to eat instead. But Cassie continued to look furious.

'What else is there to say?' Ava said at last. 'It happened. My mother died, and my biological mother doesn't even care if I exist.' She picked up her glass of wine and took a sip. 'It's time I stopped thinking there was this perfect vision of family or motherhood that's out there to save me.'

Cassie glanced over at Dylan who, unaffected by the cold, was running around the kids' play area with another boy he'd just met. It looked as if they'd known one another years. She turned to Ava and eyed her warily.

'Let's just enjoy a couple of drinks and forget the rest for now. Finding Bernice was never going to be an easy thing. You've done it now, and although it hasn't brought joy, ultimately it might bring you peace.'

Ava took another long, deep slug of her wine and remembered how she had felt in Bernice's home. When she'd marched out of the house, Ava had climbed into the car refusing to say a word. Cassie had started the engine and begun driving back to Dublin. The atmosphere had been so tense that even Dylan sensed it and stayed quiet.

'Am I right in thinking you might be in need of a drink?' Cassie had said after a couple of hours.

Signs for Dublin were approaching. In that moment Ava could think of nothing nicer than sitting in a bar with something cold and alcoholic coursing through her body.

'Yes please.'

And then that was it – Ava couldn't hold back any longer and the whole sorry story had poured out. Ava felt terrible crying in front of Dylan, but Cassie had reassured her that it was good for him to see emotion.

'We don't live in the Fifties,' Cassie declared. 'Get it all out. You've had a shock.'

Now, Ava pushed her drink away, the alcohol making her melancholy.

'I know this isn't what you wanted,' Cassie said, 'but give it time. You're still who you were before all this, nothing has changed.'

'The thing is, I think I hoped something *would* change,' Ava began, playing with the stem of her glass. 'I hoped that if I ever found my birth parents I'd feel more like a whole person, if that makes sense. As if my back story would be all nicely filled in.'

Cassie looked at her sympathetically. 'I'm sorry, Ava.'

Ava let out a bitter laugh. 'I might as well have been there to read the gas meter for all she cared. She asked the odd question out of politeness more than anything else, but she genuinely didn't care who I was.'

The contrast between Bernice's indifference to moth-erhood and Ava's deep longing for it weighed heavily. It was like two sides of a coin she hadn't expected to flip.

Cassie sucked in her cheeks, an action Ava knew she always did when she was angry.

Ava caught her eye and heaved a sigh. 'I need to accept that Steve was right, this was a bad idea.'

'I don't think so.' Cassie shook her head. 'I know you don't like what you've found but eventually you'll be grateful you can put this part of your life to bed now.'

'Maybe,' Ava muttered gloomily.

Catching sight of the barman, she waved him over and ordered a cup of tea. She needed to think clearly.

'The thing is…' Cassie said gingerly now, 'I wonder if this might help you realise that family isn't always what you think it's going to be.'

'Eh?' Ava looked at her friend in surprise.

'It's like I keep saying, family isn't always about blood.' Cassie tucked a lock of hair behind her ear and leaned forward earnestly. 'Family can be about the people you find along the way. The people at the estate were more like family to me than my own flesh and blood – that's what I was trying to get you to understand earlier. Yes, Paul has offered an olive branch, but it means nothing. There's no connection.'

Ava's heart twisted. She could see what Cassie was saying but she wasn't sure, deep down, she believed it. Family was everything. As the tea arrived she fiddled with the milk jug, needing the distraction.

'Maybe it's time to think about that,' Cassie continued. 'Bernice and Fintan were just the people that created you. But you are the one who has the power to choose what you do with that creation, who you love, who you value and protect. Anyone can get knocked up, but not everyone can raise a kid – or ought to raise a kid! There should be laws or tests before you become a parent.'

'Bit strong,' Ava said with a smile. 'But I know what you mean,' she said, pouring out the tea.

Cassie looked at her cup longingly. 'Maybe I should have ordered tea instead of a second pint.'

'You all right?' Ava asked. Her friend had seemed distracted since they had returned from Cork.

'Fine.' Cassie shrugged. 'Just Paul turning up has rocked me a bit.'

Ava had rarely seen Cassie this vulnerable. She usually kept things bottled up, always the strong one. But now, Ava could see how much this visit had unsettled her friend.

'How so?' Ava asked.

'It just makes me realise I don't want people like him in Dylan's life. He's a happy kid, I don't want anyone from my past doing a number on him.'

'Surely Dylan's asked questions though?' Ava prodded. 'I mean, he must wonder about his father at least.'

'Yes,' Cassie admitted. 'But I've been honest. I told him his dad's gift to me was him and he couldn't stick around. I've told him we're one of the special families where it's just us two and all the wonderful people we meet along the way who become our family. Found family, it's called.'

Ava stared into her cup. Could she really let go of the idea that family had to be blood? The disappointment from Bernice still stung, but maybe Cassie had a point. Maybe there was more to family than just shared DNA.

'Found family,' Ava whispered. She liked the sound of that.

The taxi ride back from the airport towards Bath felt never-ending to Ava. As she, Cassie and Dylan finally pulled into her street, all she wanted to do was get out of the car, run inside, get into bed and never get up again.

Of course, she didn't. She was a grown-up, so she paid for the taxi, smiled at Cassie, wrapped an arm around Dylan, then slipped the key in the lock and opened the door.

When Monkey wrapped himself around her legs, Ava picked up the animal and pressed his fur close to her chest, allowing her precious cat to soak up her despair.

Tactfully, Cassie and Dylan made their way to the kitchen, but for the first time since inviting them to stay, Ava wished Steve was here. He would know exactly how she felt and what to say. But the whole situation was impossible. He obviously thought so too, because walking into the kitchen there was no evidence that he had ever been here, aside from the fresh food in Monkey's bowl.

'Tea then?' Cassie asked brightly, reaching for the mugs.

Setting Monkey down, Ava nodded weakly. She was due in at work later that afternoon. She needed the morning to get her head together and take stock.

She wouldn't allow this to derail her. Bernice wasn't worth that and she owed it to the parents who had chosen and loved her to make the most of the life they had given her.

'Damn,' Cassie muttered as she peered in the fridge. 'We've got no milk.'

'I'll nip out and get some,' Ava said. She hadn't taken her coat off yet and the walk would do her good.

'Sure?' Cassie frowned, the way a nurse might look at a patient that was about to ignore doctor's advice.

Ava nodded. 'I'm sure.'

She needed to get out and breathe, do something normal that wasn't about kids or families. Before Cassie could say something else, she turned to leave.

'Won't be long,' she said, pulling open the front door.

The cool air was like a tonic for her soul. The shop was only a five-minute walk away but outside in the fresh air, alone at last, Ava could think clearly about her life for the first time since leaving Dublin.

She had known she'd placed too much emphasis on her trip and what it would mean when she found Bernice. She kept telling everyone she didn't know what to expect, that she was prepared for all eventualities, but the truth was Ava had been hoping she would come home with a brand-new family. The fact that hadn't happened hurt more than she cared to admit. She had been naive, letting herself get lost in the idea of a perfect family reunion. But now, she knew she couldn't depend on others to fill that space, she had to figure it out for herself. In the past she had always assumed the family she made with Steve would enable her to share the love spilling from her heart. Now, Ava had no idea what to do with all her excess love.

But Bernice! Ava shook her head as she turned the corner, the small supermarket at the end of the lane coming into view. To feel nothing towards your own flesh and blood seemed inhuman. Had Bernice's disinterest somehow been passed down to her? Was that why she was so incapable of having a child of her own, because her body knew something her brain hadn't yet caught up to – that she would make a terrible mother?

The wind picked up and Ava huddled into her warm duffle coat. She was torturing herself with these endless questions – it had to stop.

Just ahead of her was an elderly man about to mount a bicycle, shopping laden over his handlebars. The bike was wobbling precariously and it looked as though the man and his shopping were about to end up sprawled across the floor.

She rushed forward to help, laying her hands on the bike to steady it.

'Woah, you were in the right place at the right time,' the man said, leaning against the saddle as he turned to look at her. 'Ava!'

Ava narrowed her eyes and looked at the man again as he lowered his hood. She hadn't recognised him.

'Paul,' she said at last.

His blue eyes looked sheepish.

'I'm sorry to have turned up at your house unannounced like that,' he said. 'It was wrong of me.'

'None of my business,' Ava said, taking a step back.

She had enough family problems of her own. The last thing she needed was to get drawn into someone else's.

Paul fiddled with his bike and nodded.

'You've always been a good friend to Cass. She needs that.'

Ava said nothing. She wanted to get away but didn't want to be rude.

Paul looked down and caught the wedding ring on her left hand.

'You're married now,' he noticed. 'Have you got kids yourself?'

At the question Ava coloured and Paul looked apologetic.

'Now that was none of my business, I'm sorry.' He smiled. 'Let me try again. I suppose what I'm trying to say is that I'm grateful Cassie's got someone looking out for her and her son.' He shook his head again. 'A grandson. We never knew. All we wanted was a house full of grand-children.'

Ava was sceptical. 'That right? How did our former friend fit into that arrangement?'

Paul's cheeks reddened. 'Like I said, we all make mistakes.'

Ava shook her head. She was too tired to listen to this nonsense. 'You certainly did. You treated Cassie appallingly, no apology will ever make up for that.'

Cassie had such strong feelings of resentment towards her family, just knowing Ava had crossed words with Paul would have her scowling for a week.

'I made a terrible mistake, and not a day goes by that I don't regret it,' Paul said quietly, his eyes searching Ava's face for understanding.

'But the damage you did,' Ava said despairingly. 'You lied, said Cassie was making it all up. Caused her mother to think so badly of her you both threw her out of her home. She was a kid!'

'I know,' Paul said, still looking shamefaced. 'I want to make amends, I really do. When I read about the fire at Cassie's place, how you saved her son, I thought this was my chance to apologise.'

'I see,' was all Ava could manage. Cassie had paid a horrendous price for this man's selfishness. She wasn't sure he deserved the chance to apologise.

'I hoped the fire was a sign we could create something good out of the mess,' Paul said, 'but I see that was wrong.'

Ava watched the man gather his things on his bicycle and suddenly felt a pang of sorrow. She'd discovered only too recently how difficult family relationships could be. But if Bernice had welcomed her with open arms, even after she had told her how unwanted Ava was, Ava knew she would have been delighted to try to build a connection with the woman.

Of course, Ava knew how Cassie felt about Paul, but Cassie hadn't heard his side of things. Something in his tone suggested he was sincere. Wasn't that worth something? Ava loved Cassie with all her heart; she wanted her to be happy. Was it her place to push Cassie towards reconciliation? Something told her that Paul's regret was real, and perhaps it was time to take a risk – for Cassie's sake, even if it backfired.

'Are you free on Saturday evening?' she blurted.

Paul looked up at her in surprise. 'Yes. Why?'

'Come to the house at seven,' Ava instructed. 'I'll work on Cassie.'

At the invitation the old man's eyes lit up. 'Really?'

'Really,' Ava confirmed. 'Leave Cassie to me.'

As Paul rode off down the street, Ava took a deep breath. She already knew how Cassie would react, and it wouldn't be pretty. Her friend had been adamant that Paul was not part of her life and wouldn't ever be, but something about the old man's sincerity tugged at Ava. Cassie would be furious, probably for days, Ava knew that. But maybe, just maybe, it was worth it to try and mend old wounds. She was taking a risk, and she knew it, but Ava had learned something over the past few days: family wasn't always what you expected. Sometimes, you had to take a chance to find a different kind of peace.

Chapter Twenty-Five

Ava arrived at work that afternoon feeling surprisingly buoyant, her good mood compounded by the sight of a large bunch of flowers in the mess room addressed to her.

'When did these get here?' she asked Big Stu as she fished them out of the sink.

'Sometime this morning,' he replied.

Ava rooted around the cupboards for a vase but only managed to find an old pint glass.

'Looks like someone's been spoiled,' he added.

Wordlessly, Ava slipped open the card and read the inscription.

> *Dear Ava, Welcome home. Hope to catch up soon,*
> *Steve xx*

She smiled. Her husband had never been one of the great romantics, but flowers were a welcome surprise. Experience told her he would have gone to a lot of effort to arrange these for her first day back.

Admiring the blooms, she thought for a moment. The flowers were beautiful, but was Steve trying to make amends, or was this just a gesture? A kind reminder of what they used to be, without addressing what they had become? Still, what if this was the week people found their way back to each other?

Her thoughts turned to Cassie. Ava knew she'd have a hard time talking her friend round, but maybe she could soften it, suggest a gathering to talk about the work on the estate and afterwards a takeaway to celebrate their hard work. Then she could slip Paul into the conversation and ask her to give him a chance – just as Cassie had convinced Ava to find out more about her birth family, Ava could now convince Cassie to talk to hers. If she decided after chatting with Paul that she didn't want him in her life then that was fair enough. But Cassie should at least give herself the option, shouldn't she?

Leaning forward, she breathed in the scent of the blooms. Tea roses, Steve had always known her favourites and the fact he had remembered during such a time of crisis touched her greatly.

She fished out her phone. More than anything she needed a win, and perhaps there was a way for her and Steve to start piecing their lives back together.

> Fancy a coffee later as a thank you for the flowers? I finish at six.

A reply came back almost immediately.

> I'll pick you up when you finish.

Hugging the phone to her chest, Ava was surprised to find she was almost excited at the prospect of a date with her husband; it was as if the worst had happened and she now had very little to lose.

'You look pleased with yourself,' Miguel said, strolling into the kitchen clutching a mug. 'How was Ireland?'

She turned to look at him and sighed. 'Mixed.'

Miguel poured the remainder of his tea in the sink.

'Sorry, Ava. I take it that things didn't go as planned?'

'You could say that.'

Not wanting to relive the entire experience, she outlined the main details for Miguel, who made supportive noises in all the right places.

By the time she'd finished, he looked furious on her behalf.

'Bloody hell, Ava.' Miguel leaned against the cupboards and folded his arms. 'I don't know what to say other than I'm so sorry.'

'Least I know, I suppose,' Ava managed. 'They say the truth sets you free.'

'And will it?' Miguel asked.

Ava thought for a moment. That was something she couldn't answer. At the moment, she felt as if she'd had the stuffing knocked out of her.

Miguel seemed to notice. His eyes landed on the flowers standing next to Ava.

'They're nice. Who are they from?'

'Steve.'

She showed him the card.

'Think you two can sort things out?' he asked.

Ava shrugged and let out a small laugh. 'I don't know. I feel like at least one relationship needs to go well after Ireland.'

Miguel opened his mouth about to reply when the familiar peal of 'Mobilise. Mobilise,' rang through the station.

Emerson came bursting into the mess room with the tip sheet. 'Road traffic accident on the motorway. Sounds serious. Multi pile-up.'

Ava shuddered. Road traffic accidents always unsettled her, but there was no time for reflection. In the muster bay, her kit was ready and waiting. Stepping into it with practised ease, she made her way to the rig and saw Jodie in the driving seat. A flash of pride stirred in Ava. It usually took rookies a long time to find the courage to drive, but the fact Jodie was confident enough to try showed real progress.

'First RTA?' Ava asked, noticing the tension in Jodie's shoulders. The trainee's breath caught in short bursts, her nerves plain to see.

Jodie nodded, her jaw clenched.

'It's always tough,' Ava said softly, trying to offer reassurance. 'You don't know what you're going to find. Keep your ears and eyes open and stay calm.'

Jodie gave a quick nod, but her grip on the wheel was tight. Ava could see she was determined to hold it together, no matter how overwhelming the scene might be.

Jodie started the engine, pulling the rig smoothly onto the road. As the sirens wailed, Ava's thoughts blurred, but her instructions to Jodie were just as much for herself. No matter how experienced, road traffic accidents had a way of hitting close to home.

The journey was short, thanks to the blaring sirens. When they arrived, Ava clambered out of the cab, her heart sinking as she took in the devastation. Two mangled cars – what appeared to be a hatchback and SUV looked almost fused together, while a lorry jack-knifed just metres away. Police had already closed the road and paramedics were attending to an injured passenger nearby. The scene was alive with flashing blue lights and the hum of rescue equipment.

Without missing a beat, Ava scanned the chaos and assigned tasks. 'Jodie, Phil, stabilise the hatchback. Emerson and Big Stu, start absorbing the fuel spill over by the SUV. We need to contain it before we proceed with cuts.'

As her team jumped into action, Ava's pulse quickened. They didn't have much time.

A few moments passed and Ava keyed into her radio. 'Jodie, status on the hatchback?'

'Roof's nearly off,' Jodie's voice crackled.

'Good. Keep me updated.' Ava's gaze swept over the scene, her mind calculating the next steps.

As was typical for a major incident, Miguel had arrived at the scene, coordinating with paramedics and the Fast Response Unit. His calm presence was always a relief.

'Ava,' Miguel called, spotting her walking towards him, 'paramedics say the woman in the hatchback's vitals are stable for now, but we need to work fast. Get the equipment ready.'

'On it,' Ava replied, signalling to her team to secure the vehicle using chocks and stabilisers. Her voice was firm, steady.

Although it was unusual for any station manager to get physically involved, Ava knew that Miguel would want to be.

'Hi love, what's your name?' Ava heard Miguel ask gently as he leaned into the wreckage, addressing the injured woman.

The woman's breath came in laboured rasps. 'Helen.'

'Helen, can you move?' Miguel asked.

'I think so,' Helen whispered weakly.

'Good,' Miguel said reassuringly. 'We're going to get you out of here in time for dinner, all right?'

Helen gave a faint smile. 'Okay. My daughter's cooking cheese straws. I promised I wouldn't be late.'

Miguel backed away from the hatchback, giving Ava a look that spoke volumes. This one was going to be tough.

'How bad?' Ava asked, her voice clipped.

Miguel's face was grim. 'Not as bad as the four people in the SUV behind. The FRU is working on them with the rest of Blue Watch. Time is of the essence.'

In an ideal world, they worked to something called the golden hour, getting the injured to the hospital within an hour of the accident. But as Ava cast her eyes over the wreckage, she knew that wouldn't be possible here.

'I'll get the whole team on the family in the SUV,' she said, taking charge.

'I've got to get back to the command centre. I'll do my best to calm the crowd,' Miguel replied, casting a glance at the gathering onlookers.

'Right.' Ava nodded, noticing the group of people staring and pointing.

'What about the lorry driver?' she asked, her gaze shifting to the overturned artic where paramedics were working.

Miguel shook his head, his fingers flying over his phone. 'Suspected fatality.'

Ava's chest tightened, but she didn't let it show. Instead, she nodded curtly, shelving the emotion for later.

Within seconds, she was with her team at the SUV, taking stock of the situation.

'Jodie, Phil, focus on the family. We need to keep them calm while the cutters work.'

Jodie hesitated but quickly nodded, addressing the family inside. Ava watched her closely, impressed by the rookie's composure. Her voice was steady, asking simple questions to keep the family grounded.

'Good work, Jodie,' Ava said quietly.

'Thanks, boss,' Jodie replied, a hint of relief in her voice.

Miguel's voice crackled over the radio. 'Ava, can you get back to the hatchback? We're watching for destabilisation, and Helen's condition is getting worse.'

Ava nodded, knowing her presence was needed both for the assessment and to keep an eye on Helen.

'On my way. Let's keep things stable until we get her out.'

Without hesitation, Ava moved towards the hatchback. If the SUV behind moved, those trapped inside could be in even more danger. The grinding shriek of the cutters filled the air, causing Jodie to wince as she kept the family calm inside the car.

Ava kept scanning for any signs of destabilisation, her eyes sharp as the vehicle's roof was cut away. Suddenly, she spotted something – liquid seeping from Helen's car.

'Fuel spillage,' she barked, rushing to the rig to grab absorbent powder. They needed to contain it before things escalated.

As she worked, Ava glanced into the car at Helen. 'How are you doing?' she asked, peering through the window.

'Okay,' Helen said, though her voice wavered.

Ava could see Helen was struggling. Her breathing was more laboured, her eyelids drooping. Fifteen minutes in. The golden hour was closing fast.

'We need to get everyone out,' Ava radioed to Miguel. 'Jodie's almost done with the family, but Helen's deteriorating.'

'Copy. Ava focus on Helen,' Miguel's voice crackled in her ear. 'We'll hand her to the paramedics the second she's out.'

Ava reached into the car, stroking Helen's arm. 'We're getting you out, Helen,' she said calmly. 'Focus on those cheese straws.'

Helen smiled weakly. 'My daughter's got the recipe down. Better than mine.'

Ava squeezed her shoulder. Keeping her talking was vital. 'Tell me about your daughter.'

'Ivy. She's twelve. She's my miracle baby.'

'Miracle?' Ava asked warmly.

'Had her when I was forty-seven,' Helen croaked. 'Years of IVF. Got her on the fourth round.'

Ava's chest tightened. Helen's words hit too close to home. She blinked hard, forcing the crash scene back into focus. Not now.

Instead she squeezed Helen's shoulder once again and glanced back at the hatchback. The roof had been peeled back by the team now and the family were being gently lifted out.

To her relief she saw the boy clinging to his iPad, a sure sign he was likely to be okay. There was nothing worse than children involved in an accident.

But as she turned back to tell Helen she was next for the jaws of life, a chill swept over Ava. Helen's chest barely moved now, her breath shallow and faint. Her skin, once flushed with effort, had turned an alarming shade of white, her lips almost blue.

Panic surged through Ava as she reached out, giving the woman's shoulder a gentle shake.

'Helen? Stay with me,' she urged, her voice tight with urgency, but there was no response.

Ava leaned in closer, checking for signs of breathing. Nothing. She reached for her radio.

'I need paramedics here, now! She's unresponsive,' Ava shouted, her heart pounding. She knew they didn't have time.

Unable to wait, Ava reached through the window and opened Helen's airway, tilting her head back in the tight space. She pressed her ear close to Helen's mouth, desperate for any sign of breath. Nothing.

Chapter Twenty-Six

When Ava got home that night, her legs felt like lead as she climbed the stairs. The weight of the day's events pressed against her chest like a rock. She barely made it to her bedroom before the tears came, flowing uncontrollably for two straight hours. She had learned in her career to separate work from home, but that afternoon's accident had left her broken.

Helen had died of head trauma at the scene, her last breaths shallow and fragile. Ava had held her hand tightly, willing her to stay, even as she whispered comforting lies about her daughter waiting at home.

Deep down Ava knew it wasn't her fault, but she blamed herself. Even though she knew head trauma was rarely survivable, she couldn't help but wonder if things might have been different if she'd acted just a little faster.

The lorry driver had died on impact, his life extinguished in an instant. Two lives lost in the space of minutes. It wasn't supposed to be this way.

The family had been taken to hospital and expected to make a full recovery. It was cold comfort.

The date with Steve had been postponed to another day. Instead, Ava had fallen asleep in her clothes and had a fitful night, images of cheese straws and little girls looking for their mothers haunting her dreams.

The next morning, Ava arrived at work, feeling like the world had lost its colour. The mess room was unusually quiet, and every face around the table reflected the same weariness. Everyone had been touched by the previous day's accident. She and the rest of the watch sat in the kitchen drinking coffee in silence.

Usually after a fatality or any large incident, the watch would debrief what had happened, offering support to one another. It was an essential step before any formal counselling was offered by the station. But that morning, going over the day's previous trauma with Miguel wasn't something anyone looked forward to, especially with him taking a more hands-on approach.

'So yesterday,' Miguel began. There was a murmur around the table, heads buried. 'It was awful,' Miguel continued, 'but we had some success. We saved a family.'

'But lost a lorry driver,' Big Stu piped up.

'Who was dead on impact,' Miguel put in gently.

Big Stu nodded and there were other murmurs of assent.

'The woman,' Jodie whispered, her face ashen. 'She was a mum.'

Ava smiled sympathetically at the recruit. She knew how terrible it felt when you first lost someone on the job. So far Jodie had been lucky, but you couldn't put it off forever, even when you did your best, sometimes it simply wasn't enough.

'Firefighters are human,' Ava said quietly. 'We can't save everyone.'

'It's true,' Emerson agreed. 'I remember a member of the public shouting at me once a few years back. We were at a tower block fire in Bristol, not everyone made it out.

She screamed at me asking why I hadn't done my job properly.'

Ava winced, they had all at some point in their careers been in that position. Often members of the public were kind to firefighters and the community at large, offering tea, blankets, food and even homes and shelter to those that needed it. But just occasionally there were the odd instances when firefighters took the brunt of other people's anger, fear and frustration.

'I remember early on in my career, I'd not been on the job long, about the same amount of time as Jodie,' Miguel spoke up, 'I went to a fire at a hotel where I was working for the London Fire Brigade.'

Ava frowned, she had forgotten Miguel had worked in London.

'This was probably only about my tenth shout, but the moment I heard the peal of the station bells I was out in the muster bay ready to go.' Miguel's lips quirked at the memory. 'Couldn't wait to prove my worth. I'll never forget the moment we arrived. There was smoke as thick as brushes covering the entire area. Anyway, I went inside with the lads, used my torch to look for the injured and then I found this one little girl trapped in a wardrobe. Her parents were nowhere to be seen, she was barely breathing, her eyes closed. I couldn't leave her, so I forgot all my training, grabbed her and ran straight down seven flights of stairs with her in my arms. I got her outside and begged the paramedics to save her.'

Miguel broke off and Ava could see that in that moment he was right back at the scene.

He lifted his gaze, took a slurp of tea and continued.

'She died, despite it all. Smoke inhalation was too much for her little lungs. I was shocked. I didn't think things like that happened. Then her mum and dad came to find me at the station a few weeks later to thank me for trying.' Miguel shook his head in disbelief and Ava knew how he felt. 'I felt like I'd let them down, like I could have done more, even though I knew I'd done everything I could.'

Big Stu reached out a hand across the table and squeezed Miguel's hand.

'That's rough mate.'

'It was.' Miguel released a deep breath. 'The lads were supportive, course the boss hauled me over the coals for not following procedure, but everyone kept telling me to move on, that it was a part of the job. But I couldn't get that little girl's face out of my mind. It made me want to be the best firefighter I could be. That was the best way to honour her memory. Even now, she's the one I think of first when there's a shout. I want to do right by her and her family.'

As he tailed off, he looked at Ava. Understanding pierced her heart; she knew just how her friend felt.

–

Later that morning, Ava found herself standing next to Miguel in Helen's family home. Ava was adamant she wanted to pay her last respects, and there were items she had managed to retrieve from the smashed car she wanted to give to the family.

The husband, Igor, had opened the door looking ashen. For a moment Ava had wondered if coming so soon had been the right thing to do, but reminded herself that respect for the dead helped the living to heal. She wasn't going to shy away from that, no matter how painful.

'Would you like some tea?' Igor managed, running a hand through his unkempt grey hair, Swedish accent impacting his English.

'Not at all,' Miguel said quietly. 'This is just a welfare check. We were at the scene yesterday, Ava tended to your wife.'

Igor looked up at Ava gratefully and she saw his shoulders slump with sadness.

'Thank you. She hated being alone, my Helen.'

Ava wasn't sure if this news made her feel worse or better but she was glad Igor found the information comforting because he and his daughter were the priority now.

'She talked about your daughter a lot,' Ava said. 'Apparently she was making cheese straws at school and was going to bring them home for dinner.'

Lars smiled and gestured to a plastic box on the counter. Ava could see it was full of untouched home-baked goodies.

'Ivy couldn't wait to share them, she was excited.' He smiled. 'I know it sounds silly but we try to find something interesting or a reason to celebrate every day.'

'Doesn't sound silly at all,' Miguel said soothingly. 'Sounds lovely to me.'

Ava took that as her cue and reached into the small bag she had brought with her, pulling out a phone and a notepad. It was all she had managed to recover from the scene. She knew there was a chance other items might be recovered in future, but as this was no crime scene and the items weren't needed for evidence, Ava had taken what she could, determined for someone to be able to hold onto any memories.

'We don't want to intrude,' she said. 'We wanted to return these to you.'

At the sight of the phone, Lars gasped in delight. 'Helen's phone. Her whole life was on this. Photos of our daughter, to-do lists, things she thought about. I know she was planning an entire family road trip on this just last week.' Igor waved the phone in his right hand and pressed it to his heart. 'She wanted us to ride Route 66 during the summer holiday. All her notes, everything, her face was buried in this phone with all the planning.'

'Maybe you'll get the chance to take the trip,' Miguel said gently. 'One day.'

Igor looked stricken. 'I don't know… I don't know if I can get into a car at the moment. Not after what happened yesterday…'

There was a pause before Ava spoke.

'I know this won't help you now,' she said softly, 'but I'm living proof you can live alongside grief. Sometimes you and your daughter will feel as though there's no way you can keep going after what's happened. You'll feel guilty, bereft even, that you're here when Helen isn't.' She turned to the cheese straws and sighed. 'You won't want to eat those ever again.'

Igor nodded and she caught Miguel giving her a hard stare.

'Stop it, Ava,' he hissed.

But Ava ignored him. She knew better than anyone that pain and past tragedy couldn't dictate your life.

'I lost my parents in a fire when I was eighteen,' she explained. 'My world ended.'

Igor looked at her in surprise.

'In a fire?' he echoed.

Ava nodded. 'They're why I wanted to become a fire-fighter. I wanted to honour their memory. It was my way through my grief, and you'll find a way to that, too. When Helen spoke to me yesterday it was clear her family meant the world. All she wanted was to get back home and be here for you all.'

'Helen was adopted. Family was everything to her,' he admitted.

Surprise jolted Ava in her seat. Something else she'd had in common with Helen.

'Me too,' she admitted.

'And did it change you?' Igor asked. 'This knowledge?'

Ava considered the question.

'I don't know,' she finally answered.

'Helen was proud to have been adopted,' Igor began. 'She didn't know she was adopted until she was twenty-seven but when she found out, she asked her parents if she could look for her birth family and found them three years later.'

'Was she glad she found them?' Ava asked.

Igor nodded. 'Very. Her mother had been young, didn't have the support of her family so gave away her daughter. Never forgot her, though.'

As Igor paused, Ava gulped. This story was so unlike her own. It was something of a comfort to know there was such a thing as happy ever afters with adoption stories.

'They bonded almost immediately,' Igor continued, 'but Marta, Helen's birth mother, was quick to point out that she was not Helen's real mother, that position lay firmly with Helen's adopted mother. It was all so healthy, so well adjusted. Marta and Kathleen, Helen's adopted mother, even became friends, they still are.' Igor ran his hands over his face. 'Oh god, I need to tell Marta.'

Ava was lost for words. She had no idea how to help this bright, lovely man.

'I'm so sorry,' she whispered.

They sat in silence for a moment, and then Igor looked up tearfully at Ava.

'Thank you, for coming to see me and for bringing Helen's things.'

'It was nothing,' Ava replied. Not for the first time, she wished she had been able to do more. Helen had seemed like such a lovely woman, it was a tragedy in itself Ava hadn't been able to save her.

'We'll leave you now,' Miguel said breaking the silence. 'But if there's ever anything you or your daughter need help with please do let us know.'

As they stepped out into the cold, both firefighters carried the weight of another life lost. But Ava knew, somehow, they would find the strength to carry on. Largely because they had to.

Chapter Twenty-Seven

The ride back to the station was silent, each firefighter wrapped in their own thoughts. The RTA had hit them hard and as Ava glanced at Miguel driving them back along the A4 she couldn't bear the silence any more.

'Penny for them,' she said at last.

Miguel frowned. 'What do you mean?'

'Don't play for time,' Ava said as she scratched an imaginary itch on her forearm.

'As if!' Miguel howled.

'You forget I know you,' Ava said lightly. 'I remember you stalling for time when we went on a course together. You'd developed a weird thing about heights and were asking that instructor a million and one questions before you'd shimmy up that tall ladder.'

'Oh, and you were like a rat up a drainpipe I suppose,' Miguel countered.

At the memory Ava smiled. They were all taught through training that whenever a firefighter was needed, it's someone's worst day of their lives. It was a mantra Ava had never forgotten.

'That's not the point,' Ava said now, returning to the present. 'You've been somewhere else all day.'

She watched him, willing him to confide in her. They had known one another a long time, had been the keeper of one another's secrets more times than Ava cared to admit. But Ava knew Miguel also had pride and often that pride caused him to make mistakes.

Wordlessly he signalled right and pulled into the pub car park near the station. Switching off the engine, he looked at Ava, and she could see the pain in his eyes.

'I've really messed up, Ava,' he croaked.

'What do you mean?' she asked, her voice soft.

Miguel hesitated, the weight of years bearing down on him. 'It's everything, Ava. Xav, the job… I thought I had time to fix things, to make it all right, but now I wonder if I've left it too late.' He paused, rubbing a hand over his face. 'And then there's that girl, the one I couldn't save. I still see her face when I close my eyes.'

He shuddered, the memory weighing on him. Ava turned in her seat, giving him her full attention.

'Did you ever have counselling afterwards?'

Miguel sighed. 'You remember the old days, Ava. Back then, there wasn't much in the way of counselling. You were just expected to get on with it, to deal with the nightmares on your own like every other bloke on the job.'

'Since when have you ever been like other blokes?' Ava teased gently.

'You know what it's like, Ava. It's why we bonded so well on the job.'

Ava did know. As a woman and as a gay man they had both been minorities in the fire service. Both unaccepted, both the victims of bullying. When Ava joined, half the firefighters she worked with didn't believe she belonged there, wouldn't even help her on a shout. Instead they'd watch her carry the pumps alone, believing women weren't up to the job. It had taken years for Ava to win them round and be accepted. Miguel had suffered the same fate. But when Miguel joined Bath Fire Station, with a couple of years more experience than her, they'd supported each other through the worst, building a connection for life. With a sigh, Ava reminded herself the past was the past. She had seen first-hand how the service had changed and was delighted to see more female recruits, LGBTQ colleagues and others from diverse backgrounds all joining without question. But she also knew past hurts continued to cause pain.

'You can deal with some mistakes now, you know. Look at Xav, do you really want to throw it all away because you've grown apart?'

'No,' Miguel said, sounding almost anguished.

'Miguel, real love shouldn't be thrown away – it's worth fighting for, don't you think? And in a way isn't that a lovely way to honour that girl who lost her life when you were a trainee? By living your life to the max because she can't?'

Miguel nodded, with a glance that made him look like the young man she had once known. How much they had each seen since those days.

'I've never thought of it like that,' he said in a small voice.

'It doesn't matter, Miguel. It wasn't meant to be before now, that's all,' Ava soothed.

Miguel traced an invisible pattern on his thigh. 'When did you get to be so wise?'

'Didn't know I was.'

Ava leaned back in her chair and gazed out of the window. How was she in her forties and still dealing with drama like she was in her teens? Sometimes it felt like the more she tried to sort out, the more of a mess she made.

'And what about you?' Miguel asked now. 'How does all this impact how you feel about adoption?'

'I don't know,' she admitted slowly. 'My world feels as if it's upended. I thought finding Bernice would help me piece together who I am and what I really want, but instead it's just muddied the waters.'

Raindrops echoed on the roof of the car overhead.

'Maybe it's time to talk to Steve,' Miguel suggested. 'Let him know how you're feeling. Things are dragging on between you two. You were just supposed to separate for a few days and it's been weeks.'

'I feel like I've tried,' Ava said. 'But we seem too far apart.'

'Really?' Miguel looked surprised. 'He doesn't seem to have strayed too far to me, Ava. He's been there for you every step.'

'He moved out!' Ava said in exasperation.

'But he's been there for you. He's looked after your cat, he's listened and he cares. He wants a life with you, Ava. Look at poor Igor back there, I bet he'd give his right arm for another day with Helen. You've got that chance to sort things out and have a future.'

Ava managed a weak smile as she looked at her friend. 'I suppose I don't know what that looks like any more.'

'Maybe it's time to find out,' Miguel said gently.

'Maybe,' Ava echoed.

And then she had a flash of inspiration. Maybe it was possible to sort out all her problems in one go.

'What are you doing on Saturday night?' Ava asked.

'Wishing I lived in Mexico and was licking tequila shots off some fit thing's toned stomach and didn't have to deal with horrible, cold British winters,' Miguel quipped.

Ava raised an eyebrow and Miguel looked sheepish.

'Nothing.'

'Why don't you come around to mine for drinks? I'll invite Xav.'

'That sounds like the worst invitation I've ever heard,' Miguel said, turning the key in the ignition, the engine now purring into life. 'And Xav won't come.'

'He will if I tell him Cassie's there, you know how much he loves her.'

'True,' Miguel said ruefully.

'So you'll come?'

'Okay.'

'And you'll talk to Xav,' Ava said pointedly. 'Try and save what you have?'

There was silence as Miguel looked mutinously through the windscreen.

'Migs,' Ava said, her voice laced with persistence.

'Okay,' he said looking exasperated as he faced her. 'But what about Steve? If this is some big sorting-out party, shouldn't he be there as well?'

Ava swallowed, she'd walked right into that one. 'I'll ask him.'

'Make sure you do,' Miguel said. 'And while you're at it, can you talk to Jodie?'

'Why?' Ava asked in surprise.

'She's put in her papers,' Miguel said. 'Can't handle the job, what happened yesterday was the last straw for her apparently.'

Ava blinked in shock. 'Jodie? But she's great, really good with people, fit, confident.'

'But can't cope with seeing people die,' Miguel said quietly. 'Apparently she went home after the RTA in bits. I've had her girlfriend on the phone. And honestly, it does save me the hassle of having to make someone redundant.

The end of March is looming like a dark raincloud. I was going to let Emerson go, he's so good he'd easily get another job. Big Stu's near retirement, I don't want him to lose out.'

Ava was thrown. 'But we were told we couldn't make Jodie redundant. I don't think this solves the problem at all. I take it you've spoken to her.'

'I have,' Miguel confirmed. 'Told her the usual thing, that it's natural to feel this way after a serious accident, that your first year after training is always the worst.'

'But she's determined,' Ava mused.

'She is,' Miguel said. He ran his hands through his hair and groaned. 'On the one hand, if I'm honest, Jodie leaving solves problems. But on the other, I think it would be a shame. She's got the makings of a really good fire-fighter. As her watch manager I hoped you might have some sway over her.'

'I'll try,' Ava agreed. 'Though I'm not sure I'll be able to get through to her.'

Miguel laughed. 'I dunno, Ava, you have a funny way of getting under people's skin when you want something.'

Chapter Twenty-Eight

The following morning dawned bright and clear, a perfect, crisp early February day. As the alarm went off, Ava peeled her eyes open, a nagging sensation at the back of her mind.

Throwing back the covers, she groaned. Today was the day she had to do a lot of talking about things she didn't really want to talk about. Not only did she need to invite Steve over for Saturday night, but she also had to make sure Cassie was going to be in.

Despite her plan to talk to Cassie about Paul over a takeaway all Ava had actually done was tell her she was planning on having a few drinks on Saturday night.

Cassie had seemed keen enough when she'd mentioned it the other day. But then Cassie had probably thought the evening was just a way for Ava to discuss the future with Steve.

Which led her neatly onto the fact she needed to speak to Steve about their future and whether they even had one. Ava loved him, that much she knew. But that didn't necessarily mean they belonged together, no matter how much she might have once thought that it did.

However, Saturday night wasn't the only thing on her mind. Today, she planned to talk to Jodie about her decision to leave. If she was honest, Ava wasn't just surprised at the rookie's decision, but also a little bit hurt.

She was supposed to be Jodie's mentor as well as her watch manager, why hadn't she come to her and told her how she was feeling? Guilt tugged at Ava's heart. She'd been distracted. Her search for her birth parents, the IVF and adoption issues, not to mention her marital problems. It was no wonder Jodie hadn't felt able to turn to her.

Ava arrived at work with fresh resolve and greeted the rest of her watch before going to look for Jodie. She found the rookie in the muster bay, cleaning the equipment.

'Morning,' Ava said brightly. 'Can we have a chat?'

With a wary look, Jodie stood up and threw down her sponge.

'Is this about my decision to quit?'

Ava nodded. 'It is. I want to talk to you about it before we officially file your papers with headquarters.'

'There's no point,' Jodie said with an air of weariness. 'I've made up my mind. I'm not cut out for this.'

Ava gestured for Jodie to join her on one of the benches by the window.

'I know this job is tough,' Ava said evenly. 'There have been weeks, months, even years where I've thought I can't go on. That I'm not strong enough. But then something wonderful happens. You make a difference to someone's day, you rescue that cat from the tree, you put out a fire, you save a life. It's those wins that make the difference.'

Jodie was silent for a moment as she looked at Ava before letting out a long breath. 'I hear you, but this job, it's not what I expected.'

'How do you mean?' Ava asked.

'I thought it would be exciting!' Jodie wailed. 'And mostly it's sitting about with old blokes talking about what's wrong with vegans!'

At that Ava roared with laughter.

'Come on, that's only Big Stu, and you know he gave your vegan chilli a go last week. He said it was the best he'd ever tasted.'

'It was the only one he'd ever tasted,' Jodie pointed out.

Ava shrugged. 'Least he didn't fling it against the wall which is exactly what he did when Miguel tried to make him eat patatas bravas.'

Jodie smiled and Ava felt a flash of hope. She tried a different tack.

'I remember when I first started. It was hard for me, too. In all sorts of ways—'

'You mean the sexism?' Jodie interrupted.

'The sexism, the fact I'd just lost my parents and thought firefighting was a way to escape my grief.'

Surprise crossed Jodie's face. 'I didn't realise that was why you joined. Your parents, I mean…' Her voice trailed off as she glanced at the floor, unsure what to say next.

'It seemed like a good idea at the time. And don't get me wrong, it was,' Ava added. 'I've never regretted my decision, but sometimes the job takes over. It's all too easy to immerse yourself in it, to forget that you're a person.'

'That's not why I'm leaving,' Jodie said in a small voice. 'I don't have a mission to save people. I just thought this would be exciting, an escape I suppose.'

A stab of frustration pierced through Ava. She knew Jodie wasn't being honest, and if she had been a better mentor she knew she would have done a better job of getting through to her now.

'I've seen you in action, Jodie,' she said quietly. 'You've given this job your all. You've thrown yourself into the toughest of tasks, so I know this nonsense you're spouting about this job not being exciting enough is absolute bullshit. Time to level with me, what's really going on?'

Glancing up, Ava was astonished to see tears stream down Jodie's cheeks.

'I've never seen someone die before,' she wept. 'That poor woman, I can't forget her face, Ava. She's haunting me, and we couldn't save her. Then there's the fires, look at the estate, the RTA. The people's lives that are in tatters.' Jodie rubbed her hands over her face, smearing soapy suds across her nose. 'It's just too much for me.'

'You are good at this,' Ava said firmly. 'And I think you know that. This job is tough, but you're tougher. You put yourself through firefighter training, which we both know is not easy. I remember the first time I saw a dead body at a shout. It was a young man, he'd died of smoke inhalation, we hadn't got to him in time at a warehouse on the Bath side of Bristol. I'll never forget it, he was two years older than me.' Ava shook her head at the memory. 'It was such a waste, and afterwards I didn't just feel responsible, I felt guilty that I'd survived and he hadn't.'

'But that wasn't your fault,' Jodie countered.

'It wasn't,' Ava agreed. 'And it didn't help I only had Miguel to talk to.'

'Your work husband,' Jodie put in.

Ava laughed. 'I found a kindred spirit. But, Jodie, the thing is, if you stick at this, you will find the most incredible camaraderie. We all have each other's backs, we all love each other and support each other and if you're not feeling that yet then that's my fault.'

Jodie shook her head. 'You've had stuff going on, your husband, your family stuff—'

'Which is all stuff I shouldn't allow to spill over into my work,' Ava said resolutely. 'I'm sorry I've let you down. But I'd love to make it up to you if you'll give me and firefighting another chance.'

Jodie gave her a watery smile. 'I want to, I do. I'm just not sure I'm strong enough.'

The smell of burnt toast wafted through the air, Big Stu swearing as the others on the watch laughed and gently mocked his culinary efforts.

As Jodie smiled, Ava couldn't help but think back to Cassie's words about found family. How, sometimes, it was the people you found along the way who truly became your family. The people who were biologically connected to you weren't always the ones that deserved your love and attention. She cocked her head, the sounds of laughter echoing around the bay.

These guys were the ones who had seen her through the toughest times, more than anyone else ever could.

It had taken a long time to get here, but now they were the ones who had seen her through the thick and thin of life, the ones that had helped her cope when the chips were down, the ones that had toasted her when she and Steve had celebrated twenty years of marriage, been there for her when she coped with the miscarriages, the failed IVF and helped her remember her parents on their birthdays. And of course, taken her out to get riotously drunk on her birthday and everything else in between. Together with Cassie, these people were her family and she desperately wanted Jodie to feel the same.

'Let's just take it step by step. No promises,' Ava suggested.

Lifting her gaze, Jodie turned to Ava.

'I'd like that but there is one condition.'

'Okay.'

'Please promise me I never have to eat Big Stu's food ever again!'

Convincing Jodie to stay had been met with surprise and gratification by Miguel.

'What did you say to her?' he asked, narrowing his eyes in suspicion.

'I apologised,' Ava said simply. 'I let her down.'

She sank into the chair opposite him.

Miguel raised his eyebrows.

'You apologised?' he echoed, then scrabbled around his desk, pretending to look for a pad and pen. 'Quick let me write the date down.'

Ava laughed. 'I do apologise sometimes! I've let my personal life overshadow my work life and that was wrong. I should apologise to you as well.'

'Nothing to apologise to me for.' Miguel waved her apology away. 'We all have tough times, Ava. And Jodie's a kid. She needs to grow up a bit if she's going to make a fist of this job. It's not for the faint-hearted, she should have realised that when she undertook her training.'

'Possibly,' Ava agreed. 'But in order to grow up and be the firefighter I believe she's capable of being she needs good teachers around her. I failed her once but not any more.'

'Well, I'm pleased to hear it.' Miguel smiled as he got to his feet and pulled out Jodie's resignation letter from the pile on his desk. 'So I should bin this?'

'Maybe wait until she tells you herself. But I think so, yes,' Ava said happily then she frowned. 'This does mean someone else has to be made redundant from the watch.'

Miguel groaned. 'I know. I've thought of nothing else. You know Emerson came to me the other day – his wife's pregnant.'

'Oh no.' Ava gulped in horror and sat down. 'We can't lose him now.'

Miguel groaned. 'Which means we're down to Big Stu or Phil.'

'Or me,' Ava said in a quiet voice.

'You?' Miguel looked at her visibly shocked. 'You can't be serious.'

The idea hadn't fully formed until she spoke it aloud. But what if she did offer herself up? Sacrifice her position for the good of the team? It sounded noble, even if the thought sent a shiver of dread down her spine. Her wage was more than the others. She'd save the watch a fortune. Why shouldn't she go somewhere else? Make a fresh start? She could become part of another unit, maybe one in Bristol for a change.

'I don't know,' she admitted, the thought frightening her as it took hold. 'Maybe.'

Miguel looked down at his hands, clenching and unclenching them as if trying to physically release the weight of his thoughts.

Ava sighed. She felt clueless herself, but she did know there was no point trying to force a decision now.

Chapter Twenty-Nine

Later that morning Ava focused on the job at hand – a school visit, something Ava always dreaded. Most of the kids were bright and interested, but there were always a few with their teenage hormones running wild, more interested in making suggestive comments.

Still, community outreach was as much a part of the job as putting out fires, and supporting Miguel was part of her role.

'I'll round up the watch for the visit,' she said, feeling weary as she said the words aloud. 'You get yourself together.'

Thankfully most of them were ready, prepared for the gaggle of teens.

'It's at an all girls' school though,' Jodie pointed out on the way to the school on the south side of Bath, just a little out of town. 'Surely that means they'll be better behaved.'

Big Stu shuddered in the back of Ava's car. 'Don't you believe it, love. Those bloody girls can be vicious. Last time we came up here one of the girls ran off with my helmet and threw it on the roof. We had to get the ladders out and everything to get it back down.'

'And then there was the time one of them looked you in the eye and asked if you could still be a firefighter if you were fat,' Miguel teased from the passenger seat.

'And I'll remind you what I told them—' Big Stu said, leaning forward in his seat.

'No!' Ava said hurriedly, remembering only too well that Big Stu's suggestion of where he'd like to shove his last donut had resulted in multiple parental complaints and tears amongst the kids. 'Thank you anyway. We need to come together for the community. Show them that a career as a firefighter is great for girls.'

'That what this is, then?' Jodie asked as Ava pulled neatly into the car park. 'A careers day?'

'Pretty much,' Miguel said, getting out of the car. 'We have to do these every so often. I'm sure you remember the importance of work in the community during your training.'

'They mentioned it was important to have a positive presence,' Jodie said as she followed along behind.

Miguel nodded. 'Stay close to Ava, mirror what she does. She's usually really good with the kids!'

Ava scowled at him as they walked inside reception to be greeted by the school receptionist. As Miguel gave their names and signed them in, the smell of school canteens and polished parquet flooring was overwhelming. Why did all schools smell the same? Too much polish, big vats of tinned gravy and the stench of teenage disappointment.

Following Miguel up the stairs and into the large hall she knew also doubled as the assembly hall and school canteen, she tried to feel positive. If she could encourage some kids to think about firefighting as a career today she'd have done well.

Only, as she took her position at the trestle table in the corner where the receptionist had set them up, she felt a set of eyes boring into her. Turning around she saw Steve standing behind his own trestle table smiling back.

'Hi,' she said, making her way across the hall towards her husband. 'Didn't realise you were here today.'

Steve fiddled with a red tie Ava recognised as being one she had bought him for Christmas.

'It was a last-minute thing – Christina was supposed to do it but she had a meeting,' he admitted.

'That's code for: you've never done it mate, time to step up and take your turn.' Ava giggled.

'Something like that.' Steve looked sheepish. 'I know you said a while back you were doing this and I should have mentioned it to you. I was hoping to the other night, but we postponed…'

'No need,' Ava said quickly. She didn't want this to become another issue between them.

'Are you okay?' he asked, his expression full of concern. 'I read about the car accident in the paper. Poor woman.'

Ava said nothing. Her mind was still full of Helen and her family. Not only was she sad the woman had lost her life, but the fact she had left a child was playing on her mind.

'Look, I wondered if we could talk,' she said. 'Not here, obviously.' She cast a glance around the school hall. The kids were beginning to file in and she didn't want to leave the girls without her for too long.

Steve sighed and looked at her forlornly. 'Ava, don't you think we've talked enough?'

Ava looked at him blankly. 'I don't understand.'

'I mean we keep meeting, we keep talking, and nothing changes.'

A cold swell of fear crept through Ava's heart.

'That's not true,' she said.

'But it is,' Steve insisted. 'We need to stop talking and make some decisions about our lives. Let's face it, none of us are getting any younger. It's a tired cliché but it's true, and if we can't agree on a way forward together, well...' Steve looked at the floor. 'I think we might have to go our separate ways.'

Ava felt the air in the room shift, as though she was being pulled into a different reality. Her heart stuttered in her chest, refusing to process what Steve had just said.

'You... you want to break up?' she whispered, barely able to believe her own words.

He looked stricken, as if the full reality of his words had begun to sink in.

'That's not what I'm saying,' he said hurriedly. 'I just don't think we can keep living this weird half-life where we meet up, we're friends, but we're married. We're supposed to have a life together but I can't keep doing this.'

A wave of shock coursed through Ava's body. She glanced back at the firefighter table, saw nearly all the kids had arrived.

'I'd better go,' she said desperately.

Steve nodded, then. 'What was it you wanted to talk to me about?'

'I was going to ask if you'd come to drinks on Saturday at ours. Thought I'd cheer Cassie up. But... it's not important now.'

Steve frowned. 'I'll be there. I've got something on earlier, but I'll come by around seven.'

Ava hesitated, a knot tightening in her stomach. Something on? Steve never had things on. What could he possibly be doing on a Saturday evening? Usually Steve's plans revolved around the pub, the football or taking next door's dog for a walk when they were away. He didn't make plans, he didn't have 'things on'. She stared at him, was she losing him? Right before her very eyes?

–

Thankfully the school event passed without incident and even Big Stu managed to remain on his best behaviour. There were no letters from disgruntled parents and there were even a handful of interested girls, keen to find out more about pursuing a career as a firefighter.

Ava returned to the station feeling energised, a feeling that remained with her for the rest of the week.

It wasn't until Saturday she found herself feeling anxious and in dire need of a workout. Tonight was the night. The big drinks event she'd organised was finally happening and she was excited and nervous in equal measure – the idea of successfully reuniting Cassie with her father playing on a loop in her mind like the last scene of an ultimate feel-good film.

Hooking the barbell back onto the squat rack, Ava reached for her towel and mopped the sweat from her face. The smart speaker blared Nineties dance tracks above her head and Ava felt a burst of endorphins.

One of the perks of being a firefighter was the free gym that came with the job. Like everyone else on the watch, Ava devoted herself to staying fit so she could tackle whatever was thrown at her. Today she was feeling all over the place and she knew that only lifting heavy things would help her relax.

Yet, the day had also begun with good news when she received an email from a dealer in Bristol regarding Trooper Hakeson's medal.

Dear Ms Ryan,

Thank you for your email. I do, in fact, remember
this medal and sold it to a collector some years ago.
However, I do also have the name and address of the
person that sold the medal to me. Given you say you
found the medal in a flood, I would imagine that by
now the collector has claimed the insurance money
for this medal. If you like, I could contact the original
owner on your behalf and pass on your details?

Warm wishes,

John W Davis

Collectibles and Antiquities Dealer

Ava had been over the moon and immediately tapped out
a reply urging the collector to contact the seller. Finally,
after so many years, Ava was close to saying goodbye to an
item from her Nostalgia Nook.

Chapter Thirty

Early Saturday evening and Ava found herself running around the house, frantically pouring crisps into bowls and ensuring the wine she'd bought was chilled enough.

'Will you please relax?' Cassie begged. 'You're putting me on edge.'

'Sorry,' Ava said, automatically straightening pictures and mentally working out if she had enough ice. 'I just want to get everything ready.'

'I don't know why you're so nervous. It's just a couple of your mates coming round and Steve isn't it?'

A wave of shame crashed over Ava. But there was no time to ponder further as the doorbell rang.

'I'll go,' Cassie said firmly. 'You can keep doing that weird thing you're doing with the crisps. And Dylan,' she turned to her son who was flipping through the TV channels on the sofa, 'get up and help Ava.'

Ava watched the little boy roll his eyes and hid her laughter. The lad was nine going on nineteen.

'What can I do, Auntie Ava?' he asked. His shoulders were slumped, hands were firmly in his pockets and his hair was mussed up from too much time lying on the sofa.

'You can open those olives and put them in that bowl,' Ava instructed as Cassie reappeared in the kitchen with Miguel and Xav.

At the sight of them together, Ava's eyes lit up and she rushed forward and hugged them.

'Am I right in thinking you've patched things up?'

Miguel nodded, looking bashful as he kissed her on the cheek, just as Xav swept her into his arms.

'My sweet Ava,' he whispered.

Ava felt a rush of affection for her friend's husband and peered over his shoulder. Miguel looked so worried, her heart went out to him. A lot was riding on tonight for all of them. She wished she knew the right thing to say, but Ava was saved from any more wishful thinking by the appearance of Dylan.

'Miguel,' he cried.

Dylan wrapped his arms around Miguel's middle and Ava and Xav stood back in amused delight as they saw Miguel's face light up.

'Dylan!' he exclaimed. 'How are your tricks?'

'Good,' he said seriously. 'But Mum is making me help out with this stupid drinks thing 'cos she says we have to be nice to Auntie Ava as she's let us stay with her.'

Miguel raised an eyebrow and looked at Ava.

'Sweetheart.' Ava bent down so she was at eye level with the little boy. 'You don't have to help out if you don't want to. How about a compromise? You help me put the rest of the olives in the bowls and make sure the glasses are clean, then you can go back and watch some TV before bedtime.'

'Really?' The look of relief that passed across Dylan's face was almost funny. 'Won't Mum mind?' he asked in a small voice.

'I'll talk to her,' Ava promised. 'But I think she'll be fine. Now scoot and uphold your end of the bargain.'

Dylan went to do just that and a pair of amused faces greeted her as she stood upright.

'You're a born parent,' Xav said kindly.

'Or trained negotiator,' Miguel said with a wink.

She laughed, then caught sight of Steve looking uncertain in the doorway.

Grateful for his presence she waved him over.

'Thanks for coming,' she said, kissing his cheek.

'Thanks for inviting me,' he said formally. Then he nodded greetings at Xav and Miguel. 'What's the occasion?'

He glanced around now at the assembled guests that had gathered in the kitchen. Ava could see that Cassie had invited a few of her neighbours from the estate and a couple of her colleagues from work. Whilst she was pleased to see the place full of people, Ava felt anxious that this might make Paul feel uneasy. Then again, there was a chance Cassie might be more receptive to her father and hearing him out if there was a crowd.

'What's wrong?' Miguel looked at her as he swigged from his beer. 'You look worried.'

'I'm not worried,' Ava said defensively. 'I just want to make sure everyone has a good time. There's a few more people here than I anticipated.'

'But it's a party,' Xav pointed out. 'You can't have too many people at a party.'

'And you never said what all this was in aid of anyway,' Miguel said. 'Not that it's not lovely to be here.'

A sense of desperation began to creep up on her. A party had seemed like such a good idea when she'd come up with it. But now, an audience for Cassie's reunion with her father seemed a step too far.

Once again the sound of the doorbell rang loudly through the house.

'I'll get it,' Cassie called brightly as she passed Ava. She kissed her on the cheek. 'This was a good idea, we need some fun. Well done you for organising it.'

As Cassie whittled off, Ava turned back to look at her friends who were staring at her with questions in their eyes.

'You really have gone a funny colour, Ava,' Xav said peering at her.

Ignoring her friends she pushed past them and raced to the hallway. Cassie was standing at the front door, Paul's outline visible.

'What the hell do you mean Ava invited you?' she growled.

At the sound of her footsteps Cassie whirled around to face Ava, her face purple with rage, bewilderment in her eyes.

'Tell me this isn't true?' Cassie pleaded.

Ava looked at her friend's face and her blood ran cold. In one heart-stopping moment she realised all her romantic notions about reuniting Cassie and her father were wrong.

As Ava miserably nodded her head, Cassie's expression changed from bewilderment to hate.

For what felt like a lifetime, Ava stood rooted to the spot, watching the events play out as if she was watching a film. She pinched herself. None of this could be real because she had never seen Cassie look at her with so much hatred.

Ava took a step forward, reaching for Cassie's hand.

'I'm so sorry,' she babbled. 'Let me explain.'

Ava felt the crushing weight of her own guilt, the silence of the party mirroring the heavy emptiness growing inside her. She had thought she was helping, but Cassie's expression made it clear, she had done far more harm than good. For the first time in years, Ava truly felt like she had lost her best friend.

But Cassie snatched her hand away and instead turned to Paul.

'I don't know why you're here,' Cassie snarled. 'How hard is it to understand I want nothing to do with you?'

Paul looked stricken. 'Cassie, that was such a long time ago. I thought after your mother and everything you might think twice now.'

'Think twice?' Cassie echoed in disbelief. 'So are you here to apologise?'

At that Paul, shifted his feet. 'I just want us to make a new start, with everything that's happened lately, in your life and in mine, we deserve that. We're family, I've a grandson I don't know.'

'And never will,' Cassie said vehemently.

She folded her arms and turned to Ava. The cold, unforgiving look in Cassie's eyes shook Ava to her core. It was as if Ava was looking at a stranger.

'What were you thinking?'

'I–I.' Ava's throat went dry as she tried to speak. 'I bumped into Paul the day we got back from Ireland. I thought trying to get you two together was the right thing to do. You're family, I thought that if there was a chance you could make up then you should…' Ava's voice trailed off. Out loud she could hear how pathetic she sounded.

She searched Cassie's face for any hint of forgiveness but there was none.

The silence between them hung ominously in the air and Ava felt afraid. Cassie's cheeks were pinched red with anger, her eyes had now formed narrow slits.

'Cassie, I've changed,' Paul said, interrupting the silence. 'That's what I'm trying to tell you.'

Her father's voice brought Cassie back to the present.

'I don't care if you have changed, Paul,' Cassie snapped. 'That's the thing you're not getting. I looked up to you, you were my *dad*, and then you did the unthinkable.' Cassie finished. 'You cut me out, accused me of being a liar, a drama queen. Even got Mum to believe you. Your filthy behaviour got my own mother to disown me. What sort of father does that? I don't care if you're sorry, that you never sleep a wink because you feel guilty, I want nothing to do with you. Can you get that through to your thick skull?'

'I got it all wrong,' Paul began. He took a step into the house but Cassie was prepared. 'Cassie, I'm begging you, I've spent every day since regretting the choices I made. I know I don't deserve forgiveness, but please give me a chance to make it right.'

There was a pause. For a second Ava wondered if Cassie might be willing to let Paul inside. But then she reached forward and in one furious motion shoved him lightly back, causing him to fall onto the concrete.

'The thing is, Paul,' Cassie said lightly, 'it doesn't matter. I decided a long time ago that Dylan is my only family, that friends are my family.'

Paul looked irritated as he got to his feet.

'Now wait a minute, I'm your father. And I was invited here by your friend standing behind you who believes that people deserve second chances.'

Two sets of eyes landed on her and Ava felt a fresh stab of guilt.

'Ava wasn't in her right mind,' Cassie said abruptly. 'But you've had years to think about this. You made sure I was cast out of my family home because of your lies. Now you've suddenly decided the time is right for you to come back into my life, but you're toxic. I don't want you anywhere near me. I don't wish you any harm but I never want to see you again and I don't want Dylan to have anything to do with you either. You're a stranger now.'

There was silence as Cassie finished speaking. Paul's face flushed in anger.

'Like it or not, we're family,' Paul said sharply. 'We're related by blood—'

But Cassie had heard enough.

'Stop right there,' Cassie hissed. 'Your right to call yourself my father ended a long time ago. Now go.'

'This isn't your house,' Paul thundered.

'No, it's mine,' Ava roared, standing shoulder to shoulder with Cassie. 'I made a mistake inviting you here and now I'd like you to leave.'

In that moment all the fight left Paul. He shook his head and slunk down the road without a word. Once he had rounded the corner, Ava shut the door and rested her forehead against the back of the door. Letting a breath out she hadn't realised she had been holding she turned to look at Cassie who was stony faced.

'I'm so sorry,' Ava said. 'Truly I am.'

Ava had known deep down that this night would be the end of something. The crack in their friendship that had started with Ireland had now shattered completely, and Cassie's cold stare told her everything she needed to know before the words even came out of her mouth.

'I know,' Cassie said coolly. 'But you've gone too far, Ava. Thank you for letting us stay here, but it's time for me and Dylan to find our own place.'

Chapter Thirty-One

A week after the ill-fated party, Ava stood in the now empty guest room as she had done every day since Cassie left. The walls were still painted a moss shade of green, the plantation shutters still a gleaming white and the Nostalgia Nook was still the feature that held pride of place. But no matter how much Ava looked at the shelf, the comfort it once brought had faded. It was like holding onto pieces of a puzzle that no longer fit, memories of a life she couldn't recapture. The Nostalgia Nook had been a sanctuary, but now it felt more like a monument to the things and people she could no longer reach.

Ava was spending all her spare time in what had been Cassie and Dylan's room. She missed them more than she could ever have imagined. The day after the party, Ava had gone up to Cassie's room, armed with fresh coffee, orange juice and croissants, plus a blueberry muffin for Dylan. She had hoped to make amends, but after rapping on the door several times she had gone inside, only to find the room was empty, not even a hairband left in the gleaming en suite.

Devastation had coursed through her. Ava felt as if she had been abandoned, being left alone without Cassie felt even more terrifying than when Steve had left.

She had sunk onto the floor, spilling the orange juice and coffee onto the stripped wooden floorboards and sobbed her heart out. Now, for the first time in her life, she was truly alone.

Of course, Ava had tried to call and text Cassie but her messages had gone unanswered. She had even tried to persuade Steve to act as a go-between but he had sounded pained when she had rung to suggest it.

'Give her time, Ava love,' he had said. 'She'll come round when she's ready. I know Cassie – she won't stay mad for long, but you need to let her be.'

Unconvinced and deeply dissatisfied, Ava had done just that. Now, she found herself wishing she could go back in time. What had she been thinking, interfering in Cassie's life like that? She had allowed herself to become so consumed with the idea of blood family finding love and connection after so many years apart she had become single-minded. Cassie couldn't have been clearer about her feelings for Paul, yet Ava had disregarded her friend. She had chosen to believe that if she could find the right way to bring them together then she would bring love and light to Cassie's life. All the while ignoring the fact she had already found all the love and happiness she wanted and needed amongst the son and many friends she had in her life.

She threw her head back against the wall and sighed, just as her phone pinged with a message. Her heart skipped a beat with hope – Cassie?

But checking her phone, disappointment surged as she saw it was from a number she didn't recognise. Assuming the message was unwanted advertising, Ava clicked it open and expected to press delete, but scanning the message found her attention piqued.

> Ava love, it's Maeve McNally. I've nothing particular to say but I never heard from you after your visit to Bernice. I'm sorry for interfering but I've been worrying about you and wanted to check you were all right. I do hope you're okay. Maeve x

Ava re-read the message twice in surprise. How had Maeve got her number? Then she remembered she had enclosed it in the letter she had sent. Did she mind Maeve had contacted her? Ava wasn't sure. It felt nice to have someone show they cared. Even if she did want to shut the door on her disappointing Irish past, Ava had been brought up well and didn't want to be rude to a woman who had only ever expressed kindness. Before she could change her mind, she tapped out a message.

> Hi Maeve, thanks for your note. I met with Bernice and it was as you said. I should have taken your advice but at least I've met the woman that gave birth to me and I know the truth about my past. For that I will always be grateful. Hope you're keeping well and thanks again for all your help. Ava x

Sending the message left a strange taste in her mouth. She didn't know if Maeve's concern was a lifeline or a reminder of the family ties she wished she could forget.

Shaking her head free of worry, Ava got to her feet. She couldn't mope about all day. She had an event to get to, the only bright spot of her day. On Monday, she had bumped into Josh the barman whose ring she and Miguel had returned before Christmas.

'Ava,' he cried in delight spotting her in the supermarket. 'How lovely to see you.'

'And you,' Ava said with genuine surprise. 'How's everything going?'

'Good.' Joe beamed. 'I've been meaning to try and get a message to you.'

'Oh?'

'Me and Kira are having a bit of a drinks do at the pub on Saturday.'

'You mean an engagement party?' Ava said.

Josh looked sheepish. 'Yes. I wanted to invite you and your husband if you'd like to come. It's all very casual, just drop in if you fancy.'

'Oh.' Ava felt wrong-footed and was about to say no. After all, the last party she had attended hadn't exactly been a roaring success. In fact, after Paul and Cassie had gone, everyone else had shuffled out embarrassed, even Steve, who had smiled sympathetically, kissed her cheek and promised to be in touch, meaning they'd never got the chance to talk.

Now she wasn't sure she was ready for another party. Then again, what was that expression? If you fell off a bike you had to get straight back on. She needed to reclaim something of herself.

'All right,' Ava said.

'Great.' Josh looked relieved. 'Kira's desperate to meet you and I want to say a proper thank you. After all, it's down to you that we're engaged at all. Would never have happened without the ring.'

Ava looked embarrassed. 'Don't be daft. You'd have got another ring.'

'Not like that.' Josh shook his head. 'It starts at half-seven but come when you like.'

Now, as Ava pulled out her favourite denim jumpsuit and teamed it with a pair of glittering silver earrings, the doorbell rang. Ava scuttled downstairs to answer it. Steve was standing on the stairs holding a huge bouquet of flowers.

'For you,' he said, handing them to her.

'Again? Why?' Ava asked astounded.

'I think you've had a tough week,' he said easily.

Steve bent down to pick up Monkey and give him a cuddle, and Ava found her heart melting ever so slightly. Perhaps this night wouldn't be a total disaster after all.

'Have you eaten?' Steve asked.

Ava shook her head. In truth she had barely eaten all week, she'd been so keyed up with anxiety after Cassie.

'Fancy going to the Mexican place?' he asked, then noticing her outfit, his face fell. 'But maybe you're on your way out?'

'I am,' Ava said. 'But come with me. You'd be very welcome.'

As she explained to Steve about Josh's invitation, she arranged the flowers in a vase.

'As long as I'm not gatecrashing.' Steve frowned.

'Not at all.' She smiled, then reached for her coat. Slamming the front door behind her, Steve reached for her hand. Instinctively she linked her fingers through his and Ava suddenly remembered how Steve used to give her hand a secret squeeze during boring events, like a signal only they shared. It had been a long time since they'd felt like partners in mischief, but maybe, just maybe, they could find that again.

As they walked to the bus stop she realised how normal it felt. Despite their problems, there were some things, such as holding hands, that felt effortless.

In the restaurant the ease between them continued. But even as the ease returned, Ava couldn't shake the gnawing uncertainty beneath her smile. Could one nice dinner undo the years of tension and distance that had built up between them?

'So, you've really taken on another new client?' Ava said, taking a bite of her fourth fish taco.

Steve nodded proudly. 'Yes, and this is a big one. And the extra money will be nice.'

Ava remembered all too well the strain money had placed on their relationship. Between the long hours, the financial stress and the IVF treatments, it had felt like they were constantly wading through quicksand. Now, for the first time in a long while, they were standing on solid ground, and it almost felt unfamiliar.

'You'll hear no complaints from me on that score, not on a firefighter's wage,' she joked, trying to break the tension she felt.

'Least what you do matters,' Steve said, pulling her back to the present.

Ava blinked at him in astonishment. Compliments about her job were rare from Steve.

'You know it does,' Steve said, noting her surprise. 'You make a difference to people's lives, which is more than can be said for me. I mean, look where we're going tonight. You found a bloke's ring and reunited him with it. Now he's invited you to his engagement party.'

Ava reached across the table and squeezed Steve's hand, his cool, long fingers fitting perfectly in her palm. But in the back of her mind, Cassie's absence still gnawed at her.

She couldn't forget the hurt she'd caused, even as she tried to piece together her life, one relationship at a time.

'Thanks,' she said. 'It feels like a long time since we've been kind to each other.'

At the admission Steve offered her a half-smile. 'Maybe it's time to make a change then.'

Over the sounds of Lizzo pumping out across the restaurant, Ava held Steve's gaze and nodded.

'I'd like that.'

For the first time in a long while, she felt a flicker of hope. But deep down, she knew that mending years of cracks would take more than just one good night. Still, for now, it was enough.

—

The sound of wailing from her phone jolted Ava wide awake. As she blinked her eyes open, she saw Monkey perched at the bottom of the bed looking at her with disdain.

'What's up with you?' she croaked.

'Nothing's up with him except he's been ousted from his usual spot in the middle of the bed,' Steve replied.

Surprised, she turned her head and saw Steve lying on his side of the bed as usual. Propped up on two pillows, scrolling through his phone as if he'd never been away. Ava tried to compute what had happened.

She didn't remember inviting him back. Had he invited himself?

How much had she drunk? Quickly Ava did some mental calculations: she'd only had one glass of wine at the restaurant but at the party there had been cocktails. Inwardly she groaned. She had always been bad on cocktails.

Spotting Ava's shocked face, Steve grinned.

'I don't think I've ever woken up happier,' he said.

Leaning over to kiss her cheek, he pulled her towards him and she leaned into the familiar curves of his body.

As she did so, memories of the previous night came flooding back. They had left the restaurant jubilant and back to their old dynamic. Together they had made their way to the party and been welcomed with open arms by Josh and Kira. He had immediately presented them with super-strong Long Island iced teas, then he had pulled her to the front of the party and made a small announcement.

'Everyone,' Josh had said into the microphone. 'I would like to introduce you to someone very important. This is Ava Ryan – she's a firefighter and without her I very much doubt my beautiful fiancée, Kira, would have said yes. Thanks to Ava, I was reunited with the family heirloom I gave to Kira when I asked her to marry me. I have no doubt it was the ring she said yes to, not me—'

'Correct,' shouted Kira from the side of the room.

Ava glanced her way and saw there were happy tears in the young woman's eyes. She had felt like that when she had said yes to Steve, to the promise of a future together.

As Kira mouthed a silent thank you, Ava nodded, still dazzled by the attention.

'So please give it up for my hero and yours, Ava Ryan,' Josh finished.

While everyone clapped and cheered, the loudest whoops of appreciation had come from Steve. She laughed as she watched him jump up and down and applaud.

Afterwards, when she made her way back to him, cocktail in hand, she couldn't help feeling puzzled.

'What's got into you tonight?' she asked.

'Nothing.' Steve took another swig of his beer, having refused the cocktails.

'You seem, I dunno… energised,' Ava said, grasping for the right word but coming up short. 'Is it the new business?'

Steve considered the question. 'Yes and no. I suppose it's made me more confident.'

'I didn't know you were unconfident.' Ava frowned.

'I didn't know either,' Steve said before taking another slug of his beer. 'It's as though with everything that's been going on with us, I needed someone to remind me of my worth.'

Guilt punctured Ava's heart. Her husband was someone else she hadn't treated as well as she could have.

Noticing the guilt etched on her face, Steve reached for her hand, squeezing it in that familiar, reassuring way.

'You've done nothing wrong. Neither one of us has. We've had a lot to deal with and it's gnawed away at us.'

Ava nodded; the joy in life had been sucked from them both over the past few years.

'I've been thinking a lot about what you said,' Ava whispered. 'It's painful but you're right. We've been in limbo for months, and it's not fair. We need to take action.'

Steve nodded and pressed Ava's hand to his lips.

'I've been meaning to tell you something,' he said. 'I know it sounds silly but seeing how you threw a party in Cassie's honour to reunite her with her father got me thinking.'

Ava cringed at the memory.

'Don't,' she groaned. 'If I could go back in time and change things I would. I can't believe what I was thinking, it was stupid, arrogant and disrespectful.'

'It was,' Steve agreed. 'But I wanted to tell you not to be so hard on yourself – you did what you believed was right, and it was on the back of coming to terms with the truth about your biological family. Your heart was in the right place. In the end, Cassie will come around.'

Hope flooded Ava's eyes. 'Do you really think so?'

'You and Cassie are like sisters, you've known each other nearly forty years. She's sensitive but she's not stupid. She's as lost without you as you are without her. It might take time but she will forgive you, I'm sure of it.'

Ava wondered how different things might have been if she'd never gone to Ireland. She wouldn't have felt so lost or vulnerable. How foolish she had been not to understand that Paul only wanted a relationship with his daughter on his own terms.

'You all right?' Steve touched her shoulder.

'Fine,' Ava said glumly. 'Just realising how big a mistake I made.'

'You did,' Steve said gently. 'But you've apologised. If someone doesn't want to accept it that's not your fault. You can't make someone be your friend.'

Steve was right. And as she looked at him, another flood of realisation swept over her.

'I don't think I've been a very good friend to you lately,' she said quietly.

Steve laughed grimly. 'I don't think we've been very good friends to each other.'

Ava sighed. Maybe there was one relationship she could save.

'I think I'm ready,' she said.

Steve looked at her cautiously. 'Do you mean adoption?'

'Yes.' As Ava nodded her head, she realised it was true. That it was perhaps her destiny all along. After all, she was a child of adoption – she knew better than anyone the stigma it could sometimes carry. Perhaps she was supposed to pass on her love to another child like her, just as her own parents had done for her. Sam and Janet had never made her feel less, in fact all she had ever felt was loved.

Suddenly Steve pulled her into his arms and peppered her face with kisses.

'I've missed you so much, Ava.'

And with the heat of his lips against her skin, longing swept through her.

She kissed him like she hadn't kissed him for years.

Ava and Steve.

Lost in a moment.

Sharing their love.

Now, as he nuzzled his face in towards her, he whispered in her ear.

'Any regrets?'

Ava thought for a moment. Her headache was beginning to wane thanks to the water on her bedside table. Was there anything she wanted to change?

A bubble of happiness rose within her.

'No regrets,' she whispered back.

Turning to face her husband, she caught the look of love in his eyes and leaned forward to kiss him.

At last, something was going her way, and this time, she wasn't going to let it slip through her fingers.

The future, as far as Ava Ryan was concerned, was hers for the taking.

Chapter Thirty-Two

For something that meant so much to them both, Steve's return to the family fold passed without fanfare. The day after he and Ava woke up together, they had slipped into old patterns. If Ava was on an early shift, he got up first and brought her a cup of tea. If she was working the night shift, he'd present her with a cold beer on walking in and then they'd both eat beans on toast together before Steve went to work, the theory being they could share their first and last meal of the day and spend precious time tighter.

Ava was grateful they had found their old rhythm so easily. The saying that you don't know what you've got until it's gone, went around Ava's head in those first few days. She couldn't believe they had come so close to losing something so precious, and it was clear Steve felt the same.

It was early March when Steve returned home one Saturday evening with a bottle of wine, an Indian takeaway from their favourite restaurant and a fresh brochure from the adoption agency they had been working with.

Ava could see the nerves in his eyes as he handed her the pack. She took it cautiously, though she'd already been researching the formal Registration of Interest process. Now, as his eyes met hers, she was delighted to see he was as keen to move forward as she was.

'What do you think?' he asked.

She smiled and nodded as she leafed through the brochure. Children's faces shone from the pages and her heart flipped. Surely now they would be approved? It had been almost nine months since their last IVF attempt. Now there had been some distance, Ava couldn't honestly see her going through the process again, regardless of whether or not they were approved for adoption.

Steve saw the worry in her eyes and guided her to the kitchen, deftly taking the brochure in one hand and handing her a glass of wine in the other, looking at her sternly.

'If we overthink this we'll get nowhere,' he cautioned.

'I know,' she agreed. 'You're right. We need to stay grounded. Focused.'

She picked up the brochure again; she had so much love to give a child, how had it taken her so long to realise that having a child was the end goal, not how they got there?

'We can eat and make a start on the paperwork,' Steve said. 'Thought it might be easier this way.'

'M-hm.' Ava was lost in a sea of faces, but she knew he was right.

Her gaze roamed over the next steps in the process. The Registration of Interest was just the start. Soon, they'd begin the assessment stage with home visits from a social worker, leading to the final approval panel. But as her eyes scanned the checklist, something made her heart skip a beat: references.

'Have you seen this?' she asked, turning to Steve.

He paused mid-pour, a small frown on his face. 'What's the problem with getting references? We've got plenty of people who can vouch for us.'

'I know,' Ava said. 'But it says here they want up to five references, ideally a mix of personal and professional, and at least one of them should be from someone who knows us well and has kids.'

'My sister,' Steve put in. 'Not to mention your friend Hannah.'

'Come on, you can't be serious. I haven't seen her for years.'

'She's known you since Year Seven and you both got detention for not doing your maths homework,' Steve pointed out. 'It suggests longevity in relationships.'

'Yeah, agreed, but she's living in a commune! Don't these people want to see commitment, stability, all that sort of stuff? I mean won't it be a red flag that I'm adopted myself and don't have parents any more?' Ava pointed out.

'You're overthinking again,' Steve said, handing her a poppadom loaded with mango chutney.

Ava laughed. Steve always used food and drink to distract her. She took a bite and tried to relax.

'There's always Miguel – he'd definitely do it. And I'm sure he'd give us a glowing reference,' she added with a slight smile.

'That's the spirit,' Steve grinned.

'But we need Cassie,' she said with a sigh.

At the sound of Cassie's name, Steve winced.

'Ava, I don't think that's going to happen.'

'But she knows how important children are to us. She's huge in the community, well-respected and she's a mum,' Ava blurted. 'It's been a few weeks now, surely she might come round if she knows how important it is to us.'

Steve helped himself to a second poppadom and shook his head.

'Ava, she won't do it. I've already asked.'

Ava's blood ran cold. 'What?'

Steve was hesitant as he took a bite of his poppadom. 'I tried to talk to her last week. I took her out for lunch.'

Ava tried to process what Steve was telling her.

'I took her to see if she might want to pop round for a coffee. See if she'd thawed,' Steve continued.

'And had she?' Ava couldn't hide the hope in her voice. 'No.'

Steve clamped a hand over Ava's but she felt a wave of crashing failure. She had to change this, she couldn't live in a world where Cassie wouldn't talk to her any more. Not if they were going to bring a child into their family, she needed to make things right, no more resentments.

'Excuse me a minute,' she said.

Before Steve could say a word, she ran up the stairs and locked herself in the bathroom. She pulled her mobile from the back pocket of her jeans and stared at the screen. Then she jabbed the keypad and pressed the number attached to Cassie's name.

As the number rang, Ava felt butterflies in her stomach.

And then, suddenly, the ringing stopped.

'Ava. What is it?' Cassie's tones were clipped and clear.

Ava was initially dumbstruck. She hadn't expected Cassie to answer and had assumed she would leave one of her usual pleading voicemails.

'Cassie, hi, I, erm, I just want to talk.'

A long sigh was audible down the phone.

'I'm sorry, Ava, I don't want to talk to you. I can't forgive what you did. It crossed a line I can't move past.'

Desperation snaked through Ava's heart.

'I know. I'm sorry, it was so stupid of me, I wish I could take it back.'

'I know you do,' Cassie's voice was gentler now. 'But I'd cut my family from my life for a reason. I'm not broken, I'm not struggling with some hidden trauma and I'm not secretly hoping we'll be reunited. We're estranged for a reason – it's better this way. Some people aren't meant to be parents and mine certainly weren't.'

'I know. I fucked up. Truly, Cassie, I'm sorry. But you have to forgive me, you have to.' There was a silence. Ava took it as her cue to keep going. 'I can't remember my life before you came along,' Ava babbled. 'You're my world, my family. I miss you so much and I'm so, so sorry, you have to believe me. I'd do anything to make this right, you know I would. Just tell me what you want me to do and I'll do it, but please Cassie, please…'

Ava's shoulders shook with racking sobs, the pain of losing Cassie, her family, her sister in every way but blood, cutting deeper with every breath.

'Ava,' Cassie said, her voice softer but matter-of-fact. 'I know how much you regret what you did and I understand why you did it. I know you were hurt and confused after Ireland, it's understandable. The thing I can't let go of is how much you hurt me. You of all people know how things have been for me with my family. You were there when they threw me out, you stayed up late with me when I cried, and yet despite me telling you *repeatedly* I wanted nothing to do with my father you still thought inviting him to your house to make amends was right. I just can't get over that. Maybe if you'd talked to me before the party, told me what you had done, then maybe I could get beyond this, but you blindsided me!'

'But, Cass, you have to,' Ava begged.

'Ava, you're going to have a lovely life without me. You and Steve are back together, you're adopting now and I think that's brilliant. It'll be the making of you and I know you'll be a brilliant mum.'

'I can't do this without you.'

'I'm so sorry, Ava,' Cassie said, her voice final but kindly. 'If you're ever really in trouble and need something, I'll be there, I owe you that. But I can't be a part of your life, not any more. Not after this.'

With that, the line went dead.

Chapter Thirty-Three

As the cold swathes of winter began to disappear and the welcoming spring mornings of late March took hold, it seemed to Ava as if life was beginning to blossom. She was feeling a lot more optimistic about her relationship and life in general. Last week she had heard from John Davies, the medal dealer, and between them they had organised a lunch for her, Miguel, John and Trooper Hakeson so the medal could be reunited with its rightful owner. When Ava had picked it up from her Nostalgia Nook that morning, renewed hope had surged through her. It helped, of course, that things between her and Steve were better than ever. She had missed him more than she realised, and time apart meant they had become more honest with one another.

'It feels a lot healthier,' Ava said now as she helped Miguel organise Blue Watch's rotas.

'You two look a lot better,' Miguel admitted.

He handed her a fresh A4 folder.

'We are a lot better,' she said with a smile.

They had all gone out for drinks as a foursome the week before and there had been no sniping, no frustrated eye rolls, they had all just enjoyed each other's company.

'And any adoption news yet?' Miguel asked.

'We've made our Formal Registration of Interest and been to another of those prospective parents meet-ups again.'

Miguel raised an eyebrow. 'How was that?'

'Interesting,' she said. 'It felt easier than the last time. Some of them are lovely, just like us, they just want family, but some are so horribly keen it's nauseating.'

She laughed remembering how one couple had already told everyone at the get-together that they had baby proofed their home and they hadn't even been approved by the adoption panel yet.

'There's always one,' Miguel said as he wiped the windows for a second time.

Ava caught his reflection in the glass. He seemed tired, she thought, as if he had the weight of the world on his shoulders. She'd hoped that having Xav back in his life would give Miguel more to smile about. But even though he seemed happy enough at home, there was still something wrong. She wondered whether to ask, but despite knowing each other for over twenty years, there was a line.

Miguel was her boss at the end of the day and whilst she wished she could find someone to replace the large Cassie-shaped hole in her heart, she knew Miguel wasn't and never would be that person. In fact, she didn't think anyone would be. Her relationship with Cassie was unique. It had powered them both through all the most important bits of life: first day at secondary school, heartbreak when her first boyfriend dumped her, A levels, and of course the loss of her parents. But there had been so much fun between them, too – regular trips to Glastonbury, the way Cassie always knew to leave paracetamol by her bedside table after a night out, the long train rides to

Edinburgh where Cassie studied her master's and the hugs that went on forever when Ava stepped off the train. But that was their relationship, they spoke every day, about everything, they always had. Then, when Dylan had come into the world, he had seemed like a lovely extension of her friend. With a son to adore, as far as Ava was concerned, there was just more of Cassie to love.

Without her friend to anchor her, Ava felt lost.

'You all right?' Miguel asked catching sight of Ava's expression.

She nodded, doing her best to appear cheerful.

'So, the rebuild on the estate isn't far from completion,' Miguel was speaking but Ava had been so lost in her own thoughts she hadn't heard him.

'Sorry Migs, what was that?'

Miguel rolled his eyes. 'I was just saying that the estate will be finished soon. The residents were talking about holding a party in the spring to celebrate.'

'I thought the community centre was having problems?' she asked.

Since her fallout with Cassie, she had taken a step back from the estate rebuild, but of course she liked to keep abreast of what was going on.

'They are,' Miguel replied. 'Snags with the roof apparently. Not up to building regulations so they're having to redo it. But they reckon they'll be done by spring, though Cassie has insisted a party would be better in the pub. They've put some of the locals up so she thinks it would be a good way to give back.'

Ava winced. 'How much is that setting them all back?'

'Not as much as it should,' Miguel explained. 'A mysterious benefactor has come forward to help with the funding.'

'Really?' Ava was astounded. Such acts of anonymous generosity usually only happened in films. In her experience if someone was giving away money they wanted a picture in every local news outlet, advertising the fact they were doing good.

'Really,' Miguel confirmed. 'But it does mean the houses are almost done. We've been asked to do a home assessment.'

Panic fluttered through Ava's chest at the word we. She had no place up at the estate, not any more.

'Can you take Big Stu?'

'Yes. But I'm also taking Emerson and Jodie,' Miguel said patiently. Then catching sight of the worry in Ava's eyes, he continued softly, 'Ava, you have to be professional. Besides, you've apologised until you're blue in the face. I don't know what else you can do. If Cassie won't accept your apology – your very many apologies I might add – then that's not your problem, it's hers. And I certainly wouldn't let it stop you from doing your job.'

Ava listened in astonishment to her boss's outburst. He had said very little about Cassie so far, but she knew he was right. She might be hurting but she couldn't let the row with Cassie derail every part of her life.

'All right,' she said.

Surely if she told herself enough times she could live without Cassie then she would start to believe it one day.

Throwing her sponge in the bucket she glanced at the time.

'Bloody hell, it's nearly twelve, we've got to be in Bristol by one.'

Confusion flickered across Miguel's face. Ava could see their lunch with the medal dealer and Trooper Hakeson had slipped from his mind.

'We're being treated remember,' she said.

'You get changed, I'll be up in a minute,' he said quickly. 'Worst case scenario I'll find some blues and twos and you can stick 'em on the Astra.'

Ava laughed as she walked towards the stairs. 'Like your thinking, but I don't think a sacking is the easiest way to sort the cutback problem. Let's just hope the traffic to Bristol is kind to us.'

—

Thankfully the traffic was kind, and Miguel and Ava found the restaurant at the top of the city with ease. It was a venue that had recently opened to much fanfare and Miguel had regaled Ava all the way there about how hard it was to get a table.

Usually Ava enjoyed her friend's incessant chatter, but today she felt anxious and needed to ground herself. Taking a deep breath as they reached the restaurant entrance, she pushed the door open. Giving her name to the waiter at the front of house, they were led to a table at the back of the room.

As they got closer, a tall man with thinning white hair dressed in a neatly tailored navy blazer and chinos smiled warmly at them. Ava guessed this was John and returned his grin but couldn't help noticing how fearful the younger bald man, sporting an almost identical outfit, looked.

'Such a pleasure, I'm John,' said the older man, standing to clasp Ava's hand and pumping it furiously. Turning to Miguel he did the same and then gestured to the man behind him.

'And it is my great pleasure to introduce Simon Hakeson,' John said.

'Pleasure to meet you, Simon,' Ava said.

'And you,' Simon said politely, though his face told a different story. 'Shall we sit?'

'Of course,' John said.

Over starters of bruschetta and olives the foursome chatted amiably. Or at least Miguel, Ava and John did. Simon stayed strangely silent. He refused the wine that was offered, preferring instead to stick to water. Ava tried to coax him out of his shell, asking him about what he did for a living and his time in the army with the Household Cavalry, but was met with monosyllabic answers.

Ava couldn't understand it. Nerves was something she had plenty of experience with, but Simon was bordering on rude. He hadn't asked her one thing about herself, he hadn't even mentioned the medal or the effort she had made to reunite him with what was rightfully his.

By the time the coffee came she'd had enough. They were here for a reason and Ava felt it was time to discuss the matter they had all gathered for. Leaning down into her bag, she reached for the wooden box and rested it on the table.

'So, I think this is yours,' she said gently.

The table fell silent. Simon's eyes looked hesitantly at the box while John's face shone.

'The medal,' he gasped, then looked at Ava and Simon for confirmation. 'May I?'

They both nodded and John opened the box, letting his eyes roam admiringly over the medal inside.

'Beautifully preserved,' he said. 'Look, Simon.'

John presented the box to Simon who couldn't take his eyes off the medal.

For a moment he paused and Ava wondered what on earth he would do. Did he even want the medal? Would he snap the box shut? But to her surprise he lifted it from the box and held it to the light.

'There's a small chip here,' he said, running his finger over the rim. 'From when I smashed it in rage, but other than that it looks as good as new.'

Simon had smashed his medal? Ava exchanged puzzled glances with Miguel who seemingly had no answers either.

'It's all right, Simon,' John said gently. He took the medal from Simon's hand and placed it back in the box. Then setting it down on the table he gave the military man, a warm smile. 'It's back with you now. Yours to do whatever you want with.'

Simon nodded. Ava shot John a concerned glance, feeling terrible that the sight of the medal in the flesh seemed to have upset him.

John smiled at Ava, as if to reassure her, and then turned to Simon. He was about to speak when Simon raised his head.

'I'm sorry, Ava, you must think I'm a right grumpy sod,' Simon said bluntly.

'No, not at all,' she began, then added gently, 'well, only a bit.'

'Forgive her,' Miguel said good-naturedly. 'She graduated from charm school a few years ago, her manners have become a bit rusty.'

Simon and John laughed.

'No, it's me,' Simon admitted. 'I've got mixed feelings about this medal, and I've been worried about this meeting since we arranged it.'

'That's understandable,' said Ava. She lifted her coffee and watched Simon. It was a relief to hear him start to talk normally.

'To be honest, I'm not sure I want this medal back,' Simon declared.

Ava paused, coffee cup midway to her lips.

'It's not that Simon's not grateful,' John said hurriedly.

'No, I am. Very grateful,' Simon said earnestly. 'I'm sorry, I'm making a proper hash of this.'

'You're not.' Ava set her coffee down and looked at him, her eyes filled with kindness. 'It's your medal, you do what you want with it.'

'Exactly,' Miguel agreed. 'After all, you sold it once, you could sell it again.'

Nobody laughed and Miguel looked away a little embarrassed.

'I was medically discharged after I was diagnosed with PTSD. Every loud noise felt like a bomb going off.' Simon grimaced. 'I couldn't walk down a busy street without thinking of the war. It got to the point where every day felt like a battlefield. I tried to hold down jobs, worked in a chocolate factory, but the smallest bang would set me off, throwing me straight back into the Gulf.'

'I'm sorry,' Ava said gently.

But Simon was lost in his story as he continued his retelling of the past. 'I turned away from everything and everyone I knew. Eventually I turned to drink, it was the only thing I had any enthusiasm for. My wife got fed up, she left me in the end. Took the kids.'

Simon looked up, his knuckles white from balling his hands into fists.

As Simon spoke, Ava couldn't help but feel a strange sense of connection. They had both been forced to confront their pasts and rebuild their lives – each in their own way, battling ghosts no one else could see.

'After that, everything unravelled,' Simon continued. 'All I wanted was money for booze. I started selling everything in the house. The telly, the furniture, the medal.' His eyes strayed warily to the box on the table. 'I didn't care how much I got for it, I just wanted money. John didn't want to sell the medal for me at first. But I told him I was adamant I didn't want it any more. Too many bad memories. Eventually John agreed, but asked me to keep in touch. This was before mobiles and emails so I gave him my address. He came looking for me one day when he'd sold the medal to give me my money. Couldn't find me and one of the neighbours told him the house had been repossessed and I'd last been seen sleeping near a retail park.'

'When I found him, I felt terrible,' John recalled, taking up the story, his face grave. 'Simon was a man of honour, he'd fought for his country. To see him in that state was shocking. I'd had a brother with PTSD. He'd served in the Crimean war, ended up almost suicidal, and I recognised the signs in Simon.'

'So John came to my rescue,' Simon continued. 'He offered me a job as a trainee dealer at his antiquities business.'

'More like dogsbody at first,' John chuckled.

'You gave me a home.'

'It was nothing,' John said, waving away the compliment. 'It was a couple of dilapidated rooms above the shop.'

'It was a home,' Simon insisted again. 'And a fresh start, and without you I'd never have got back on my feet. I'd forgotten about the medal. Then you got in touch, John knew it was mine straightaway but he wasn't sure whether to tell me or not.'

'But of course, he did,' Miguel put in.

'I did,' John confirmed. 'It was up to Simon what he wanted to do.'

'It was a shock,' Simon said. 'I'd moved on since I sold this medal. My kids are back in my life, I'm friends with my ex-wife, I've moved out of John's flat, I manage my PTSD and have a new relationship, but suddenly all those memories came flooding back. The war, my friends, the men we lost.' He closed his eyes and Ava could see that Simon was right back in the Gulf again. 'But I knew this had happened for a reason,' Simon continued, blinking his eyes open. 'A chance to face my past.' His hand strayed to the wooden box and he ran his fingers across it.

'How do you feel now?' Ava asked softly.

Simon smiled. 'This feels like a lifetime ago. I was worried that this medal would take me back to some very dark corners but actually I think I feel lighter for having it – it's a relief in a way. This medal felt like a burden back then, but now, it's a reminder, not just of the men I served with, but the very private battle I faced and survived. I think getting rid of it was probably part of this medal's journey.'

With that Simon snapped open the box, lifted the medal out and pressed it to his heart.

'I don't know what I'll do with it now,' he admitted, turning to look at Ava. 'Maybe one day, I'll pass it on. But that's for the future to decide. If nothing else, I can finally make my peace with the past, and that is priceless.'

Chapter Thirty-Four

The lunch with John and Simon had weighed on Ava's mind for weeks. She questioned whether contacting Simon was the right choice, knowing the medal stirred such conflicting feelings. Yet in the end, Simon had seemed genuinely pleased, perhaps finding peace with the past.

If only Ava could say the same. It was now the middle of April and she was still no closer to feeling better about Cassie. She kept replaying Simon's story. How had he managed to weather such wounds in his life and come out smiling? If only she had half his fortitude.

Reluctantly, she turned back to Jodie's training log. The recruit was still some way short of fulfilling the units that needed to be completed. It was a worry, not just for Jodie, but for the state of the fire station itself. Was it a sign that they weren't busy enough to need two stations in the city?

'You look happy,' Miguel said gruffly as he walked into the kitchen and found Ava hunched over the table frowning.

She sighed. 'Just thinking.'

'I won't ask what about,' Miguel said, glancing at Jodie's logbook. 'Anything I can help with?'

But before Ava could answer, the station tannoy began blaring. 'Mobilise. Mobilise,' rang through the station.

'Shout!' Jodie yelled as she hurtled down the pole, tip sheet in her hand.

Ava smiled. Despite the empty logbook, Jodie was blossoming.

'What is it?' Ava asked. She shimmied down the pole and into the muster bay, then stepped into her protective clothing in seconds.

'Hotel fire,' Jodie said excitedly. 'The one in Queen's Square.'

'Bacons?' Miguel exclaimed. 'Shit, that place is ancient. How bad?'

'Not sure,' Jodie said. 'This was all the information available.'

Ava felt Miguel's eyes on her.

'It's a major incident so I'll be up at the bridgehead with you. That all right?' he said quietly.

She gave him a brief nod of the head and Miguel was in the rig in seconds.

It was common knowledge around the station how much Ava hated hotel fires. Thankfully they were rare, but they always brought back terrible memories of the way Ava lost her parents. Now, as she clambered into the rig beside Big Stu and gave him a stiff smile, she promised herself that whatever happened, she was ready.

-

As they neared Bacons Hotel, thick plumes of black smoke soared into the sky, and Ava's pulse quickened. The engine rounded the corner, revealing flames licking the front and sides of the building.

A crew from Bath North were already on the scene, and Miguel headed straight for the bridgehead on the second floor to coordinate with the other station manager. Ava focused on her own watch. Adrenalin was coursing through her body but she didn't want to be treated any differently. This was a shout like any other, and it was down to her to manage the watch.

She turned to Blue Watch – Jodie had already teamed up with Emerson and Phil, leaving Ava to work with Big Stu.

'You three,' she pointed to Emerson, Phil and Jodie, 'get your breathing apparatus on.'

The trio did as instructed and Ava waited for further information from the bridgehead over the radio. The hotel believed they had evacuated all the guests but there were a few unaccounted for.

Ava gave a quick scan with the thermal-imaging camera at her side, but the heavy smoke made it impossible to rely on sight alone. They'd have to trust their instincts and training in the remaining rooms.

'We're working on the right of the building,' Ava instructed her watch. 'There are five floors, we'll cover the lower tiers, you do the top. You three go first.'

Wordlessly Emerson, Phil and Jodie marched swiftly towards their destination.

Meanwhile Ava took in the scene. Scores of firefighters were running about the building like ants while a large group of hotel residents gathered at the designated fire zone staring up at the blaze. Some were weeping and being consoled by other hotel guests, others were staring in disbelief at what was happening.

A hive of activity caught her attention. A pair of firefighters had brought down two men and a woman all in their mid-fifties. Their faces were ashen as they choked and spluttered, desperately trying to fill their lungs with fresh air. As paramedics led them to the back of the ambulance to check them over, she looked over at another group standing to the side by the staff entrance. All dressed in the hotel uniform of purple and black, she could see they were shaking and pointing to the eaves of the hotel. The manager was doing their best to appease their worries, but looked as concerned as the rest of her team.

Turning to look at the bridgehead she could just make out Miguel together with the group manager and the Bath North station manager, heads bent in discussion. Being a major incident, it was no surprise to see them out in full force. She knew they would be discussing strategies, the best way to ensure everyone got out alive.

Ava closed her eyes and for a second allowed herself to be transported back to the Portuguese island that had claimed her parents. Not for the first time, she wondered if her mum and dad had fought to leave, scratched at the door like rats trying to escape a sinking ship, or if they'd gone quietly, asleep in each other's arms.

'This isn't like the fire that took your parents,' Big Stu said quietly. Ava flinched, but when she looked at him, all she saw was kindness.

'I know.'

'Do you?' Big Stu pressed. He gestured to the blaze in front of them. 'You can sit this one out if you want to, Ava. Nobody would blame you, least of all me. Just be watch manager, you don't have to get involved.'

Could she really leave this to Big Stu? For a moment, all she wanted was to step back. But Ava had been a firefighter for over twenty years – she wasn't about to back down now.

Smiling gratefully at Big Stu, she nodded. 'I'm all right. I promise.'

'Okay,' Big Stu replied. 'But if you're not, that's okay too.'

Ava checked the telemetry screen, a digital display showing real-time data on her team's air supply. Jodie and Emerson's levels were dropping steadily, the green bars shrinking as they worked deeper inside the building. They had just a couple of minutes before they came out and then it was her and Big Stu's turn. As she waited, she scanned the area again. The creaking overhead wasn't a good sign. The fire had clearly weakened parts of the structure, and she didn't like the way some of the beams sagged.

'We'll need to keep an eye on the ceiling,' she called to Big Stu. 'If it starts coming down, we're out of there fast.'

When Jodie, Phil and Emerson emerged into the light, Ava picked up her breathing apparatus and Big Stu did the same.

'Upper floors are clear, but it's intense in there,' Jodie said, her cheeks pink from the heat. 'We cleared what we could.'

'Stairwell's heating up, watch your step,' Emerson warned, wiping the sweat from his brow.

'We're on it,' Big Stu said.

Ava gave a tight smile and together the two walked inside. Ava felt the wall of heat instantly hit her, sweat forming under her protective gear. The water-slick floors were treacherous, and the air was thick with smoke along with the acrid scent of burned fabric and chemicals.

Her mask filtered out most of it, but the metallic taste lingered in the back of her throat.

There was no light thanks to the debris that had blocked the windows, but it was possible to make out some signs of life. The smart speaker on the reception desk was untouched, while the jacket of a receptionist hung on the back of one of the chairs.

As the flames grew hotter, she realised there was a chance she could walk into this building and never come out again, that this fire could be the blaze that would finally claim her life. Hadn't she cheated death several times over in her life already?

She shook her head free of the unwelcome thoughts and carried on behind Stu to the floor they had been assigned.

'The fire inside the building is out now,' Miguel's voice burst into life over the radio. 'Just the outside for us to put out now. Concentrate on checking the floor for signs of life.'

'Copy,' Ava replied into her radio.

Wordlessly, the two firefighters made their way through the hotel rooms, using their shoes to stamp and sweep their way through each one, ensuring the area was safe and hazard free. The scene of devastation was much the same in every room: smoke-stained walls, sodden beds, some broken in two, wardrobes burnt to the ground and televisions hanging onto walls or smashed to bits on the floor. As Ava trampled carefully through the wreckage of each room, she felt her heart grow a little lighter with every step. There had been no casualties and no rescues needed. She checked her breathing apparatus gauge; there was just five minutes left. Soon she and Big Stu would be back out into the sunshine and away from this hellish mess.

Turning to look at her colleague, he gave her a thumbs-up and she could see that he was as relieved to leave the hotel as she was. There was something eerie about the place. Ava didn't know if it was the age of the building or its size, but there was a weird energy in the building that she would be glad to leave behind.

There was just one last room to check between them, and Ava gave the door a push and stepped inside. Carefully, but deftly with her left foot, she kicked the debris and stamped just as she had a million times before in her career. She glanced briefly over her shoulder, double-checking the exit route they'd need if things went wrong. The door was still clear, and the hallway behind her looked passable, at least for now.

But as she did so, she felt the wall beside her give way. Startled, she looked to her left just as the Georgian stone beside her came crashing down. She stepped back instinctively and reached for her radio, her voice sharp.

'Bridgehead, this is Ava. We've got a partial collapse on the left wing. Be advised it's unstable inside.'

Fuelled by adrenaline, Ava whipped around, searching for Stu. A sharp crack split the air and then above her, the ceiling gave way. She felt a wave of horror as she saw a large air conditioning unit coming away from the wall.

'Stu!' Ava shouted, spinning around, but he was gone. Panic surged, where was he? She took a step back into the room, but debris scattered beneath her feet, throwing her off balance as the unit hurtled towards her.

'Fuuuuuuuuuuck,' she screamed, all the while trying to wrench her foot free from the twisted debris, but it was wedged tight.

And then, with a deafening ripping noise, the screech of metal tore through the air. Ava lunged, her heart pounding, but the heavy unit plummeted straight towards her, too fast to avoid.

–

Ava's initial sensation was a pounding in her head, swiftly followed by a suffocating weight pinning her down. She struggled against the heavy mass pressing on her chest and instinctively felt around for anything to use as leverage. But the air conditioning unit wouldn't budge.

Stuck in a hotel, whilst flames burned all around her, she sunk her head back onto the ground. Ava reminded herself of her training, focusing on her breathing and trying to slow her rapid breaths. She knew that getting upset wouldn't help, but no matter how hard she tried to remain rational she couldn't. Images of her parents and their last moments flooded into her mind. Had they felt this frightened as they faced death? Was her fate the same as her parents?

A soft, almost imperceptible whimper escaped from her lips as she thought about her life and all the things she hadn't achieved. She hadn't been to Australia or learned a second language. She hadn't hiked Scafell Pike, she wasn't a mum, and most despairingly of all she hadn't made up with Cassie.

In the darkness Ava's imagination went into overdrive. Was this how it was going to end for her? With a lifetime full of regrets?

'Ava,' Big Stu's voice cut through the darkness.

'Stu,' she croaked.

'Bloody hell!' he cried. 'Me and Miguel have been looking all over for you. We didn't see you because of this bloody air con unit.'

Flicking on his pocket torch Ava winced, blinded by the sudden light.

She let out a gasp of surprise.

'You all right?' Big Stu asked concerned.

'I can't move,' she croaked.

'I can see that,' Big Stu replied, then reached for his radio.

'Miguel, I got her. Give us a hand mate.'

The station manager arrived within seconds, ignoring protocol to look for her. One look at his grave expression told Ava how serious the situation was. With a shared nod, the two men got to work, communicating quickly and efficiently to shift the air conditioning unit. Within seconds she was free, but Ava's ordeal was far from over, as she tried to stand and found her legs wouldn't hold her.

'Don't try and move,' Miguel said warningly.

'I can't stay here,' Ava rasped in between panicked breaths. 'Please.'

Big Stu locked eyes with her and a flicker of understanding passed across his features.

'We're getting her out now,' he said decisively.

Reluctantly, Miguel took Ava's legs and Big Stu held her arms. Before lifting, they quickly checked her breathing apparatus, ensuring her mask was secure and her air supply intact. As gently as possible, the two men walked through the rubble, taking care with every step not to cause more injury.

Ava could see the worry on Miguel's face as they made their way across the room. But even though Ava was in agony, and it went against all her training, she couldn't bear to stay a moment longer in the hotel fire. They were outside in minutes, and the moment Ava saw the sunshine-flooded Bath skies, relief rushed through her. No matter what her injuries, she had lived long enough to see the outside world once more. She wasn't going to end her days alone and in the darkness. Once again, her mind strayed to her parents. Had she been their last thought, in the way they had been hers? Would they have risked life and limb to see her one last time? Or had their guardian angel never showed up, not affording them the opportunity to fight for life once more?

Doing her best not to cry, she saw the outline of an ambulance and Gayle, the paramedic who had looked after her so well at the estate fire, standing in wait.

'Not you again,' she said cheerfully.

'Afraid so.'

'You got a death wish or something?' Gayle clucked, helping Miguel and Big Stu transfer her fluidly onto the stretcher.

'I'm beginning to wonder that myself,' Miguel said, his lips pressed into a thin, tight line.

Ava turned to look at him, astonished to see he was so upset.

'You can talk all right then?' Gayle asked as she began to perform a cursory exam.

'I think so,' Ava rasped over Big Stu's cough.

Gayle frowned at Miguel and Big Stu. 'You two want looking at as well. I don't want you going in there doing any more heroics. It's bad enough this one keeps gambling with her life, never mind you two joining in.'

'I'm all right—' Big Stu began, only for Gayle to cut him off.

'Ambulance next to me. Now,' she said in a tone that brooked no argument.

Shuffling off towards the neighbouring vehicle, Miguel gave Ava a comforting smile. Gratitude and love went out to her boss and friend. In all the years they had looked out for one another, worked together, this was above and beyond. He and Big Stu had risked their lives to save her in an act of generosity and kindness. It was something she would never forget.

'Thank you,' she mouthed, as Gayle wheeled her into the back of the ambulance.

As the door slammed shut, Ava's eyes grew heavy. And for the second time that day she felt the darkness close in on her.

Chapter Thirty-Five

'Visitor for you.'

The nurse swept back the curtain that hid Ava's hospital bed from the rest of the ward and gave her a warm smile. Ava sat up in bed and tried to look cheerful, but it was tough. Her head was still sore and she tired easily.

It was no wonder. The air conditioning unit had clipped the side of Ava's helmet before slamming against her chest, her helmet absorbing the brunt of the blow. At the hospital, doctors discovered that although Ava hadn't suffered any internal injuries as Miguel had first feared, she had sustained a depressed skull fracture and needed an operation straightaway. Thankfully, the surgery had been minor and had gone well. Ava was expected to make a full recovery in about three months.

It had now been a week since the surgery, and she was starting to feel better. So much so, she was due to be discharged the following day. The doctors had wanted to monitor her for any lingering neurological symptoms like headaches or dizziness, and while her recovery seemed positive, Ava knew the road ahead would be slow.

Miguel had been to see her the previous day and told her that in two weeks, she could start light duties at headquarters while she continued to heal. After three months and following a full medical assessment, she could return to the fire station and resume her normal role as watch manager.

Ava had been disappointed but knew it was for the best, that she needed time if she was going to heal and get back to a normal life, though it still felt like a bitter pill to swallow.

Steve appeared from behind the overly bright nurse and she was delighted to see his hands were full.

'Oooh chocolate,' she said, almost snatching the bar of Dairy Milk from his hand.

'And a voucher for a new book,' he said brandishing her e-reader. 'I didn't want to pick you something as I got it so wrong last time.'

They both shuddered at the memory of the Christmas before last when Steve had bought Ava one of the best-sellers about a gruesome serial killer who burned his victims. She had started reading it that morning but by lunchtime was in tears and could hardly touch her roast dinner, Steve protesting all the way he thought she would enjoy it because it was about fires!

'Thank you,' was all she said now.

Putting the chocolate and voucher to one side, she looked at her husband as he sat opposite her.

'Any news?' she asked hopefully.

She had only been in hospital just over a week but it already felt as if she had been cut off from society for a lifetime.

Steve frowned as he thought for a moment.

'Our adoption home visit has been postponed. I explained the situation and asked if they could delay it until you were feeling stronger. They were really under-standing about it. Nikki said it was best to wait until you're fully ready, rather than rush anything.'

Ava's face fell. 'You did what?'

'It's for the best, sweetheart,' Steve said. 'Come on, let's get you well first.'

Ava nodded miserably, knowing he was right.

'What did they say?'

'They were very supportive and understanding,' Steve said. 'We've already been assigned a case worker named Pru.' He rolled his eyes and grinned. 'She's very jolly hockey sticks. Reckoned you were "darned plucky".' He made air quotes with his fingers.

Ava laughed. She liked the sound of Pru already.

'Not been called that before.'

'And hopefully you won't be again,' Steve said leaning back in the hard upright chair next to Ava's bed. 'So are you ready to come home tomorrow?'

Ava had never felt more ready. 'I can't wait.'

'But you're not going back to work until next week at least,' Steve warned.

'I know.' Ava rolled her eyes. 'But I'm going to need something to do to keep me occupied.'

'Agreed,' Steve said. 'It's called rest.' He reached for Ava's chocolate bar and tore off the wrapper, snapping off a piece for himself and her. She took it and allowed the sweetness to melt inside her mouth as she thought.

'I suppose I could sort out the bottom of the garden,' she mused. 'And Monkey needs his biannual check at the vet. Oh, and if I was really smart, I could get a load of batch cooking done for when I go back to work.'

'Or you could just rest, Ava,' Steve cried in frustration.

'Good luck getting that one to do as you say,' a voice blurted.

Ava and Steve looked up.

There at the bottom of the bed, clutching a houseplant, was Cassie.

Ava's jaw dropped open in shock. Cassie? She didn't even know if Cassie knew what had happened to her, never mind cared. What was she doing here?

'Er, have a seat, Cass,' Steve said getting to his feet.

'Thanks.' She took the chair, looking awkward as she sat down.

Ava's heart went out to her. It would have taken Cassie a lot to come here.

'I heard about the fire,' Cassie whispered. 'I had to see you.'

Ava nodded. She hardly dared breathe. What did Cassie's visit mean?

'Thank you,' she managed. 'That means a lot.'

Steve shuffled awkwardly at the foot of Ava's bed.

'I'll just nip to the canteen, I think. Get a coffee. You want anything Cassie?' He jerked his thumb in the direction of the doorway.

Cassie shook her head. 'I'm not staying long.'

'Okay. See you later.'

As Steve disappeared, Cassie set the plant on Ava's beside table and leaned forward in her chair.

'I was worried about you, I couldn't believe it when I heard.'

Ava said nothing, she felt as if it would take too much energy to say everything that was in her heart. Of how her biggest regret if she had died would have been that she would have gone to her grave having never made things right with her friend.

'I'm okay,' was all she could muster.

Cassie reached for Ava's hand and squeezed it firmly.

'I've missed you so much.'

'Me too,' Ava whispered.

The tears that had been pooling in her eyes were now cascading down her face, but this time, they weren't just for the hurt. They were for the relief that, despite everything, she hadn't lost her best friend forever.

She wiped them away with the back of her free hand, not wanting to break the connection with Cassie. She had thought that things were over between them, that she would never enjoy this simple pleasure of seeing her ever again; she didn't ever want to let her friend go.

'I overreacted,' Cassie whispered, her voice catching slightly. 'I should have understood what you were trying to do, Ava. You'd been through so much – that trip to Ireland brought up all kinds of feelings, of course it clouded your judgement. I should've seen that.'

Ava shook her head. 'No. It's my fault. You were right, I should never have interfered – I don't know what possessed me.'

'Grief,' Cassie said softly. 'I'm sorry, Ava, the last thing you needed was me turning my back on you.'

'I deserved it,' Ava said miserably.

'You didn't. You deserved a row, and you deserved me tearing strips off you, but not being cut out my life. If nothing else, I only caused myself pain!' Cassie laughed and then squeezed Ava's hand again. 'I've been so stupid, when I heard about the fire… I thought I'd lost you. I didn't know what I'd do without you. It hit me how stupid I'd been.'

Ava clamped her free hand over her friend's.

'I'm just glad you're here.'

'Me too.'

With that the two women fell on each other, wrapping each other up in a hug that neither one wanted to end.

Eventually the pair pulled away and Cassie looked at Ava with affection in her eyes.

'How's the adoption going?' Cassie asked brightly.

'Fine,' Ava said flatly. 'Or at least it was until Steve cancelled the home visit next week.'

'Probably best, Ava,' Cassie said. 'You need to make a good impression and I hope it might give me a chance to make amends. I should have written you that reference to the adoption panel. I'm sorry I didn't, that was childish of me.'

'It doesn't matter,' Ava replied. 'The way things were between us we should never have asked.'

'You were right to ask,' Cassie insisted. 'I should have put our differences aside and got myself together. It was unforgivable of me. If for no other reason than you'd be a great mum, proper helicopter parent.'

'You think?' Ava asked in amusement.

'I know!' Cassie said. 'And that's what a kid being adopted will want. They've had enough trauma in their lives, enough independence. They need someone to swoop in and take charge and that's what you'll do. I'm only sorry I might have deprived a child of having you as their parent, because that's a terrible thing to have done.'

'It's okay,' Ava replied, sinking her head back onto the hospital pillow. 'I just wish I hadn't been injured. I'm worried the adoption people will think I'm too reckless to take on a child.'

'They won't think that,' Cassie scolded. 'They'll think you're brave, just like I do.'

At that Ava smiled wryly. 'I don't feel very brave.'

'You, Ava Ryan, saved my son single-handedly. You faced a hotel fire even though something similar killed your own parents. You're the bravest woman I know –

you need to own that,' Cassie said. 'Because your found family will make sure you do.'

The words hung in the air as each woman allowed themselves to feel the pain and loss they'd experienced in the last few weeks. Each of them suffering without the other. As the spring sunshine streamed through the ward window, Ava caught sight of the locket that hung around Cassie's neck.

'I'd never have taken this off, no matter how much I thought I hated you,' Cassie said softly, catching Ava's glance. 'We might not be related by blood Aves, but you're my sister in every way that counts, always have been, always will be, this locket is testament to that.'

Chapter Thirty-Six

Ava reached instinctively for her winter coat, the one she'd relied on through the long, bitter months. As her fingers brushed the wool, she hesitated, realising the early May morning sun streaming through the window made it unnecessary. Spring had arrived, and with it, a welcome warmth that felt almost foreign, much like her current job. For the past two days Ava had headed to the station as normal, only to get halfway down the road and realise she was heading to the wrong place.

This morning, finally, she remembered where she was meant to be going and was delighted to have done so. She could only put it down to the fact she was feeling more like her old self. Life felt calmer, though in truth she hated being chained to the office on light duties.

'It's not forever,' Miguel promised her later that morning when he came to visit headquarters for a meeting.

'I know, but I wasn't built to push paper,' Ava grumbled, as she shoved a sheaf of papers away with one finger.

Miguel sighed. 'Ava, you were seriously hurt. You need to take your recovery seriously and this is part of that recovery.'

'I know.' Ava folded her arms. She felt like a petulant teenager.

'Want to go for a coffee?' Miguel asked. 'I've got something I need to talk to you about.'

'Okay.'

They headed towards the cafe at the corner of the park and ordered two Americanos.

'What was your meeting about? The redundancies?' Ava asked as she sipped her drink, fully aware that the middle of May was just days away. Miguel had to make his mind up.

'Sort of,' Miguel said. He sighed and stopped by a bench under a large oak tree. 'I've partially solved the redundancy problem.'

'Oh?' Ava asked taking a sip of her coffee.

'I'm leaving,' Miguel said bluntly.

Ava dropped her coffee, the hot liquid seeping across the hard ground but she didn't care. Miguel couldn't be serious. The fire service was in his blood. She looked at his face, the grey shadows under his eyes that he'd been sporting over the last few weeks had disappeared and he had a sparkle in his eye Ava hadn't seen for some time.

'You're joking!' she spluttered.

'I've been thinking about it for a while,' Miguel admitted. 'But when I saw you under that air conditioning unit… it just clicked. I can't keep doing this. Watching you that day, I realised I didn't want that to be me. It was the final push. I'm forty-six, Ava. There's more to life. There's people, there's family, there's hobbies and holidays. You nearly died, and it made me look at things differently. I want to do something new while I'm still young enough to enjoy it.'

The ground beneath Ava's feet began to shift. This was all so out of the blue.

'I don't know what to say,' she said at last, her voice barely above a whisper. 'I can't believe you're really leaving.'

Miguel wrapped an arm around her shoulders. 'Say you're happy for me. I'm going to travel the world, me and Xav are going to spend time together, I'm going to take up pottery!'

Ava forced a smile, but the thought of Miguel leaving filled her with an unexpected sadness. He had been her anchor at the station, the steady force in a job that often left her feeling off-balance. Without him, what would her days look like? The station wouldn't be the same, and the weight of that realisation made her chest tighten, but now wasn't the time to say it.

'Now I know you're taking the piss,' Ava said, nestling into her friend's shoulder. 'I'll miss you.'

'You'll still see me!' He kissed the top of her head and let her go.

But Ava could already feel the distance between them grow as they sat together. Silence descended across the pair of them, each lost in their own worlds.

Leaning back into the bench, Ava watched the trees sway gently in the spring breeze. The last time she and Miguel had gone for a walk in this park the branches had been bare, now they were lush and green. Change happened whether you wanted it to or not.

'I'm pleased for you,' she said at last.

Turning to him, she caught the surprise in Miguel's features.

'Thank you,' he said slowly.

'I mean it,' she said. 'You've given so much of your life to the service. You deserve a break.'

'Well, so have you,' Miguel said softly. 'But it doesn't seem to have affected you in the same way. I feel ground down by it all. Every day we're surrounded by disaster. As firefighters, we're always there for someone's worst day of their lives. I don't want that any more.'

Ava nodded, understanding. There was always a tipping point for firefighters – Ava had seen it happen time and time again, and she knew she would see it again. She just never expected it to happen to Miguel.

'Have you thought any more about leaving?' Miguel asked now.

Ava shook her head. 'I know I suggested it a few weeks back but lying in that hospital bed work was all I could think about.'

'But what about when you have kids?' he asked.

Ava sighed. 'Then they'll have a mother with a passion.'

'Touché.' Miguel laughed.

'It's my world,' Ava said softly.

'I thought it was mine too.' He got to his feet, tossed his empty cup in the nearby bin. Ava joined him, and together they fell into step, side by side towards headquarters.

'I'm sorry to see you go,' Ava said. 'Life won't be the same without you.'

'Change isn't a bad thing. You can still love something and decide to let it go.' He looked at her.

'What do you mean?'

'I mean that when I joined, I loved the fire service. But over the past year I've realised there is another life out there, other challenges, other priorities that will satisfy me, probably more than firefighting will. If you'd told me I'd give it up at forty-six when I joined I'd have laughed.'

'Me too,' Ava quipped. 'I thought once you got to forty, you were old, decrepit and irrelevant.'

'Bit like how Jodie feels about us now,' Miguel teased.

'Something like that.' Ava laughed.

It felt good to smile and lighten the mood.

'The point is, that we all change, including you.'

She looked at him in surprise. 'I haven't changed.'

'You have. Since Dublin. You're stronger somehow.' He chuckled softly under his breath. 'As for me, I didn't see any of this coming but it feels right. This is my next chapter and I'm ready for it.'

Ava felt her heart swell with love and when they reached the building, Miguel pulled her into his arms and hugged her tight.

'This isn't the end,' he whispered into her ear. 'It's the start of something new.'

Ava nodded, but as Miguel turned to walk away and she watched him go, she felt restless, her mind full of questions she didn't yet have the courage to ask.

–

Ava couldn't stop thinking about Miguel's decision to leave and had started questioning if she would ever feel the same way. She was coming up to twenty-two years of service and wondered if it was because she was still a firefighter, albeit a watch manager, that made a difference.

Miguel was bogged down in decisions, sometimes life-and-death decisions. Ava had never done that, not in the same way.

Now, as she finished her shift, she packed up her bag and prepared to head home.

'You off?' Colleen poked her head around the door, interrupting Ava's thoughts.

'Yes,' she said. 'It's our adoption home visit tomorrow so I'm working a half shift to make sure we're ready.'

'Of course, good luck.' Colleen nodded in approval.

As Ava walked outside, she was pleased to feel her life beginning to return to normal. The home visit was the first thing on that list to get out of the way, and then in another six weeks she would be declared well enough to have made a full recovery and would be returning to the fire station – it couldn't come a day too soon. Paperwork was valid, useful and needed but Ava couldn't wait to be amongst the cut and thrust of day-to-day fire work. Even if that sometimes meant doing nothing more than memorising road maps and helping Big Stu make a less than terrible spaghetti bolognese.

She had almost reached the bottom of the headquarters car park when she heard footsteps hastening towards her. Ava turned around and saw Colleen was almost upon her.

'Everything all right?' she asked in surprise.

'Fine,' she said. 'I just want to ask you something, away from prying eyes.'

'Go on,' Ava encouraged even as her heart sank. Was Colleen about to tell her she couldn't go back to the fire station she loved?

'Don't worry, you'll be out of headquarters soon enough,' she grinned, correctly guessing what she was worried about. 'I want to talk to you about Miguel.'

'Oh?' Her heart quickened with hope. Perhaps this meant he wasn't leaving? Had there been a change of plans?

'I know Miguel has told you his plans to leave but I wondered if you'd ever given any thought to stepping up as station manager?'

'Me?' Ava asked in surprise. 'No. Why?'

Colleen looked slightly exasperated at the question.

'Because everyone at headquarters thinks you would be perfectly placed to take over. You'd have to apply of course, go through the process, and of course Miguel isn't leaving for six months, but I can tell you that your application would be looked upon very favourably.'

Ava's head spun. She already felt as if she couldn't keep on top of things in her life. After so many hurdles, the adoption home visit was tomorrow. She and Steve had agreed to take the afternoon off to blitz the house and get everything together before Pru the social worker came round. Now she was being asked to step into her old friend's shoes. For a job she didn't think she wanted.

'That's a lot to think about,' she said honestly. 'Can I take some time?'

'Of course,' Colleen replied, her wide, open face brimming with understanding. 'We all know you've been through a tough time, but everyone thinks very highly of you, not just at your station, but here at headquarters as well.'

Ava was lost for words. 'Thank you,' was all she could manage.

With that, she got into her car and drove away, aware of Colleen watching her in bemusement. Making her way along the A-roads, her mind was full. So much so she almost went straight through a red light, only just managing to hit the brakes in time. As she waited at the traffic light, her heart raced with adrenaline thinking of what might have been. And as she did so, something clicked. If there was one thing she'd learned in life it was that you never knew what was around the corner. You could do your best, make plans, but ultimately chance played a huge part so what was the sense in worrying? All you could do was cope with whatever was thrown at you as best you could. If there was one thing she had learned in the past few weeks it was that.

Chapter Thirty-Seven

Just over forty minutes later she walked through the door of her home to find Steve frantically scrubbing the oven.

'What on earth are you doing?' she asked.

'Everything's got to be clean, Ava,' Steve blurted in a panicked tone. 'We don't want the social worker thinking we've got a dirty home, we didn't get around to this yesterday.'

She walked up behind him and took the Mr Muscle from his hands. Pulling him gently away from the oven she wrapped her arms around her husband's middle.

'Our home is more than clean. We've got more than enough space, we've got everything a kid needs,' she whispered.

'But are you sure?' Steve looked frantically around the kitchen. 'What if the house is just an excuse. Maybe they'll meet us and say we're not good enough, what then?'

Ava shook her head. 'Not going to happen. We're just who they want.' She gestured to the oven. 'Though they might question why you're cleaning the oven by hand when it's self-cleaning.'

Steve looked at the oven in surprise. 'It is?'

'Yes.' She laughed and pulled him over towards the kitchen island. Setting him down on one of the bar stools, she pulled two beers from the fridge and handed him one.

'We can't drink beer,' he spluttered.

'We can and we should,' Ava said, pulling the tops off each. 'Besides, they're alcohol free.' She took a long hard pull on the bottle, enjoying the cooling effect as it travelled down her throat. 'You need to relax. And so do I, come to that. All we need to do is create a warm, pleasant space where a kid would feel welcome.'

'It doesn't feel like enough,' Steve said. He took a gulp then started picking the label off his bottle.

'It has to be enough,' Ava said firmly. 'We've got a lot to offer a child, but panic isn't one of them.'

Steve looked at her with suspicion in his eyes.

'Why are you so calm? You've been stressing about this for weeks.'

'I know. But I've realised that you can't plan for everything. We're good people, Steve. We're well adjusted, calm, confident, solvent with a lot of love to give. If the social worker can't see that then I don't know what else we can do. I do know she's not going to decide on whether we get a kid or not based on if our oven is clean.' Ava smiled at her husband, leaned over and kissed him. 'We have to be enough Steve.'

Their eyes met and she felt a rush of love for the man that had been by her side for almost thirty years. Steve was enough, always had been. She had been foolish not to realise that.

He pulled her into his arms and in that one simple form of human affection, Ava felt the pain of the miscarriages, the torture of the failed IVF, all slide away. Cassie had been right, Ava realised, family came in all forms and if she and Steve were only ever meant to be family to each other then she knew she would have done pretty well in life.

-

Ava watched Steve hand round the plate of biscuits, his hand shaking as he did so.

'We've got two types,' he said nervously. 'Chocolate digestives and bourbons.'

Pru smiled and shook her head. 'Thanks but no thanks. Too much sugar.'

'Oh, absolutely.' Steve snatched the plate away and put it behind the sofa as if it was on fire. 'We don't eat much sugar either, do we, Ava? I mean we certainly wouldn't encourage any child that was placed with us to eat sugar.'

'That'll be a tough one,' Pru laughed. She pulled out her pen and started making notes on a pad with a large unicorn on the front of it. 'In my experience kids love sugar, if you tell them they can't eat chocolate in your house, they might not want to move in.'

Steve stared at Pru open-mouthed in shock, but Ava caught the glint of humour in the social worker's eye and laughed.

'She's teasing, Steve.' Ava nudged her husband playfully in the ribs.

'Oh.' Steve plastered on a fake smile and tried to relax. 'Course, sorry, bit on edge.'

Pru put her pen down and looked up at the two of them.

'I'm on your side. I want to help you find your family – you don't have to put on airs and graces with me, you don't have to pretend to be something you're not and you don't have to pretend you don't eat sugar. The only reason I say no is because I see a lot of people and they all want to give me biscuits. If I said yes to them all I'd be the size of a double-decker bus. Best to leave it in my experience.'

'Well then you won't mind if I have a couple,' Ava said reaching for the plate behind her husband. 'I've not been back from work long and I'm starving.'

'Be my guest.' Pru chuckled before turning back to her notepad, and Ava felt Steve relax.

She had to admit Pru was a breath of fresh air, so much nicer than she had anticipated. Tall, slim, with a no-nonsense attitude and ready sense of humour, Ava felt at ease in her company.

'So, Steve you run your own company and Ava you're a firefighter? How exciting for you both!' Recognition dawned on Pru's face as she looked at Ava. 'Are you the firefighter that was in the papers for rescuing that little boy last year from the estate?'

Ava quickly swallowed her mouthful of biscuit. 'We don't usually do stuff like that. It was very unusual.'

Pru nodded. 'Sounded very dangerous.'

'As Ava says, it's not something she does very often,' Steve put in, looking a little flustered.

'I hope not, for Ava's sake. Being a firefighter must be terrifying enough without making unusual saves a daily thing.'

Pru smiled again and Ava really did believe she was on their side.

'But Ava's working in the office now,' Steve said.

'Oh?' Pru looked at Ava expectantly.

'It's just temporary,' Ava said. 'I had an accident a little while ago. I'm on light duties for a while.'

'But it could be permanent, it's something you're thinking about, isn't it?' Steve said desperately.

Ava looked at him perplexed. 'No,' she said slowly. 'I can't stand paper-pushing, you know that. In fact, I've been asked if I want Miguel's job when he leaves.'

'Miguel is…?' Pru asked.

'Miguel is Ava's boss, he's station manager,' Steve said desperately.

'What a positive role model you'd be, Ava,' Pru said smoothly. 'Someone that puts the needs of others above your own, I'd say that's a jolly fine example for any kid. And now a promotion!'

Pru looked so impressed Ava found she felt a swell of pride.

'Have to say I think this will go down very well with the panel.' Pru winked again at Ava before she turned back to Steve. 'If Ava wants to be promoted then that's wonderful, if she doesn't that's also wonderful. You both strike me as a very loving couple that has everything a child could ever want.'

'Really?' Steve's shoulders dropped an inch.

'Really,' Pru promised. 'Now relax and let me just check the house out, make sure there are no death traps and then I've got enough for my report.'

'Steve's a bit worried about the cleanliness of our oven,' Ava giggled through a mouthful of biscuit.

Pru stood up, looked across at the oven and shuddered.

'I can see I've spotted my first death trap.'

'No, it's not like that,' Steve said leaping to his feet as both women giggled.

Realising he'd been had, he exhaled noisily in relief.

'Looks as clean as a pin to me,' Pru said sweeping past them. 'And I say that as someone who keeps jumpers in their oven.'

'You don't cook?' Steve asked aghast, following her through the house.

'Good grief, no,' Pru exclaimed. 'I'd be lost without the Indian takeaway on the corner of my street.'

An hour later, Pru had left with a warm smile and all the information she needed, assuring them they were well prepared for the next step: the adoption panel. Her easy confidence put Ava and Steve at ease, though Ava couldn't shake the flicker of nerves she felt whenever she thought about facing the panel. She knew they had done everything right, but there was always that niggling doubt. What if they weren't enough?

As Steve shut the door he breathed a sigh of relief. Reaching for Ava's hand, he guided her into the kitchen and pulled her towards him.

'Well that went okay, didn't it?' he asked.

'If you don't count how neurotic you were, then yeah.'

'Oi!' Steve prodded her in the ribs. 'I was nervous.'

'Yeah, we got that,' Ava said gently.

Steve sighed. 'I'm sorry. I can be a nob sometimes.'

'Sometimes?' Ava teased, earning herself a growl from her husband.

'I was just really worried about today.'

'I know,' Ava whispered. 'But Pru seems lovely.'

'She does,' Steve agreed. 'She must think I'm nuts.'

Ava smiled, her head beginning to throb. She was almost back to normal but the bumps and bruises she had endured from the hotel fire still troubled her when she was anxious.

'I imagine she sees it a lot.'

Pulling away from her, Steve reached into the fridge and helped himself to two beers, this time alcoholic. He passed one to Ava.

'Are you seriously thinking about the promotion?' Steve asked, his tone light but edged with curiosity.

Ava paused, twisting off the bottle top slowly. The question lingered – was she? 'I think I am,' she said slowly. 'When Miguel told me he was leaving, I was too shocked to even think about the future. But people change, life moves on.'

She took a swig from her beer. She felt she'd earned the precious nectar slipping down her throat.

'I think I'm ready for the next step.'

Steve leaned against the fridge and cocked his head to one side as he regarded her.

'I think you are, too.' He raised his beer with a soft smile. 'To you, Ava, here's to whatever comes next.'

She smiled and held her own beer aloft.

'To both of us and the new beginnings we deserve.'

Chapter Thirty-Eight

It was July when Ava walked back into Bath City Fire Station with a spring in her step. She couldn't help feeling as if all was right with the world. After a couple of weeks' break following her time at headquarters, today marked the start of her return to her real job. And as if to further prove she was on the right path, the sun was shining and Big Stu had even brought her a coffee and welcome-back muffin from the bakery around the corner.

'You shouldn't have,' she said kissing his cheek.

He reddened, looking embarrassed as he waved her affections away.

'It was nothing,' he said, then looked thoughtful, 'though by rights, you should have brought cakes. It's tradition when someone starts a job.'

'I haven't started a job, I've been doing this for years,' Ava said.

She took a bite of the muffin and sank down into her favourite chair in the break room. It was good to be back.

'I think he means *my* job,' Miguel said, as he swept into the room.

'Well, look at you,' Ava marvelled. 'You look about ten years younger since you handed your notice in.'

She wondered if she could ever feel the same peace when her day came.

Miguel grinned. 'That mean you're getting ready to look ten years older?'

'Haha!' Ava said as she spat muffin crumbs at him. 'Anyway, how is my promotion common knowledge already? I only told Colleen I'd go for your job when I got back off holiday yesterday.'

'Subject to appropriate interview,' Miguel said, raising an eyebrow. 'We all know procedure must be followed.'

'Yeah, yeah,' Big Stu said. He flicked on the kettle and reached for the pound cake he'd bought earlier that morning. 'We all know that's a formality. Ava's getting the job just as she should.'

Ava chuckled, but inside, she knew that even a formality required her to play by the book. There would still be an interview, an official process to go through. And as much as her colleagues believed the job was hers, Ava wasn't one to take anything for granted. She'd have to prepare and prove she could balance command with everything else life was about to throw at her.

'Too right,' a voice agreed.

Ava turned around and saw Cassie standing in the doorway of the break room with a huge box of chocolates in her hand.

Cassie enveloped Ava in a hug. 'How does it feel to be back?'

'Fine, I think,' Ava replied, her voice muffled as she spoke into Cassie's hair. That familiar scent of CK One and baked beans already making her nostalgic for simpler times. 'What are you doing here?'

Cassie handed her the chocolates as she pulled away.

'For you. To say welcome back and good luck.'

'Thank you.' Ava was touched.

Although she and Cassie had made up, things weren't quite the same as they had been before their fallout. They were taking things slowly. They'd had lunch a couple of times and she and Dylan had been out to the cinema when Cassie needed a last-minute babysitter. Cassie had texted as well after the adoption home visit, asking how it had gone, but something had shifted between them.

Ava supposed it was understandable. There were hurt feelings on both sides, but to see Cassie now, recognising what a momentous day this was for her, felt wonderful. She gave Cassie a warm smile as she opened the chocolates and began handing them around.

'Long way for you to come today,' she said.

'Cassie's not just here to wish you luck,' Miguel pointed out. 'She's here to discuss the last few stages of the party tonight.'

Ava inwardly groaned. She had been so caught up in her own world she had totally forgotten about the estate party.

'Of course,' she said easily now. She didn't want to let her friends know how such an important event had slipped her mind.

'It's all right, I'd have forgotten too if I'd gone through everything you have,' Cassie said generously.

Ava grimaced while Miguel chuckled.

'You're more forgiving than me,' he said. Then, clapping his hands together, he looked at them expectantly. 'Shall we?'

Ava followed them both to the meeting room next door. She felt nervous suddenly, sensing a change in the atmosphere. When she took a seat at the table and Miguel and Cassie continued to gaze at her, she knew she was right.

'What?' she asked, rubbing her chin wondering if she had that morning's porridge on it.

'Thought you might like to take the meeting,' Miguel said casually. 'Seeing as this is what you'll be doing in a few months.'

'Eh?' Nerves suddenly crashed through her stomach. This wasn't what she had been anticipating at all. She wasn't ready for this, surely Miguel was joking. But judging by the smile on his face, which she could see now wasn't jeering but was encouraging, happy, she could tell he was serious.

'All right,' she said slowly.

She picked up the binder that lay on the table in front of her. So many improvements, so much that the estate had got right. It seemed fairly straightforward, nothing that they wouldn't do for any other new or renovated building.

Snapping the folder shut she beamed at them both.

'So, I recommend a general fire safety talk to all the residents?' Ava suggested. 'Now the community centre is ready, perhaps we could do it before the party if there's time?'

'Good idea,' Miguel nodded his approval. 'We won't need much to get set up and I think everyone will be so happy to get back to their homes they won't need much from us.'

'It's been wonderful welcoming everyone back, I have to say.' Cassie reached for a biscuit from the plate in the middle of the table. 'Though I've been so busy, I've had to put poor Dylan back in breakfast club at his school for a couple of days a week. He's not impressed.'

Miguel and Ava let out wry laughs.

Cassie beamed in between bites of her bourbon and Ava felt a flood of relief. The fact Cassie was here, eating biscuits, was surely a sign that things between them would be back to normal soon. A natural cynic, Ava usually struggled with positivity, but recently she'd found it came more and more easily to her.

After their home visit with Pru, the adoption panel decision hung over their heads like a final test. They felt they'd done well at the panel last week, with Steve answering questions about their IVF journey and hopes for a child with quiet determination. But now they had to wait for the official decision.

She'd also kept in regular contact with Maeve since that first text, which had been a surprise.

They now routinely checked in on one another, and when Ava had been in hospital, Maeve had sent her a get well card and wished her a quick recovery.

It was nice knowing that someone over on the Emerald Isle was thinking well of her. And if she was honest, Ava liked knowing Maeve, who had been so kind to her when she was born was still watching over her now.

Work was still a bit of an issue. The thought of taking over from her friend still left Ava feeling conflicted. The only consolation to it all was that Miguel seemed lighter.

In his heart, Ava could see that he had already left the fire station and was more than ready for a new adventure. In fact, only that morning Xav had driven him to work, ten minutes late in a brand new sports car.

'So, can I take you out to lunch?' Cassie asked, interrupting Ava's reverie.

Startled, the firefighter came back to the present.

'Oh god, I'd love to, but I can't,' Ava said quickly. 'Me and Steve are actually going to an adoption workshop this afternoon. It's sort of a picnic in the park with other potential adoptive parents. A chance to meet people going through the same thing, chat through experiences and questions.'

She paused, wondering if she sounded too casual. It wasn't just a picnic, after all. This was the next step in their journey, and the idea of getting one step closer to their family made her heart race.

Miguel and Cassie's eyes widened in surprise.

'That sounds heavy,' Miguel remarked.

Cassie looked at him sharply. 'And also lovely.'

Once again Ava felt a flush of pleasure her friend had come to her aid.

Cassie got to her feet and threw her arms open for a hug. Ava walked around the table and allowed herself to breathe in Cassie's joy.

'I'm happy for you. It's about time this all happened for you and Steve,' Cassie whispered.

Ava squeezed Cassie a little tighter, grateful for the way things were slowly falling back into place between them. Their friendship wasn't as effortless as before, but this moment felt like a step in the right direction.

'I'm happy, too,' Ava said.

And for the first time in what felt like years, she meant it.

–

In typical British fashion the summer rain poured down that Friday afternoon, forcing the adoption get-together indoors to a pub rather than the local park.

Ava didn't mind, but she had to admit that rain aside, the event was a bit of a washout. Only a handful of people had turned up, and those that did had already managed to adopt. Nobody was like them, waiting for that final seal of approval.

All she'd heard from people since arriving was how lucky and blessed they felt that they'd been chosen. Given Ava and Steve couldn't say that themselves yet, they both spent much of the party feeling frustrated.

'Sure you don't want something stronger?' Steve asked, as Ava asked him for her third sparkling water.

Ava shook her head. 'Working tonight, remember.'

'Oh, what do you do?' Hiram, one of the other adoptive dads, asked.

'I'm a firefighter,' Ava explained patiently. She was sure she had told them before what she did, but the words seemed to have fallen on deaf ears as coos of interest and curiosity rippled around the table.

She answered questions as politely as she could, nodding and smiling, but possibly for the first time in her life Ava wanted a break from the world of firefighting. She'd wanted this afternoon to be about her desire to become a mum and so, when Steve returned with her sparkling water, she drank it down as if it were a large gin and tonic.

The rest of the afternoon passed in a blur of questions about the adoption process, how difficult it was and how it had taken everyone much longer than they anticipated to find the family they hoped for. There were tales of the social services changing their minds after approval of an initial placement, parents coming back into the picture and even prospective parents themselves having a rethink after discovering that many of the children they would be adopting would have possible mental health and behavioural issues.

By the time Ava and Steve left she had to confess she felt rudderless. The afternoon had been about trying to inject some positivity in their new search for a family, but all Ava could see were problems.

'Just because that's their story doesn't mean it's ours.'

They were walking back to the car, Steve slightly merry after three pints of bitter.

'I know.'

Ava started the ignition, trying to find the positive. The adoption process seemed different than the last time they had begun exploring this avenue, and she knew that this time it was because she was all in. Now, she found meaning in everything, just waiting and hoping for the moment they were connected with their child.

'You looked as if you wanted to thump Hiram when he told you how it took him three years and two failed placements before he and Sheila were placed with Amber.'

Ava laughed. 'Would you judge me if I told you that you were right?'

As Steve leaned over the gearstick and kissed her softly on the cheek Ava felt herself relax. Even in moments of frustration, she knew the process, flawed as it might be, was still worth every step. All the waiting, the setbacks, they wouldn't stop her from wanting the family they'd dreamed of.

'I always judge you,' he said, softly, 'but usually you pass the test. To be honest, I was close to punching Hiram myself.'

'And Elaine.'

Steve groaned. 'All that talk of how you spend most of your time as a parent of an adoptive child taking them to counsellors and doctors or avoiding tantrums.'

'It was awful!' Ava exclaimed. 'I wanted to turn around and say, hey, I was adopted and I didn't have any of these experiences.'

'That's because their experiences are the only exciting things that have happened in their lives,' Steve muttered darkly. 'I wish you had told them your story, but then again, they're so fixated on their own version of events that they wouldn't be interested in hearing how positive your experience was.'

'I know.' Ava sighed. 'I just wanted to hear something positive. I mean we know most of these kids have problems, we know most of them won't be babies, but regardless, we want to give these kids the best start in life and be their cheering squad, just as my mum and dad were for me.'

Chapter Thirty-Nine

A few minutes later, Ava switched off the car and got out. She reached for Steve's hand.

'I'm sorry. I don't know why I'm so upset.'

'I'm upset, too,' Steve said. 'You said you were going to drop me home!'

With a start Ava looked out of the window and realised she had driven straight to the community centre.

'Oh god. I'm sorry. I was on autopilot back there.' She checked her watch. There was still time to take Steve home and make it back in time for the pre-party talk she and Miguel had planned to give.

'If we go now I can drop you.'

'Ava, I'm kidding.' Steve laid a hand on her forearm. 'To be honest I'd quite like to hang around, and it saves me coming back later. I can watch you and Miguel in action and toast Cassie's success.'

Ava looked around her, astonished at what she saw. The progress was incredible. The little houses were fully repaired and restored, painted cheerful shades of every colour in the rainbow, while the community centre, always at the heart of the estate, was the crowning glory with its huge glass doors that breathed light into the function and sports rooms.

Ava held her breath. She couldn't believe the transformation.

'You okay?' Steve asked her.

'Fine.' Ava exhaled. 'It's surreal in a way to see it like this after so long – it was just a ruin that caused disaster for so many.'

'But now look.' Steve threw an arm around Ava's shoulder. 'So much light and hope.'

Ava recognised a figure in the distance.

'Cassie,' she called waving at her.

Hearing Ava's voice, Cassie smiled and waved back, quickening her pace towards the two of them.

'You all ready for tonight?' Steve asked.

Cassie rolled her eyes. 'You'd think it was the coronation the way some of the residents are going on. They've invited all their mates, the local paper's coming to do a piece on the fact we're like a phoenix rising from the flames. It's madness. You'd think they'd be happy just to have their homes back, but not this lot!'

'You love it,' Ava teased. 'You're just as excited.'

'You're right.' Cassie let out a peal of laughter. 'I do love it! Honestly, I've been so excited for this day.'

Ava couldn't help but smile at Cassie's excitement. The party was more than just a celebration – it was a testament to the resilience of this community, rising from the ashes just as the estate had. It made her hopeful for her own new beginnings, too.

'Steve, you're here too!' Cassie said, cutting through Ava's thoughts as she embraced her husband.

'Nowhere else I'd rather be,' Steve said sincerely, as he looked behind Cassie. 'Where's Dylan?'

'With Miguel,' Cassie said. 'He's decided that he wants to be a firefighter!'

'What! Really?'

Ava was astonished. Dylan hadn't said a word.

'What's brought this on?'

There was a twinkle in Cassie's eye. 'You. Wants to be a hero just like his Auntie Ava!'

'I suppose you did rescue him from a burning building,' Steve remarked.

'Very true,' Cassie said solemnly. 'You're a very good role model for him, Ava.'

'But a firefighter?' Ava said. 'You're all right with that?'

Cassie looked nonplussed. 'Ava, he's nine. Last week he wanted to manufacture Barbie dolls for dogs.'

'Wow, kid's got ideas,' Steve observed.

'He has. Not always good ones,' Cassie said wryly. 'But I like to tell him nothing's off limits. He can do whatever he wants to do.'

'Not every parent feels like that,' Ava said lightly.

'Your mum and dad did,' Cassie countered. 'They were supportive of all your choices. Even when you decided to cut your own fringe!'

Ava groaned at the memory. She was seven and had cut all the hair off her Girl's World. Convinced she was going to be a hairdresser, she had thought she'd practise on her own hair. Unfortunately, Ava's scissor skills had left a lot to be desired and she'd cut such a huge chunk out of her fringe her mum had wept all night.

'It was a look,' Ava said mutinously.

'That took months to grow back,' Cassie laughed.

'You joined me in solidarity, if I remember rightly,' Ava said softly.

A laugh bubbled up out of Cassie's mouth at the memory.

'I'd completely forgotten that.'

'I hadn't,' Ava countered. 'You did it after those girls in the year above bullied me. Your mum went mental.'

Cassie shrugged, memories flooding back to her in a flash. 'I felt sorry that you felt so bad. I came into school with the same chunk of hair missing and said we were a club. Only cool kids could join.'

'Bloody hell!' Steve laughed shaking his head in disbelief. 'How many kids were going around with chunks of hair missing from their fringe so they could be like you two?'

Ava and Cassie exchanged knowing looks.

'Er, just us two.'

They erupted into laughter and Ava knew that it was only a matter of time before they fell back into their old relationship. Their bond was too strong to ever be broken.

'Oh look, there's Miguel and Dylan,' Steve said, interrupting the spell.

Spotting Miguel and Dylan walking up the hill towards them, the trio waved.

'Know all there is to being a firefighter then?' Steve asked.

Dylan shook his head gravely.

'Uncle Steve, there's a lot to learn. And you've got to be really fit.' He turned to his mother. 'Can I start going to the gym, I need to do press-ups.'

The adults chuckled.

'I think you're a bit young for that yet,' Ava said gently. 'Tell you what, you can come and work out with me sometimes at the fire station gym.'

Dylan's eyes lit up.

'Can I use the barbells?'

'No!' she and Cassie said in unison.

'But maybe Ava'll let you walk on the treadmill if you're not getting in someone's way,' Cassie countered.

'Plus, there's the other great skill you need as a fire-fighter,' Miguel said seriously. 'You can practise that a lot at the station for us if you want?'

'What?' Dylan begged.

'The ability to make a really good cup of tea,' Ava said, as Miguel gave her a wink.

As the adults laughed again, Dylan let out a howl of anguish and Cassie pulled her son in for a hug.

Together they all walked down the hill towards the centre, with Ava delighted life was finally settling down.

Chapter Forty

The yawn at the back of the room echoed through the hall. Ava did her best not to take it personally, as she finished talking about the advantages of installing a fire alarm in your home.

She was more than used to people nodding off when she discussed the merits of fire safety. She had, however, hoped that her biggest cheerleader, Dylan, might stay awake.

Watching him now, leaning against his mum's shoulder, gentle snores reverberating through his body, Ava felt herself melt.

'So, in conclusion,' she said hastily, 'I think I speak for both myself and Station Manager Fernandez when I say enjoy your new homes and if you have any questions at all don't hesitate to contact us.'

The group suddenly came to and broke into a round of applause, jolting Dylan wide awake.

'When's the party?' someone called from the middle.

'Now,' Cassie said, getting to her feet to address the group. 'But I thought we'd go across the road to the pub first, where the landlord has put on a little spread for us all as a gesture to say he appreciates all we've been through.'

With that there was a mass exodus. Ava laughed, she couldn't honestly blame them. This group had waited long enough to get their homes back. Realistically, this was probably completely the wrong night for a fire safety talk.

'You are coming to the party, aren't you?' Cassie looked at them anxiously as though there was a chance that either might say no.

'Course we are,' Steve said now. He stretched his arms above his head and released a huge yawn as he walked from the back of the room towards them.

'That was you!' Ava exclaimed.

Guilt passed across Steve's face. 'Sorry, to be fair I have heard it several times before.'

Ava was about to protest when she realised he was right. He had done more than his fair share of listening to her fire safety talks and demonstrations not only when she had been a young trainee and had practised them in the mirror, but when she had delivered them to groups and individuals across the city.

She kissed his cheek at the memory.

'You're forgiven,' she said.

'Aww young love,' Cassie beamed.

Miguel glanced at Cassie and shot her a worried glance. 'And now I'm worried about you, have you had a bump on the head?'

'What?' Cassie exclaimed. 'I'm pleased they're back together.'

'Me too,' Ava said as she nestled into her husband.

And she was. She couldn't remember a time she had ever been this happy. She was about to say so, when the sound of Steve's phone ringing burst the silence.

He looked apologetic as he reached into his jeans pocket and fished out his device.

'It's Pru.'

Butterflies filled Ava's stomach. What did their social worker want at this time on a Friday? Had some unforeseen problem arisen after their meeting with the panel?

'Answer it,' she hissed, unable to bear the suspense.

Steve needed no further encouragement.

'Hi Pru,' he said smoothly down the phone. 'Everything okay?'

Ava watched, her heart in her mouth as her husband nodded and grunted non-committally. It took all the strength she had not to tug and pull at her husband's sleeve and demand he include her in the conversation.

After what felt like a lifetime, Steve ended the call and turned to Ava. His face looked pale in the evening sunshine and she felt her heart sink.

'Well?' she demanded.

'We've been approved!' Steve shouted in excitement.

He reached for her hand and Ava felt her pulse race.

'You're sure?' Ava whispered. It was more than she dared hope.

'It means we've passed, Ava! We're going to be parents.'

Ava's hands flew to her mouth as her heart thudded. Could this really be happening? The chance they'd been waiting for seemed almost too good to be true.

For a moment she allowed her mind to run wild. She imagined holding a child's hand and running along a beach, playing football in the park, hoisting him or her up on her shoulders as she showed her child off at the fire station. Steve reading them bedtime stories, holidays together – a family.

Her eyes shone with tears and to her surprise, she saw everyone else's did too.

'I'm so pleased for you,' Miguel said warmly.

Cassie stepped forward to hug Ava. 'It's finally happening, Aves! I knew it would. What did I say?' Cassie pulled back and Ava wiped the back of her eyes with her hands.

'That found family is often where you least expect it,' Ava replied.

'We haven't got our child yet. And it's a long road,' Steve warned. 'We need to be realistic.'

A ball of fierce determination burned brightly in Ava's chest.

'I don't care,' Ava said firmly. 'If this is how our family is meant to be, then this is what we do. But I know it's just the start. We still have to wait for the match, but I'm ready for whatever comes next.'

There was a silence as Ava willed her husband to see her point, to understand where she was coming from.

Leaning down towards her, he pressed his forehead against hers.

'All right, my love. But let's just take it one step at a time.'

Happiness bubbled up inside her. She knew she shouldn't get her hopes up but something told her that her own child was on their way.

'So this is all very nice,' Cassie teased, 'but before you two completely steal my thunder, this is actually supposed to be a celebration for the estate.'

'Oh, shut up,' Ava said good-naturedly as she linked her arm through her friend's.

'How about we celebrate together? Looks like we've got a lot to be happy about.'

'Finally,' said Dylan.

And together the little group made their way down the hill towards the pub.

Chapter Forty-One

'Am I getting a cousin?' Dylan asked later that evening.

The group were sitting at a table in the corner, the pub thronging with life as everyone from the estate laughed and cheered at the joy they felt in being back at home again.

'Are you what?' Ava turned to Dylan who was sandwiched between her and Miguel.

'Am I getting a cousin? You're my auntie, so does that mean that if you get a baby then I get a cousin?' Dylan asked.

Ava raised an eyebrow and looked at Cassie for help but her friend was too busy chatting with Steve about something to notice.

'Not yet,' Ava said delicately.

'Look, Dyl, it might take them years. You might be long gone at uni by the time these two get their hands on a kid,' Miguel said bluntly as he reached for the glass of fizz he was currently drinking.

In addition to the spread the landlord had laid on, Cassie had arranged for a free bar all night thanks to some leftover proceeds from all the fundraising efforts. The money raised had stretched to several bottles of cheap Prosecco.

'Charming,' Ava said to Miguel as Dylan looked at her puzzled. 'I think what Miguel means is we have a lot of hoops to jump through yet before we can officially welcome anyone into the family,' Ava explained.

Dylan sipped his juice and thought for a moment. 'When you get your baby, I could babysit – once I'm a bit older, of course. Mum says it's a good way to start earning pocket money.'

Ava burst out laughing. 'Sweetie, we are definitely a long way from that but I promise you that when the time comes, you can definitely babysit.'

Dylan looked mollified and Cassie bounded over.

'What's going on?' she asked.

'Your son's demanding money with menace,' Miguel said, taking another sip of fizz.

'Is he?' Cassie looked cross. 'What have you done?'

'Nothing, Mum,' Dylan groaned. 'I was just saying that when Ava and Steve get a baby I can babysit. And I'll do it really cheap, too.' He took a sip of her drink. 'At first, of course.'

Ava howled.

'You've raised a monster.' Miguel chuckled.

'I've raised a little boy that needs his bed,' Cassie said.

'Oh no, Mum. It's early. I don't want to go yet,' Dylan protested.

'Oh look, the terrible pre-teens have come out already.' Cassie groaned. 'Come on,' she said firmly. 'It's half-past eight. It's late.'

'Are you coming back?' Miguel asked.

Cassie nodded.

'Dolores from next door has offered to babysit until eleven, which is more than late enough for me,' she said reaching for Dylan's hand. 'I'll only be a few minutes dropping this one back and then we can get the party started.'

At that Dylan's eyes widened with dismay. 'You mean you'll have a better time without me?' he asked incredulously.

Laughing, Cassie pressed a kiss to her son's cheek. 'Never in this world, my love!'

And then giving everyone a quick wave she left, leaving Ava with a million and one questions about just how much Dylan babysitting was going to cost her. She had to admit it was a nice feeling.

–

An hour later and the party was in full swing. Ava had been thrown around the makeshift dance floor more times than she cared to count, the sounds of The Human League and Kylie Minogue ringing in her ears.

'Happy?' Steve asked, setting a fresh glass of Prosecco in front of her.

She was sitting at their original table in the corner, enjoying a breather. Miguel and Xav were offering impromptu dance lessons. Ava looked over and winced as Miguel scooped one woman into his arms and then invited her to twerk alongside him. Like her boss, the woman was no spring chicken.

'I am now I'm off that dance floor,' she said, bringing her gaze to meet Steve's. 'Someone looks like they're about to put a hip out.'

Steve laughed and shuddered as Xav tried to beckon him onto the dance floor.

'It feels like our family's slotting into place.' A smile spread across his face. 'If you'd told me this time last year we would be this happy I never would have believed you.'

Ava knew what he meant. A year ago it felt as if their relationship was hanging on by a thread, their dreams of a family in jeopardy because Ava had been so intent on having her own baby.

She didn't recognise that person now. Why had she been so fixated on creating a baby of her own? All at the cost of her own physical and mental health? Because of a long-held childhood dream she was unwilling to move on from? Looking back, it seemed crazy. She knew more than anyone that biology didn't matter. Meeting Bernice had proved that. And now here she was, with the chance of her own family. To raise a child right, just as her own parents had done.

'I was wondering actually,' Steve said lightly. 'If you'd given much thought to finding your biological father's grave?'

'Fintan?' Ava was surprised at the question.

Steve nodded.

'No.' Ava was emphatic in her response. 'I know enough. I'm not bitter any more, I actually think they did me a favour. I was brought up shrouded in love, Bernice and Fintan were the very opposite of that. I don't think finding out anything more about them is going to help.'

Steve clamped an arm around her. 'For what it's worth I think you're right. I think meeting Bernice has helped you lay some ghosts to rest, but I wish I'd been there for you.'

'We've been through this,' Ava said gently, lifting the glass of Prosecco to her lips.

As far as Ava was concerned, what was in the past was in the past. Tonight, she wanted to focus on the positive.

As the sounds of 'Spinning Around' came to an end, Ava saw Miguel and Xav walk away from the dance floor towards their table, faces glowing with joy. Miguel was holding onto a bottle of Prosecco and liberally topped them up, splashing fizz onto the table. He'd clearly had one too many.

'Easy,' she remarked. 'Some of us have got to get up for work in the morning.'

'Ah whatever,' Miguel said with a sashay of the hips as he took a seat. 'You only live once.' With that he leaned over to kiss Xav on the lips. 'We've been talking about our new life.'

'Going to be booze-filled, is it?' Steve asked wryly.

'I bloody hope so.' Miguel chuckled and opened a bag of crisps that were on the table, tearing them down the middle so everyone could share, he took a handful.

'I'll miss working with you, Ava. You've been more than a pal to me the last twenty years, you've been my confidante and I know you're going to make a fabulous station manager. Look at you now, everything you wanted. It's nothing more than you deserve sweetheart and I couldn't be happier for you.'

'Ah, you're really pissed.' Ava giggled.

Miguel nodded and rested his head on Xav's shoulder.

'Maybe just a bit. I'm happy, Aves. For you, for me, for all of us.' He held his glass aloft. 'To happiness,' he shouted.

The entire pub joined in with his cheer.

'To happiness,' they cried.

Miguel basked in the unexpected delight around him, then started looking for something around him as if he had forgotten it.

'Where's Cassie?' he asked suddenly. 'She left ages ago. She can't still be putting Dylan to bed.'

Ava checked her watch. Miguel was right. How had she not noticed the time – Cassie had been gone almost two hours.

'Maybe there's problems with the babysitter?' Xav mused.

'She would have let us know.'

Ava reached into her bag for her phone expecting to see a text message or missed call, but there was nothing.

Ava was worried. This was so unlike her friend. Usually Cassie would text her just to tell her what she'd had for lunch. If she was going to be late or had problems with Dylan she'd have said so. Gnawing her bottom lip she brought up Cassie's number on her phone and rang.

No answer.

She thought for a moment then got to her feet.

'I'm going to find her.'

'I'm sure she'll be fine, Aves, you're over-worrying. She's probably having trouble settling Dylan. That boy drank a lot of juice. Probably too much sugar left him hyper,' Steve put in.

Ava shook her head and pressed a kiss to his cheek.

'You keep these two company. I won't be long.'

'Ava,' Steve protested.

But Ava wouldn't be persuaded. She knew her friend, and she wouldn't rest until she found her.

Ava had only just left the pub when she heard the sound of uneven footsteps behind her.

Turning around, she saw Miguel walking unsteadily towards her.

'Can't let you go alone, not gentlemanly,' he hiccupped.

Ava laughed. 'You're not much help.'

'It's for Xav's benefit,' Miguel said, walking straighter. 'He loves it when I let go a bit. You know what it's like in a relationship – sometimes you have to do things for them to keep them happy. I've left him and Steve talking about Britpop.'

'Well that'll only make them maudlin!' Ava exclaimed as Miguel linked arms with her.

Before long, they reached Cassie's place and Ava rapped softly on the blue wooden door.

'Hi,' she said when Dolores opened it seconds later. 'Is Cassie about?'

'No.' Dolores looked confused. 'Is she supposed to be?'

'Well, we thought she was coming back to the party,' Miguel said.

'Yes, that's right,' Dolores said checking her watch. 'She left a good hour ago.'

'She's not here?' Ava's heart pounded faster. This wasn't like Cassie. Her friend would have called, texted, something. A creeping sense of dread settled in her stomach.

'No,' Dolores replied looking alarmed. 'She's not at the party?'

Ava thought for a moment. The estate was a safe place, it was unlikely any harm had come to her.

Dolores frowned. 'She did say she was going to go past the community centre on her way back. She thought she'd left the lights on.'

Relief flooded through Ava as she smiled at Miguel.

'I bet she's still there,' Ava said. 'No doubt got caught up in some daft task that doesn't need sorting.'

Miguel laughed. 'Time to fish her out and take her back to her rightful place in the pub.'

'Well, I'm glad we've worked that out. You'll let me know if you can't find her won't you,' Dolores said, shutting the door.

'Course,' Ava promised.

And together she and Miguel set off towards the community centre.

A couple of minutes later they saw the bright spark of light beaming out from the newly restored building.

'What a surprise,' Miguel exclaimed. 'That girl is a workaholic.'

Pushing open the door to the centre, Ava called for her friend.

'Cass, where are you?' she called.

'Oi, Cassie!' Miguel yelled, walking in the opposite direction. 'You're being a crap hostess, there's loads of people that want your attention.'

As Ava made her way into the main body of the hall, she saw it was empty. Strange, she figured that was where she would be. Perhaps she was in the ladies', Ava reasoned, touching up her make-up before making a return visit. But peering into the loos, the room was not only in total darkness but empty.

'Have you found her?' Miguel asked appearing in the hallway.

Ava shook her head. 'I take it you haven't either.'

'No.' Miguel looked as if he had gone straight into station manager mode. 'Let's check the perimeter. It's possible she decided to deal with something outside.'

'But we'd have seen her,' Ava reasoned as Miguel pressed the torch on his phone on.

'Not if she was round the back.'

Miguel set off at a pace and Ava followed, quickly catching him up.

Rounding the corner, she gasped.

'What?' Miguel asked.

'Look,' she said, pointing to the back door of the centre.

'I can't see anything,' Miguel said.

For a split second, she hesitated. What if this was real? What if something had actually happened? But before she could stop herself, her feet were moving again. Wordlessly, she started to run.

'Ava, what is it?' he called.

But Ava didn't speak, too keen to reach her destination.

And then she saw it. At the back of the centre, something caught the light – Cassie's locket, the one Ava had given her, glinting like a beacon in the darkness. But it wasn't just the locket.

Cassie lay in a crumpled heap beside it, eyes closed, unmoving. Almost like a lighthouse, beaming a warning that something wasn't right.

Chapter Forty-Two

Ava crouched by Cassie's side, dread twisting inside her.

'Cassie,' she said loudly, stepping into firefighter mode. 'Cassie, can you hear me?'

In the light of the community centre, Cassie's skin took on an eerie orangey hue. Despite the warmth of the night, Ava shivered as Miguel knelt beside her.

'Is she responsive?' Miguel asked.

Ava shook her head, grateful they had both shifted into professional mode.

'Cassie,' she tried again, louder this time, but nothing.

Miguel leaned forward, placing his fingers on Cassie's neck, feeling for a pulse.

Ava watched him, her heart in her mouth, as she saw a flicker of surprise and then alarm cross his features.

'No pulse,' he whispered.

The words hit her like a punch in the chest. This was Cassie, her sister in all but blood. This couldn't be happening.

'I'll start compressions,' Ava said, her voice trembling but determined. 'You call for an ambulance.'

As Miguel dialled 999, Ava began chest compressions, placing her hands in the centre of Cassie's chest and pushing hard and fast, at least two inches deep, just as she'd been trained. She could almost hear the rhythm of 'Stayin' Alive' in her head – the mental trick she always used to keep the pace steady. She tilted Cassie's head back slightly, checking her airway was clear, before giving two firm rescue breaths.

Come on, Cassie.

Miguel came off the phone.

'They'll be here within ten minutes,' he said, sounding tense.

Ava nodded, that was fairly quick for a Saturday night in Bath when drunken stag dos and hen parties were usually at their highest.

'Come on, Cassie,' she urged, 'you will not bloody die on me, do you hear, you DO NOT DIE!'

Ava looked desperately up at Miguel, who was watching their friend for any signs of life.

'Keep going,' he ordered.

Ava had no intention of stopping.

Cassie was everything. Her world, the kindest, bravest, funniest, smartest person she knew. Cassie had to live, not just for Ava and Dylan but for the space she took up in the world. She was a shining star who made everyone that met her light up with joy. Cassie wasn't going anywhere, Ava was going to make sure of that.

Ava pushed against Cassie's chest, pouring everything into each compression. Miguel's eyes stayed locked on her, monitoring every move.

'Careful, Ava, you'll break her ribs. Let me take over,' he said gently.

Ava didn't argue, stepping back to watch Miguel work.

'This is taking too long,' she said, her words tumbling out in a rush.

Miguel had been doing compressions for just over a minute.

'Not helpful, Ava,' he said. 'Let me work.'

Her gazed turned to Cassie's body.

So helpless, so still. She looked as if she was sleeping, Ava thought with a shudder as the familiar peal of sirens got louder and louder. The paramedics were here at last. As the ambulance rounded the corner, the flash of headlights lit up Miguel's face and Ava could see the emotion in his features while he worked away on their friend.

'How long since you started compressions,' one of the two paramedics asked as they rushed from the ambulance.

'Eight minutes and seventeen seconds,' Miguel said with precision, glancing at his watch. Details mattered in emergency care, something that had been drummed into Ava during her training. Every minute, every second counted and she knew every precious moment would matter for Cassie.

'Any idea how long she was out?' the other paramedic asked.

Ava shook her head. 'We just found her. She'd been in the pub a couple of hours earlier than that so we think she could have been here a good hour.'

Saying the words aloud unleashed the torrent of fear she'd been holding at bay as reality dawned. There was only so long the human body could cope without oxygen to the brain.

Looking at Cassie still lying on the ground, it was hard to believe that just two hours ago she had been the life and soul of the celebrations. Cassie had given so much of her life to the estate, now it was back on its feet it seemed as if Cassie had given enough.

Ava wasn't having it.

Everything was working out. She and Cassie had made up, they were friends again. Ava was going to be a mum, Cassie was going to help her. Their next chapter was going to be exciting, a whole new adventure as they took on the world.

This was a nightmare. A very sick and twisted way of her brain letting her know she was under too much stress and needed to relax. All she had to do was wake up and this would be over. Cassie would be safe and well and so would she.

But when she gave her cheek a hard pinch, Ava didn't wake up. The acidic taste of bile at the back of her throat reminded her that this was real, and her friend was in serious trouble. Ava stepped back, watching as the paramedics worked with practised efficiency.

One continued compressions while the other checked the defibrillator. His expression tightened as he spoke, 'Her heart's not in a shockable rhythm.'

Ava's stomach dropped. She knew exactly what that meant. Flatline. Without a pulse all they could do was keep pumping, hoping to restart her heart through compressions.

Another paramedic placed a mask over Cassie's face, squeezing the attached bag to push air into her lungs. The team worked in sync, but the seconds dragged on.

'We'll take her to the hospital. Can you follow on behind?' the first paramedic said. It was an order not a question.

Miguel flicked through the apps on his phone and ordered a cab. 'Two minutes,' he said softly to Ava, walking towards her and wrapping an arm around her shoulders.

Together they watched the ambulance disappear into the distance.

'Cassie's going to be okay, isn't she?' Ava begged. Her knees were weak and she felt empty inside.

Miguel hugged her tight. 'Course she is,' he said in an overly bright voice.

But Ava knew that as he said the words he didn't believe them any more than she did.

–

'We need to tell Dolores and Dylan what's happened,' Miguel said as the taxi pulled up outside the community centre.

Ava nodded and climbed into the back.

'I'll text Dolores but won't mention how serious it is,' Ava said, aware her voice was trembling. 'After all, we don't know what's happened and there's no sense worrying them when we don't have all the information.'

'I agree,' Miguel said, sitting beside her.

'I mean Cassie could just be hurt, or it could just be a really bad asthma attack,' Ava said desperately.

'Even if that's the case, which I hope it is,' Miguel said gently, 'Cassie will likely be in hospital for a long time. She'll need her son.'

Ava thought for a moment. Her instincts were to protect Dylan from whatever dreadful thing was happening to his mother in that moment.

'We'll go to the hospital first,' she said quickly. 'Assess the situation. If it looks as though we need Dylan, I'll get Steve to collect him immediately. At least Dolores will be prepared for a night-time visitor if I text her now.'

'All right,' Miguel agreed.

As the taxi sped through the city, Ava messaged Dolores and then rang Steve to fully outline the truth of the situation. Everything was so unreal, she felt as if she was an actor playing a part. By the time she put the phone down, the taxi had arrived at the hospital.

She and Miguel all but flew out of the car and into the casualty department.

'Hi, you two,' a nurse welcomed them, Lola. Ava knew her from various hospital visits, personal and professional, over the years.

'I think you had a patient brought in recently. Cassie Hope.' Ava's pulse thudded in her ears.

Lola frowned and looked up the name on her computer.

'She a friend of yours?'

Ava nodded.

'We found her at the community centre and called the paramedics,' Miguel explained. 'How is she?'

Lola sighed. 'Doctors are working on her now. Has she any family we can call?'

'She has a nine-year-old son, Dylan,' Miguel said.

'Anyone else?' Lola asked.

'Yes, me,' Ava said, her voice laced with desperation and urgency as she said the sentence she hoped she would never have to say. 'I'm Cassie's next of kin.'

Lola's brown eyes looked searchingly at Ava before she scanned the notes. She seemed to find the confirmation of Ava's insistence as she gave a brief nod of approval.

'I'll let the doctors know you're here,' Lola finished.

'Thank you,' Ava mumbled.

Miguel steered her towards the chairs in the waiting room and went to get coffees from the vending machine.

Ava sat on the edge of the chair and tapped her feet up and down. She was used to hospitals, she spent so often inside them. The smells, the pace of life, even the drunks didn't bother her. But tonight, as she looked around, she saw things through new eyes. Opposite her, a father was sitting with what she guessed was his drunken teenage

333

daughter, his expression both annoyed and concerned, whilst his daughter sat on the seat beside him, a cardboard kidney-shaped bowl on her lap, vomiting, all the while claiming her drink had been spiked. Two seats along sat a lone man rocking backwards and forwards muttering something about aliens, and behind him an elderly woman was whispering something in her husband's ear, clutching his arm looking a deathly shade of white.

Her heart went out to all of them. If there was one thing Ava had learned throughout her life it was that you could never predict where it was going to take you next.

Just then Lola walked past her.

'Any news?' Ava asked.

'The doctors are coming now,' she replied.

Ava recognised Lola's tone. Gentle but matter-of-fact. Ava's chest tightened, instinctively she knew that whatever was coming next wasn't going to be good news.

'Should I call her son?' Ava whispered.

'I think it's time, yes,' Lola replied gently.

Ava fished her phone out of her bag and dialled Steve.

'Can you get Dylan please?'

'Going now,' Steve replied and hung up.

Miguel returned with two scalding hot coffees, spotting the alarm in Ava's eyes.

'Have you heard something?'

At the question, Ava's breath caught in her throat.

'Lola suggested we call Dylan now. That the doctors will be out in a minute.'

'Okay.' Miguel sat beside her and handed her a paper cup. His brown eyes met hers, and like Ava's they were brimming with tears.

They sat in silence. Every passing moment felt like a weight pressing down against her shoulders, the uncertainty as to what would happen next wrapping itself around her like a spiky blanket, threatening to extinguish any remaining hope. Clutching the cup of coffee, Ava found herself whispering prayers to a God she wasn't sure existed.

Please let Cassie live, please. I'll do anything, and I mean anything, but please don't take her from me, not yet.

With each bargain, Ava knew she was willing to make any sacrifice, with anyone, if only it meant she didn't have to say goodbye.

Sure enough, the security controlled double doors to the rooms beyond opened, and through them walked Doctor Barnaby, an A&E doctor she had known for years, her face serious.

'Hi,' she said softly. 'You're here for Cassie Hope?'

'That's right,' Miguel said. He reached for Ava's hand and she took it, grateful for the warmth and reassurance of his touch.

'As you know Cassie was brought in by paramedics and was unresponsive,' Dr Barnaby explained. 'We know you performed CPR for several minutes as did the paramedics.'

Ava nodded. 'How is she?'

Doctor Barnaby paused. 'We did everything we could. I'm sorry, but Cassie didn't make it.'

In that moment, Ava felt the world around her shift. It seemed to lose its sharpness, fading into a hazy backdrop of muted colours and indistinct shapes as she struggled to comprehend the enormity of the loss. Every sound, every movement, was distant and muffled, as if she were immersed in a thick fog of grief she wasn't sure she would ever emerge from.

Ava felt Miguel grip her hand. The boniness of his knuckles digging into her flesh bringing her back to the present.

'But there was no accident, no fall, she hadn't been injured,' Miguel pointed out, his voice full of confusion.

'I know,' Doctor Barnaby agreed. 'We can't find an obvious cause of death at this point. We believe she may have suffered sudden arrhythmic death syndrome.'

Ava's heart sank further. She'd heard of SADS. It was a rare, silent killer. The kind of thing you read about but never expected to strike someone you loved. There had been no warning, nothing she could have done.

'We'll do an autopsy,' Doctor Barnaby continued gently, 'to see if there's something we missed, but I suspect that's how the coroner will record her death. Once again, I really am so sorry.'

With that the doctor's eyes softened in sympathy and she returned through the double doors behind her.

After she'd gone, Ava sank to the cold, hard floor. Time seemed to stand still, she was suspended in a haze of disbelief and sorrow. The world continued to turn, but for her, everything had ground to a halt. She was adrift in a sea of pain, struggling to find her bearings as the overwhelming waves of pain threatened to engulf her completely.

Everything that Ava knew up to this point was a lie. How could there be a world without Cassie in it?

Miguel crouched beside her.

'I don't understand.' Miguel's voice shook. 'Cassie was fine. She just left us to drop off her son. What if we'd stayed with her? What if we'd taken Dylan home ourselves? Maybe she wouldn't have collapsed. We could've been there sooner. I should've known something was wrong. We should have…'

His words tumbled out, and Ava could feel the weight of his guilt crashing down on him.

Miguel was sobbing now, his whole body shaking with grief and shock. Ava turned to look at him. She felt numb.

'You know as well as I do that may not have made any difference,' Ava said slowly.

She watched Miguel crying and couldn't understand why she wasn't joining in. It was as though she couldn't connect what was happening on earth to what was happening in real life.

A voice brought her swiftly back to the present.

'Auntie Ava?'

Wriggling free from Miguel's grasp she turned around and saw Dylan bathed in the black of night holding Steve's hand. With his hair mussed up from sleep and still in his pyjamas the sight of him caused Ava to sob in a way she never had before.

Chapter Forty-Three

Ava had been staring at her Nostalgia Nook for the past hour. The necklace that she had gifted to Cassie took pride of place, its pendant glowing as the warm sunshine bounced off it. The funeral director returned the necklace after Cassie was released to their care, but wearing it now felt wrong.

When Ava had given the necklace to Cassie, she had seen it as a connection, a talisman that kept them together. Now she wasn't sure what it was, but she knew she couldn't part with it.

She turned her attention to the window. How could it be so bright when in her heart there was so much darkness?

It had been a week since Cassie's death and in that time Ava had returned to a place she had never wanted to revisit: grief.

Every waking moment was filled with thoughts of Cassie. The last time they had laughed together, the last film they watched, even the last cup of tea Cassie had drunk in their home. The mug Cassie had used was now a cherished, prized possession, with nobody else able to touch it.

Even now, Ava kept going into the spare room – or Cassie's room as she liked to think of it – just to remember her. Every square inch held a memory. The way she'd pulled out dresses from that wardrobe to go on dates, the way she and Dylan had laughed late on Saturday nights when they all huddled up together to watch Netflix.

Only now, it wasn't Cassie's room. Now, for the moment at least, it was Dylan's room, and the only reason Ava was sure that she hadn't let her grief consume her was because of Cassie's son.

At the hospital, Ava had scooped Dylan up into her arms and held the little boy as he cried.

They had gone into the relatives' room, a cold, miserable room in every hospital as far as Ava was concerned, and she and Steve had gently explained that his mummy loved him very much but she'd gone to heaven.

'What's heaven?' Dylan had asked between tears.

Ava felt hopelessly ill-equipped. Cassie had talked to Dylan about death, but what could she possibly say now, when everything felt so final?

She thought for a moment as she looked into Dylan's confused blue eyes. What had she needed to hear when her parents had died? Admittedly, Ava had been eleven years older, but she had still been lost. If it hadn't been for Cassie who helped her, offered her guidance and love when she needed it most, she didn't know where she would be. She cast her mind back to that fateful plane journey to Madeira. She had been mute with grief and Cassie had been silent, holding her hand throughout the journey, never once letting go. It had been the anchor Ava needed and instinctively Ava knew this is what Cassie would want her to provide her child – an anchor, a place in heart and mind that her son could always call home.

And so, Ava had allowed Cassie's love for them all to guide her as she and Steve took the little boy home. Just as her best friend had done all those years ago, Ava had slipped her hand around the little boy's and hadn't let go all night.

Naturally, social services had been in touch right away. Thanks to their suitability for adoption, Ava and Steve had been able to step in as Dylan's temporary foster parents under an emergency placement. Still, fostering was a different process, and they knew his long-term arrangements were yet to be fully decided.

For a time, Ava had worried Paul would reappear, but so far he'd kept his distance and Ava was grateful. Just the thought of seeing the man that had caused Cassie so much pain was enough to make Ava's blood boil. She wasn't sure what she would do if she laid eyes on him again.

Now, in the days that followed, and the grief began to settle in like a well-worn coat, there was the aftermath of Cassie's death to deal with. Because Ava was Cassie's next of kin, Ava had taken charge of identifying her body. The coroner's report, following the post-mortem, confirmed that Cassie had died from a sudden arrhythmic cardiac episode. There was no obvious warning, and it would have claimed her life in moments.

'She would have known very little about it,' Lola had told her kindly when Ava returned to the hospital.

'I know,' Ava said in a small voice. Ava had witnessed sudden deaths like Cassie's before, but nothing could have prepared her for losing her best friend this way. But Ava also knew that whatever feelings she had about her friend's death, and how rudderless she felt, she knew that she had to put her own feelings on hold. At least for a while. Dylan was the one that was important now. He needed someone he could rely on to navigate life's hurdles. And one of those hurdles was his return to school that day. With just a week to go before the school broke up for the long summer break, Ava wanted Dylan to have some sort of normality to his life.

Snapping herself back to the present she smiled at Dylan, who was looking at her expectantly, dressed in his school uniform.

'Are you looking forward to seeing all your friends?' Ava asked in an overly bright voice.

Dylan nodded, his eyes still red and pinched from the morning's tears.

'Nancy says she'll look after me today. Her mum's giving her two cupcakes, one for me to cheer me up.'

Ava sent a silent prayer to Nancy's mother and Nancy for making the little boy's return to school so easy.

'How lovely.' Ava beamed. 'Make sure you save a bite for me.'

'No way!' Dylan gave a half-smile.

Ava thought her heart would break at his bravery. All she wanted to do in that moment was hold him and protect him from any more pain, shield him from the world's cruelty. But she knew hiding away from grief wasn't the answer. They would have to face this new reality together, one day at a time.

Ava gave him a mega-watt smile. 'I'll just have to make my own then!'

Dylan said nothing but simply reached for Ava's hand. Unquestioningly the firefighter wrapped her large palm around Dylan's smaller one and gave it a squeeze. She wanted him to know that she was always with him in his heart, even when she wasn't with him physically – just like Cassie.

'I thought you were working today,' Dylan said at last.

Checking the time Ava saw there were just a couple of minutes before they had to leave for school. Ava was taking him that morning and then going to work to start her tour.

'I am. But I reckon me and Big Stu will still have time to make a huge chocolate fudge cake and we'll eat it all up by ourselves.'

Giving his hand a final squeeze she let go and straightened his tie.

'There, you look perfect.'

He nodded. 'Mummy used to always do it like that.'

A lump formed in Ava's throat at the 'used to', and she squeezed Dylan's shoulders.

'Come on then. Let's get you off to school,' she said.

'Auntie Ava, will you bring me a slice of that chocolate cake?' Dylan asked as they walked down the stairs.

Ava laughed inwardly. In the last week there had been a lot of sugar consumed, they had all definitely been eating their feelings. But as far as Ava was concerned now wasn't the time to worry about it.

'I'll see what I can do. Now, shoes and coat.' She kissed Dylan's cheek and steered him into the hallway where she saw a letter on the mat.

Picking it up, the solicitor's stamp on the front of the envelope caused a lump of dread to settle in her stomach. As well as being Cassie's next of kin, she was also executor of her will. The solicitors she had spoken to a couple of days ago had said they were in the process of putting together the paperwork and would be in touch. This must be the start of it, she thought, remembering the shock of having to deal with her own parents' affairs when she was not much more than a kid herself.

Once Dylan was ready, the two set off in the car towards school. All the way there, Ava kept up an endless stream of chatter the little boy hardly replied to. By the time they reached the school gates Ava had a horrible feeling Dylan would be glad to get to school just to see the back of her.

Waving him off, Ava set off for work. She turned on the radio but every song seemed to remind her of Cassie and she couldn't face another morning of arriving at work with her face covered in tears and snot so she settled for silence.

Pulling into her usual space she turned off the car and took a moment to breathe. She would get through this, she reminded herself. Whatever happened, she would survive.

Leaning back in her seat Ava heard the sound of rustling in her pocket.

The letter.

Fishing it out of her pocket she turned it over in her hands and unfolded the letter, her eyes scanning the formal, typed words. The solicitor explained that Cassie had left specific instructions for her, a message recorded shortly before her death. It was described as personal, urgent, and something Cassie had been adamant Ava should hear directly. The letter included a secure link to the recording, along with a brief note from the solicitor urging Ava to listen at her earliest convenience. For a moment, Ava just stared at it, her heart pounding. Whatever was on that recording, it had been important enough for Cassie to arrange all of this.

With fumbling fingers she followed the instructions to download the recording and in seconds, Cassie's voice filled the car.

Hey Ava
Well, this is bloody weird isn't it? The voice note I never thought I'd leave, never wanted to

put together and definitely the one I hope you'll never listen to. Because if you do hear this, then I suppose we can take it that the worst has happened. I've gone. If I am dead, then please know that the last thing I ever wanted to do was leave you, Aves. You're my everything. Ever since that first day we met at school until now, and beyond. I couldn't have got through life without you. I know you think it was me that looked after you when your mum and dad died, but the truth is it was always you looking out for me. You knew the best ways to save money, how to write a stroppy letter of complaint, how to deal with Dylan's bullies, and most of all, how to talk to me and make me feel connected with another human. Some may think it's a shame I never found 'the one', but I think I did, Aves. You were my 'one', and I am so grateful to have found you and had you in my life.

I hate to think I've put you through more grief and pain. Believe me, if you're reading this, I'd have fought whatever it was that killed me. I loved life, and I loved my life with you and Dylan in it. We might not have been a family in any way that's legally recognisable or even conventional, but to me we were family.

I'm saying all this aloud just after coming back from seeing you in hospital. Your near brush with death has made me realise two things. Firstly, I need to get my own affairs in order, and secondly, I'm so glad we made up. I was a mess without you and I'm so sorry we fell out in the first place. I was hurt and I overreacted. I took it too far, but I think you know this already. Living without you *for those few weeks were the most miserable of my life, which is why I'm sorry I've left you to deal with my death alone.*

It was then Ava pressed pause on the recording. It all felt too real, too raw. She couldn't breathe, hearing Cassie again hit home to her how much she missed her friend, how she would do anything to have just five more precious minutes with her. They would laugh one last time, share a glug of wine and tell each other they were the very best thing that happened to the other in life. For a second, all Ava could do was breathe, but she knew she had to listen to the rest of her friend's message – she had to know what was so important and so with a sense of trepidation she pressed play and once again Cassie's voice boomed into life.

I think, however, the worst thing you can do when you die is leave others to guess what you wanted or how you felt, which is why I'm saying all this now. I know we always talked loosely about you being my next of kin, but I don't think we really talked about the full implications of what that meant. With you trying for your own family, it seemed like too big a subject to bring up. But, well, death does spur you on a bit, doesn't it, and now I've no choice but to ask you for rather a large favour.

The fact is, if I've died someone has to look after my little boy no matter how old he is. If he's a grumpy teenager or stroppy twenty-five-year-old then please keep an eye on him. If he's still my baby, then what I really want is for you to look after Dylan permanently. I know you adore him as much as he adores you, but I also know you're the perfect mum for him. You're like his second mother already! I don't know if Dylan will fit into any family you go on to have, or if you'll have the space or room to take him on. But Ava, I really hope you'll say yes just as much as I'm hoping you'll never read this letter. But if you want to know why I'm choosing you to be my little boy's guardian, it's not just because I love you, it's because you fight. Not just fires, but for people, their hearts and their loved ones. That's who I want looking after my boy, someone who cares enough to put their own feelings aside, the consequences that might be faced somewhere along the line, all for the sake of others.

Cherish my child for me, Ava. Kiss him, hug him, encourage him, raise him right. Tell him that there are scary men on street corners, but some of them might be heroes. Remind him of the value of caring for yourself so you can care for others, but most of all, tell him to make memories because it's those memories that will power you through life when it's as tough as it no doubt is in this moment.

I love him Ava and I love you. Please look after Dylan for me. All my love forever, Cassie.

Chapter Forty-Four

Cassie's voice note had been burning a small hole in Ava's heart for the last week. Even before the funeral, the note and its wishes had been weighing on her mind. In some way, she had expected Cassie's request. After all, she and Cassie had been family in every way that mattered. She knew Dylan and loved him, who else would care for him in the way Cassie wanted?

After listening to Cassie's voice note, Ava hadn't moved for an hour. She had simply thrown her head against the steering wheel and sobbed, huge, ugly great sobs, her heart breaking with every freshly shed tear. She found herself going round and round in circles asking the same questions, but there was only really one she came back to and it could be summed up in a single word: why?

If it hadn't been for her job, Ava wasn't sure how she would have got through those terrible first few days of loss. Just as when her mother and father had died, firefighting had given her something to hold onto, a life raft to cling to as she weathered uncertain seas. Miguel had suggested she make use of the firefighters' counselling service, but Ava wasn't ready to open up. All she wanted to do was get through Cassie's funeral, and then she would start facing up to the reality that her friend was no longer by her side.

But today had been Cassie's funeral – a humanist ceremony with a woodland burial just as she had asked for.

The ceremony had been surprisingly uplifting, even for Ava who had held onto Dylan's hand throughout, only pausing briefly to let the little boy throw a clod of earth onto his mother's coffin.

It was now, at the wake in the estate's community centre, that the power of grief threatened to take hold. She couldn't shake the memory of the last time she was here, those tragic moments when she had found her friend lying motionless on the floor.

Clutching a cup of tea, as someone from the estate expressed their condolences, Ava's gaze drifted across the room and landed on Steve. He was doing the rounds, the polite 'hello, how are you, thanks for coming' routine, continually ensuring everyone's drink was topped up.

Her heart swelled with love. Ava may have lost a lot of love in her life but she had also gained a lot too. How blessed she had been to find not just one anchor in Cassie but another in her husband. She sipped her tea and felt an ache in her chest. Since Cassie's death, Steve had quietly fallen into step behind her, anticipating Ava's every need before she even knew what she needed herself. Not only was there always a cup of tea waiting for her when she woke but he had guessed when she was hungry, when she needed time to watch trashy television and lose herself in terrible plot lines.

Now this, asking him to join her in parenting Dylan for the rest of his life, seemed like an extra ask. She knew that he would say yes, but she wondered where that left them with their adoption journey.

There was something else worrying her, something she couldn't put into words – it was just too terrifying. As if sensing her needs now, Steve walked towards her with a plate of sandwiches, crisps and, if she guessed correctly, a teacake nestled on the side.

'How are you doing?' He set the plate in front of her and sat down opposite. 'It's been a good turnout.'

Ava glanced at the community centre. The place was heaving with at least two hundred mourners all dressed in their finest black to pay their last respects. Ava had kept an eye out for Paul and thought she had seen him standing at the back of the crowd, but he never attempted to force his way inside or connect with Dylan. Their eyes had briefly met, and they gave each other a polite nod. It seemed that it took Paul the death of his daughter to truly understand her wishes and keep a respectful distance from her in this pivotal moment of her last journey on earth.

Cassie had touched the community in ways Ava had never known, with people she had helped coming from as far afield as Scotland and Wales to pay their respects.

It was something that would have astonished Cassie, but Ava wasn't surprised. Cassie had always been special. She had a quality that drew people to her like a magnet, and although she wasn't here any more, Cassie had left a legacy across the estate that would leave an indelible mark on the community for good.

There had been talk of erecting a plaque on the community centre in her honour. Something Ava had a feeling would have delighted and horrified Cassie in equal measure.

Now she turned back to look at her husband and gave him a brief smile.

'It was never going to be anything else for Cassie was it?'

'No,' Steve said.

Ava saw the sadness mirrored in his eyes, deepening the ache of her own grief. She gave him a half-smile. Sometimes she forgot it was hard for him as well, that he had been Cassie's friend, too. She could only hope that the funeral would help them all deal with the unbearable loss.

It had been down to Ava to organise the funeral and she had wanted to involve Dylan as much as possible in the funeral choices. He was, after all, not just Cassie's son but her world, and so she had tried to find out what Dylan thought.

'She would just want everyone to be happy,' Dylan said as he looked up from his homework. 'Mum hated it when people were sad.'

Ava's heart had gone out to the boy. He had seemed to morph into an adult overnight.

'But you know it's okay to be sad. Especially when something like this happens.'

Dylan nodded. 'I am sad, but Mum said you can feel lots of things at the same time, so I'm sad and trying to do happy things too, Auntie Ava.'

And so, Ava had kept the funeral arrangements simple – picking things purely because she knew Cassie liked them. 'Boys Don't Cry' by The Cure played out as the coffin was brought in because it was Cassie's favourite song. Hydrangeas stood at the end of the rows of chairs in the community centre just because Cassie loved them. And Dylan had been allowed to sit wherever he wanted rather than being made to stand up front because Ava knew Cassie wouldn't have wanted it any other way.

Steve looked around, the last of the stragglers were leaving now with only Dylan, his friend Nancy, and her parents, Peter and Millie, beginning to tidy up.

'We should go and help,' he said. 'Then get you back home with a stiff G&T.'

Her cup of tea was stone cold now. She set the half-full mug on a nearby table and met her husband's eye.

'There's something we need to talk about.'

Concern flickered across Steve's face.

Ava reached into her bag for her phone and handed him a pair of headphones.

Wordlessly he took both things, and as he did so Ava pressed play on her phone.

As Steve listened, she watched his face crumple as Cassie's voice filled his ears.

'Oh,' he whispered, when he'd finished.

He removed the headphones from his ears and handed them back to Ava along with her phone. As he ran a hand through his greying locks, Ava stared at him.

'Well?'

'I mean yes, obviously.' Steve glanced at her phone as if it was a hot poker. 'When did you get this voice note?'

'A week ago,' she mumbled looking sheepish.

'And you only thought to tell me now?' Steve exclaimed.

'There's been so much going on. I wanted to get the funeral out of the way. And of course, we're going through the adoption process.'

Steve let out a large sigh.

'I know. But Ava, whatever happens with our adoption journey, we can't let Dylan down. We have to talk to the adoption people and let them know.'

Ava nodded. 'I know. Dylan has been through so much.'

'And what do you think?' Steve asked.

'Me?' Ava looked astonished at the question. 'It's obvious, surely? We have to give Dylan a home, raise him as Cassie asked.'

Steve broke out into a big smile. 'I can't imagine the house without Dylan in it now.'

'I feel the same,' Ava whispered. 'But what if it's not what Dylan wants?'

She gestured to Nancy, Peter and Millie, who she had to admit had been a huge help since Cassie had died. Not only had Nancy become Dylan's biggest protector, but Peter, who ran a yoga studio, managed to pick up Dylan from school with Nancy when Ava or Steve were working and couldn't get away.

Steve shook his head.

'No chance. He adores you. You have to explain to him that this is what his mother wanted, but the decision is ultimately his.'

She knew Steve was right. She also knew this was something that couldn't be put off any longer. Spotting Dylan as he hugged Nancy tight, she waved at him and he walked towards her and Steve.

'Can we have a chat?' she asked gently.

Dylan nodded.

'Sit down, sweetheart,' Steve said pulling out a chair next to him for Dylan to sit on. 'You okay?'

'I think so,' Dylan said. 'It's just sad.'

'It's horribly sad, Dyl,' Ava said.

'But I'm trying not to be sad all the time,' Dylan said in a voice that sounded oddly grown-up. 'It's what Mum would have wanted.'

Ava took her moment. 'And speaking of your mum. She left me a very nice voice note before she died. It's all about you.'

'About me?' Dylan asked.

Ava nodded. 'Yes. About what she wanted for you if anything bad were to happen to her. She wanted you to come and live with me, Uncle Steve and Monkey.'

'What do you think?' Steve asked.

Ava shot him a look. It was for Dylan to talk. He needed space to think.

'If you're my new mum and dad does that mean I was never Mum's little boy?' He scrunched up his face, as if trying to piece together a puzzle too big for him to solve, confusion sweeping across his features.

Heartache coursed through Ava.

'No sweetheart, that's not what it means at all,' she said tenderly. 'It just means your mum can't look after you any more, but she will always be with you. All she wanted was to make sure you were properly looked after if she couldn't do that any more.'

'By people that will love you as much as she did,' Steve added gently.

'So, what do you think?' Ava asked. 'Do you want to give it a try?'

There was an agonising pause as Dylan looked from one to the other.

'Yes please,' he said in a small voice.

And with that Ava leaned forward and wrapped her arms around Cassie's son. She never wanted to let him go, knowing that this was just the beginning of a new chapter for both of them. One filled with love, challenges and Cassie's unwavering love in their lives.

Chapter Forty-Five

The end of October brought with it, as it often did, blustery cool weather, the previous month's Indian summer sunshine a distant memory. As Ava took her seat in what was now Miguel's old office she felt a stab of nervousness. She had never been looking to become station manager, but now that she was, she wanted to do a good job and do the station proud. This wasn't just a promotion; it felt like stepping into a new phase of life altogether. A chance to build a foundation for the future, not just for her team, but for Dylan, Steve and herself, too.

The process had been rigorous, a mix of interviews, assessments and leadership evaluations, but in the end, Ava had been chosen. Now, the responsibility weighed on her, but so did the pride of stepping up for her team.

Today was officially Miguel's last day, but he had already finished a fortnight ago and had immediately gone on holiday with Xav for a fortnight in Brazil.

Ava had been reluctant to move into his office straightaway. To her, it felt a bit like jumping into your grandmother's grave but Miguel had insisted. So, she had been moving a few bits into his office to make it feel more like hers. Now, as she added the finishing touch, a photograph of her, Dylan, Steve and Cassie, taken last year, she felt a flash of pleasure at the simple scene of her family on her desk. There were so many changes that had happened in the past twelve months, she could never have predicted any one of them, but this one, station manager, was a new one. It was now her job to make sure she looked after her work family as well as the family she cared for at home. They had reluctantly withdrawn from the adoption process. Social services, particularly Pru and Nikki, had been supportive, but Ava knew the legal process for adopting Dylan would take time. For now, they were focused on creating stability for him, knowing the paperwork would follow.

But life wasn't all bad and had still continued to take unexpected turns. Later that day, Maeve was flying into Bristol airport to see them and Ava was looking forward to welcoming the Irish woman into her home.

They had continued to exchange messages and, shortly after Cassie had died, Maeve had lost Gerry. The messages had turned into phone calls then, as the two women became each other's support system as they each worked through their grief.

Today was also about her work family, who were planning a celebration as Jodie had now passed her training period, making her a fully-fledged member of Blue Watch.

'Knock, knock.' Miguel rapped on the door loudly, making Ava jump.

At the sight of her friend she beamed and threw her arms open in welcome.

'You're back!' she gasped.

'Easy, tiger.' He chuckled but Ava noticed he was clinging onto her just as tightly. 'Just thought I'd check in on you before I leave. Answer any last-minute questions.'

'I think I'm okay, but no doubt I'll have a million when you do finally leave,' she said into his neck.

He let go of her and surveyed the office. 'Looks like you've made yourself at home here,' he said.

Ava felt a stab of guilt. 'Miguel, I'm sorry. I didn't mean to tread on toes.'

'You didn't, you daft cow.' Miguel slapped her on the back. 'I'm teasing.'

Relief ran down her spine. 'You know I still feel weird about this,' she said. Then, walking over to the window, she gazed outside and saw Xav chatting to Big Stu and Jodie. 'He looks happy,' Ava commented, noticing the bright smile on her friend's husband's face.

'He should be, he's just had two weeks in Brazil!' Miguel pulled out his phone and thrust it in front of Ava's nose. 'Look! Best holiday ever.'

Taking the phone from Miguel's hand, Ava flicked through the photos. There were dozens of the two of them sitting on sandy beaches in front of crystal-clear azure waters beaming at the camera. They were both so relaxed.

He shook his head, clearly still marvelling at the memories and then put his phone back in his pocket.

'So it went well then?' Ava walked back to the desk and gestured for Miguel to sit opposite.

'Ava, I don't know what to tell you,' he said with a relaxed sigh. 'I can't remember the last time I went away and felt so relaxed. I know it sounds cheesy but I've finally realised there is more to life than working here.'

As he trailed off he glanced around his old office, his lips slightly curled and Ava couldn't help laughing.

Delighted as she was to see this new lease of life, she also knew it was unlikely to last. As for Miguel, he looked as if he was about to protest, then thought better of it.

Miguel leaned forward in his chair.

'So seriously, anything I can help you with before I go? I'm just here to hand in my kit, collect a few bits.' He glanced around the office and saw the photo of Steve, Ava, Dylan and Cassie on the desk.

'How's the family?' he asked softly.

Ava beamed. 'Good. Dylan's adjusting well to living with us. It's hard, for him and for all of us. I keep catching him crying in his room at night but the community at the estate have been wonderful. He still goes up there and plays, sees his old mates, and of course Dolores is always happy to babysit so he's still connected to his mum.'

'That's got to help?' Miguel murmured.

'I think so,' Ava said. 'That boy has a lot of love in his life. There's nothing I can say that will bring his mum back. I just have to remind him we have a different kind of love, right here for him and it will never go away.'

This feeling was one Ava understood more than most. She could still feel the aching void her parents had left behind, but she also knew that grief softened in time. She would help Dylan find his way, just as Cassie had once helped her.

'Oh Aves, that's tough,' Miguel whispered. 'I don't know where you find the strength.'

'You just have to, I guess,' Ava said softly. 'Cassie did it for me when I lost my mum and dad.'

There was a pause as both reflected on the unbearable losses Ava had suffered. She had been through so much pain, but now Ava was determined that such heartbreak wouldn't define her. She would rise, and so would Dylan. She would make sure of that.

'I think they call it life, Ava,' Miguel said as, with an air of reluctance, he got to his feet. 'I'll just collect the last few bits of my stuff and I'll leave you to it.'

Ava felt her nerves return.

'I'm really not sure I can do this,' she called as he walked towards the door.

'Course you bloody can!' Miguel exclaimed. 'I don't want to listen to any of that. You need to believe in yourself more. I believe in you, always have. Look how far you've come from that timid firefighter looking to find purpose and meaning in life because she'd lost her parents. You found it and a lot more besides, you found family.' Miguel extended his arms, gesturing to the fire station that surrounded them. 'You know I'll always be a part of that family, even though I'm not here.'

It was then Ava felt the tears fall. She couldn't help herself and rushed towards her friend and the two fell on one another, both of them feeling heavy with the emotion of the situation.

'God, this is stupid,' Ava wept. 'I'm going to see you at the weekend.'

'And no doubt before then,' Miguel laughed, hugging her tighter. 'I'm always here for you.'

'And me you,' she whispered.

The sound of footsteps outside her door made the two of them spring back. There was Big Stu loitering apologetically. Ava wiped the tears away with the back of her hand.

'Sorry.' She laughed. 'Just having a moment.'

'I saw nothing,' Big Stu said so solemnly, Ava almost believed him. 'But I have got Colleen here ready to officially welcome you on your big day. Shall I bring her up?'

'Yes, please do,' Ava brushed the last of her remaining tears away and smiled.

'And I'll go downstairs and say my goodbyes,' Miguel offered.

As Big Stu walked away Miguel followed before turning in the doorway.

'Time to look forward not back,' he said.

Ava nodded. 'Forward,' she echoed.

And with that, Miguel turned and walked away, leaving Ava finally feeling ready to face whatever life had to throw her way next. As she stood at her desk, her fingers strayed to her neck, to the necklace that had been a faithful talisman throughout her life. Leaving it to the fate of the Nostalgia Nook seemed wrong somehow. The more she had stared at the jewellery the more she felt as if the piece was meant to be hers once more. As if the very act of being reunited with the necklace was not only keeping her connected to her mother but also to Cassie. Two incredible women she had been blessed to have in her life whether for reason, season or lifetime.

Naturally the meaning of the jewellery had changed over the years, but Ava was grateful for the constancy of love it had always represented. She felt the weight of the necklace not just as a keepsake, but as a reminder of the love that had shaped her life, from her mother to Cassie. It was a love that didn't die, but was carried forward, lived through the people who remained. Her thoughts turned to the woman that had given it to her all those years ago. What had this necklace meant to Maeve? What had made her want to share something so precious with Ava? Could this talisman actually be like the medal she had held onto all those years ago? Was Maeve really the rightful owner, and were she and – for a while – Cassie, careful guardians of a treasured keepsake? Theirs to hold onto briefly, a fleeting connection to remind them of their purpose?

Ava realised she had never asked Maeve these important questions, too wrapped up in her own disappointments to find out what had made Bernice's friend want to stay connected to Ava. Now, as Ava clutched the necklace tightly in her hand, the sharp metal of the clasp pressing into her fingers, she wondered if it was perhaps time to find answers. Maybe the time had come to find out more about the memories that connected them and in turn, perhaps, invite even more people into the found family Ava was proud to call her own.

Acknowledgements

Writing a book is a strange old business. You spend months (sometimes years) holed up with people who don't exist, trying to wrestle a story into shape while wondering, often far too loudly, why on earth you ever started. *The Holder of Hope* has been no exception, and I owe a great deal to the people who helped me see it through.

To my wonderful agent, Kate Burke, thank you so much for your faith in this story, for your honest feedback, and for managing to steer the ship even when I was convinced it was sinking. And to my incredibly talented editor, Emily Bedford, your calm, clever notes (and miraculous ability to read what I meant to write, rather than what I actually did) made a difference.

To everyone at Canelo, thank you for being so supportive, so encouraging, and for making me feel like part of something special. It's genuinely appreciated.

To the readers who picked up this book, whether you've been with me from the start or this is your first time, I really do meant it when I say thank you. It's a leap of faith, trusting a writer to take you somewhere for a few hundred pages, and I'm so grateful that you've chosen to come along for the journey.

And finally, to the friends and family who've had to put up with me talking about this book for what probably felt like years, you're saints. Truly.

I love hearing from readers and if you'd like to get in touch you can find me at instagram.com/fionafordauthor. Praise and book chat always welcome, one star reviews, no need to tell me!